D0950332

"From icy gales on the Chilkoot Trail to the mud and festering greed in booming Dawson City, *At the Mountain's Edge* gives new life to one of the most fascinating chapters in Canada's history. Fast-paced and full of adventure, this novel is an exciting take on the raw emotions that make us human and the spirit required to endure."

Ellen Keith, bestselling author of *The Dutch Wife*

"Graham continues her worthy crusade of recounting pivotal Canadian history in this poignant story [about] the travesties of war both on the battlefield and the home front."

RT Book Reviews, on *Come from Away*

"The talented Genevieve Graham once again calls upon a fascinating true story in Canadian history to remind us that beneath the differences of our birth, and despite the obstacles we face, we're all human underneath. Vividly drawn and heartwarming, *Come from Away* is a beautiful look at the choices we make in the face of both love and war."

Kristin Harmel, *New York Times* bestselling author of
The Forest of Vanishing Stars

"At once dizzyingly romantic and tremendously adventurous, this novel also serves as a poignant reminder of the senseless toll the violence of war can take—and the incredible lengths of heroism humans will go to in order to survive and rescue the ones they love."

Toronto Star, on *Promises to Keep*

"Graham has delivered a book that reads like a love letter to a time and place that figures largely in our national identity: Halifax in 1917."

The Globe and Mail, on *Tides of Honour*

BLUEBIRD

GENEVIEVE GRAHAM

Published by Simon & Schuster
New York London Toronto Sydney New Delhi

Simon & Schuster Canada
A Division of Simon & Schuster, Inc.
166 King Street East, Suite 300
Toronto, Ontario M5A 1J3

This Simon & Schuster Canada edition April 2022

SIMON & SCHUSTER CANADA and colophon are trademarks of
Simon & Schuster, Inc.

For information about special discounts for bulk purchases, please contact Simon &
Schuster Special Sales at 1-800-268-3216 or CustomerService@simonandschuster.ca.

Manufactured in the United States of America

1   3   5   7   9   10   8   6   4   2

Library and Archives Canada Cataloguing in Publication

Title: Bluebird / Genevieve Graham.
Names: Graham, Genevieve, author.
Description: Simon & Schuster Canada edition.
Identifiers: Canadiana (print) 20210269332 | Canadiana (ebook) 20210269359 |
ISBN 9781982156657 (softcover) | ISBN 9781982156664 (ebook)
Classification: LCC PS8613.R3434 B58 2022 | DDC C813/.6—dc23

ISBN 978-1-9821-5665-7
ISBN 978-1-9821-5666-4 (ebook)

To Dwayne

"I think if one knew beforehand what all this was going to be like one would hardly want to face it, but somehow you're glad to be there."

Diary of a Nursing Sister on the Western Front, 1914–1915

"Nothing so needs reforming as other people's habits. Fanatics will never learn that, though it be written in letters of gold across the sky. It is the prohibition that makes anything precious."

Mark Twain

BLUEBIRD

prologue
CASSIE

❦

— Present Day —

Cassie Simmons rolled her shoulders back, then her neck, wishing she'd restocked on Tylenol. She could always tell when a storm was on its way because its threat squeezed everything in her body tight. This one was coming with a vengeance, darkening the museum windows as if she'd closed the curtains. Fingers crossed that the rain would hold off a little longer, so she could run to her car without getting drenched.

She finished sweeping the floor in front of reception and was about to tidy the back room when the main door creaked open. She gritted her teeth, wishing she'd locked the door, even though it wasn't quite five o'clock. All day long she hadn't seen more than the mailman and a couple of couriers, and *now* someone walked in? Probably another delivery or a lost tourist. She pasted a smile on her face and turned toward the front desk to see a man entering the room, almost completely covered in a layer of fine white dust. She tried not to notice the white boot prints he left behind on her clean floor as he walked toward her.

Watching him, her brow twitched with curiosity. He was hardly what she'd come to expect as a guest of the Maison François Baby House museum. As an assistant museum curator in a National Historic Site of Canada, she was used to answering questions about Windsor's part in the War of 1812, the Battle of Windsor, Prohibition, and the area's Francophone heritage, as well as responding to requests to see the archives. Normally she tried not to judge in advance, but this guy didn't look like someone interested in history. He was tall and broad, and around her age, she thought. He might be handsome, but she couldn't be sure because his attention was on the pack he was carrying, which was also coated in dust. A construction worker, she surmised. He obviously wasn't here for a tour.

"May I help you?" she asked.

"Hey! Yeah. Thanks," he said, sounding a bit flustered. He looked up from the bag and caught her eye for the first time. A smile cut through the mess on his face.

Yes. He was definitely handsome. Just filthy.

"I'm sorry," he said. "I have no idea what I'm doing here."

"That makes two of us."

A dark eyebrow flicked, acknowledging her quick answer. "Well, I'm renovating an old house just outside of town, and I found something. Maybe an artefact, but I'm not sure. I figured the best thing would be to find an expert, so I checked Google, and this museum came up. I thought I'd start here and see if I could speak to a local historian or archivist, but this is all new to me. I'm not from around here, so maybe I've come to the wrong place . . ." He trailed off.

Cassie couldn't yet tell if what he carried would be interesting or not, but her head was still pounding from the headache, so she hoped it wouldn't take too long. All day, she had been craving her tidy little apartment, a glass of wine with her dinner, maybe a movie, hiding away from the impending storm.

"Can you help me?" he asked, and she reconsidered her plans, noting her visitor's deep brown eyes. She could do all that a little later.

"I'm happy to, if I can," she replied. "People often bring in things that they've found, but I'll be honest with you: they're usually duds. But who knows? What did you find?"

"Uh, it's an old whisky bottle. I know whisky, but this one is new to me for sure. I polished it up a bit. I hope that's okay."

He reached inside the pack, pulled out a dark green glass bottle, and placed it carefully on the desk in front of her.

Cassie's heart leapt with an unexpected surge of interest. The bottle's round body and sloped shoulders looked like other whisky bottles she'd seen before, but most these days were brown glass, not green. And this one came with a badly corroded cap and an ancient-looking label. At first glance, she realized the bottle dated back almost a hundred years, to the age of bootleggers and Prohibition, a rip-roaring era that had put Windsor on the map in a big way. She hadn't seen anything like this in a very long time.

Careful not to overreact, she asked, "Where was this?"

"Inside one of the walls. I broke one bottle, but there are lots more."

"How many?"

"I'm not sure. I haven't finished the renos and didn't want to break any more of them, so I left them in the wall. Dozens, though."

Her fingers wrapped around the cool bottle—she could tell right away that it was full of liquid—and drew it close to read the print.

Bailey Brothers' Best

1920

Windsor, Ontario, Canada

Her pulse hammered in her temples, overpowering her headache. She'd seen one or two of these before, but only in photographs. "This was in your wall?"

"Yeah. I knew it was whisky right away, because when I smashed the wall the whole place suddenly smelled like a distillery. I wonder if it's still any good. I've never heard of Bailey Brothers' Best before. Have you?"

Cassie's mouth had gone dry. Oh yes, she had. "Starting back in the 1800s, there were a number of smaller distilleries around this area," she said, easing around a direct answer. "In the 1920s and '30s, this area was the busiest port for bootlegging in the entire world. May I ask where the house is? What's the address?"

When he told her, Cassie's heart lodged itself in her throat. What were the odds? Just last week she'd driven past the old place. The FOR SALE sign sticking out of the tall grass had stood there so long it had practically become part of the landscape, so the bright red SOLD sticker in the top corner had come as a surprise. For a moment, she'd been tempted to stop and peer through any possible holes in the boarded-up windows, but she reminded herself she had no business at that house anymore. She'd pressed her foot on the accelerator and kept going.

"The place looks and smells like no one's been there in decades," the man was saying. "Not bad, just kind of musty. But so far, I think it's in pretty good shape. I got it for a steal."

She nodded, her thumbs slowly stroking the label. She knew how much he'd probably paid for the house. How often had she held that price tag up against her bank balance, only to admit defeat once again?

"Aren't you gonna write the address down?"

"Of course," she said. She grabbed a pen and wrote the familiar address on her notepad underneath her latest to-do list. "Can I get your contact info as well?"

"Matthew. Matthew Flaherty," he said, then recited his phone number. It was a 780 area code, which she didn't recognize. "I just moved here from Alberta," he explained.

With effort, she attempted nonchalance. "I'm Cassie Simmons, the museum's assistant curator. Would you like to leave the bottle with me so I can research it?"

"That would be terrific. Should I bring the rest over? I don't know what to do with them."

"Could you leave them in the wall for now? I'd like to see where you found them, maybe take some photos for the archives. Then I can bring them back here for safe storage."

"Fine by me. I'll just work in a different room."

After they arranged that she would come by in the morning, Matthew started to leave.

"Mr. Flaherty?"

He turned back. "Yeah?"

She hesitated. "Have you told anyone else about this?"

"About finding the bottle? No, why?"

"I think that this bottle might actually be a pretty special piece of local history." She chose her words carefully, uncomfortably aware she was crossing a professional line. She had already decided to make this her pet project. No need for Mrs. Allen, the museum's curator, to trouble herself over it. "But we won't know its significance—if there is any—until I've done some research."

He nodded conspiratorially. "This is just between you and me, then."

She locked the door behind him then returned to her desk and stared at the bottle, still stunned.

She knew the stories. She'd heard them since she was a little kid on her grandmother Alice's knee as she leafed through the family scrapbook with its peeling pages, telling her about the two generations of brothers who had gone off to fight in both world wars. But Cassie's favourite tales were the ones that included Model Ts, flapper dresses, and bootlegged whisky. Her grandmother knew that as well, and she would give Cassie a guileful smile whenever she began. *Prohibition was a wild age*, she would say, *and my father and his brother were right in the thick of it, or so the stories go*. She would gather Cassie closer. *Now, where should I start?* Then she'd recite the stories she'd learned in her own childhood and fill Cassie's world with tales of whisky and money, adventure, and love.

But there'd never been any talk about bottles being hidden in a wall.

All the questions from her childhood bubbled up like she'd popped a cork from a bottle of champagne as she studied the label, with its neat typeset and a sweet illustration of a bird in the top right corner. Bailey Brothers' Best, founded by Jeremiah Alexander Bailey and John Joseph Bailey, former World War I tunnellers turned bootleggers.

And Cassie's ancestors.

The bubbles fizzed in her chest. "What else did you hide, boys?"

PART
— one —

one

ADELE

∽

— June 1918 —

No. 1 Canadian Casualty Clearing Station, near Adinkerke, Belgium

Adele focused on the tips of her fingers, numb from being clamped around a metal surgical bowl for so long, then she shifted her attention to the wrists supporting them and silently demanded they stop shaking.

"Lieutenant?"

She held out the bowl. "I'm sorry, Dr. Bertrand."

Tink. A tiny sound of victory as a metal fragment dropped in. Adele steeled herself, determined to remain still as stone. Dr. Bertrand's use of her rank had that kind of effect. She'd never felt entirely deserving of the official title, but every one of the Canadian nurses had been given the same one upon enlisting. "Lieutenant Savard" gave Adele a perceived position of authority, which came in handy around some of the soldiers she tended.

Adele had never assisted with a trepanning before, an ancient procedure where a hole was cut into a patient's skull to relieve pressure and gain access to any foreign matter lodged within. What was throwing her off wasn't the sight of the poor man's exposed brain or the blood. That rarely bothered Adele anymore. It was the exhaustion that rattled through her bones like a train. She'd been on her feet for sixteen hours today, eighteen yesterday. In between, she'd curled up in the nurses' tent, grabbing a few hours of sleep before returning to duty. For the past ninety minutes, she'd been standing next to Dr. Bertrand, holding the bowl as he fished bits of shrapnel out of the soldier's brain. She couldn't understand how he managed to stay awake long enough to do it.

A boom sounded in the distance, and she shifted her weight. Stationed as they were so close to the French border, less than an hour from the busy port of Dunkirk, she was no stranger to the thunder of the big guns.

"That should . . ." Dr. Bertrand murmured, peering into the site.

Adele raised her chin, then let it drop. If she saw what Dr. Bertrand was doing, she would want to ask questions. He was a nice man, but he wouldn't have the energy to operate on a man's brain and answer a woman's questions at the same time.

His dark brow creased with concentration. "No, wait. Magnet, please."

Clutching the bowl in one hand, Adele passed the magnet to him with the other. A new blast jostled a lamp overhead, sprinkling the workspace with a light shower of dust, and Dr. Bertrand paused for a moment, waiting for it to settle, before returning his attention to the man on the table.

"Ah, there it is. I'd never have found it without the magnet."

She saw his smile lift behind the cloth mask as he held up the forceps again, a tiny sliver of metal clamped between its tips. He dropped it into Adele's bowl then stepped back so his surgical assistant could close the site.

Dr. Bertrand slid his mask beneath his chin and nodded at Adele.

"Excellent job, Lieutenant. I think you've earned a good night's sleep. I'll see you in, what, four hours?"

She huffed a laugh, feeling the tension release as she lowered her aching arms. "Sounds about right." Then, out of habit, she cast a worried glance at the patient, still unconscious.

"Time will tell," he said. "These types of surgeries are so intricate. Even if he survives, we have to hope nothing critical was injured in the brain. Just keep a close eye on him."

Adele untied her apron and deposited it in the laundry bin along with so many other pieces of bloody cloth, then left the main hospital tent, stepping into the early summer chill of night. The air carried a suggestion that rain was, once again, on its way. Behind her, the agonized howls of men and the concentrated voices of doctors and nurses faded away as the thuds of explosions travelled across the landscape beyond. Bursts of light blanched the distant battlefield, but Adele didn't bother to stop and watch the spectacle. She'd seen it before. Besides, her vision was blurring around the edges with fatigue as she made her way through the endless maze of sheets and bandages drying on lines, then around temporary huts, buildings, and tents toward the nurses' quarters.

No. 1 Canadian Casualty Clearing Station was more than a hospital, it was a village unto itself—a square mile of various structures surrounded the main hospital tent, all of which could be relocated depending on the proximity of the fighting. Since Adele had arrived three years ago, the clearing station had already moved to a few different spots between France and Belgium, always as close as possible to a railway so they could treat the injured men coming from the battlefields.

Inside her tent, Adele found Hazel and Minnie sound asleep, Minnie's snores a soothing hum. Lillian wasn't in her bed. She was likely still in the hospital tent, tending to some poor soul. Not one of the hundreds of Nursing Sisters who had come to Europe from Canada would ever leave a patient in need of medical care or a compassionate ear, and Lillian was no exception. It was in her blood to care for the broken and bruised, just as it was in Adele's.

Before the war, Adele had been eager to see the world beyond her quiet town of Petite Côte on the Detroit River. When her mother had encouraged her and her sister, Marie, to attend nursing school in Toronto six years ago, Adele had jumped at the chance. Two years later, the war broke out, and a year after that, Adele told her mother that she was going to enlist with the Canadian Army Medical Corps. Marie was content to stay in Toronto, working in the hospital and hoping to get married at some point, but Adele wasn't ready for that. She wanted more. Joining the Nursing Sisters as a qualified nurse was the only option for a Canadian woman wanting to serve overseas, and since officials had realized the demand for nurses would be far greater than what the Sisters could provide on their own, they had opened the application process to women who were not nuns. Her mother had pleaded with her not to go, but Adele had gently turned down every one of her arguments.

"I'm going for the country, Maman," she said. "It's my duty."

It was only after she said she wanted to go to honour her father, who had died serving in the Boer War thirteen years earlier, that her mother admitted defeat. Guillaume, her mother's second husband, and the man who had raised Marie and Adele as his own daughters, wholeheartedly approved of her plan, though his farewell hug felt tight with regret.

Out of the two thousand applications submitted that year, Adele was one of only seventy-five nurses chosen, and that was due to her exceptional nursing skills, citizenship, physical fitness, and high moral character. Maman couldn't help but smile with teary pride the day Adele received her uniform. As soon as she put it on, anticipation had buzzed through Adele, all the way from the top of her stiff white veil to the hem of her official blue gown.

On the ship bound from Canada to England, Adele had met the three girls with whom she would soon be sharing a tent at a clearing station. Hazel and Lillian both hailed from New Brunswick, and Minnie was from Nova Scotia. What a relief to discover they were kindred spirits, and they all got along famously. As nurses, they would be in the war in the dual capacities of medical workers and caring women. They would be the first to greet wounded men coming off the trucks and trains from the Front, and their duties would include everything from cleaning and dressing wounds, dispensing medicine, delivering tetanus vaccines, and assisting in surgery and post-op care, to the often overlooked necessity of simply listening and comforting their patients. It wasn't long before the soldiers came to affectionately call the nurses "Bluebirds" whenever they caught sight of their cheery blue uniforms.

Despite all her training, nothing could have prepared Adele for the front lines of war. It wasn't just the horrible wounds from bullets, shrapnel, or fire. Men came in all conditions: delirious with trench fever they'd caught from hoards of lice, gasping for breath through pneumatic lungs, weak from dysentery, crippled by numb, gangrenous feet from living in fetid water with rats, and so much more. Adele had never imagined the horrors she would see, the gore she would handle, or the grief that would tear through her when another man died.

In her early moments of despair, Nurse Johnson, their steely-eyed matron, had drawn Adele aside and gently told her there was an art to staying sane here, day after day, month after month, year after year: stay busy and stay focused on medicine. Don't get too close to the men on a personal level. But as much as Adele tried to think of the patients as statistics rather than scared and suffering men, she couldn't. She became a mother bird, comforting them and caring, even if she knew some of them were fated to die under her watch.

Would she have come if she'd known the devastation that awaited her? She'd asked herself that question many times over the last three years, wondering if she was as courageous as her family claimed. Her answer was always yes. Unequivocally yes. Despite everything she'd seen and done, she'd come back here if she was needed. As much as Adele hated everything about this place, it was exactly where she was supposed to be, and that knowledge never failed to boost her from whatever dark place enveloped her. That, and the loyal camaraderie between her and her friends.

After peeling off her tired uniform, Adele folded back the rough grey blanket on her bed and crawled beneath its scratchy fibres, too tired to even contemplate writing in her journal. There was no comfortable spot on her lumpy pillow, but it didn't matter. A rock would have been just as welcoming. As she closed her eyes, she felt the slightest bounce on her cot, then the velvet touch of her new friend nuzzling in around her neck like a hot water bottle. The General, they called him. The tiny black kitten with startling green eyes had followed Minnie to the tent a week before and now graciously permitted all the girls to give him attention when he wasn't busy batting an imagined toy. Minnie might claim him as hers, but he made the perfect end to Adele's day.

It seemed she had just dropped into sleep when the door to their barracks swung open.

"Everybody up!"

Adele's eyes felt glued shut, but she forced them open. Beside her, Minnie grumbled something about it being only five o'clock, but Nurse Johnson marched in and started tugging blankets down. Lillian hadn't even returned from the previous night's shift yet.

"It's all hands on deck this morning," Nurse Johnson announced.

Booms rolled in the distance, closer and faster than mere hours before. Adele heard rain pattering against the canvas walls, then the sharp orders of men. The girls dressed quickly, grabbing their capes on the way out. As they sprinted to the hospital, heads ducked in the freezing rain, they passed two ambulances hitched to filthy, defeated horses. The wet animals swayed at the front of the wagons, their heads hanging low, their hooves partially submerged in icy mud. The nurses stood to the side as a long line of stretchers carrying wounded men snaked out the backs of the ambulances and into the clearing station.

All that day, ambulances ferried soldiers from the Front to the hospital. They arrived soaked and shivering from the wind and rain, broken and bleeding from enemy machine-gun fire or shells, some crying, some silent from shock. Adele heard snatches of conversation from those who were conscious, some claiming the Allies had won the battle, others merely shaking their heads with frustration and defeat. Adele rushed to triage them, supporting men who could walk to a bed, directing stretcher-bearers for those who could not. She unwound bloodied bandages, cleaned and treated wounds as best as she could while the men waited for a doctor, then she wrapped them up again. The hours blended together in a rancid swamp of blood, tears, and exhaustion.

"Excuse me, Sister?" a voice called.

Adele had just finished a difficult *débridement*, clearing necrotic tissue from a case of gas gangrene on the inside of a man's thigh, and she turned toward the speaker as she removed her rubber gloves. He was tall and dark-haired, and the fibres of his uniform were stiff with dried mud and blood, but she could see no obvious wounds.

"Are you injured, Corporal . . . ?"

"Bailey. John Bailey. No, Sister. It's not me." He pointed at a man on a cot across the tent. "You see the fella there at the very end? Is he all right? Will he be all right?"

"I'm sorry. I really don't know. I haven't had a chance to go to him."

"He's my brother," he said quietly. "Please help him."

She'd heard that before. *He's my brother. He's my friend.* Those beautiful, terrible words tore men apart and scarred her every time.

"Why don't you go sit with him? I'll be right there."

"Thank you," he said, then took off like a bull toward his brother.

Adele paused to give her patient with the gas gangrene a reassuring touch, but he barely moved in acknowledgement, then she went for a fresh pair of gloves, a bucket of water, and a clean cloth from the trolley before making her way to her new charge.

The chart at the end of the bed read *Corporal Jeremiah Bailey, 1st Canadian Tunnelling Company. Facial lacerations, multiple fractured ribs.*

So these men were tunnellers. Members of the courageous breed who dug *beneath* the trenches, blocking and bombing the Germans. She'd never seen a tunneller before. Not a live one, anyway.

John was hovering over Jeremiah, gently trying to rouse him. The corporal's face was wrapped in stained linen, so Adele got to work, peeling back the dirty bandages and cleaning the skin underneath. She didn't want to touch the wrong place and accidentally do more harm, but she had to be thorough. The doctor would need the patient to be clean before he could help with anything. With forceps, she tugged at a piece of gauze, but it was stuck to dried blood. Jeremiah gasped and his eyes flitted open.

"I'm so sorry, Corporal Bailey," she said, cutting the cloth free with scissors instead.

"Jerry?" John said.

Jeremiah's eyes rolled to his brother. "I'm all right."

The words rode on an exhalation, squeezed through motionless lips, husky and quiet, as if made with the least possible effort. But there would have been a great effort made, Adele knew.

"Jesus, Jerry," John whispered.

She felt the cheek quiver slightly under her cloth in acknowledgement of the sentiment and felt a vague twinge of shame, listening in on such an intimate offering between the brothers. She focused on wringing out the cloth, darkening the water in her bucket to a dull copper brown.

After a few minutes, the left side of Jeremiah's face was recognizable. It was bruised, and there was a small cut on his brow, but that was all. The damage must be on the other side.

"I'll just switch spots with you, if you don't mind," she said to John.

Once in place, she pressed tentatively against the bandage covering the right side of Jeremiah's face, feeling for the definition of bone. She'd seen jaws blown off before. The shock of that terrible wound had sent her behind the tent, retching the first and second times. She was more prepared now, but always nervous.

"I'll be very careful, Corporal Bailey," she promised, loosening the bandage with a syringe of warm water.

"Jerry. Just call him Jerry, would you? He's Jerry. I'm John. We're the Bailey brothers."

"Of course." But it was so hard to think of the men in here like that. To give them names and homes and families. It made it so much more difficult to say goodbye.

"Jerry," she said gently, "I'm going to start under your chin and work my way up, all right?"

He looked at her through clear grey eyes the colour of winter storm clouds, then he blinked slowly before regarding his brother.

John laughed. "Nothing wrong with your vision, I see."

Adele raised an eyebrow. "Did I miss something?"

"No, Sister," John said, but she could tell what it was from the guilt in his expression.

It wasn't the first time she'd heard these kinds of comments or felt the men's lonely energy. She was aware of them watching her, thinking about her in ways they ought not to, but she didn't really mind, especially after all they'd been through. There was no harm in their glances. If any of them got the least bit out of hand, all she had to do was touch her veil, and they'd leave off, and so she rarely corrected those who thought she was a nun anymore.

To her relief, Jerry's jaw was whole. That left his cheek and temple, where the bandages were suffused with dark, almost black blood. Adele straightened, stretching her back, then went for fresh water. When she returned, she set her bucket down and looked at John.

"Would you mind putting your hand on his arm?" she asked. "The pain often makes them reach for the wound, and it will be much easier on him if I can get this done quickly."

He placed his hand on Jerry's forearm, but only rested it there. Maybe he didn't understand.

"Hold tight," she advised.

John shook his head, unconcerned. "He won't move."

She wanted to tell him that he had no idea, that she'd seen it a hundred times, but she didn't feel like lecturing. How hard it must be to see his brother like this. She couldn't imagine watching Marie suffer. It would be so much more difficult than being in pain herself, she thought.

Jerry's eyes had closed, though she saw movement beneath. He let out a long breath, preparing himself, and she did the same.

She started slowly. The veins in Jerry's neck pulsed with effort, but his brother was right. He didn't cry out, and his hands never reached to stop her as she removed the gauze, revealing two very deep cuts. One carved a straight, horizontal line from beneath his ear and through his bristled cheek, so that she could see the bloodied white of his teeth. Miraculously, the damage had stopped beneath his nose, on his lip. The second laceration ran from almost the same spot under his ear and passed across the bridge of his nose, terrifyingly close beneath his eye.

"How did this happen?" she asked. "It looks like shrapnel. Weren't you underground?"

"We were, but Germans broke through, set off a *camouflet*," John said, sagging slightly. "That's how they got in."

"Germans were in your tunnel?"

"They dig their own, and our paths can cross. Sometimes it works in our favour. Not this time."

"Aren't those tunnels quite narrow?"

"Yes, ma'am. About three or four feet wide, maybe five feet from the floor to ceiling. The hard part is knowing in the dark who you're standing beside. You don't want to kill the wrong man."

"How can you tell who's who?"

He tapped his shoulder with one hand. "The Germans have epaulettes on their uniforms. We don't. We feel for them."

Adele stopped, speechless. In her mind she saw the men in the murky blackness underground, fumbling desperately for that extra bit of fabric on the shoulders of the enemy's coats.

A huff of air escaped Jerry's nose, and she turned her attention back to him.

"I didn't find out until after we killed the Germans that Jerry'd been hit by the blast," John went on. "He'd been thrown back, but the shrapnel caught him on the way. He was buried when I got to him."

She shouldn't have asked. Somehow, out of necessity, she'd hardened herself to the things she saw in the hospital day in and day out, but hearing how the wounds before her had been inflicted made them so real.

"Thank God you found him," she whispered as she wrung her cloth out one last time.

Considering the extreme damage, the pain resulting from her tender touch should have been practically unbearable, and yet Jerry hadn't flinched. She hoped there wasn't nerve damage.

"The doctor will be by soon to stitch you up. He's very good, but you will have a scar, I'm afraid."

"Too bad, Jerry. Like I've always said, you'll never be as handsome as me."

"Some ladies like scars," Adele teased.

John's low-throated laugh filled the hushed room. Jerry closed his eyes, and she thought maybe he was smiling inside.

"I gotta get back," John said eventually.

Jerry stiffened. Adele saw the pull between them as if it were a rope drawn tight. John clearly wanted to embrace his brother but settled for a light pat on the shoulder, then Jerry lifted a hand and his brother clasped it.

"Don't worry. I'll be careful," John said, then he turned to Adele. "Look after him, all right?"

"I will," she promised.

Jerry watched John until he disappeared, a sparkle of tears at the corners of his eyes.

"It's okay, Jerry," she said. "You're safe. I'll take care of you."

But later, as she gave him morphine in preparation for his surgery and his eyelids grew heavy with the drug, a terrible thought came to Adele. If only Jerry had been hurt more severely. If he had lost a limb or more of his face, they'd send him home. If he recovered from this wound, he'd be back at the Front with his brother in short order, facing death once more.

two

JERRY

❧

Morning came to Jerry in the middle of the night. The darkness was the same as it had been when he'd first arrived at the clearing station, but he was not.

He couldn't remember much about what had happened in the tunnel, just that they'd thought the muffled thumping in the walls wasn't cause for worry. After so many hours, how could a man possibly determine if he was hearing shell fire in the distance, the thudding of an enemy shovel only inches away, or his own heartbeat? Then the world had exploded, cutting through him, burning, then burying—until there was only blackness and a great, gasping weight pinning him down, invading his nose, his mouth, and his lungs until John's fingers clawed him out. Then fragments. John's clenched jaw fading in and out of Jerry's view as he carried him to the ambulance. An unspeakable dread spilling through him that this might be their last moment together.

But today Jerry was alive. He knew that much at least, though it was a foggy certainty. The bandage they'd wrapped around his head covered one eye, so his vision was restricted, and the muted sounds of conversation seemed very far away.

But he still heard the anxious, ragged whispers of the men in the tunnel in the moments before it had all happened. *What do you hear? What is it? Shell fire? Digging? Which is it, man?*

Slowly, Jerry ran inventory of his body. He began by wiggling his toes, assuring himself that they were there. If he still had his feet, that meant he had his legs, too, and if he could move his toes, he could walk again. His chest was restricted, but from the uniform tension around it, he figured it was bandages. He wouldn't be surprised if he'd busted some ribs or something. When he reached his neck, he paused, remembering the simple sensation of a cloth following the line of his throat, caressing his jaw. The nurse in blue. The sense of being looked after was so out of place these days. In those moments when she'd touched him, he'd been a boy again, cared for, cared about. Now that he lay alone, he craved that comfort again.

He continued his self-assessment, his eyes still closed. With effort he lifted his hand and followed the path of the cloth on his face. He carefully touched what he could of his upper lip, swollen to twice its size. Stranger still was the fact that it and half of his face were numb. He felt nothing but hot skin against his fingertips. He walked his fingers up his cheek to where the skin was tight and inflamed, but still insensitive to his touch. Foreign. The inside of it swelled, and the stitches felt like the seam of a coat, puckered and rough. His mouth was sticky with the coppery taste of old blood. Though it was painful, he used the tip of his tongue to explore the thread looping over and over through his cheek, trying to count how many stitches it had taken to put him back together, but it was hard to tell from the inside, and he had no mirror. Not that he was eager to see his face.

He was whole. That's what mattered.

Assessment complete, he became more aware of the sounds around him, the metallic *tink tink* of metal being dropped into pans, the dull monotone of voices. So calm here, he thought blearily. So quiet compared to the relentless fighting and killing outside of this place. Somewhere nearby a man moaned, then began to sob, but it was all right. It wasn't the same as the screams of terror he'd lived with at the Front.

Shifting his head ever so slightly, not wanting to disturb the field of stitches stretched over his skin, Jerry slowly opened his eyes. The room came into a dreamlike, grey view, a slowly moving landscape of bodies. Individual cones of light lit the crowns of doctors and nurses bent over wounded men. He wondered vaguely if he knew any of those men. It didn't matter. He wasn't about to talk with anyone. Considering the state of his face, he wondered if he'd ever be able to speak normally again. Not that he'd ever been a big talker, but still.

"You're awake," came a woman's voice. She appeared before him in her robin's-egg-blue dress and white apron, a few blond wisps of hair peeping out from under her veil. "Remember me?"

Did he? The hours were fuzzy, but yes, she had been there, a pillar of reassurance standing across from John. A ridiculous wave of shyness came over him, and he worried that if he tried to speak, he'd come off as a total fool. He wanted to smile at her, to thank her for the care she'd given him, but he gave up the thought. He had no idea if the part of his face he couldn't feel still moved when he told it to.

"I bet you'd like some water," she said. "I'm going to sit you up straighter so you can drink on your own. Your face is still numb, so that might be a challenge, but I'm here to help."

Before she moved behind him, he caught her name tag. *Sister Adele.* A nun. The world could be a very cruel place sometimes.

She raised the back of his bed gently, and he winced slightly as his torso adjusted to the angle, reminding him he'd broken bones as well as his face, then she put the cup in his hand. "Here you go. Just small sips."

The lukewarm water came straight from heaven. He wanted to drain the entire cup, but his face felt heavy, awkward around the tin.

She dabbed at his chin with cloth. "That's enough for now."

"Uh," he managed, mortified to discover that water had dribbled out of his mouth. He hadn't felt a thing.

"Don't worry. That's to be expected. But you must be feeling better if you're concerned about what I think. Drink a little more, then I'll need you to open your mouth as wide as you can so I can look at the stitches."

The skin of his face, his jaw, his cheekbones, and everything else above his shoulders screamed with defiance when he did as she asked. But Jerry would never complain. After peering inside his mouth with a little lamp, she straightened and smiled. She had a pretty smile, he thought. It reached right into those blue eyes of hers.

"You know, I have seen much, much worse. Dr. Bertrand did an excellent job stitching you up," she said. "I don't think I'll get you a mirror just yet, but eventually I think you'll be pleased. We don't want you to speak for a while, since we have to let your face heal, but I can read to you if you'd like. We do have a small lending library."

He made a little sound of approval, hoping she understood.

"I'll fetch the book I'm reading."

She came back with a worn copy of *The Thirty-Nine Steps*. He knew the book—or rather he knew of it. Jerry had found what was left of his sergeant slumped on his chair, his copy of the book still open, facedown on his desk. The man had blown his brains out rather than climb back down the shaft and enter the tunnel.

Jerry didn't care what she read, he just wanted her company, and he listened with half an ear. Something about her gentle, matter-of-fact voice drew him in more than the words. Like the cloth on his throat, the soft flow of her voice was a balm. He shut out the sights and sounds of the hospital, letting his mind follow the cadences. Somewhere behind her, the wind sent a gust of pelting rain against the side of the tent, but he was safe inside, her voice an undulating river, stretching and twisting as he slipped deeper beneath the surface.

At the Front, Jerry would have given anything for sleep. Out there, he dug for ten or more hours at a time, hunched within the tunnel, constantly vibrating with the uncertainty of living beneath the war while hundreds of thousands of boots and hooves and weapons and trucks rumbled over his ceiling or blasted through it with shells. Behind him in the dark, men hammered in timbers at the side and ceiling to shore up the tunnel, but no one could guarantee they'd hold. He blinked through dirt. He listened through dirt. He breathed through dirt.

After his shift, bleary-eyed and aching with weariness, Jerry would climb the ladder to the surface and emerge into a world of burnt-out trees and barren ground. Even up there, he didn't trust setting his feet flat on the ground. He knew about the deep, treacherous paths that wound beneath, because he'd dug them. He knew the whole thing could cave in and swallow them all. In those brief moments when he had an opportunity to sleep, he could not. Because he always had to be listening. Listening through the dirt in his ears and the dirt in the walls.

Underground, the only sounds the men wanted to hear was the air pump, giving them life, reminding them they were human, and the quiet cuts of their shovels. If for one minute, in those millions of dank, claustrophobic minutes, a man forgot to listen, he might never hear anything again.

On the day it happened, Jerry had been loosening clay with his spade and passing it back for disposal, thinking of nothing at all. He had forgotten to listen. Then he did, and he froze, paralyzed by the *feeling* that he'd heard something—a thumping, a vibration, a hushed German word beyond the tunnel wall—but it was too late. An explosion burst his eardrums, threw him backward. Bits and pieces of men, clay, metal, and blood spun through the darkness. Then nothing.

"Corporal Bailey?" Sister Adele stood over him, concern etched on her face.

He blinked, confused. Muddled by the nightmare.

She held the back of her hand to his forehead. "You were dreaming," she surmised gently. "I'm sorry. I should have let you sleep. It's just that you cried out, and I was worried."

He was glad he couldn't speak. He didn't want to have to explain that sleep was his enemy, no matter where he was.

Over the next few days, his wounds began to heal. The taste of copper on his tongue went away, replaced by careful sips of water, then broth. The sharp pain dulled to an ache, though a lot of his face was still numb. They cut back on his morphine, which he was mostly glad of. He preferred gritting his teeth to feeling trapped inside the drug, though sometimes he regretted that steely determination. He'd love a hit right at this moment. One of the nurses had adjusted the head of his cot so he could sit up, and the sharper pain had returned with a vengeance.

Sitting was better than lying down, though. It felt more active. Like he was closer to life than death. And from this position he got his first real view of the hospital: the rows of metal bed frames, the endless flow of doctors, nurses, patients, orderlies, and stretchers. Most of the patients were flat on their backs, some moving, some not. Many had tubes coming out of their bodies. The nurses tended to them all in turn, checking stitches and changing gauze, flitting from one man to the next like those little blue butterflies he remembered from summers at home.

The thought of home brought a wave of longing. He wondered how his parents were, and if John had gotten word to them about his injury. Mail was so unreliable out here.

He missed his mother. The cool days when he stepped inside the house and was instantly soothed by the warm, welcoming aroma of her baking. The familiar sight of her in the sunshine, hanging laundry, pins clamped between her lips. The light of adoration in her eyes whenever she looked at either of her boys. Those pretty, pale grey eyes they had both inherited from her. And the laughter that came so easily to her. Especially when his father waltzed her around the living room floor.

His father was a big man, strong like his first son, introspective like his second, and he always smelled of fermenting grain from the whisky still he ran. Since childhood, Jerry had been fascinated by the process of distilling whisky and the science behind it. Every day after school he waited for his father to come home from his accounting job so they could work on the still together. He would give anything to be by his father's side right now, filling the copper vat with barley mash, lining up bottles to be filled and corked.

Most of all, Jerry missed his older brother. Being with John was what Jerry had always known. When he thought of John being back in the tunnels without him, his heart ached with guilt. While Jerry rested here, John fought for his life.

"Good morning, soldier." Sister Adele stepped up to his bedside, her smile bright and encouraging. "Big day today. I think the bandages might be coming off for good this time. We shall see. Ready?"

She reached for one end of the gauze, and he felt a lightening around his head as she carefully unravelled the bandage. The second time her hand passed across his mouth, he spoke his first word to her.

"Thanks," he mumbled.

She stopped, surprised. "Why, you're welcome! How nice to hear your voice. You must be feeling better."

"Thanks to you." His tongue felt heavy, but he was relieved that he could say some words without moving his mouth.

"We do what we can. Would you like some water? Maybe a little oatmeal if you can manage?"

"Yes, please." He still couldn't move his upper lip much, so he had a hard time pronouncing anything with a b, p, or m in it, but he tried. "Please" came out as more like "tlease," but she didn't take any notice of his embarrassment.

"All right." She handed him a cup of water. "I'll go get you some breakfast and we'll see how that goes."

It was awkward at first, aiming the spoon where it was supposed to go since he couldn't feel his mouth properly, but she gently guided his hand until it came as naturally as it should have all along.

"Where's home?" she asked after a bit.

"Ontario." He was so pleased to finally be able to speak with her. He wasn't usually much of a talker, but he'd missed conversation since coming here. And he wanted to know more about her. "Windsor. Do you know it?"

She sat back. "Do I know it? Why, I grew up in Petite Côte!"

His gut clenched automatically at the memory. *Frank*. Over a decade had passed since that day on the river, and Jerry still felt something more complicated than grief for his friend. Regret. And a whole lot of guilt. Of all the places for her to mention.

He took another careful bite of his oatmeal. "Ten miles from my parents' house."

"Isn't it a small world? You've probably never been to Petite Côte," she said. "It's so tiny compared to Windsor. It's nice to meet someone from my neck of the woods, though."

"I've been there," he said, wanting to keep the conversation going, but it was difficult. How much could he say without bringing it all back? "John and I played hockey on the river when we were kids."

"My sister and I used to watch. I wonder if I ever saw you," she replied. "When was the last time you were there?"

"March of '05." He knew the date exactly.

She shook her head, wistful. "Those were the days. The world sure is different now, isn't it?"

He grasped at the opportunity to change the subject. "Is your sister a nurse, too?"

"She was, but she got married a couple of years ago. She and her husband and their new baby live in Toronto. I plan to visit her when this is all over. What about you? What will you do after the war finally ends?"

"My pa's an accountant, and I'm good with numbers. I worked with him before I came here, so I'll probably go back to that."

She reached for his empty bowl then dabbed a wet cloth around his stitches. He noted with surprise that for the first time, he could actually feel her gentle touch on the bridge of his nose. He must be recovering, as she said. He wondered what he looked like these days.

"And your father? What does he do?"

"My stepfather is a whiz with engines. He's always fixing something."

He studied her. "Stepfather?"

"My father died in the last war. I was just seven. I don't really remember him. My stepfather fought beside him, but he was the only one who came back."

"I'm sorry," he said, not knowing what else to say.

"Oh, there's no reason to be sorry. He's a wonderful father." She smiled. "And he adores my mother."

He almost smiled at that. "Yeah, my parents are like that too. They're always together. They married real young, and it's been over twenty-five years. He still takes her dancing. He'll dance with her at home some nights. When he built our house, he made sure there was a big room downstairs just so they could dance whenever they wanted."

"How romantic. Tell me about your brother. Is it just you and him?"

"Yeah. Just us."

"What's he like? I only met him briefly, but he seems like a good man."

"John's older than I am. He's always the loudest voice in the room. He doesn't hold back. People love him. He's rarely alone."

But he's alone now, isn't he?

"It's difficult, isn't it?" she said. "Being out here, away from our families, I mean."

He nodded carefully, but his attention had shifted to the elegant smoothness of her neck. She might be a nun, but how could he not admire her? She was beautiful.

"Why did you become a nun?" he asked, then he immediately regretted it. "I apologize. That's none of my business."

She cocked her head to the side in thought before softly replying. "I'm not a nun." She touched the stiff white material at the side of her face. "This is just the uniform. Originally, they only had Nursing Sisters out here, but they needed more help, nuns or not. They had to take that requirement out."

"That's good. That you're not a nun, I mean."

This time she laughed. "Is it? What a thing to say, Corporal Bailey."

His face burned. "This is why I shouldn't talk. I apologize again. I don't mean to be fresh."

She reached for her book, smiling slightly. "Would you like me to read?"

She was letting him off the hook. Very kind, he thought, abashed. "I think that would be wise."

"Where were we?"

"Chapter Five. He crashed his car, and the Scot gave him his bike."

"That's right." She started flipping through pages until she found it. "Chapter Five."

She had just begun reading when her name was called from across the tent.

"I'm sorry. It's the matron," she said, rising. "Would you like to keep reading yourself?"

"Nah," he said, missing her company already. "The story's better when you read it."

She looked pleased. "I'll be sure to come back later then."

He watched her leave, then he picked up the book, careful not to lose her spot. Growing up, he had loved to read, though he hadn't gravitated toward fiction. But so many things had changed for him since those days, he thought, running his fingertips over the cover. He was a different man from the boy he had been. He had killed, and he would do it again as soon as he had to. The truth, it turned out, was no longer something he wanted to think about. Maybe fiction was safer for him now.

It struck him that Adele's book felt out of place here, its pages fragile in his calloused fingers. Its words belonged in a different world. One in which things made sense. Suddenly afraid the pages might crumble in his grasp, he rushed to put the book aside, wanting to keep it safe.

three
ADELE

Adele closed the book, her gaze on Jerry's sleeping face. Her reading had lulled him, and she liked to see the calmness on his features. He deserved the peace.

She'd finished her rounds hours ago, choosing to read to him rather than retire to the nurses' tent. Now all her charges were sound asleep, their fresh white bandages glowing within the darkened hospital tent, and it was past time that she go to bed.

Over the past few nights, she had stayed beside Jerry well past her shift. They had spoken into the late hours, their conversations hushed in the lamplight—really, she had done most of the talking, but she could tell from the alertness in his dove-grey eyes that he was listening closely to her. She had overdone it, not sleeping when she should, but there was something about Jerry Bailey that made it difficult for her to leave. Covering a wide yawn, she waved goodnight to the night shift and headed out of the hospital tent toward her own.

The fact that Jerry didn't talk a lot sometimes made him difficult to read. She wasn't sure if that was his natural state, or if it was simply due to his injured face. She knew other parts of him were hurting; like so many others, he politely refused to talk about anything that had to do with the war and his part in it. From his shuttered reaction she'd learned early on not to broach the subject. He would talk about John, though, and those conversations were his most animated. He clearly loved his brother, and it was difficult for him that they'd been separated by this. As terrible as his life was at the Front, Jerry wanted to be there, keeping his brother safe.

Inside her tent, Adele found Minnie, Hazel, and Lillian sitting in their nightgowns around their small table, intent on a poker game. It was almost eleven, but time often didn't matter. They were all used to living on a few hours of sleep. A card game at the end of the day helped take their minds off the things they'd seen and done.

"Should I deal you in, Delly?" Minnie asked. Her back was to Adele, her riot of short black waves glinting in the lamplight. She set a card down then squinted up at Adele through the smoke twisting from her cigarette. As if he was copying her, the General roused himself from Minnie's lap and climbed up to stare over her shoulder at Adele.

Adele noted the toothpicks the girls were using as poker chips, most of which were piled in front of Minnie. Lillian pursed her lips in warning. Evidently, Minnie was on a rampage.

"No, thanks," Adele said, slipping off her shoes. Her feet tingled with relief. "I owe my mother a letter. But I will take a cigarette."

Minnie held out a pack for Adele then turned back to the game.

"I should write a letter too," Hazel said, propping her glasses higher on her nose and looking ready to throw in the cards. She was the meekest of them, and usually Adele ran interference for her on nights like this. But tonight Adele was too tired to try.

"Sit, Hazel. Don't you leave me alone with Minnie," Lillian said. She was an excellent nurse, and as organized a human being as Adele had ever met. When she dressed up for the occasional party, complete with scarlet-red lipstick, she looked like a movie star. "I'm in. Three sticks."

Hazel set her cards down. "I fold. I haven't had any good cards all night."

Adele turned away from the girls to change for bed. She removed her veil, folded her blue gown over the foot of her cot, and slipped on her nightgown. Once she was under the covers with her pen and paper propped up on the pillow in front of her, she lit her cigarette and took a long drag, feeling the tension in her body release. After a moment, she took up her pen.

Dear Maman, she wrote.

I am thinking of home tonight, imagining we are together by the boathouse listening to crickets and the river. It's been raining here for days, and the dampness of the air seeps into our bones. At least the Germans have left us alone for now.

My charges are all recuperating. Some of their friends have been sent to the main hospitals in England and France for their own, lengthy convalescences. Of the twelve in my care, I expect half will be going back to the fight next week. The others are still confined to their beds. If it would only stop raining, we might roll them outside during the day. We all are craving sunshine.

Remember the soldier from Windsor that I mentioned before? He's rather charming, in a quiet, thoughtful sort of way. Sometimes we talk about home. It's nice to have someone here who knows the same places I do. It's as close as I can get to being there, I suppose. His face is healing well, though he will most definitely bear scars for the rest of his life. So many will. It makes me wonder what awaits us on the other side of this war.

She paused, tapping the pen against her lips, the image of Jerry Bailey hovering in her mind. She hadn't really owed her mother a letter; she'd just written last week. She did owe one to her sister, Marie, whose correspondence practically glowed with happy tidings of married life and motherhood. Adele had yet to meet Marie's husband, Fred Everett, as they'd married a year after Adele had gone to war. All she knew was that he was a lawyer and worked for the war effort in a government office. He sounded like a good father to their baby girl, whom Adele couldn't wait to meet, then spoil.

"Oh, Minnie." Lillian sounded exasperated. "You bluff so well."

"You sure I'm bluffing?"

"Come on. I finally have good cards," Hazel whined. "If you're only bluffing, give me a shot!"

"Where's the fun in that?" Minnie teased, blowing out a stream of cigarette smoke. "Don't worry. You'll do better next week when I'm away on that hospital ship." She looked at Adele. "Listen, Delly. I can't thank you enough for letting me switch with you. It's going to be perfect timing for me to meet up with my cousin. I haven't seen Jeanette in forever. She's my best friend—other than you three, of course. She and I always get into the best kinds of trouble."

Adele smiled. "I'm happy it worked out," she said, and she was. It would have been a nice break for her, but since the ship was only going to Halifax and back, the timing of the trip would be too short to permit her to go to Toronto and see Marie. "I'll go another time. Is it a full ship?"

"Something like fourteen nurses to look after six hundred wounded."

"Busy!"

"Yeah. It's a quick trip. Jeanette and I will have to make the days count. Then I think we come back here with two hundred men, hale and fresh for the front line." She paused. "Such a waste."

A beat of silence stretched between them until Adele broke it. "Well, we'll miss you when you're gone."

Minnie winked. "I'll bring back souvenirs for everyone. Even the matron."

With a chuckle, Adele stubbed out her cigarette and returned to her letter.

Would you please thank Madame Fournier for the generous gift of twenty (!) pairs of socks? When they arrived, I sent them directly to the dressing station via ambulance, and from there, they were distributed to the fighting men in the trenches. You have no idea how grateful they are for what we used to consider small kindnesses. How the war has changed us all.

Did I tell you—

"Do you hear that?" Hazel whispered.

They froze, their eyes rolling to the ceiling of the tent. A low, buzzing sound in the distance was building rapidly, just like the adrenaline rushing through Adele.

"Helmets!" Minnie ordered, abandoning her cards.

They dove under their beds' metal frames, grabbing helmets and wrapping blankets around them as shields. Across from her, Adele saw the slight flick of the General's tail, held tight in Minnie's arms. When a shriek pierced the air, Adele curled up as small as she could, hands over her ears, then the first bomb dropped, shaking the earth beneath her.

A moment later she felt Lillian prodding her arm. "Come on. We have to go."

Adele pried herself off the floor and joined the others. In their nightdresses and helmets, they ran toward the hospital tent, lit by a few glowing lanterns. The first time they had been attacked was in France two years earlier, and it had felt counterintuitive to dash into the night as madness rained down. It still did, but it was easier now.

Above them, Adele saw the lights of incoming planes beaming through the night sky, and she willed her legs to run faster. More than four hundred wounded men lay in the hospital tent, helpless and vulnerable inside such a huge target. She had to get to her patients. Another deafening explosion rocked the camp, much closer to the hospital this time, making Adele's pulse skip. She shuffled to the side, letting a couple of stretcher-bearers past, then ran to catch up to her friends.

Nurse Johnson stood by the hospital entrance, a stalwart, solid presence amid chaos. Beyond her, a blur of blue gowns and white coats rushed from one bed to the next.

"You know the drill, ladies. The hospital is too easy to spot from the sky. We must move all the patients," the matron bellowed over the noise. As commanding and in control as she appeared, Adele noticed her hands were shaking. "Take the most seriously wounded to our personal barracks. Any who can bear it can be temporarily stationed within the trees."

"The trees?" Hazel exclaimed.

"Orderlies are setting up tents as we stand here, wasting time. Now, you must get—"

A blast hit near one corner of the hospital, crashing into the earth so hard they all swayed sideways and grabbed at each other for balance. Dirt and medical supplies blasted into the air and vanished into thick black smoke, and a shrill ringing pierced Adele's ears, blocking out all other sounds. People's mouths were moving, but she could make nothing of what they were saying. She opened her mouth wide, trying to clear her ears. When at last words started to take shape, they felt thick, buried in mud.

"Get to your stations!" Nurse Johnson yelled, breaking through. "Now! Watch those coal heaters. We don't want the whole place to go up in flames."

The hospital was more crowded and hectic than it had ever been, and the hot summer air reeked of fear and cordite. Squeezing past staff and patients, Adele wove her way to the back of the tent and the men for whom she was responsible. Overhead, the shelling continued, and she ducked reflexively, but other than the corner that had initially been hit, the tent remained undamaged so far. She took heart as she neared her section and saw the dark shapes of the men, their various appendages wrapped in bandages. A few were out of their beds, trying to help each other. Just then, Sergeant Taylor staggered toward her, his face contorted with panic. He'd been there a few weeks, recovering from a terrible injury to his back, but she'd known from the beginning that most of Sergeant Taylor's pain came from deeper within. *Shell shock*, the doctors called it.

"Take cover! Take cover! Take cover!" he cried.

She grabbed his arms. "Sergeant Taylor!"

He struggled to get loose, not recognizing her—in his mind he was in No Man's Land, the mud sucking at his boots as he sought shelter.

"Sergeant Taylor!" she shouted, gripping him more tightly. "It's me, Sister Adele."

He didn't appear to hear her, and he squirmed out of her grasp. Relief rushed through her at the sight of burly Sergeant Hatch, one of the unit's dentists, returning from outside.

"Sergeant! I need help!"

He was at her side immediately, reassuring Sergeant Taylor as he led him toward the exit. Adele had no time to watch them leave.

"Help me? Help me, please, Sister?" a voice called.

Adele turned to see Corporal Brown, leaning back on his elbows, terror cutting deep lines into his young face. The eighteen-year-old had already lost one leg, and the doctors were unsure if they could salvage the other. He was utterly defenseless.

"Of course, Corporal. Let me just see to you first. Your leg—"

"It's all right. Please, please just get me out of here."

She nodded and set up a stretcher, gesturing to a couple of her better recovered patients. "Help! Over here, please!"

The two men loaded Corporal Brown onto the stretcher then raced toward the exit.

Wiping sweat off her brow with the heel of her hand, Adele scanned the smoke-filled tent and spotted Jerry, his bandages white in the grey dim. Between his damaged face and those broken ribs of his, she didn't think he was well enough to be on his feet, at least not without support. She took a step toward him, but just then, everything exploded. The impact shoved her back against an empty bed, and she hesitated, waiting for her head to clear, but the noise was a solid wall of panic, though she heard it all as if through a wad of cotton batten. Confused by the billowing smoke, she clambered to her feet, hoping to determine which direction she faced, but the scene was chaotic. Anyone mobile was rushing to help those who weren't, and a crew hustled toward a fire blazing in the back—directly where she'd been heading. Her helmet had come loose, so she held it firmly on her head as she moved with purpose toward the flames, her skin burning hotter the closer she got.

The third time they were hit, the blast came from behind, hurtling scissors and scalpels and bandages through the tent like weapons and driving Adele headfirst into the foot of one of the beds. When she came to, she was lying facedown on the ground, the world shifting around her, the muffled roar of fire and panic overwhelming. Her helmet lay six feet away, upside down, and was still spinning. Clenching her teeth against the effort, she clung to the bed frame for balance and struggled upright again. Sensing an unexpected warmth on her brow, she pressed a soot-smeared hand to it. Her fingers came back bloody, but the wound didn't feel bad enough to keep her from helping. She set her helmet back in place, tugging the strap tightly under her chin this time, then she sought out her charges through the smoke. There was Reilly, leaning on Stowe. Their wide eyes met hers, and she clamped down on her fear. They needed her to be their strength.

"Make your way to the exit. They're setting up temporary shelters."

"Do you need me to come back?" Stowe shouted over the bedlam. "I think I can help."

"If you feel strong enough, that would be very much appreciated."

She continued forward, spotting Corporal Thomas trapped in his bed. Then there were Grant and Kerr, their hands clamped onto a stretcher as they lugged Clifton out of the chaos. She didn't see Jerry. Had he gotten out already?

"I've got you," she told Corporal Thomas, helping him stand. He'd lost an entire arm and shoulder the week before, but it was his persistent chest wound that had kept him mostly horizontal. She guided his remaining arm around her, taking on his heavy weight. This was what she was there for. This was her duty. Taking care of these men was everything.

It felt like an excruciatingly long time before the two of them made it to the exit, and an orderly took Thomas from there. Adele turned back to the fray, passing the blurred shapes of Dr. Bertrand, Hazel, Minnie, Lillian, and the others clearing the tent as she made her way back. By now she was using her entire forearm to clear the blood that ran freely from her forehead into her eyes.

Nurse Johnson appeared out of the smoke, her cheeks smudged, straggling wisps of brown hair loose beneath her helmet. "The planes are coming around again. We need to get out now. Are all of yours out?"

"Nearly," Adele replied, counting off their names. "Taylor, Brown, Thomas, Grant, Kerr, Clifton . . . Have you seen Clarkson and Arthurs?"

"Bailey brought them out, and he kept going back in. I don't know how many he and the others managed." As she spoke, one corner of the tent collapsed, and she grabbed Adele's arm. "We have to go. Now."

"I'm missing Bailey and Trent."

"There's no time. Let's go!"

"I'm sorry! I can't!" She twisted away, heading to the maze of beds, shouting their names over the noise.

"Here!"

She spun toward the sound and spotted a grimy hand waving over the top of a mattress. Out of reflex, she grabbed bandages as she ran. At the back of the tent, she found Jerry Bailey on his knees, pressing a darkening wad of bedsheet against Ian Trent's neck. Trent's bloodshot eyes darted desperately between Jerry and Adele, and his pale lips formed words no one could hear.

"Shrapnel," Jerry said gruffly. Sweat streamed through the dirt and blood on his face. "I couldn't find bandages, and the stretcher's way over there."

Adele saw right away that Trent wasn't going to survive this no matter how many bandages and stretchers they could gather.

"Corporal Bailey, I—"

His gaze held hers, piercing even in the heavy smoke. "I'm not leaving him to die alone," he said quietly.

Trent's mouth was still moving, so Adele leaned down, holding tight to the young man's cold hand. "Say it again, Ian," she urged.

"Edith," he grunted, tears sliding down the sides of his face. "My Edie. Tell her I love her. Tell her I tried."

"I will, Ian. I will."

How many times had she witnessed the choked agony of a man's last words, the pain and fear contorting their expressions until it gave way to grief, even guilt? They wept as they entrusted Adele with their final farewells to their wives, girlfriends, mothers, fathers, sisters, brothers. They'd promised they'd come home. They'd promised to be with them forever and ever. They'd broken their promises. *Tell her I love her.*

It didn't take long before Ian's hand went slack in hers, and she laid it gently on his unmoving chest.

"We'll have to leave him here. The planes are coming back."

Jerry shook his head and reached for the fallen man. Gently, as if he might disturb Trent's permanent state of sleep, he laid the body over his shoulder then looked at Adele. Before she could react, his fingers went to her brow.

"You're bleeding," he said, showing her proof.

"It's nothing."

"I don't think so," he said. He tried to press a clean corner of Trent's bedsheet against her brow, but she took it from him and dabbed at the cut herself. She was surprised by the amount of fresh blood.

"I don't even feel it."

"Adrenaline," he said, slowly rising to his feet as he adjusted Trent's weight. "You'll feel it later. It's gonna be a big bump. Careful when you get up."

She shook away his offered hand, but the ground beneath her shifted, and she almost fell. His free arm wrapped firmly around her waist, and somehow, he held both her and Trent against his body as they limped forward. Suddenly, she was so tired. Exhaustion battled her head wound for dominance.

It was his voice in her ear, husky yet somehow reassuring, that kept her upright. "Come on, Bluebird. Let's get outta here."

four
JERRY

❧

Jerry cracked his eyes open then squeezed them closed. It wasn't worth the effort. Smoke from the night before had seared his corneas and still smouldered within. He didn't need his eyes to know who in the temporary tent was making careful sounds of optimism. Amid all the coughing, he heard the weary, hushed voices of doctors and nurses evaluating the situation. Apparently, the hospital tent had not been entirely wrecked, so some of the patients had been returned there the following morning, but many, including Jerry, had not, as the whole back section needed to be rebuilt.

A whole new side of the war had been revealed to Jerry last night. Before then, he had assumed the soldiers at the Front were the only ones fighting to stay alive, day in and day out. Now he understood how hard the doctors and nurses fought, not only to survive but to keep their patients alive. Last night, their bravery had been on full display, he thought, picturing Nurse Savard's smudged, bloody face.

He hoped she was all right. When they had reached the hospital's exit, Sergeant Hatch had rushed over to take Trent's body and help them get out of range. By the time Jerry delivered Adele to the matron, he could tell that she was more than a little woozy. Nurse Johnson had looked her over with concern then directed him to take Adele to the nurses' tent, assuring him she'd be in good hands there. When he knocked on the door, a stocky, no-nonsense nurse with short black hair had answered.

"What have you done, Delly?" she'd said, examining Adele's forehead. "My, that's a good one you got there."

Adele groaned, stepping into her care.

"Nurse Johnson says it's a concussion," Jerry said, watching as the woman handed Adele off to someone else inside. "You'll check on her, right? She shouldn't sleep too long."

"Yes, we know about concussions here. Thanks for taking care of her." She tilted her head. "Hey, I saw you in there. You gotta be worse off than she is. How many times did you go back in?"

He swallowed hard, remembering the hot pulse of Ian Trent's blood on his own hands. He couldn't help thinking that if he'd just gotten up, grabbed bandages, pressed harder, done *something* . . . His hand went to the side of his own neck in reflex, but there was no blood there. Just his pulse.

"Trent died."

The tight lines of her face eased, as if she understood what he was thinking. "You saved a lot of lives, Corporal. You can't save them all."

It wasn't the comfort he needed, but it never was.

"I promise we'll take care of her," she said, then she offered a private smile. "I'll tell her you were concerned, shall I?"

He hadn't wanted to go into that, to tell her how important it was to him that Nurse Savard be all right, so he just gave a little nod, said goodnight, and wandered back into the crowd. Someone found him and assigned him to temporary barracks, where he'd squeezed in with eight other men and fallen into an uneasy sleep.

Now, he kept his eyes closed, listening to the sounds around him. He knew the moment Nurse Savard entered the tent and spoke to the doctor, her singsong voice clear despite everything she'd survived. A few minutes later, she was by his side.

"How are you this morning, Corporal Bailey?" she asked.

"I should ask you the same thing," he replied.

He heard a quiet trickle of water in her bowl, then felt a cool wet cloth, pressing gently against his burning eyelids.

"I'm fine, thank you," she assured him. "All stitched up and ready to go."

He couldn't resist peeking up at her. She had a bandage across her brow and a pretty impressive black eye beginning to bloom on one side, but she was still beautiful.

"Do they attack the hospital often?"

"Not a lot, but enough. We were hit more often in France than here in Belgium. I think this was one of the worst ones, though."

"Did everyone make it?"

She held his gaze. "Everyone but Corporal Trent. That was a good thing you did last night, bringing him out."

"I couldn't have if you hadn't come back."

Something in her expression changed slightly, softening, and he felt a shift within himself. *She came for me*, he realized.

"I was wondering how you'd feel about a shave," she said, changing the conversation.

"That would be great."

She unfolded a small towel across his chest, then turned back to her bowl. He hadn't noticed the straight razor on her table before then.

"You've done this before?" he asked.

Her eyebrows shot up. "Really? You're going to question my shaving skills after all this?"

But she wasn't offended. Her poor, bruised eyes sparkled as she leaned in and brushed a lather of shaving cream over his cheeks and chin, and beyond it he caught a whiff of her clean, slightly floral scent.

"Smells good," he murmured.

"It does. Nice and clean. We just got this cream delivered last week. We'd run out a while ago."

She set the brush aside then picked up the razor, unaware that he was talking about her.

"All right. Close your eyes and relax, soldier. Tilt your chin up just a little. That's right. Now don't move. This blade is very sharp."

Baring his throat required a certain level of trust, but she made it easy, placing her cool fingers on his skin just so. He imagined her focused expression as she followed the blade over his skin, and he surrendered to her caress.

"I'm almost done," she said after a little while. "I'm usually pretty quick at this. You've just given me"—He opened his eyes. There was something endearing about how she bit her lip with concentration—"a few different angles to work on." She sat back. "There you are. It's not perfect, but it will do."

"Can I see?"

"You want to see how you look? Oh, it's rather early for that. You're still fairly swollen."

"That's all right. I'd like to see."

Reluctantly, she brought him a mirror. "Keep in mind that you're still a work in progress. There was a lot of damage, and the swelling will take a while to come down," she explained, hugging the mirror to her chest. "But there's no unhealthy redness around the stitches, and that tells us you're on the right track. Things could have been so much worse."

He took the mirror from her and looked within. Though he was determined to be objective, he hadn't been prepared for the possibility that he wouldn't recognize his own reflection. He struggled not to avert his gaze.

The fierce bruising on the right side of his face was sliced by two long, zigzag lines of stitches as black as his hair and beard. Some had disappeared within the swollen fabric of his cheek, and his nose almost seemed to have sunk into his face. The right side of his mouth was larger than the left, making his lips look lopsided. Jerry pulled the mirror closer, trying to find the face he'd known from birth, but it was buried deep inside.

"You'll be handsome again, soldier. Don't worry."

"Good," he mumbled, "'cause I wasn't before."

She looked at him coyly. "Oh, I doubt that very much."

He felt the oddest compulsion to laugh. At a time like this, and with a face like his, she could flirt? Then again, he supposed, why not? Just because she worked in a miserable tent that stank of death and worse, tending a bunch of bloody, hacked-up men at the end of the world, did that mean she was dead herself? She was just a girl, after all, and he was just a boy.

"You need your eyes checked," he said.

She laughed it off, tucking the mirror into her apron pocket, then she looked away. He followed her gaze, but there was no one there.

"Hey," he said. "Everything all right?"

Her eyes were a deep blue, swimming with concern. "I think they'll be sending you back soon. You've done so well." He'd have had to be deaf not to hear the sadness in her voice. It twisted in his chest. "I will do all I can to keep you here as long as possible."

Jerry sank back into his cot, chilled by the reality of returning to the Front and descending below once more, and a dark thought came to him unbidden. If only he'd been just a little closer to the wall when it had exploded. If only he'd been buried deeper than John could ever find him. He'd never have to go back there if he'd only died.

But if he had, he would have left John standing alone. And he never would have met Adele.

He paused, then he said the first thing that came into his head. "Maybe we could meet again, when this war is over and we're back home."

A sweet smile lit her face. "I would like that very much."

"As long as I can still walk by that point, I'll take you dancing. How would that be?"

"That sounds wonderful."

When she'd gone, he closed his eyes, feeling strange. He'd been sheltered here, and now he had been reminded of the greater world awaiting him outside this hospital. How long had he been here?

"What day is it today?" he asked the room.

"Wednesday?" came an uncertain response. "June something."

So Tuesday night had been the bombing of the hospital. Slowly the days began to click back into place, earmarked by one or two things out of the ordinary. It had been two weeks since John had carried him from the tunnel. His face still had a way to go before the swelling was gone, but he was walking now. Adele was right. They'd send him back soon. Apprehension rumbled to the surface from the depths of his memory, where he'd buried it in the dirt, drawing him back. War, with its endless array of perils, was reaching for him. This time, he told himself, he would be extra careful. He had to at least keep his legs while he was out there. After all, he had a dance with a Bluebird, and he wasn't about to miss out on that.

five
ADELE

J ust put that box over there," Adele said as Hazel entered the storage
building, dripping wet from yet another rainstorm. Honestly, she
couldn't recall the last time she'd seen the sun. "Wherever you can find
space. Are we getting near the end?"

"This is the last one," Hazel reported, setting the salvaged supplies
down and peeling off her wet cape.

After the bombing, the entire camp—including any wounded men
strong enough to help—had gotten to work rebuilding the clearing
station. Large sections of the hospital tent would be replaced when
new shipments arrived, but for now they did what they could using all
the resources they had in their little village. It had fallen to Adele and
the other nurses to do an inventory of the supplies that hadn't been de-
stroyed. With Adele's concussion, she'd been assigned the lighter work
of cataloguing and filing everything into the correct cabinets while the
others collected and carried.

"Where shall I start? Where does it all go?" Hazel asked, opening
the box.

Adele pointed to a table on her left. "Metal instruments on that side for now. I haven't gotten around to all those, but I'll have to separate them eventually. Bandages here, but we have to divide them up. This whole section over here is for medicines, and—"

"What a job! Don't worry. I'll figure it out." Hazel shook her head and started unpacking her box. "Just Minnie's luck to miss out on all this, isn't it?"

"I hope she's having more fun than we are, that's for sure," Adele said. "We'll have to find something equally as tiresome for her to do when she's back."

Minnie had left on the hospital ship headed to Halifax on the day after the attack. She'd been reluctant to leave them in such a state, but her help was also required on the ship, and she'd made a commitment to go. In true Minnie fashion, she'd winked at Adele as she stepped onto the transport truck. "Don't you run away with Corporal Bailey while I'm gone," she had said, making Adele burn with embarrassment. After they'd waved farewell, Adele had felt a stab of regret. She'd loved to have left this place, if just for a little while. Then again, if she'd gone, she'd have missed Jerry Bailey's return to the Front, which would happen any day now. She couldn't have gone without seeing him off.

She'd been so careful not to make these kinds of connections with the men. She thought she had, anyway. When he'd suggested they might see each other again after the war, she had entertained the thought against her better judgement, imagining dancing with him, holding his hand, and making him laugh. What would he look like with a full smile? She'd never seen it, and oh, she wanted to. She wanted to finish the book she was reading to him then start another and another, just so she could be with him.

She wound up a length of mostly clean white gauze and set it in its proper place, telling herself to concentrate on the task. It was easier on her heart to keep working and not think about him.

About a half hour later, Lillian poked her head into the room. "Nurse Johnson has called us all to the meal hall for an announcement."

"What about?" Hazel asked, looking up from an array of scalpels and scissors.

"How should I know?"

"Come on, then," Adele said, pulling on her rain cape. "Time for a break anyway."

"Maybe she's planning a surprise party for Minnie when she gets back," Lillian said with a smirk. Everyone knew Minnie's favourite thing to do was get on the matron's last nerve.

Adele dodged a puddle. "You know, she'd never admit it, but I think she misses Minnie as much as we do."

In the meal hall, Nurse Johnson stood at the head of the room, hands locked in front, her expression even more pinched than usual. She was pale, except for the red skin around her eyes and nose.

"Has she been crying?" Lillian whispered, astonished.

"Ladies, please take your seats."

Nurse Johnson watched them all sit, then she dropped her gaze, her fingers busy on her cuffs, fussing with the stiff white material. No one spoke.

At last she lifted her chin. "There has been a tragedy. One which affects us all," she announced, her imperious voice wobbling. "A U-boat attacked the *Llandovery Castle*, the hospital ship upon which Nurse Minnie Donnelly was traveling, along with thirteen other nurses and over two hundred soldiers. Their ship went down off the coast of Ireland."

Adele's breath caught in her throat, and she heard a strangled cry from Hazel. She reached blindly to her sides to squeeze her friends' damp hands.

"They attacked a hospital ship?" Lillian exclaimed.

Others joined in. "Why? Weren't they marked? Didn't they know?"

Nurse Johnson held up a hand for quiet. "I've been informed that it happened during the evening when most of the passengers were asleep. The ship was lit by regulation Red Cross lights and markings to protect it from attack under international law. Evidently, the Germans paid no attention. They fired a torpedo into the ship. All fourteen nurses were able to board a lifeboat, and other lifeboats were filled as well."

Adele let out a sigh of relief. Minnie was all right after all.

Then the matron cleared her throat and spat out the rest of the report rapid fire. "But the U-boat rammed and fired upon the lifeboats. It is my terrible duty to inform you that all the nurses aboard the *Llandovery Castle* perished when their lifeboat was swept into a whirlpool beneath the sinking ship."

The air around Adele vibrated with a stunned silence. Then slowly the whispers began, rising through the disbelief, building to sobs as everyone in the room was hit by the full realization of what Nurse Johnson had said.

Minnie, their dear, cheeky Minnie. With the cigarette bobbing in the corner of her mouth, her smug yet affectionate, sideways smile as she teased Hazel to bits over cards. Her gentle touch as she tended Adele after the bombing, and the words with which she had soothed her. Always the one with a laugh or a hug when someone needed it most.

Adele stared at nothing, held in place by shock. She couldn't fathom the idea that such a sparkling, vital soul was dead.

Hazel choked out a sob, jarring Adele from her stupor. In a daze, she rose and staggered out of the meal hall, needing to be anywhere but here. When she stepped outside, the rain was falling in a steady shower, but she barely felt it. Hazel and Lillian caught up, catching Adele's arms and trying to direct her to the quiet, dry shelter of their tent, but she shrugged them off. She needed air. She needed space. Half running, half stumbling past the hospital, she picked her way between the temporary tents in the trees, only stopping once she was beyond them. Hands shaking, she took out a cigarette and tried to light it, but the rain kept dousing her lighter.

Grief washed over her like a tidal wave. Suddenly weak, she fell to her knees, drowning in the weight of every loss she'd known in this place. She sobbed helplessly for every man under her care who hadn't made it, whose eyes had lost their light. And now for Minnie.

Minnie, who wasn't even supposed to be on that ship.

"Adele?"

She was aware of him kneeling beside her, the stark, crisscross scars from his stitches dark against his face. She couldn't speak, so she reached for him instead. She felt Jerry sink into the puddle with her, then he held her tight while she wept, her cold, wet face pressed against the warm comfort of his shirt and the heartbeat beyond it. His arms were a solid promise, holding her together, shielding her from the storm as well as he could.

"Minnie," she managed, loosening her arms from around his neck, needing to see his face. "My friend Minnie. She was on a hospital ship, and a U-boat—" On a gasp, she caught the next words in her throat, unable to speak them out loud.

"I'm sorry." Sympathy swam in his silver eyes. "I heard the news from one of the men inside. They were defenceless. What the Germans did was . . ." He closed his eyes, and she could tell from his strained expression that he was seeing the attack almost as if he'd been there. He knew the brutalities of war better than she. All Adele ever saw were the outcomes. "I'm so sorry."

Her throat ached, swelling against more tears. "She had my ticket. I was supposed to be there, not her. It's my fault she's dead."

"No. Not you. A U-boat killed her," he said, his voice gentle but firm.

He didn't understand. "But if I had only . . ."

"Only what, Adele? If you'd only gone instead?" He touched his cool fingertips under her chin, raising her face to his. "Listen to me. If I'm in a tunnel and someone passes me and gets shot, that was his bullet, not mine. You might have had a ticket, but your friend held it. She got on that ship, not you. The U-boat killed Minnie. You didn't."

Oh, she wanted to believe him. If only she could.

"The only time anyone should feel guilty is if they are directly responsible for a death. If they caused it, they deserve to live with that guilt for the rest of their life." His jaw clenched as if he was reliving a memory, then he blinked it away. "But you have never done that. You are a good person, Adele. You do all you can to save lives. What happened to Minnie is a tragedy, but it is not your fault. It's this damned war."

Deep down, she knew he was right, but Minnie's happy face as she packed her things kept coming back to her. "It should have been me." She faltered, ashamed to admit the truth, but then the words rushed out, and all she could do was pray he would understand, not despise her for what she needed to say. "But Jerry, in a small, horrible way, I'm relieved, because I wasn't on that ship. I'm still here, still living in this godforsaken place. I know I should feel fortunate. But how can I when the only reason I'm alive is because she's dead?"

"I wish I knew," he said softly. "I've seen so many men die. Friends, and men I never knew. I'll never understand why it wasn't me lying there in the mud. Sometimes I almost wish it *had* been me, because I can never stop seeing them there."

There was no judgement, only understanding. The knots of tension strung through her body began to loosen just a little. So she could breathe again.

"I miss her so much already," she whispered.

"Yeah," he said.

She laid her cheek against his chest again, listening for the reassuring *thu-thump, thu-thump* of his heartbeat, and he rested his chin on the top of her head.

"You're going to be all right, Bluebird. You just gotta keep moving forward."

She took a deep breath, and he tightened his arms around her. For a moment she let herself believe him that maybe, just maybe, everything would be all right someday.

After a while, she drew away, suddenly shy, and mumbled that she needed to get back to work. He nodded, then helped her to her feet, and they walked back through the trees, the only sound the falling rain. When they reached the storage building, she stopped, and he opened the door for her. She stepped inside, out of the rain, and he gave her an encouraging smile, then she watched him walk away.

No one was inside the building, and she was glad of it. For the next two hours, she counted and sorted the inventory into orderly piles. She lost herself in the work, leaving no room in her mind for murderous submarines or lost friends. Eventually, the smell of supper carried through the air, but she couldn't stomach the thought of eating. Instead, she walked through the camp and passed the mess hall, deciding to go to bed early. When she reached the tent she had shared with Minnie, Lillian, and Hazel for so long, she put her hand on the door and braced herself for what would be missing inside.

Adele had been alone in their tent so many times, but it had never felt this quiet before. Never this empty. In a daze, she floated over to Minnie's corner of the room and sat on her friend's cot. Minnie's bedside table was cluttered with letters, a couple of photos from her family, a half-empty pack of cigarettes, and her lighter. Adele picked it up and flicked the trigger until a little flame sprang to life. Minnie must have forgotten to take it with her, she thought.

Tears filled her eyes again. "I'm sorry I gave you that ticket," she whispered.

She was distracted by the pitiful sound of a tiny meow, coming from near her toes. She lowered her gaze just as the General hopped onto Minnie's bed then sat, his little black tail curled around himself. He focused his green, unblinking eyes on Adele and mewed again. It sounded like a question.

"She's gone," she told him. "I'm sorry."

The kitten observed her a quiet moment, as if he was trying to make sense of what she'd said. Then he placed his tiny black paw on Adele's palm, still watching her. Without a word, she scooped up his warm body and gathered him against her chest, stroking his back as she stared through her tears at the ceiling of the tent.

It's not your fault, she heard again. *You're going to be all right, Bluebird.*

I will try, she promised him.

Tomorrow she would pack up Minnie's things. She would write to her friend's mother because that's what Minnie would have done for her. Then she would keep moving forward, just as he'd said.

An hour later, Hazel and Lillian returned and nudged her awake. She'd fallen asleep on Minnie's bed, the General in her arms.

"We need a toast," Lillian said, handing her a glass. In her other hand, she held a bottle of whisky she'd taken from their secret cabinet under the table.

Sitting up, Adele held out her glass while Lillian poured. When the three glasses were full, they all stood and raised them toward each other.

"To Minnie," Lillian said, the slightest quiver in her voice. She was the toughest of them now. Before it had been Minnie, and now it was Lillian.

"To Minnie," Hazel whispered. "It won't be the same without you."

Adele swallowed back the tide of emotions that threatened, then looked both her friends in the eye, one at a time. "Here's to Minnie, a wonderful friend, and a wonderful nurse, who inspired me to be a better person. Here's to smiling when the chips were down, and always looking on the bright side, even after the lights went out." She paused. "I don't want to lose that now that we've lost her. I want us to make her proud." She raised her glass a little higher, and they did as well. "Here's to our friend Minnie, the best of us."

"The best of us," the other two agreed, clinking all three glasses together.

The next morning, Nurse Johnson came to see them. "You three were closest to Minnie. You should take some personal time. We have things under control," she said.

Adele exchanged glances with Hazel and Lillian. "With all due respect, Matron, we would rather do something useful than mope around. That's what Minnie would do."

Over the next few days, Adele threw herself into her work, but she had a hard time sitting with her patients. Even Jerry. Because whenever she stopped moving, her mind would wander back to Minnie, and though she had believed him when he said she would be all right, she wasn't ready for that. So when her shift in the hospital tent was done, she hid away in the supply building, organizing and reorganizing the inventory until Lillian came in and said she had to stop.

But there was another reason she was having trouble sitting with Jerry, and every time she passed his bedside or saw him walking the grounds, she burned with guilt over it. She saw his questioning look, and she knew he didn't understand why she was avoiding him, but she didn't know what else to do. It wasn't fair to him, she knew, but the truth was, she had come to care deeply for Jerry Bailey. Far deeper than she ever imagined she could. Despite the fact that he made her feel more alive than she had in a very long time, and that he had been the one person to make a difference in her despair over Minnie's death, she wished she had kept her distance. If she had, she would have avoided the pain of losing him, of walking into the hospital tent and seeing another man lying in Jerry's cot. Because the reality was that his stitches were all healed up, the swelling was gone, the bruises almost entirely faded away. Beneath it all, he had revealed himself to be a strikingly handsome man, dark and quiet, the bones of his face strong despite the fragility of its surface. Frankly, that made it even harder. He would be leaving soon, heading back to the worst of the war zone. She'd probably never see him again. She saw the irony, of course. Just when she should be savouring her dwindling time with him, she was afraid to. She simply couldn't bear to be hurt again. To lose another part of her heart.

In the morning he caught her eye as she passed the foot of his bed. She wished it wouldn't, but her face burned at his attention. She stopped and said good morning.

"I hate to ask, but do you think you might have time to give me another shave?" he asked, rubbing a hand over his cheek. "I'm getting a little scruffy."

"I can bring you a razor and a mirror," she offered, feeling awkward.

He smiled, one side of his mouth lifting higher than the other, and she found it painfully endearing.

"Please," he said. "I'm positive I won't be able to work my way around all these detours as well as you. I'll make a mess of my face all over again."

With a cheeriness she didn't feel, she went for the shaving kit then returned to his side. She set up her bucket and cloth, then placed a towel across Jerry's chest, aware of his eyes on her. He seemed to sense that she didn't want to have a conversation, so he simply sat calmly, waiting. When all was ready, she tilted his chin up and placed the blade against his beard. *I will miss you very much*, she thought, slowly scraping off the bristle, but she had to push those thoughts away. She couldn't do her work if her eyes blurred with tears. Not if he was to escape her razor without an extra cut or two.

Dr. Bertrand had done a very good job, considering the mess he'd had to work with, but Jerry's scars would never completely fade. They cut his cheek into sections and drew a ragged line under his eye then across the bridge of his nose. The path would show when she was no longer around to shave his beard. When he was back out there, facing the guns.

He'd been there before. That's where he'd come from, after all, when they'd first met. And she reminded herself that even with such a horrible wound, he'd survived. He'd seen men die, and yet he had not. Maybe he would survive again. He wanted to become an accountant. He wanted to take her dancing.

But first, he had to go back. He hadn't said anything to her about being afraid, or of being shy about people seeing his scars. He was moving forward, just as he'd said. She wished she could be as courageous as he, she thought, but she didn't know how. As the razor followed the line of his cheek, she briefly looked toward his eyes, which were closed. He was enjoying her touch. She was giving him the pleasure he needed, and suddenly, she understood.

When she was done, she gave him a genuine smile. The first one she had raised in days. "You look good."

"There's that vision trouble of yours again," he said kindly.

Adele reached for a mirror. "See for yourself."

When Jerry saw his reflection this time, his expression barely changed, though she saw a clinical kind of curiosity in his eyes now that the swelling was down. He brought the mirror closer, angling his face slightly so he could follow the line where the stitches had been. A frown passed briefly over his brow.

"What do you think?"

"Same as ever," he said, handing the mirror back. "Just a few lines added for variety."

She set it aside then folded her hands in her lap, forcing herself to meet his gaze. "Jerry, I am sorry I have been staying away."

"I wondered if it was my imagination," he said. "Or if I'd done something to upset you."

She shook her head. "Exactly the opposite. I am going to miss you very, very much, Jerry Bailey."

His smile faded, taking in her confession.

"We are trained not to get personal with our patients. There are far too many hazards to doing that. But somehow I forgot all of them after I met you."

"You're not the only one," he said. "I'm gonna miss you, too."

"I've been selfish, staying away with hopes of avoiding the pain of separation. Turns out all it did was make me unhappy."

He reached for her hand. "This will all be over someday, Adele. And when it is, I'll come looking for you."

She pressed her lips together, trying valiantly not to cry. "I hope it's soon," she managed.

"So do I."

"Corporal Bailey."

Adele pulled her hand from Jerry's, and her stomach sank, seeing Dr. Bertrand approach. She knew what he was going to say, and once again, she felt her heart breaking.

"You've made a tremendous recovery, son," the doctor said, then he set a hand on Adele's shoulder. "Due in part to the special care you received from Lieutenant Savard, I am certain. She has done all she can to keep you here, but it's time I be the bad guy and send you back to the fight. The truck will be heading out tomorrow morning."

Jerry's jaw flexed. "Yes, sir. Thank you for everything."

They didn't speak as the doctor walked away, then Adele took a breath and tried to keep her voice steady. "We never got to finish the book," she said, remembering the nights when they'd set it aside, more interested in each other's stories than the one on the pages. "I suppose you'll find another copy when you're back there."

"It won't be the same," he said.

———

The next day, she found it difficult to get out of bed. Outside, the sunshine was blinding. The first day in weeks without rain, and the irony of that hurt Adele deep inside. Soon Jerry would be gone, and to make it all worse, he'd take the sunshine with him.

When she entered the hospital, his gaze found hers, and she noted with a pang that he was already dressed in a new, clean uniform, ready to leave.

"I'm sorry to see you go," she told him.

"I bet I'm sorrier," he replied quietly.

Of course he was right. Because while she stayed here and worked, he was headed back to hell.

"You'll be all right," she said with forced optimism. "Though I can't imagine what it must be like out there. You're so brave."

"I don't know about that. Courage only applies when you have a choice. We do what we must, that's all. Just following orders."

"Fighting for us."

He held her gaze, a soft light in those grey eyes. "I'll always fight for you, Bluebird."

For a moment she couldn't look away. Then they both did, wishing they could say more, wishing they already had. Because it was too late now.

Outside the hospital, she watched him join the other returning men in the back of an open truck, using her hand as a shield to block out the sunlight and shadow the tears welling in her eyes. Some of the soldiers in the truck were bent over, their faces in their hands, resigned to their fate, but Jerry was looking up at the sky. From this angle, she couldn't see the scarring. Then he lowered his gaze to hers, and she saw the face she'd grown to love. As the truck's wheels jolted forward, she raised her hand in farewell. He lifted his briefly before letting it fall, but his eyes held hers until the truck bumped out of sight.

PART
— two —

six

CASSIE

—Present Day—

Cassie turned her ancient Prelude onto the long gravel drive she knew so well, and her stomach rolled with anticipation. As she passed between half a dozen hundred-year-old elms, she leaned closer to the windshield, eager to catch sight of the house. When she was a little girl, this place had seemed massive, with its two stubbled acres of cornfields, the grey barn, and the stately two-storey house just past the big sinkhole, complete with a wraparound porch. Almost like a palace, to a little girl. Seeing it now as an adult, everything looked a little diminished—the fields were abandoned, the barn appeared slightly crooked, and the once bright blue shutters of the house had faded. Even the sinkhole behind the barn looked less dramatic, though she still thought it was an interesting part of the geography, like someone had forgotten to cement in a pool.

The day she'd left the place for good, it hadn't felt like a palace. She'd been only a kid, but she remembered how the house had looked shrunken from her perspective inside the police car, how the upstairs' windows were like eyes, sad to watch her go.

A lifetime had passed since then, and just like the house, Cassie had changed. She took a deep breath as her car rolled past the barn toward the house and felt a mix of anxiety and anticipation tingle in her chest. The last time she'd driven by, the windows and doors had been blocked with plywood, but they were open now. Despite all the years and general decay, the house stood proud. Like an unflinching old farmer overseeing his land, pretending to be unaffected by the arthritis ravaging his bones.

She parked beside what she assumed was Matthew's navy-blue F-150. Avoiding the puddles left by last night's storm, she wrestled four black plastic storage bins from her trunk, then climbed the porch's two uneven stairs. She paused in front of the door, beside the big bay window, trying to prepare herself for the moment she'd come face-to-face with the long, shadowed staircase she'd seen in her nightmares for almost twenty years.

The sound of hammering interrupted her thoughts, and she let the memories go. Hitching the storage bins higher on her hip, she knocked on the door with her free hand, determined to appear confident no matter what her stomach was up to. Seconds later, she heard shoes thumping down the stairs, then the door opened.

"Hi," Matthew said, running a hand through his hair and creating a small cloud of drywall dust. "Good to see you, Miss Simmons."

Suddenly, she was nervous. Hugging the tubs awkwardly against her chest, she gave him what she hoped was an easy smile. "Oh, it's Cassie. Please call me Cassie. May I come in?"

"Of course. Here, let me take those for you."

They angled around one another, with him trying to take the tubs and her trying to release them, and they ended up dropping everything onto the floor. He flushed with embarrassment as he picked them up, but she only laughed, grateful that whatever ice had existed between them had broken.

"Come on in," he said, leading the way to the living room. "This is . . ."

He was still talking, but Cassie didn't hear him. She felt like she was stepping back in time, the empty room before her filled with furniture, photographs, and the brown, upright piano in the corner where her father used to play. The same old chandelier from decades before still hung from the ceiling, though it was coated with dust. Some might say it was a little gaudy compared to today's chic styles, but she was unreasonably glad to see it was still there.

Her inspection stopped at what was left of the wall dividing the living room from the kitchen. It was mostly broken plaster and splintered two-by-fours, and Cassie could see the familiar, sage-green kitchen cupboards through the remaining framing. Before coming here, she had thought she would hate the demolition Matthew had mentioned, but she was pleasantly surprised that it was quite the opposite. The kitchen was flooded with light from the big window in the front room. It was a beautiful change.

"Wow."

He turned to face her, misinterpreting her reaction. "I'm sorry. It's a disaster zone in here." He set down the tubs then gathered broken chunks of wall from the floor and shoved them into a half-empty garbage bag. Three others were already full and lined up along the wall. "This room was supposed to be an easy reno, but then I found the bottles and—"

"It's so bright like this," she said, taking it all in. "So open."

"You've been here before?"

She sidestepped his question. "So this is the famous wall. What made you take it down?"

"I don't know, to be honest. It wasn't load bearing, and it just felt like it didn't belong. Actually, I think it was put up later—the trim was different from the rest of the room. Plus, I figure people are more into open concepts these days." He hesitated. "Do you think it'd be worth more if I leave the rest as is? Maybe just spruce it up?"

"You're planning to sell the house once you're finished?" she asked, her heart falling a little.

"That's the goal. I'm trying to decide what I should upgrade."

She felt a little insulted on behalf of the house. Then again, why should he feel emotionally attached to the place? He had bought it, but it wasn't really his, after all. At least he was trying to improve it; another buyer might have leveled it entirely.

"I don't know anything about real estate, but I'm sure most people would want new floors, and probably a new kitchen," she conceded. "Personally, I hope you don't change it too much. I like the authenticity—though I'm a museum curator, so I like original things. But the house obviously needs work. It's been empty for so long."

"My realtor told me it's been twenty years, but it looks like a time capsule from long before then with all the vintage fixtures. Parts have been updated, but a lot hasn't. I'm new to renovating houses of this era, but I read up on it. Some of the electrical systems from the '20s aren't even grounded. This one isn't. It's amazing there hasn't been a fire. If I hope to sell it, I'll have to update all that."

She turned back toward the broken wall, spotting a glint of dark glass within. "I'm not surprised. This house is a piece of history. It was built by Robert Clyde Bailey in 1890 and has been passed down through the Bailey family for five generations."

"Ah. The Bailey family," he echoed. "Sounds like you've researched it."

"A bit."

"So, Bailey Brothers' Best comes from right here then," he mused. "They didn't make the whisky in the house, though."

"No. It was during Prohibition, which was a really busy time for whisky makers and buyers. Especially around these parts. The still would have to have been well hidden and far from here to keep it safe from others," she explained, digging out her phone. She flicked on its flashlight, then leaned over the ragged edge of the broken wall to peer into the tangle of two-by-fours, plaster, and glass. "Being a bootlegger at that time was dangerous. Things could get pretty violent, just like in the movies. Everyone carried a revolver, they raced Model Ts down twisty roads in the middle of the night, there were flappers and gambling, millionaire gangsters . . ." Her light flickered over the dust, glinting off the sleeping bottles. "It was an exciting era."

"So why'd they do it, if it was so dangerous?" he asked.

She began snapping photos of the wall, the hole, and the bottles, imagining it as a later display in the museum. "I think partially because the men coming back from war generally wouldn't be inclined to follow the old rules. They'd just come from the worst possible place, and they wanted to enjoy themselves. But I also think it's because some of the vets couldn't find work. Once they saw how much money they could make, it was a natural."

He scratched the bristle of his beard. "And these Bailey brothers were veterans?"

"Ever heard of tunnellers?"

"The guys who dug underneath the trenches?"

She nodded, impressed he already knew. "That's what the Bailey brothers did. It was incredibly dangerous work. After surviving that, I don't think rum-running seemed risky to them at all. They had a reputation for trouble, but it's hard to know what's true and what's not. What's a legend without its share of exaggerations, right?"

He raised his eyebrows. "Legend, eh? Anything in this legend about hiding bottles in walls?"

"No, none of the stories about the Baileys mention this," she replied. That little detail had bothered her since Matthew had brought the first bottle to her. How had she not known about this?

"Cassie?" he asked, breaking her train of thought. "You okay?"

She looked up at him, noting his deep brown eyes. "Sorry. I was just thinking. It wasn't uncommon for bootleggers to hide a stash of whisky for safekeeping from rivals. They would have sold the booze eventually, though. Unless something happened to prevent that, I guess." She reached inside and touched a bottle. "You said there are about fifty?"

"I think so. I might have missed some in the back. A few of them look empty. Condensation, I guess."

She stood back, surveying the room again. "Maybe this was their secret vault. Their 'just in case.' If you hadn't gotten creative with your renos, we might never have known they even existed."

"I aim to please," he said, flashing her a truly handsome smile, his laugh lines deep in his tanned skin.

"Then maybe you can help me pack the bottles?"

"Happy to," he replied, and they got to work.

She'd lined the tubs with blankets to keep the bottles from breaking. Together, they carefully lifted the bottles from the wall, wrapped them, and layered them inside the tubs.

"You know," he said, bundling up a bottle. "The more you talk, the more interesting I find the whole idea of this place. The rum-running and stuff, I mean. Does the museum have an exhibit or something on Prohibition?"

"We do. People are often surprised to learn that Prohibition happened in Canada, not just the U.S." She stopped. "Are you sure you're interested in this? Because I could talk all day about it."

He nodded. "I am. These days we live in the 'now' so much that we kind of forget the world was full of stories long before we came along."

That made her smile. "That's a beautiful thing to say."

"Is it?"

"I think so. I guess that's why I love my job at the museum. It's about bringing old things back to life and finding their stories along the way."

"So tell me some stories from Prohibition times," he prodded.

She didn't need to be asked twice. "Well, it was an age when legends were born. The big names like Al Capone and Bugs Moran were across the river, in the U.S. But here in Canada we had our own kingpins. Like Hiram Walker, though he came along earlier, in the late 1800s. Ever had Canadian Club whisky?"

"Once or twice," Matthew said. "My last name's Flaherty, remember. Irish and whisky go together."

"Right." She laughed, feeling more and more at ease. "Walkerville was his town, just east of here. Hiram was a grocer in Detroit, and he distilled whisky on the side, as so many people did back then. His Canadian Club whisky was the bestselling whisky on the market, and he made so much money he built himself a castle with a swimming pool and a barbershop inside it. All to the disapproval of the temperance movement people."

"The teetotallers."

"Those are the ones."

As they worked, she told him how the temperance movement had pushed for Prohibition, which began federally in Canada in 1918. "It was flouted initially as a way to save money during the war. Every province made different rules, but people found ways around the regulations. A lot of the local police were paid off, for one thing. If the runners needed to go underground, they literally did. There used to be tunnels and hidden rooms under a lot of the restaurants and taverns. Oh, and if you happened to go to your doctor and tell him you had a headache, he would no doubt write you a prescription for whisky or whatever you wanted."

"All of a sudden everyone came down with mysterious illnesses," Matthew quipped.

"Exactly. Most of the supply came from big companies like Hiram Walker's, but there were a lot of private distillers, too. Like the Baileys."

"But the big money was in selling to the Americans, right?"

"You know your history," she said, impressed. "Prohibition went on all across the country, but this seventy-mile stretch along the Detroit River was the busiest. We shipped more booze and brought in more money than anywhere else in Canada—seventy-five per cent of the total illegal liquor that passed from Canada to the U.S. happened right here, between the Windsor area and Detroit," she said, reciting the facts she knew so well from the museum tours. "There was no bridge yet between the cities, because it wasn't opened until 1929—at a staggering cost of more than twenty-three million U.S. dollars—so the river was the only way across. I've read that it was like a highway back then, with boats of all kinds in the summer, skaters or cars when it was frozen."

Matthew's jaw dropped. "The rumrunners drove over the river? It must freeze pretty hard."

"It does, but not all of them made it. That was part of the risk. Some guys bought cheaper cars for something like five or ten dollars, but they were slow and not as dependable. Some drove Whisky Sixes—"

"Drove what?"

"Whisky Sixes, or the McLaughlin Buicks. They're called that because they had six cylinders in their engines. They could outrun everybody except motorcycles, and they were so big they could blow through blockades."

He grinned. "What an amazing time that must have been. Just like in the movies."

"For sure. The American authorities were overwhelmed, trying to chase them down. Prohibition made big-money gangsters out of thugs. There was this one guy, Harry Low, who had a fleet of all the fastest boats—he even bought an old minesweeper and a patrol boat from the war. Those things were super fast, they were hard to sink, and they held a lot of liquor."

"A minesweeper? I'd love to see that."

"It's gone now. The cops finally caught up to him."

"When you say 'big money,' what are we talking?"

"Put it this way. The average workingman's income at the time was about two thousand dollars a year. In the case of the rumrunners, an average boat made about a hundred and fifty a day. And some could feasibly cross every single day."

Matthew whistled. "I can see the attraction." He studied the last bottle with new appreciation before wrapping it. "I can't believe all this happened right here in my house. Are there a lot of places around the area with mysteries to them?"

She put the lids on the tubs and got to her feet, brushing dust off her jeans. "Not anymore. There are still some neat old houses that have hidden rooms and tunnels from back then, but most are gone now. Either they burned down or they were demolished."

"That's a shame. These old places have great bones. I'd never want to knock one down. Though I may have bitten off more than I can chew with this old house." He looked at her, an idea in his eyes. "Hey, would you like a tour?"

Her heart did a little bump at the thought of revisiting those places she'd tried so hard to forget, but in the end, she couldn't pass up the opportunity to see her childhood bedroom. Besides, Matthew sounded so excited, it was difficult to resist.

"Sure," she said, telling herself she'd be fine. It was all in the past. "That'd be fun."

"Great," he said, jumping to his feet. "Maybe we'll find something else that'll interest you."

As she followed him, she forced herself to remember the happy memories. Climbing up these stairs for bed, holding on to her mother's hand. Sneaking down early on Christmas morning, eager to see what Santa had brought.

He held out his arm. "After you."

She took a breath then placed her hand on the handcrafted bannister, its wood smooth and dark like it always had been. It felt strange to set foot on these stairs again, at once familiar and new.

"Did you say you came here from Alberta?" she asked to distract herself as they ascended.

"I was working at the oil rigs, but I left that."

"What brought you to Windsor?"

"Oil was a temporary thing for me. I was always more into construction—my first job was working with my dad on houses. When I lived in Alberta, I made some pretty good coin working on the rigs, and I was on my own." He paused, making her wonder what he wasn't saying. "Anyway, I decided to leave and start something new, maybe try flipping houses. I liked the sound of Windsor, and this house kind of called out to me when I saw it online."

She smiled to herself. "I can see that. What does your dad think of this project?"

The enthusiasm in Matthew's voice faded a little. "He's not around anymore."

Cassie bit her lip. "Oh, I'm sorry."

"It's okay. He passed away last year in a crash, hit by a drunk driver. My parents had divorced years before, when I was young, and my mom remarried a guy out in BC with kids, so I always lived with my dad. When he died, there were too many memories. I had to get out."

Cassie understood. "I'm so sorry to hear that, Matthew. I lost my dad when I was little. Cancer." She reached the top of the stairs, keeping the rest of the story to herself.

He headed down the hall, letting her explore on her own, having no idea she used to know every part of this house. She hesitated then walked into her old bedroom, feeling as if she had crossed through time when she reached the window. The sill was dusty, of course, but she skimmed her hand over the old wood, covertly studying the peeling paint. *There.* With her fingertip she touched the tiny, faded lines of ink where she had once printed her initials. She'd only just gotten proficient at her alphabet by that point, so she'd decided to leave her mark.

"The house has three pretty big bedrooms," Matthew said from the doorway. "A large place for the time. They even added on a bathroom, probably in the early- to midtwenties. The plumbing's pretty ancient, though. I'll need to update that, too."

He had his work cut out for him, she admitted, following a few feet behind, so she decided to divulge a slice of family lore in the hopes that he'd keep as many of the original fixtures. "The bathroom was rumoured to be a wedding gift for a new bride—Robert's daughter-in-law."

He chuckled, walking into the bathroom. "A whole different slant on romance."

Cassie hung behind, wondering if she could just walk past it, right to the master bedroom. "I bet she appreciated it, though. Beats having to go outside in the middle of the night."

"True."

But she didn't move as he walked out of the bathroom and around her, heading toward the expansive master bedroom.

"I'm just starting to work on the mouldings in here," he was saying. "The detail work is fantastic."

Cassie wasn't listening. She stood paralyzed in the bathroom doorway, seeing her mother exactly as she had on that day twenty years ago, hunched over the toilet, retching, her whole body arching with effort. Ten-year-old Cassie had backed away, suddenly afraid of the woman her mother had become.

"It's okay, baby," her mother had slurred. She put her hands on the toilet seat and struggled to her feet. "Come here."

This wasn't the first time Cassie had seen her mother drunk. After Cassie's father had died, her mother had found solace in the bottle more and more. Cassie's grandmother Alice had moved in to help, but she'd died of a stroke a month before. After that, it was just her mother and her in that big house. But while Cassie had reached for comfort in her mother's arms, her mother had reached for the bottle.

Cassie had run to the stairs that day, thinking that if she could get to the telephone and call 911 like her grandmother had taught her, everything would be all right. Help would come. But when she glanced back over her shoulder, she saw her mother staggering behind her on the stairs. She panicked and ran even faster.

Now Cassie was back in the same place where it had all happened, and suddenly, everything felt too close. Heart racing, she backed out of the room. "I'm sorry, Matthew," she called, trying to keep her voice even. "I have to go."

He poked his head into the hallway, but she was already halfway down the stairs. "Is everything all right?"

She ran down the rest of the stairs then backed away from the bottom, just as she had that day long ago, after her mother had taken one wrong step and crashed down the staircase. How many times had Cassie imagined how different her life might have been if only she'd stayed at the top of the stairs with her mother? If only she'd stopped her from taking that terrible plunge.

"Cassie? You okay?"

"Yes. Yes, I'm sorry. I just forgot that I have a meeting to get to," she lied. Short of breath, she went to the living room to collect one of the heavy tubs. She had to get out of the house.

"Oh! I'll come help you load up your car," he called after her.

Careful not to jostle the bottles, she heaved one container onto her hip and started for the door. Once she was outside, her pulse began to slow, and she took some deep breaths.

Matthew caught up to her, two tubs in his arms, his brown eyes etched with concern. "Are you okay? You look like you've seen a ghost."

For just a second she was tempted to tell him the truth, but the impulse vanished. "I'm fine. Thank you. Just lost track of time."

Matthew went back in for the last tub, and when they were all safely packed in the trunk, he went around and opened the car door for her.

She climbed in, turned on the ignition, and put the car into drive, needing to get away. "Thank you again. For the tour. I'll give you a call, let you know what I find out about the bottles, all right?"

"That'd be great. I love a good mystery."

"I don't know how much I can solve, but the discovery itself is notable. A hundred years, and you're the first one to find anything."

"Yeah," he said, holding her gaze. "I gotta say, I'm feeling pretty lucky."

As she drove down the long driveway, she glanced in her rearview mirror, watching Matthew turn and re-enter the house. Then her eyes flitted up to the windows, which seemed once again to be watching her leave. So many years had passed since she'd last been here, and she'd thought the nightmare was gone. Now it was back, and her hands clamped onto the steering wheel, seeing it all again. The memory of that little girl, curled into a ball by the front door, weeping as she stared into her mother's dead, open eyes. The screaming sirens, the stretcher carrying her mother's body to the ambulance. Then the older, bald police officer with a kind face who had taken her hand and led her to the back of the police car so she wouldn't witness the end of her family. But she had, anyway.

It was only when a tear touched her upper lip that she realized she was crying. Wiping her face with the back of her hand, she accelerated, eager to put more distance between her and her past, along with all its grief, loneliness, and guilt.

seven

JERRY

☙

— December 1918 —

Windsor, Canada

Jerry hopped off the train's bottom step and joined John on the platform, where his brother breathed into his cupped hands, lighting a cigarette. Tugging his scarf a little higher to shut out the cutting wind, Jerry peered down the platform at the small crowd. There weren't a lot of people here, just a few tired soldiers disembarking into their family's arms, a couple of brisk-looking gentlemen in black bowlers with briefcases swinging in step, and a hunched caretaker standing against the wall with a broom.

"You see them?" Jerry asked.

He'd written home in plenty of time, telling their parents when to expect them, so it was odd that no one had come to greet them.

"Maybe Ma got the dates mixed up," John said, blowing out smoke.

Hoisting their bags over their shoulders, the two began walking in the direction of home. It was a cold, still afternoon. The only sound in the air was the crunch of frosted leaves beneath their feet, and that was all right. They were used to the quiet between them.

When the war had ended, everyone had celebrated with cheers and toasts, but no one had discussed much of any substance, and he understood why. They were all still in shock. Because how was a man supposed to return to "How do you do?" when he'd just spent the past four years blowing others up? Jerry had asked John about that when they were on the ship heading home, their bunks side by side, but the conversation hadn't gone much further. They'd gotten in the habit of keeping their mouths shut when they'd been underground together, living like moles, nibbling on rations. Talking in the tunnels was the easiest way to get killed.

They'd experienced each other's terror. No need to talk about that, either. What was there beyond that? A world of pain.

Now outside in the crisp December air, walking beneath a cloud-filled sky that suggested snow, it was John who broke the silence.

"Think Miller's acorns made it all the way back?" he asked.

Lieutenant Leslie Miller, a signaller they'd met on the train ride home, had told the Baileys that this past fall, as he'd walked in the shadows of ancient oaks in Vimy, France, he'd come upon a carpet of acorns, which he scooped up and packed into his bag. When Jerry asked what he planned to do with them, Miller declared he was going to plant them back at his farm in Ontario.

"They'll be my Vimy oaks. I'll name my farm after them."

The trees would be beautiful. Of that, Jerry had no doubt. But every rustle of leaves or fallen acorn would be a reminder of where they'd come from. Jerry didn't want to remember anything about Europe. He'd have left those acorns right where they were.

"He's probably planting them right now," Jerry said.

Miller's bright plans for the future had gotten Jerry thinking about their own prospects. Now that they were back in Windsor, they'd have to adjust to an entirely different world, and they'd need jobs. Four years ago, Jerry had worked with his father in an accounting office, and there'd be available positions, he was sure. Back then, John had worked across the river with Ford for five dollars a day, but could he settle back into that old life? John was the funny, handsome, popular brother who lived in the moment, a heavy lifter, a man at the railway, on the docks, or in the warehouses, putting his muscles to good use. But he wasn't the same man that he used to be, and Jerry didn't think his brother could fit into assembly line work anymore. He might look as if he had it all together, but Jerry had seen the echoes of the war flare behind his brother's eyes. Jerry carried the brand of war on his face for everyone to see. John wore his scars on the inside, out of sight.

It felt strange, turning down the long, familiar driveway after so much time. The saplings their father had planted in 1912 were all grown up, and the military boots the brothers had so proudly worn two years after that were now shabby and broken.

"Guess they'll be surprised to see us," John said as they passed the barn, nearing the house.

Jerry imagined their mother's fluster. "Ma'll be all over herself, apologizing."

"I hope there's enough supper for us. I could eat a horse."

Jerry rubbed his cold hands together and sniffed the air, seeking the comforting scent of burning woodsmoke. He found none, which was strange. As soon as they settled, he'd bring in some firewood.

The house was looking good on the outside. Pa had covered it with a fresh coat of white, though the big bay window needed a wash. The wooden step to the porch creaked under Jerry's weight, and a thousand memories rushed through him. As he reached for the front door, John clapped Jerry on the back.

"We made it," he said, grinning. "We came back, just like we promised. I can't wait to just . . . sit."

The door swung open the moment John's knuckles struck the wood. The brothers exchanged a glance; it wasn't like their parents to leave the door wide open.

"Could be they went for a walk," Jerry reasoned.

"Ma?" John called inside. "Pa? Anybody home?"

There was no answer. Both boys dropped their bags, then John reached under his jacket and pulled out his pistol. Jerry's was still packed. He was so tired of guns.

He gestured to John and shook his head. "Put it away."

John ignored him and slid silently inside the house. Jerry followed close behind, his pulse accelerating as if he was back on the battlefield. They turned left into the living room and stopped short.

Sunshine poured through the big front window and filled the wide space of the room, illuminating millions of tiny dust motes as they coasted through the air. There was no heat in the house, and from the stillness of the air, no fires had been lit for a while. Jerry ran his finger along the mantelpiece, and it came back grey with dust. The sober faces in the framed photographs said nothing.

John led the way into the kitchen, usually the busiest room in the house. It felt abandoned. Jerry's stomach rolled with apprehension as they headed upstairs to check the bedrooms, but there was no sign of their parents there, either.

"The cellar," John said.

They returned to the kitchen and opened the little door leading underground. Jerry's chest tightened as they climbed down the stairs, the cellar's clammy air closing in around him as if he was back in a tunnel. The only thing he didn't mind about being down there was the familiar, heady stink of alcohol that invaded his senses. Their father had stored his whisky in the cellar their whole lives. Jerry would always associate that smell with him.

But their father wasn't there, and neither was his liquor. Something was wrong. Nerves coiled inside Jerry like a snake.

"Let's get outta here," he said.

"The barn," John said, his foot already on the stairs.

Jerry caught up to his brother just as he flung open the barn door, spilling the last rays of sunlight through crisscrossing cobwebs and onto the dusty black surface of a brand-new Ford.

John let out an admiring whistle, running his palm over the sloped hood, clearing a swath of dust. "Oh, Pa. Nice car."

Jerry lifted the hood, also distracted. "Nineteen seventeen Ford Model T Touring Sedan Roadster," he murmured, ogling the inner workings.

"It's like new. The leather's perfect." The car tilted as John stepped onto the running board then slid onto the front seat. "He must have just got it. What would he have paid for it?"

"Around four hundred and fifty dollars." Jerry had read up on everything he could on that long train ride home, including advertisements. There was a lot they didn't tell a man when he was a hundred feet underground. "Fifteen to twenty miles to the gallon, top speed around forty miles per hour." He closed the hood then crouched so he could see underneath. "Electric lights. She's gotta ride so smooth with these springs."

"Springs feel good in the seats, too."

Jerry frowned through the windshield at his brother, whose fingers were curled around the polished wood steering wheel. "Why would Pa leave a new car to get dusty in the barn?"

For once, John didn't have an answer.

Heart pounding, Jerry climbed in the passenger side. "Uncle Henry will know where they are. Drive."

Their mother's sister's family had a hog farm west of Windsor between Sandwich and Petite Côte, just a short drive away. Growing up, the brothers had spent a great deal of time there, hanging around with their cousins Walter and Charlie. Enough time that the farm almost felt like a second home. Leaning back against the Ford's soft leather, Jerry glanced at his brother, his dark hair ruffling in the wind, and all at once it was ten years earlier, except instead of grabbing their bicycles or running on foot through the trees, they were driving their father's Ford.

It wasn't right. Pa should be behind the wheel. Or else sitting in the back, coaching John on how not to crash the car. It made no sense that Pa wasn't here.

His concern didn't ease as the idyllic sight of their uncle's farm came into sight, with the pigs snuffling in their pen and chickens scratching in the grass, looking like nothing in the world was out of place. But before John had even shut off the engine, Aunt Judy came running out of the house toward them, her face a mess of emotions. Jerry had to brace himself against the onslaught of feelings as she came closer. Her flyaway curls and pale grey eyes looked exactly like those of his mother, her twin sister.

"Oh, aren't you two a sight for sore eyes!" she cried, meeting them between the two big oaks in front of the house.

Aunt Judy was swallowed up by John's wide embrace, and from over his brother's shoulder, Jerry saw her face was flushed and shiny with tears. He was used to the red tinge of his aunt's skin when she was emotional, but the colour was more pronounced now that her curly hair had gone almost entirely white. Had his mother's hair gone white, too?

She reached for Jerry next, squeezing him tight. In the woolly fibres of her dark green sweater he smelled the barn, her sweat, and much of his childhood, along with a tired hint of Lifebuoy soap. When she released him, her expression softened, and her calloused thumb reached for the pink scars that held his face together. He drew back. He didn't like to be touched.

"I'm so happy to see you both," she said, her voice catching. She let her hand fall away. "But what a welcome this must be."

Apprehension gnawed at Jerry's gut. What did she mean?

"Where are they?" John asked.

Her hand flew to her mouth. "Did you not get my letter?"

Jerry exchanged a glance with his brother. "We've been travelling. We haven't had mail for a while. What's going on, Aunt Judy?"

"It was the flu," she gasped. "About a month ago. End of October. I'm so sorry, boys."

Jerry's chest squeezed, and his arm shot out, reaching for the oak tree at his side; he didn't think he could stand without it.

"It was terrible, terrible," she said, over and over. "It swept through and killed so many people. We were all right out here, but . . ."

He barely noticed when she touched his cheek again. "Your mother and father were in the midst of it all, working with the church to help the sick. They seemed to be doing all right." She shook her head. "Oh, it came on so fast. There was nothing anyone could do."

Jerry knew about the Spanish flu. He'd come down with it in September. He'd been stuffed into a hospital tent, one cot among dozens filled with more ailing men. He'd seen men collapse midstep and never get up again, bloody tears in one's eyes, and dried, flaking trails of blood leading from another's ears to his neck. He'd heard the rantings and screams when fevers and hallucinations spiralled out of control.

Jerry knew that terror personally. He'd become certain that the doctors and nurses had a secret plan to do away with him. John had stayed by his side, calmly promising him that his paranoia was coming from the fever, assuring him the medical staff was there to heal him, not kill him. And then there was the music—Jerry hadn't been able to understand why no one else heard the singing. When he'd grabbed John's arm and insisted that he listen harder, his brother only chuckled and told him that all there was playing in the background were moans and groans. Two weeks later, Jerry sat at John's bedside as his brother wallowed in his own sweat and hallucinations.

When they finally walked away from that hospital, much thinner than they had been, their skin retaining a pasty grey shade for a while, they understood how lucky they'd been. The flu had killed thousands of soldiers all over Europe, and every village they visited was littered with bodies of the dead. But Jerry had never thought about it reaching Windsor, Ontario. Their hometown had seemed so far away. So safe.

"What did you do with—" John's voice was choked. "Where are they now?"

"We buried them."

Buried.

Cold, hungry clay suddenly flooded Jerry's mind, bled into his veins, sucked him under. He could taste it, gritty and foul and stinking of blood, crusted onto his face, his lips . . .

John gripped Jerry's shoulder, bringing him back. He understood what no one else could.

"Where?" he was asking.

"Windsor Memorial," Aunt Judy said. "It—it was a nice service, John. Your uncle put up a stone."

The old cemetery with the moss eating into the stones, the skeletons beneath. Jerry clenched his fists, fighting memories of the dirt falling on him, covering his face, filling his nose and mouth. He couldn't think about his parents' rotting bodies. He needed to focus on reason, on reality. But the realities he needed were the very things that were gone from his life forever.

His mother, with her chipper voice and warm heart, her apple pies and cornbread muffins. Pretty eyes that should have been overflowing with tears of joy today, accompanying bubbled words of relief and a deep but reassuring sympathy for Jerry's scars. If she'd been here, he would have held her tight and breathed in her scent. He would have known he was really home.

Their bull of a father would have been standing back and watching their arrival, arms crossed, pride brimming from his smile. He would have lit a pipe that night, then sat by the fire with his boys, drinking beer and laughing; he would have asked them about the war, compared their stories with his time spent in South Africa. Jerry had never planned to talk about what happened overseas with anyone afterward, but on the journey home he'd thought about telling his father about it. To see what he thought. Maybe to let out some of the pain.

Aunt Judy forced her smile back. "Come in, boys. I imagine you're hungry. Food will help. You can go to the cemetery later."

They followed her wordlessly, and Jerry's empty stomach cramped with urgency as he inhaled the fragrant warmth of the fireplace and the smoky smell of bacon. A little brown terrier with a much greyer muzzle than he remembered snuffled wildly around his boots, her whole body wriggling with recognition.

"Hey, Daisy," he said, picking her up. She smothered him with kisses, oblivious to his ruined face.

"She missed you," Aunt Judy said. "We all did."

Jerry and John were different in a lot of ways, but there was one thing they'd both mastered, and that was holding back tears. *Once you let yourself cry, you've lost control*, his father had said. Jerry had held on so tight to that lesson that the only tears he'd shed during the war had come privately, after John had left him in the hospital.

Here, with Daisy nuzzled into his neck, the air filled with the aromas of family, and an orange glow snapping behind the metal fireplace grate, it was almost too much.

"It must have been hard on you, losing Ma," Jerry said, his voice hoarse.

Aunt Judy's smile was weak but determined. "Better now that you're here. Your mother had said you were all right, but I just couldn't trust it until I saw you again."

"Uncle Henry?" John asked.

She sighed. "Same as ever, the old fool. Gave me a scare a few weeks back, but he's all right now. He's with the pigs. He'll be in soon. Sit, sit, and let me get you something to eat."

They did as they were told, waiting while Aunt Judy disappeared into the kitchen. She returned with a loaf of bread, a brick of cheese, and a plate of bacon. After another look at the boys, she brought over two bowls, along with the pot of stew she had simmering on the stove.

John and Jerry were quietly helping themselves to seconds when Uncle Henry barged through the door, bringing with him the stink of hogs. He stopped short at the sight of them, his wide face crinkling into a smile.

"Our brave soldiers are back at last!" He sat down with his nephews, but wasn't quite quick enough to hide his shock at Jerry's scars. His eyes were soft as he gazed up at his wife. "Judy, I think this homecoming calls for whisky."

"Of course," she said.

She retrieved a bottle and glasses and began pouring. Once they were all seated, Jerry studied the table crowded with food, unable to ignore the two empty chairs. He swallowed, unsure how to ask about his cousins.

John felt no such compunction. "Where are the boys? Is it all right to ask?"

Aunt Judy nodded. "We've been so blessed, your uncle and I. They both came home early."

Jerry dropped his gaze to the tabletop. There was only one reason men came home early from the war, unless they were in a coffin.

"What happened to them?" John asked.

Uncle Henry's expression was pinched. "Walter got hit by mustard gas. It was touch and go for a while, and he spent a few weeks in a hospital in England. Took a while for his eyesight to come back, but thank God it did."

"It's in his lungs now," Aunt Judy said quietly. "The doctor says it's chronic bronchitis, and it's permanent. You'll hear him coughing a lot, and he gets short of breath."

Her husband nodded. "But he's been keeping busy with the

rum-running lately, making good money. Charlie is down to one leg and one hand, and he's nearly deaf, but it could have been worse." He looked fondly at his wife. "Judy's been helping Charlie learn to write with his left. His penmanship was so bad before I can't really see much difference."

"Rum-running?" John echoed.

Aunt Judy's smile was contrite. "It's not legal, but there aren't a lot of other jobs available, to be honest."

"Michigan's dry," Uncle Henry said. "You knew that, right? The rest of the States will be soon, but for now it's just here. A man can make a lot of money running booze to the Americans. Your dad was starting to do pretty well at it. You might want to look into it."

Jerry could practically hear the wheels turning in John's mind. The idea would be right up his brother's alley. Running booze might even be up Jerry's alley, but he couldn't think about that yet. His grief was too raw. He stared at the table, leaving the talk to his brother.

"I'll tell you what," their uncle went on. "When you're ready, the boys'll come over, take you out on the town. There's a lot to do in Windsor these days. Prohibition's changed everything."

Aunt Judy placed her hand on Jerry's. "It might be good for you. Help you get your mind off things for a little while."

"You could hit a couple of blind pigs, see what it's all about," Uncle Henry agreed. "Walter and Charlie know where to go. Hell, the two of you deserve to have some fun after everything."

"I've heard that term," Jerry said. "Blind pig. What's it mean?"

"A juice joint. Same as a speakeasy but for working stiffs."

"Meaning?"

"Meaning according to the law, no one's allowed to drink booze in public anymore, but you are allowed to head into a tavern and pay to be entertained by a blind pig or a talking bird or whatever they have going on in there. Or else you pay to get fed. If you're at a speakeasy, you have to dress nicer, and you'll get dinner and entertainment while you're there. Either place, while you're at it, you'll receive a complimentary drink or two."

John turned a hopeful smile toward Jerry. "We should go."

Jerry let out a long breath, then nodded. Life went on, after all, despite everything. He just had to keep moving forward.

"Tomorrow night. Tonight, we got somewhere to be. We gotta say goodbye."

eight

ADELE

❧

— November 1918 —

Portsmouth, England

Adele clutched at a lamppost at the end of the dock, her other hand
pressed firmly on her wide-brimmed hat, bracing against a cold blast
of wind. The war was over. Everyone was going home. The General had seen
the tents being taken down, and after pacing nervously for two days the little
cat disappeared mysteriously into the night. The empty hospital tent had
been packed up and sent away, taking the long-dried bloodstains and echoes
of agonized cries with it. Where did someone store an old hospital? Adele
wondered vaguely, tugging her coat tight around her. After all the years it
had stood strong, protecting those within, what was it good for now?

The weather was miserable, the wind and rain making a bad day
worse, and the dark water around the Portsmouth docks was laced with
white. Adele reminded herself the war was over, that there were no more

U-boats or torpedoes to fear, but all she could think about were Minnie's last moments on the *Llandovery Castle*.

"Come on, Delly!" Hazel shouted from the ship's deck. "It's raining cats and dogs! Lillian's already inside. Let's get out of here."

"Coming," Adele replied, not moving.

She could hear noisy conversations on board, the hundreds of soldiers and nurses eager for warm, loving reunions with family and friends. This was ridiculous. All the terrible things Adele had survived, and she was afraid to board a ship? No more battered bodies, she told herself. No more amputated limbs or broken skulls. No more stink of blood. No more screams of men day and night. Instead, she would get some real, quality sleep. She'd see Marie and her baby. She'd eat Maman's cooking again.

At last, Adele took a bracing breath and stepped onto the gangplank, then onto the big grey ship.

The sail went without a hitch despite all her fears. She didn't sleep much; the movement of the ship kept the three of them up most nights, but they arrived in Halifax without any difficulties. The rain was still coming down when they landed, as if the storm had chased them over the sea, and by the time they were through customs, the rain had hardened to sleet. The three friends walked as far as they could together, then stopped under an overhang, trying to stay dry.

"Well, this is it," Lillian said, reaching for Adele.

Lillian and Hazel would stay here. They were meeting up with their families then driving home to New Brunswick. Adele would be going on alone on the train. She closed her eyes, hanging on to her friend's embrace as hard as she could, already missing her. It hardly seemed real, saying goodbye after four years. She knew these girls almost as well as she knew herself.

"It's going to be so strange not seeing you every day," she said, sniffing against Lillian's coat.

Lillian backed away, making room for Hazel. "It's not forever," Lillian assured them all, but her eyes were red from crying. "We'll stay in touch, won't we?"

"I'll write to you all the time," Hazel promised, giving Adele a teary peck on the cheek.

The three of them stood looking at each other, hesitant to break apart.

"You'd better go," Lillian said. "Your train's leaving soon."

Adele bit her lower lip. "I'll miss you both so much."

One more hug for all three, then Adele picked up her trunks, ducked her head under the brim of her hat, and sprinted toward the train, dodging the throngs of uniforms.

"Can I help you, ma'am?"

She glanced up from under her hat. A black man in a red porter's uniform stood before her, soaked from the top of his cap to the toes of his shiny boots. His eyes were tired, but a patient smile stretched across his face.

"Oh, that would be lovely," she said, gratefully handing off her cases. He took them with a nod then carried them toward the train, as if they weighed nothing at all. Once on board, she found a seat, and the porter stowed her things.

"Can I help you with anything else, ma'am?" he asked after he'd taken her wet overcoat and hat.

"No, no," Adele replied. She dug into her little purse, pulled out a dime. "I'm just so glad to be here, dry and warm. Thank you for your help."

He gave her a nod of thanks, then headed back out into the storm.

Adele turned to her seatmate, a young woman with a charming bob haircut. "Hello, I'm Adele."

The girl put down the book she was reading. "Bridget. Nice to meet you." Her sharp gaze rose over Adele's head, assessing the people still coming onto the train. "I hope you paid George well."

"I'm sorry? George?"

"The porter. They're called George."

Adele peered back down the aisle. Porters were moving smoothly between the door and the seats, but the man who had helped her was gone.

"What do you mean? All of them are called George?"

Bridget nodded and opened her book again. "They're not paid. They live off tips, so every time I see one, I'm as generous as I can be."

Adele thought about the $4.10 she'd been paid every day she'd served in the war. She hadn't really had much of an opportunity to spend any until today when she'd bought her train ticket to Toronto. She looked down the aisle, then stopped a porter as he was passing by.

"I'm so sorry," she said. "There was a porter who helped me get on the train, but I don't know his name, and I wanted to thank him properly."

He gave her a lost kind of look, and she realized that she was taking him away from his work. Disconcerted, she dug in her purse and handed him the first four coins that touched her fingertips.

"Here. Please accept this."

"It wasn't me that helped you, ma'am."

She closed her fingers around his, trapping the coins within. "I know, but I still want you to have it. What's your name?"

"George, ma'am."

"I'm sorry. Your real name."

He hesitated. "Roy. Roy Bell."

"Well, Roy, thank you for all you do. I hope you have a good day."

Smiling, he touched his cap then returned to work, and Adele sank back into her seat, not the least bit satisfied. The very idea that the porters were not only unpaid but had also lost their individuality just because of the colour of their skin, was abhorrent. It wasn't the first time she'd learned of such inequality either. She knew of a Canadian battalion made up entirely of black men; they had wanted to serve, to fight alongside the white men, but instead they'd been relegated to the No. 2 Construction Battalion, where they worked in the lumber mills overseas. The wood they cut was used in the trenches, made into walkways over the mud, as well as supports for the tunnels and the observation posts. Though she had never seen any members of the Construction battalion come through her hospital, she knew they were crucial to keeping so many alive. She hoped they had survived the war and were headed home, just like her.

The thought of home brought Jerry Bailey's face to mind. The sweet soldier with the grey eyes hadn't come back through the clearing station in the past six months, which could mean one of two things. Either he hadn't been injured again and was on his way home now too or . . . She chose to believe it was good news.

The train whistle blew, and the locomotive jerked forward, starting its long journey to Toronto and after only a few minutes, Adele felt her eyelids grow heavy. The jostling of the train wasn't nearly as disruptive as the swaying of the ship, and she woke hours later feeling more refreshed than she had in a long time. When a porter walked past, she handed him a nickel for a newspaper and twenty cents just because. She wanted to catch up on what was happening on this side of the Atlantic.

Schools across Ontario had closed because of the flu, she read, which had killed over fifty-six hundred Ontarians in just two months. Even more alarming was *The Globe and Mail*'s estimate that over six million had died of the virus worldwide in the span of twelve weeks. Adele had seen the disease firsthand; some of the dead had been her own patients. Miraculously, she had not fallen ill herself.

Turning the pages, she scanned the articles, taking in more news. POWs and other British and Canadian civilians were being freed from camps and repatriated, just as Germans held in Canada were being sent back to their own country. She was horrified by a story of forty British POWs finally returning to their homes, sick and skeletal after being imprisoned in a Turkish camp without common decencies for three years. And then there was the whole Prohibition mess, and the fact that the provincial government was planning a referendum about whether to permit the sale of alcohol now that the soldiers were at last coming home.

She set aside the paper and pulled out a novel she'd taken from the hospital's library before she'd left, hoping fiction would help the journey go faster. Bridget had obviously planned for the trip because she focused on her book then moved on to the next, barely uttering a word to Adele the entire way. Unfortunately, Adele was disappointed with the novel she'd brought for herself. Virginia Woolf's *The Voyage Out* was a strange, dark story, and she'd had enough of that. Instead, she chose to close the book and watch the landscape flitting by.

Soon they would arrive in Toronto, and she'd finally see her sister again. So many things had changed since Adele had left—not the least of which was the fact that Marie had married and become a mother. In Belgium, Adele had pinned her dear little niece's photograph on the wall of her tent alongside Marie's wedding photo and a portrait of Maman and Guillaume, wishing for the day when she could put her arms around them all. She'd be at Marie's apartment for only one night, and though she knew it wouldn't be nearly enough time, she told herself she'd go back to visit again soon. Right now, her heart longed to be home in Petite Côte.

The train screeched into Union Station in the late afternoon, and after picking up her luggage, Adele started toward the terminal. Just as she headed inside, she heard her name being called. She turned with a rush of joy and spotted a feather on a wide brown hat, bobbing as Marie jumped up and down.

"Marie!"

She couldn't get to her sister quickly enough. With tears in her eyes, she threw her arms around both her and the baby on her hip.

"Oh, I've missed you!" Marie cried, squeezing Adele tight.

"It's so good to see you," Adele said. Wiping her cheeks, she held out her hands. "And look at you, ma petite Madeleine. Why, aren't you the most beautiful thing? My goodness, you are going to be every bit as stunning as your mother."

Madeleine reached out her pudgy hands in reply. Soon her warm little body was nestled against Adele, and she wondered if she'd ever felt anything so wonderful in all her life.

"How are you?" she asked Marie, needing to hear everything all at once.

"I'm much better, seeing you," Marie said, dabbing her own tears away.

"How's Fred?"

"Oh, he's fine," Marie said, flapping a hand. "He's probably arriving home just about now."

"I'm looking forward to finally meeting him."

"I hope you like him."

"I'm sure I will. But let's walk slowly. I want you all to myself for as long as I can get."

They stored Adele's larger trunk at the station, since her stay would be so short, and that meant she and Marie could pass a drowsy but happy little Madeleine back and forth between them. They talked the whole way on the streetcar, barely stopping for breath. Adele could hardly believe any of it was real after all this time. It felt like a completely different world.

Inside Marie's apartment, Adele put down her small bag and gazed around, admiring the neat living room with its matching flowered drapes and sofa cushions. It looked like a page from *Ladies' Home Journal*. She took off her coat and hung it next to her sister's.

"What a beautiful home," she said, but Marie didn't seem to hear. She was already walking ahead and calling for her husband.

"Adele's here, Fred! Come meet my sister!"

A tall, slender man appeared from another room, his chestnut-brown hair combed over to the side. He was rather pale, even sallow, in person, and he wore thick, round spectacles over a thin moustache and a somewhat small, pinched smile. Somehow he'd looked better in photographs, she thought, though she'd keep that to herself.

"I shall be right back," Marie said, the baby in her arms. "Madeleine needs a change."

"Wonderful to meet you at last, Adele," Fred said, shaking her hand. "May I call you Adele? Really, what an honour this is. What stories Marie has told me about you, the family's very own heroine!"

Adele had known people would ask about the war, but she hadn't quite figured out how to respond. The truth was far too much for those who had not been there.

"Oh, it's not like that at all. I'm just glad I was able to help."

"I imagine all those poor, unfortunate men were pleased you were there as well. A pretty little bird fluttering about in the middle of all that devastation."

"I hope so. I did what I could."

"You must have seen a lot of terrible things."

She nodded tightly, hoping he'd get the message, but he seemed determined to continue.

"Personally, I believe it was an unthinkable crime to have sent ladies over there." He pulled a flat silver case from inside his jacket, selected a cigarette, and lit it, never once taking his eyes off hers. She waited for him to offer one to her, but he did not. "It should be obvious to anyone that the fairer sex would not be able to tolerate such violence and horror."

Ah, so that explained the way he was watching her. Somewhere between disapproval and a dare. He'd probably been waiting a long time to challenge her about this. She glanced over as her sister returned to the room, but Marie was depositing Madeleine into her high chair, then was off to the kitchen.

"The whole war was a crime, wasn't it? Difficult for everyone," Adele replied. "Fortunately, the thousands of women who did, voluntarily, serve both overseas and here tolerated it just fine."

"But still. The things you saw and did, that would certainly upset the natural order of things."

"What does that mean?"

"Why, that you have now seen men in all conditions and states. A travesty for women to witness those things. Not to put too fine a point on it, but how could a man possibly wish to marry a woman who has seen such things? There's no state of dignity left for either the man or the woman."

She forced a smile. "I'm afraid marriage wasn't the first thing on my mind when I was out there, Fred."

"Aha, but there's the problem. Shouldn't it be, after all? You're two years younger than Marie, correct? Twenty-four? Now that you're back home, it certainly will be, and while I understand modern women feel entitled to work—"

"Fred!" Marie exclaimed, rushing from the kitchen with a steaming tray in her hands. "I've asked you before to please not bring up your archaic principles." She looked at Adele with kind eyes. "Don't listen to him. Come and sit. I made us a new recipe that I hope you'll like. I can hardly wait for these rations to end so we can eat real food again. Wouldn't that be nice?"

Adele slid into her chair, but she couldn't escape her brother-in-law's stare, so she turned her attention to Marie.

"What did you make? It smells delicious."

"You'd never know this wasn't a roast of pork. They call it a camouflage roast. Really, it's just breadcrumbs and ground peanuts, onion, an egg, flour, milk . . ." She frowned briefly. "Yes, I think that's all. Oh, and I made corn bread. Wait. I'll go get that."

Fred seized the opportunity. "The whole process of going to war—"

"Forgive me, Fred, but where was it you served? I'm sorry. I can't recall."

Fred smoothed his tie. "I was needed here."

"Bureaucracy," Marie breezed, bringing the corn bread. As soon as she sat down, she broke off a little piece and put it on the tray of Madeleine's high chair. "Who knows what goes on behind those government doors."

Fred's chin lifted. "A lot of very important things that I'm certain would not be of interest to you, my dear."

Adele took a bite of the roast, surprised by how good it was. It didn't taste like pork, but after years of rations, anything that had flavour was welcome. "This is delicious. You can hardly tell the difference."

"Thank you," Marie replied. "I'm sorry we can't pour a little celebratory wine. Tea?"

Marie's letters had made it clear that since becoming a married woman, she had also joined the Woman's Christian Temperance Union. That had struck Adele as funny at first. Throughout their lives, various towns and villages around the province had been "dry," but Marie and Adele had always enjoyed some of Guillaume's own brand of sweet wine around the table with him and Maman. Back then, Marie's laughter had been the loudest. But nowadays, she appeared serious about abstaining.

"So you really can't buy alcohol anywhere?" Adele asked, holding out her teacup. "I read something on the train about a referendum."

Fred nodded. "Next year sometime."

"It just made sense since the world was at war, and the provinces all agreed to it," Marie said, pouring the tea. "We needed to tighten our belts, after all, to support the fight."

"Not Quebec," Fred reminded her shortly. "They didn't participate."

"I can't imagine Guillaume following that law," Adele said, laughing. "I can't wait to ask him when I get home."

Marie and Fred exchanged a look. In her high chair, Madeleine was stuffing corn bread into her little mouth and happily kicking her feet.

"What? What is it?"

"It's nothing, really." Marie waved a hand, but Adele recognized the nervous blush in her sister's cheeks. It was *not* nothing.

"Go on, tell her," Fred prompted.

"Tell me what?"

"Oh, you'll think it's silly. But Fred and I were talking, and we were hoping we could convince you to stay here in Toronto a little longer. Maybe even move here. There are so many opportunities for nurses."

Adele set down her fork. "What are you talking about? Move to Toronto? Why?"

Fred chimed in. "A lot of things have changed since you went away. Especially in Windsor. We would be happy to have you stay here with us for a while."

"You could see Madeleine all the time," Marie added. "It would be so nice to spend more time with you."

"I'm not sure I understand," Adele said slowly.

Marie let out a breath. "The truth is Windsor has become a hot bed for smuggling liquor. You know how everyone has always made their own out there, and there are those bigger places like the brewery in Walkerville. Well, instead of stopping production, the manufacturers have actually made *more* during Prohibition. Taking booze across the river to Detroit is a profitable business. Now those thirsty Americans are practically taking over Windsor."

"Windsor is a dangerous place," Fred agreed. "And that's why Marie and our little cherub will not be travelling there anytime soon."

Adele was stunned. Her mother would have said something if she felt Windsor was unsafe. She turned to Marie. "You won't go to Windsor? What about Maman?"

Marie inspected something invisible beside her plate. "She was here when Madeleine was born."

"Not since then? Marie, she must be heartbroken," Adele said softly.

"Please don't say that. Fred and I have discussed this. It's simply not safe to take an infant to Windsor. We just hope you'll see the wisdom in staying here yourself."

"It would be for your own good," Fred finished, as if all was decided.

For the rest of the meal, Adele focused on Madeleine, soaking up every moment she could with her precious niece. She had to, now that she knew she wouldn't be seeing her for a while. After Fred took his last bite, he retreated to another room, newspaper in hand, and Marie began collecting the empty dishes. Adele rose to help, and as they washed the dishes side by side, she cast worried glances at Marie. Did she really agree with Fred's decision? Or had he steamrolled over any counterviews? Her letters had never hinted at any strife between them. If anything, they were effusive. But maybe that was a front. It bothered Adele that she could no longer tell which it was.

Once Madeleine had been tucked into bed, the sisters settled onto the sofa with a fresh pot of tea. Adele was secretly glad that Fred had disappeared under the excuse of an early morning. She'd thanked him for his hospitality, but all she really wanted was to have more time alone with her sister.

"What do you think of Fred?" Marie asked, pulling out her cigarette case and offering one to Adele.

Adele chose her words carefully. "Honestly, he's not entirely who I pictured you ending up with, but he seems to care deeply about you and Madeleine."

"Yes, he does," she said, smiling as she lit their cigarettes.

"And you're happy?" Adele pressed.

"Yes, I am." Marie tilted her head a little, blowing smoke to the side. "Oh, I know he's got some strong opinions, but don't let him upset you with all that talk about you being overseas. He's a little fixated on that. It all started when women won the right to vote. That really bothered him. You know about that, right? It happened while you were gone."

"Of course. The Nursing Sisters were the first women in Canada to cast a legal ballot." She still remembered how proud she had felt, dropping her ballot into the box. "I thought of you while I did my duty."

"How wonderful. I wish I could have seen it." Marie's brow creased slightly. "Adele, I am serious about you staying here. I've been writing to Maman for months now, trying to convince her and Guillaume to come, too."

Adele raised an eyebrow. "And how has that gone?"

"Not well." Marie allowed herself to laugh, giving Adele a welcome glimpse of the sister she remembered. "I told Fred you wouldn't like the idea either. But selfishly, I want you here."

Adele put a hand on Marie's. "I know, but your home is here with Fred and Madeleine. Mine is with Maman and Guillaume in Petite Côte. I appreciate you wanting to take care of me, even though you don't have to anymore."

"True. You survived a war, after all." She held Adele's gaze. "Would you consider staying just one more night? There's a temperance meeting tomorrow, and I thought you and I might go together."

"I think by that time, I will be enjoying sherry with Maman," Adele teased, ashing her cigarette.

Marie scowled. "I am kind of surprised that you aren't concerned about what's happening back home. Surely you know how dangerous alcohol is, disrupting businesses and families."

Adele thought back to the nights she and the girls had huddled around a tiny lamp, toasting the end of a disastrous day or praying the next bomb would not find them, shaking so badly that the precious, clandestine whisky in their hands almost washed over the rims of their glasses.

"I suppose I see things a little differently now," she said. "War can do that."

"But what about all those men coming back from Europe now, drinking, being violent, staggering through the streets, causing trouble in—"

Adele stopped her. "I understand the dangers of alcohol, Marie, but I have to say, you do a disservice to the men with your exaggerations. And since we're being honest, I will admit I enjoyed a glass or two when things got a little tense over there. I believe the men coming back deserve to let loose a little after everything they've been through. *I* deserve to let loose. You can't imagine what it was like over there."

Marie's cheeks flushed. "So because you went and I didn't, you are more morally correct than I am? You know more than I do? More than the authorities?"

"I never said that."

"We all have our own responsibilities. I have a family now. I have different concerns. I believe alcohol is bad for society, and as part of the temperance union, I have a duty to stand up for those beliefs."

Adele looked at her teacup, the china unchipped. The sight of it felt unfamiliar, like it was from another era of her life. How simple it must be for Marie to let the truth pass unacknowledged while it ate Adele up inside. What a privilege to be able to discount something she knew nothing about. Marie was right: Adele did know more than her sister, at least about this. The fact remained that the same government that had banned alcohol had sent millions of men to war.

"I'm not saying I am better in any way," she said, hearing her voice waver. "All I'm saying is that you do not know what we went through over there. Those men deserve to put their feet up with something stronger than a cup of tea, if only to temporarily forget what they will never forget. Those men who still have feet, that is."

Marie was studying her with concern, all hostility gone. "Are you all right?"

She glanced down, uncomfortably aware that her hands were shaking. She laced her fingers together to still them.

"I don't know. Sometimes I am." She met her sister's eyes. "One thing the war has shown me is how short life can be. And I don't want to live my life depriving myself of the things I want. So please, let's not do this. I'm just so happy to see you, and we have so much else to talk about."

Marie's expression softened. "I'm sorry. You know how stubborn I can get. I worried about you every single day, and I will always be proud of you for doing your duty out there. Maybe someday you can tell me about it."

"Thank you." Adele swallowed the lump in her throat. "Now tell me about Madeleine. What's it like being a mother?"

Adele sat back to listen for as long as she could stay awake, warmed by the sight of Marie's shining eyes every time she spoke of her daughter. But the journey was catching up to her, and her attention drifted more and more until Marie took notice and led her to the guest room for some much-needed sleep.

In the morning, Marie brought her back to the train station and they had a long, loving hug while Madeleine squirmed between them.

"Please think about coming to Windsor," Adele said. "Before Madeleine is all grown up."

"I'll think about it," Marie allowed. "I'd have to talk with Fred."

"If anyone can convince him, it's my beautiful, stubborn sister."

Marie nodded, and after one last squeeze, Adele boarded the train, her heart a little heavy now that she knew something so unimportant in the grand scheme of things had caused a rift in their family.

Hours later, Adele arrived at the station in Windsor, and she bit her lip against tears as she scanned the faces waiting on the platform. She squeaked involuntarily when she spotted Maman and Guillaume in the small crowd, then she sprinted into their open arms as soon as the train stopped. After a long moment, she reluctantly pulled away. Their cheeks were sparkling with happy tears that matched her own. It had been three long years since she'd seen either of them, apart from in the photographs she had treasured.

"We missed you, *chérie*," Guillaume said, picking up her trunks.

Her mother linked her arm in Adele's. "I may never let you go again. Come, I've made your favourite, *tortière*. You're skin and bones."

Adele happily let them lead her to their car, and as they drove away from the station, past the winding roads and fallow fields, their crops cut to stubble, she peered out the window, eager for her first glimpse of the river.

Later that night, after they had toasted Adele's return, she lay in her childhood bed, her stomach and heart full, and her head resting on an unimaginably soft down pillow. She breathed in the fresh scent of the wind on her quilt, and she knew her mother had hung it outside despite the cold, just so Adele could smell the clean air of Petite Côte. It smelled different from the air she'd breathed over there. Such a faraway place. Such a different world.

When she had stepped onto that ship and departed Canada's shores, she had been searching for more meaning in her life. A chance to be useful in a place that needed help. She had donned a blue gown and pinned on a veil, then she'd rolled up her sleeves and experienced so much more than she had ever imagined possible. Horrors, yes, but there had also been friendships. She thought of Minnie, then of Lillian and Hazel, and even Nurse Johnson. She hoped they were bundled up as comfortably as she was right now.

Just before sleep could pull her under, Jerry Bailey's poor, scarred face came to mind. Not for the first time, she wondered where he was. She had allowed herself no option but to believe he had survived the remainder of the war. And now? Was he at home, only a few miles from here? Were he and his brother sitting with their parents, maybe dancing to the gramophone in that big room he'd spoken of? She smiled at the thought, letting herself imagine she was there as well. She pictured the moment he offered his hand to her. She saw the way he watched her, wrapping his arm around her waist so they could move to the music. And for a moment she wished would never end, all she could see were those dove-grey eyes.

nine
JERRY

❧

The Windsor Memorial Cemetery was a quiet place. The wind held its breath as Jerry and John passed beneath the arched iron gates, their boots crunching softly on the frozen grass. A couple of chickadees provided the only other sounds, chattering and whistling to themselves as they darted between the shrubs lining the edge of the grounds. The last time Jerry had been here, it had been to visit Frank's grave. He glanced toward the spot where his childhood friend had been buried thirteen years before, then he turned away.

Uncle Henry had said their parents were buried toward the north end. From across the cemetery, Jerry could see rows of fresh graves along the tree line, the rounded mounds of dirt a silent evidence of the recent influenza scourge. Many of the graves lacked headstones, several were marked by wooden crosses, most were layered in fallen, frost-burned leaves. Their aunt had mentioned putting up a stone, so the brothers scanned the few markers, searching for the Bailey name. When his gaze landed on the large grey stone at the head of two graves, their humped surfaces dried to hard dirt by the wind, Jerry felt a sharp twist in his chest.

ROBERT CLYDE BAILEY
1869–1918

ELIZABETH FRANCIS BAILEY
1873–1918

The names were carefully painted in black with a small red heart connecting them, likely their aunt's loving handiwork. A dry, faded clutch of late wildflowers lay at the base of the stone.

"John," he called softly, and his brother came to his side.

Slipping off his tweed hat, Jerry knelt and traced the painted lettering with his fingertip, feeling as numb as the cold stone itself.

John placed a hand on his shoulder. "I'll go in the morning and hire a mason," he promised. "See that they're marked properly."

Jerry nodded, absently turning his cap in his fingers, remembering. Four years ago, when he and John had waited to board the train, his nerves had buzzed with a youthful eagerness, and his only thoughts had been of what might lie ahead. Standing on the platform in his crisp new uniform, he'd kissed his mother's damp cheek while his father stood stoically by her side. Back then, they'd all thought that if anyone was going to die, it would be one—or both—of the brothers, not their parents. The very idea of coming home at the end of it all had been far from his mind. But even if Jerry's thoughts had gone forward in time, he never could have imagined a homecoming like this. He would give anything to hug his mother one last time, to hear his father's rumbling voice.

He scooped up a handful of dirt and sifted it through his fingers. *Dust to dust*, he thought. All those days and nights underground, his body aching, his soul strung tight with dread. Above the tunnels, in the fetid, smoky air, the dying had lain submerged alongside the dead, floundering in the mire. When all that mud finally dried, it would feel like the dust in his hand. Eventually the bones lost within it would as well. What had any of it been for?

"Ready to go?" John asked.

Jerry looked up at his brother and took in the tight, closed lines of his face. He knew the torment going on beneath the surface. He knew it like he knew his own.

"Yeah, there's nothing for us here," he replied, rising. Dusk had closed in while they were here, he realized. It had been a very long day. "It's just you and me now."

But if there was nothing for them on the cold ground of the cemetery, Jerry felt the opposite as soon as they walked through the door of their house. Memories clung to every object in every room; echoes of laughter hung in the empty air. For a moment, the brothers stood side by side in the living room, barely breathing, then John broke away. He strode toward the shelf on the wall and grabbed a bottle of whisky by its neck, then he swept past Jerry and up the stairs to his bedroom, slamming the door behind him.

Jerry couldn't move. He swore he could still hear the gramophone playing. In his mind he saw his father curl a strong arm around his mother's waist, leading her in a dance. Jerry had sat right here on the old blue couch so many times, memorizing the 1-2-3, 1-2-3 pattern of his parents' feet, as well as the sure way his father's hand pressed against the small of his mother's back. The love he saw between them, warm and certain and full of light.

All of it gone now.

Weighted by weariness and aching with loss, Jerry lowered himself onto the couch and reached for a cushion his mother had once embroidered with small pink flowers. He remembered the hours she'd sat by the fire, squinting in the dim light over her needlework. Closing his eyes, he hugged the cushion to his chest and rested his chin on the petals, needing just a moment. To rest. To quieten the memories.

He awoke with a start, alarm roaring through his chest when he realized he wasn't gripping his rifle. The Germans could have—

The familiar room swam into focus: the floral wallpaper, the pale drapes, the rows of books on the shelves. The cushion that had soothed him to sleep had fallen off the couch. He reached for it then tucked the pillow under his head and lay back down. His bed seemed impossibly far away.

Jerry was stiff but slightly rested when he woke the next morning to the sun spilling yellow into the living room. He stepped outside and walked toward his father's shed, noting along the way that the barn was empty; John must have already taken the car to the stone mason. He was glad his brother had taken that job on. Jerry didn't want it. At the shed, the door's rusted hinges creaked, then the yeasty scent of the still filled his senses. His father hadn't been gone long enough for it to dissipate altogether.

Inside, Jerry gazed around with a kind of wonder. If not for the complete silence, he could almost believe his father was still there. He'd left everything as he always had, including the neatly arranged wall of tools with the screwdrivers in one row, wrenches in another, all ordered from smallest to largest. Above them were the little boxes fastened to the wall, filled with nails and screws. A few empty wooden crates were still piled precariously in the corner, and the floor was littered with swirls of shaved wood and the occasional rusted nail. And of course, there was the still.

"How do you keep everything so tidy?" he remembered John asking their father many years before. The boys had been sorting screws for him while he sat on his stool writing in his leather journal. "I never know where anything is."

Smiling gently at John, their father had closed the black book then slid it into a drawer at the side of his workbench. "That's why this book goes here, and those tools go there. Everything has its own place, and you have to put it back before you walk away from it. That's why you run into trouble, John." He tapped his pencil against his temple. "If you pay attention to the little things, the important ones will fall in line."

It was just a moment in time, but it was one Jerry knew he would cherish forever.

Now Jerry opened that same drawer and wrapped his fingers around the book he remembered so well. His thumbs skimmed over the soft leather, recalling the last pair of hands to hold it. Then he settled onto his father's stool and cracked the book open, taking in the familiar handwriting. The outside world fell away.

"I thought I might find you in here."

Jerry looked up, vaguely surprised to see John in the doorway, and even more surprised to note the daylight behind his brother was fading. He'd lost all track of time, hidden away here in the shed. He studied John's suit, curious.

"You look dapper."

John brushed an imaginary fleck of dust off his lapels. "I do, don't I? What's that?"

"Pa's old journal."

"Oh yeah?" John reached inside his coat pocket, tapped a cigarette from its package. "What did he write about?"

Jerry held out a hand, so John lit two cigarettes and handed one over.

"A lot of stuff. Notes to himself. Ideas. Lists. Us." Jerry took a deep drag of the cigarette. "He also wrote about Prohibition and the rum-running business. That's what the last pages are about: lists of suppliers, sellers, and other key contacts. I was thinking it might be something for you and me to consider."

"Uncle Henry did say there was good money in it," John said. "Suppose we can ask Walter what's what tonight."

"Tonight?"

"Did you forget? Charlie and Walter. We're all heading to town." He lifted an eyebrow at Jerry's worn shirt. "They'll be here soon."

"Right. I'd better get changed."

His mind still on the journal, Jerry headed back to the house, drawing a bucket of cold water from the well as he went. In his room, he poured the water into a white porcelain bowl, grabbed the cake of soap his mother always left there, and scrubbed off the dirt he'd worn for the past couple of days. How very like her, he thought with a pang, to leave it out for him, knowing he'd need to clean up when he returned, whether she was there or not.

From his bag he retrieved his razor, then he leaned close to the mirror, lifted his chin, and set the blade on the crooked terrain of his face. It felt like a luxury, this clean water, this clear mirror. This quiet time to himself. As he guided the razor up his cheek, he thought of another blade scraping cleanly through his beard, held by a smaller but confident hand. As he had so many times, Jerry closed his eyes, praying Adele Savard had made it home.

By the time he was ready, Walter and Charlie were waiting downstairs. Jerry could hear their voices bouncing off John's, punctuated by Walter's coughing fits, and he felt an odd tremble of nerves in his chest. Part of it, he knew, was the eagerness to see them. The boys had grown up together, but it had been four very long years since they'd shipped out and gone their separate ways. So much had happened. All of them would bear their own scars, whether he could see them or not. They'd all be strangers somehow.

"Hey," he said, coming down the stairs. The three were sitting in the front room, glasses of whisky in their hands.

Walter stood to greet him, looking every bit like a younger version of Uncle Henry with his light brown hair slightly mussed and a toothpick dancing in the corner of his mouth.

"Hey, Jer," he said, pulling him in for a hug. Jerry heard the hint of a wheeze in his voice. When they parted, he nodded toward Jerry's face, but not critically. "Dad mentioned you went for a new look. I like it. Adds a bit of mystery."

"Jerry," Charlie boomed, reaching for his cane as if to rise.

"Don't get up," Jerry said, going to him instead.

Charlie held out his left hand, since his right was gone, along with most of his forearm. The right sleeve and trouser leg of his brown tweed suit were both folded and pinned out of the way, but his hair was just as curly as it had always been, though he'd tried to slick it back tonight.

"It's good to see you, Jerry." Charlie's smile quivered, and Jerry detected the unrest in his eyes. "Awful sorry about your folks."

"Thanks, Charlie. I'm sorry for what happened to you, too."

"I got hit at the Somme on the first day," Charlie said. "Could have been worse, right? That's what people keep saying. What about you? How's your face feel, Jer?"

"A lot better than it did. Some spots are still numb."

"Eh?"

"He said he can't feel all of his face," Walter said, raising his voice. "Charlie can only hear through one ear, so you gotta speak up if you're not on his left."

Charlie nodded. "I'm getting better at reading lips, though."

John handed Jerry a glass of their father's amber hooch. "We're having a toast." He looked at the other three and raised his glass. "To coming home."

"I'll drink to that," Walter said, and they all tossed back the whisky as one. Then, for just a heartbeat, no one spoke a word. Jerry's chest constricted with the memories of where they had been, all they had lost, and a bittersweet gratitude that they had made it through.

"Yeah," Charlie said softly, as if he was thinking the same.

"C'mon," John said, offering Charlie a hand up. "Let's go. I'm thirsty."

"Only if one of you drives," Walter said. "We've been itching for a spin in your dad's new Ford."

"Deal," Jerry said, grabbing his flat cap.

John and Walter squeezed into the back of the Ford, letting Charlie ride up front where there was more space for his cane, and Jerry slid in behind the wheel. Driving the familiar roads into town, he felt more at home than he had in a long while. All those times he'd feared he'd never see this place again, and here he was.

About twenty minutes from the house, he turned onto Sandwich Street, then slowed a bit, intrigued by the bustling sights and sounds. When they'd left Windsor for the war, the streets had been quiet, women had worn ankle-length dresses and were always accompanied by a chaperone, and the mood was nothing special. None of that could be said tonight. Prohibition had made this place a lively town, and laughter and music filled the air.

"Busy little place," John said.

"Yeah," Walter said, then he coughed for a few seconds. Neither he nor Charlie commented on it, so Jerry didn't either. "It's nice to see it getting busier."

Jerry studied the crowds along the side of the road, taking in the crutches and the pinned trouser legs like Charlie's. He got the impression there were more women out here than he'd seen before. Or maybe it was just a lot fewer men.

"When I got back in '16, everyone was pretty tense," Charlie said loudly. "The town was walking on eggshells, afraid to talk about the war in case someone's boy got killed or wounded. It's better now that everyone's home. Everyone who's coming home, anyway."

"Look at the women!" John exclaimed, leaning out the window and watching a group of ladies, their midcalf, colourful dresses swaying in the streetlights. "Look what they're wearing! The world sure has improved since we've been gone."

"Pull over there," Walter told Jerry, indicating an open spot at the side of the road.

It was only six o'clock, but as they crossed the street toward a large, well-tended building and yard, Jerry could already hear music coming from inside.

"Sounds like a party," John said.

Charlie grinned. "It's always a party at the Edgewater."

"The Edgewater Thomas Inn," Jerry read from the sign out front. "I don't remember this."

"Sure you do," Walter said. "Used to be a little restaurant."

"That little three-room place from before?"

Walter nodded. "The very same. Now it's a speakeasy."

Jerry whistled as they got closer, admiring the construction that had gone into the building. "Someone's put some money into it since then."

"A *lot* of money. It's one of the more sophisticated speakeasies around," Walter said. "The Edgewater belongs to a gorgeous dame by the name of Bertha Thomas. Food's good, drinks are good—"

"And it sounds like a great band," John said, picking up his pace. "I'm gonna let loose in here."

"In we go," Charlie said as Walter opened the door.

Instantly, they were swallowed up by the animated voices of men and women straining to be heard over the music, which came from a circular, raised island in the middle of the busy dance floor. The air Jerry breathed was thick with the stink of fermentation, and his shoes sank so deep into the thickly padded carpets he felt like he was walking on a pillow. Peering over heads, he took in the room's bright white interior, the matching white tablecloths, and a low, white fence dividing the large oak dance floor from the tables. In case that wasn't fancy enough, someone had planted half a dozen imitation palm trees around the circumference. And the guests—the room itself danced, brought to life by men in fancy dark suits and women swishing past in colourful, beaded dresses, laughing and flirting, glasses held in the air. Beyond them, at the other end of the room, Jerry spotted a mirror behind the bar, where the largest crowd milled. All shapes and sizes of liquor bottles stood on a shelf, the coloured glass reflecting the lights in the mirror like jewels.

With everything coming at him, Jerry's senses were bombarded. The close squeeze and the noises of the crowd threatened to drag him back toward the mud, but he forced himself past the danger point. He stuck to John, quietly concerned about the rapid movements of his brother's eyes, and they followed his cousins to an open table. Almost immediately, a waiter appeared to take their supper order, including their free drinks, and while John ordered whiskies all around, Jerry scanned the room, observing the lights, the faces and bodies, the movement. The place had its own pulse, he realized, but instead of fear, there was laughter. Instead of darkness, magic glinted off bottles. This might be wild, but it wasn't dangerous. One breath at a time, the tension in his shoulders began to melt away.

By the time Jerry sat down, John was already enjoying himself, exchanging smiles with a gorgeous brunette a table away. He hooted out a laugh. "Hell, I think I'm gonna like this place." Then he lifted his glass and met Jerry's gaze. "Here's to us, brother. Let's drink to our new lives."

Jerry shot back his drink, wanting to share John's joy, and as the whisky burned down his throat, the whispers of war began to slip beneath the noise of the people.

"Thing about Prohibition," Charlie yelled happily, signalling the waiter for a second round, "is that I drink more now than I ever did before. I hope booze is never legal again."

Jerry turned to Walter, his mind shifting to the possibilities he'd seen in his father's journal. "So how's it all work? I mean, booze is illegal, but I'm sitting in a public place drinking whisky. The noise can be heard out on the street, and yet there isn't a policeman in sight."

Walter's face cracked into a broad smile. "I thought you'd never ask."

Jerry lit a cigarette then nudged John, who dragged his attention away from the brunette, and both brothers leaned toward Walter, all ears.

"Let's start from when we walked into this place," Walter said. He started to cough, but just then the waiter brought their drinks, and Walter drained his glass to clear his throat. "You wouldn't have noticed, but there's a spotter watching the entrance from an upstairs window. Bertha used to get visits from the law more often, but then she took in a young kid named Louis. The kid does his homework up there, and while he's at it, he looks out for the police. If he sees them, he signals to another fellow in the little shack in the parking lot. That guy presses a button that flashes the lights on and off inside the building. That way everyone knows what's coming."

Jerry gestured to the open booze on the table. "And if they get past the kid? What happens with all the liquor?"

Walter stomped his boot on the thick carpet underfoot. "The minute there's a raid, everybody dumps their hooch."

That explained the plush, soft floor, Jerry thought. And the smell.

"And see the long tablecloths on every table? Underneath each one there's a bucket for the glasses, but the tablecloths block the view. The best part is the bar itself." He pointed toward the mirror behind the bar. "One little tap of a stick and those shelves tilt, sending the bottles down a chute. Soda magically appears where the booze used to be. Everything is quick and slick these days. It's a riot."

Jerry stared across the room at the bar, impressed by the mechanics.

"There are buzzers and false walls everywhere around here," Charlie chimed in, having read Walter's lips. "This place has more hidden passageways and tunnels than all of Europe, and they're all for the liquor. People over here are making a fortune selling over in the States. I know of one rumrunner on this side of the border who bought a case of cheap scotch for eighteen dollars, then sold it across the river for a hundred and twenty."

John's eyes widened. "You don't say."

"Yeah. Over there, everything about booze is illegal, but that don't mean folks aren't thirsty, if you follow me."

Jerry frowned. "But Prohibition's still in place here, ain't it? Or did I miss something?"

Walter tilted his head from side to side. "It is and it isn't. During the war, the making, importing, and exporting of liquor were all illegal federally, but they're planning a referendum on that soon. I'm taking bets on which way that goes, but I'm fairly sure they'll throw Prohibition out. Then there's the provinces, and they set their own rules. They're all different. Here in Ontario, our distillers and breweries can manufacture booze, but we can't legally buy it here. We *can* buy it from another province, though."

John snorted. "Government."

"Yeah, well, they got nothing to complain about now. They're raking it in since the States are going dry. While the American authorities are doing their best to shut rumrunners down, the Canadian border men are behind it all the way. As long as the sellers pay the Canadian export tax, they don't care where the booze ends up."

Jerry's mind returned to the rows and columns of names and numbers his father had written in his journal, creating a business plan for his sons. "What about producing it independently? That still illegal?"

"You gotta have a federal permit." Charlie grinned. "Or be real quiet about it."

Someone hollered something, and Walter nodded toward the staircase at the far end of the room. "Take a look! There's Miss Bertha Thomas herself."

The speakeasy's owner was a tall, slender woman not much older than Jerry's twenty-four years, wrapped in black and draped in furs. A low cloche hat covered most of her face, but he saw a flash of a smile when the men around her raised their drinks in her direction.

"What's she like?" John asked. "Have you met her?"

"A couple of times. She's a nice enough gal, but she's a big shot, so folks try to stay on her good side. She's better as a friend than an enemy, or so I've heard."

"Has she ever been arrested?" Jerry asked. "I mean, as glamorous as all this is, even with a spotter out front raids do happen—here and at the docks, right?"

"She's been raided," Walter agreed. "But never arrested. She might get a fine or two, but she's so rich, those are like mosquito bites to her. She's paid most of the coppers off, so they stay away."

"What's upstairs?" John asked, indicating the stairway she'd just descended.

"She lives up there. And she's got rooms for important fellas who needed their palms greased, you know? Private gambling, drinking, girls, whatever they want. Bertha doesn't like the general public to know about that, though."

"So how do you know? You one of them important types?" John teased.

"I hear things," Walter said mysteriously, wiggling his eyebrows. "I ain't exactly been sitting around twiddling my thumbs since I've been back."

"What's that supposed to mean? You in the business already?"

Charlie laughed. "He sure is!"

Jerry and John exchanged a smile. "So, Walter, tell me," Jerry said. "How does—"

"Well, well, well." A shadow fell over their table, punctuated by the glowing end of a cigar. "If it ain't John Bailey."

John's smile hardened to a sneer. "Willoughby."

"I figured the Krauts would shoot you first thing," he said, then he turned to Jerry and let out a laugh. With a fat cigar pinched between two fingers, he pointed at Jerry's scars. "My, oh my. They got you anyway. You look like Frankenstein."

Jerry resisted the urge to snap the finger Ernie Willoughby was waving in his face. Didn't seem fair since he was already missing three on his other hand. But he sure asked for it. There was a time when Jerry and John had been best friends with Ernie and his brother, Frank, but ever since the day on the ice when the frozen water beneath their skates had given way, a rift had hardened between them. While Jerry had buried his feelings of guilt over Frank as best he could, Ernie was reminded of it every time he looked at his damaged hand. It was on account of his hand that Ernie hadn't gone to war, and from the looks of it, that had definitely been to his benefit. The past four years appeared to have been good to him. He was dressed to the nines in a spotless black suit, his dark hair pasted smoothly back, the shine of money practically glowing off him.

Jerry took a moment, taking a deep drag of his cigarette then letting the smoke slip through his lips. "I see you made it through the war just fine," he said through gritted teeth.

"I sure did." Ernie's dark eyes slid to Walter, who was studying his empty glass. "Just ask your cousin. Hey, Wally?"

Walter looked up at him but said nothing.

"What's this?" John asked.

Ernie towered over them. "What, you didn't tell the boys you work for me? Now, why not, I wonder."

"For crying out loud," John muttered under his breath, and Walter dropped his gaze to the tabletop.

"Beat it, Willoughby," Charlie barked.

Willoughby held a hand behind one ear. "What's that, Charlie? I can't quite hear you." Then he turned to Jerry. "Say, I got a new name for you. Jigsaw Jerry. How do you like that?"

John shot to his feet, and Willoughby drew back slightly, taken by surprise.

"You know how that happened to my brother, Witless?" John's voice was a steel blade. Jerry could practically see it, like a bayonet twisting into Willoughby's brain. "Nah. You wouldn't, because you didn't make it to France, did you? Didn't make it out of this town." He spat to the side. "Coward. You got the guts of a rabbit."

Willoughby's nostrils flared. "You'll want to be careful what you say to me, Bailey. I run this town now." He made a show of scanning the room. "I got guys who could kill every single one of you right now."

"Is that so?" John asked. "For what?"

"For breathing my air," Willoughby seethed.

"Makes sense that it's your air. It stinks in here."

The noise of the band might have covered their words, but the anger rising between the men was drawing attention. A trickle of patrons headed toward the door, casting uneasy glances at their table as they passed.

"John," Walter said nervously, and Jerry saw what he had: the bulge of John's pistol, tucked into the back of his trousers.

But John wasn't backing down. John never backed down. "You gonna have other guys kill me for you? Can't do it yourself? Sounds about right."

Jerry stood and tossed some money on the table for the waiter. "That's enough. Leave it, John. We didn't lose Frank just to kill each other in a speakeasy."

At the mention of his brother, Ernie's eyes narrowed. "You don't get to speak his name, Jigsaw. You don't even get to think it. It's your fault he's gone." He lifted his chin at Jerry's face. "You got what was coming to you."

John lunged at Willoughby again, but Walter held him back. "We saved you, didn't we?" John growled. "What a goddamn mistake that was."

"Let's go," Walter urged.

"Good idea," Charlie said. "Lots of other places around here where Willoughby ain't. All the way up the shore."

John downed his drink and slammed the empty glass on the table, never taking his glare off Willoughby, who watched them as they left.

Suddenly, all Jerry wanted was to get outside, but as he stepped through the door, the night air didn't clear his head like he needed it to do. Instead, the chill brought him back to that beautiful day thirteen years before, when four young boys had laced up their skates in the early spring sunshine, but only three had come home.

John gripped Jerry's arm and pulled him aside. "I know what you're thinking about. I see it on your face. Let it go, Jerry. It was an accident, and it was a long time ago. He drowned, and you couldn't have done anything to save him. We all know that."

But acid churned in Jerry's stomach, along with a deep, inconsolable hurt. "Doesn't matter whether it was an accident or not. Frank's dead. Our parents are dead. Millions of people died in the war, then millions more from the flu. I know more people who are dead than living." He flicked his cigarette to the ground and stamped it out. "Sometimes *I* feel more dead than alive. You heard Willoughby, and he ain't all wrong. I look like Frankenstein, a monster created from the dead."

John paled. "That ain't true."

"Sure it is."

"Well, you wouldn't look that way if it wasn't for me," John said, his voice strained. "You shouldn't have been down there when it blew up, and you wouldn't have, if I hadn't begged for a little more sleep that day. Your face is my fault."

Jerry stopped. They'd never spoken about that day. Now everything Jerry had tried so hard to forget came rushing back: the blast of dirt and rock, the crack and roar of the world caving in, then a sudden, terrifying paralysis as he was buried alive and suffocating under a solid blackness. How long had it taken before John realized Jerry was trapped? How long to dig him out of the devastation before carrying him to the outside world? It didn't matter. All that mattered was that he had.

In truth, Jerry had been glad it was he who had been injured. He couldn't have imagined seeing John hurt.

He looked John in the eye, making sure he understood. "Listen to me. The explosion did this, not you. You dug me out. That's what matters."

"I couldn't have left you there," John said. "You're my little brother. I'll always watch out for you. I just wish—"

"I wish you wouldn't blame yourself, is what I wish. What's done is done, and it's nobody's fault but the Germans. At least we still have each other." He glanced over John's shoulder at the Edgewater's doors. "Willoughby can't say that."

"He's saying a lot of other things though."

"Don't pay Willoughby any mind."

Willoughby could be a jackass. Still, as much as Jerry despised him, he couldn't help but feel sorry for him. Jerry could live just fine with his battle scars as long as he had his brother by his side. Willoughby would never have that again.

Jerry patted his own face, wanting to shift the conversation. "Look, it's better this way. Gives you a better chance with the ladies. I won't be overshadowing you anymore."

John gave him a cheeky smile. "The blast must have damaged your brain, Jerry. I've always been the handsome one."

"Hey!" It was Charlie, waiting across the road with Walter. "We going for a drink or what?"

For a moment, the Bailey brothers held on, absolution and understanding solidifying between them. Then they turned and crossed the street toward their cousins.

"Where to next, Walter?" Jerry asked.

"Chappell House," he declared, and the four of them piled into the Ford.

From the back seat, Walter directed them to their next stop, then to another, and another, and with each glass of whisky that Jerry drank, the dead faces from his past faded away. With them went the image of the lone grey stone in the cemetery, painted with a little red heart in the middle. For a little while, even the memory of John's desperate grimace as he'd carried Jerry from the mud to the ambulance was washed away by the liquor. Maybe not forever, but for a little while at least.

ten
ADELE

— December 1919 —

The door to Butler's General Store swung open just as Adele's mitten reached for the doorknob, and a familiar face peered out.

"Why, Miss Savard. How lovely to see you. Come in out of the cold before you turn into a snowman."

"Mr. Butler. It's very good to see you." Adele stepped into the warm shop and stomped her snow-covered boots on the mat. The fire burning in the stove, right in the centre of his store, smelled divine, and she slipped off her mitts to appreciate the warmth. She caught the scent of something fruity, and Mr. Butler nodded with efficiency.

"I'll get you some mulled cider, shall I? It's piping hot. I'd say it's just what you need."

"That would be lovely," Adele said, holding up a list. "I need to pick up a few things for my mother."

Mr. Butler passed her a cup and took her list in exchange, then he disappeared into the shelves. Breathing in the spicy apple steam, Adele gazed around her fondly, remembering. She and Maman had shopped at Butler's for as long as she could remember, and it was nice to see that at least some things had remained the same in this new, livelier version of Windsor.

This morning she'd driven Guillaume's truck into town, urged by her mother to get out of the house. What a liberating feeling, driving by herself! One of the orderlies in Belgium had taught her to drive in a rare moment of leisure, but this felt very different from puttering around the clearance station's grounds. As she'd rolled down Pitt Street, she'd taken in the bright store windows, the taverns with their doors swinging wide open, and the sheer number of people along the sidewalks. It was all so different from the quiet, almost staid mood of the place before, and it reminded her of Marie's warning. Before she'd gone away, she couldn't remember hearing much more noise than the clanging of the streetcar bell. Now everything clanged, it seemed. It made her curious about what went on after sunset, when the blind pigs and speakeasies were in full swing.

As the cider warmed her hands, she thought about the two letters in her pocket. She'd just picked them up at the Windsor Post Office, one of the oldest structures in the city. The building boasted a beautiful fountain at the front door that was dedicated to the memory of Windsor heroes who had fallen in the Boer War. Heroes like her father.

One of the letters was from Marie, who had proven to be an enthusiastic writer, perhaps in an effort to make up for staying away. Adele had repeatedly assured her that all was well in quiet Petite Côte, but she didn't seem likely to budge anytime soon. It broke Maman's and Guillaume's hearts, but they were resigned to accept her decision. Their girls were of equally stubborn stock, a fact they'd realized years before.

Marie's missives were full of stories about Fred's busy job, her own temperance work, and little Madeleine. Adele read closely, looking for signs that Marie might be unhappy, but all seemed well. Adele did her best to reply as regularly, but she'd had her ups and downs since returning home a few months ago, and sometimes it was difficult to pen a cheery reply. She wasn't about to confess to Marie that she had practically locked herself in her room for the first couple of weeks she'd been home, grappling with a sense of emptiness she didn't understand.

She wanted to be home, didn't she? She didn't want to be in the war, risking her life every day and night, stinking of blood and worse, up at all hours to dig inside a man's body.

Except, in a way, she realized, she did. And she was ashamed to admit that, even to herself. In Europe, she'd been useful. She'd spent every day surrounded by people who needed her. Now that she was safe at home, she'd tried to find that feeling again, but she just couldn't. Despite all the love she received from Maman and Guillaume, she felt very much alone.

She didn't tell Marie or anyone else about that, though she was certain her mother sensed her gloom. To ease her mind, Adele had started writing in her war diary again, sometimes working deep into the night to get it all out. Afterward, she felt a brief sense of relief, and it seemed to hold back the nightmares for a little while at least.

The other letter was from Hazel, and a feeling of longing had swept over Adele, seeing her friend's exacting handwriting. Hazel and Lillian were the only people in her life who understood what Adele had been through, and she wished they were closer. Lillian had written to her last month, saying she was back to work in a hospital. Then she'd dropped the exciting hint that she might have to quit soon because she had a new beau who she thought "might be the one." Sometimes they let their feelings out a little more, even speaking about Minnie. *What do you think she would be doing today?* Adele had asked, and Lillian had written back, *Still beating us at cards!*

Unlike Lillian, Hazel had put away her nursing gown for good. "No more blood and guts for me," she had told them on the voyage home. "I've had enough of that for two lifetimes."

At the time, Adele had agreed with Hazel, but lately, she wondered if she had made the right decision.

Her cider now cooled, she took a tentative sip, then another, savouring the tangy sweetness.

"Miss Savard?"

She turned and saw the kindly face of Dr. Knowles. "Good afternoon, Doctor. Lovely to see you."

He was a sweet, patient man with jolly white tufts of hair over his ears and under his nose, and he had been her doctor her entire life. Adele was sorry to see that he appeared both smaller and older than when she'd last seen him. But behind his smudged spectacles, his eyes sparkled just as brightly as she remembered.

"I understand you're newly returned from overseas," he said.

"I have been back for a year. It's good to be home."

"I can imagine. You must have seen a great many things over there."

Her smile felt strained. "I did, sir. A great many."

"Your mother has told me of your correspondence, and I must say, you have more courage in one of your little fingers than I do in my entire self."

It felt strange, hearing how people regarded her now. She was no longer just Adele, the inquisitive little girl from Petite Côte, but some kind of hero, though that felt far from true. She had done well over there, and saved a lot of lives; however, it was impossible not to remember all those she'd failed to help. The papers estimated the war had caused over forty million casualties, and half of those were deaths. Canada alone had lost over sixty thousand men, and thousands more would spend the rest of their lives suffering injuries both physical and emotional. Adele could still see some of those faces so clearly, watching her work, listening to her talk, trusting her to send them home in one piece. She'd let so many of them down.

"I don't know about that," she said, offering her standard response, "but thank you. It was an honour to be there. It was the least I could do."

"How is it being back?"

"Oh, fine," she said, because she couldn't bring herself to admit the truth. She took another careful sip. "The food is much better."

Dr. Knowles tilted his head in sympathy as if he saw through her bravado, and she dropped her eyes to the floor.

"It's an adjustment," she admitted quietly. "I'm getting used to it."

"Here we are," Mr. Butler said, appearing with Adele's groceries in two paper bags. "That will be seven dollars and eighty-two cents. Cider's on me. Consider it a thank-you for your service overseas."

"Thank you, Mr. Butler," she replied, counting out the coins. "It was nice seeing you, Dr. Knowles."

"You as well," he said with a nod. He went to open the door for her, then stopped. "You know, Miss Savard, my office is much busier these days. I could use an experienced nurse if you're interested in a position."

Her heart leapt at the words, and she almost dropped the groceries.

"It's not as exciting as the Front," he continued, "though recently I am seeing a noticeable increase in gunshot wounds. Stabbing victims as well. All of which would be familiar to you. Of course, there are the standard infections, inebriation, illnesses, and all, but I imagine you would be more than qualified to handle any and all of those things."

Adele hesitated only a moment, imagining what Hazel might say, then she smiled, a sense of purpose, of readiness, bubbling through her for the first time in a long time.

"Thank you, Dr. Knowles. I would truly appreciate the opportunity," she said. "When would you like me to start?"

eleven

JERRY

༜

— December 1920 —

Jerry leaned over the old Chevy's gas tank, watching closely as the big Frenchman pointed out what he claimed was his most brilliant innovation. Having followed the mechanic around for the past ten minutes, learning things about vehicles that he'd never known, Jerry easily understood why John had dragged him downtown to the man's garage.

If the brothers were serious about selling whisky to the Americans—and they were—one of the most important cogs in the operation was figuring out how they would run the booze from their still to the docks and across the river fast enough that no one would catch them. That's where the Frenchman—he insisted they call him that—came in. Jerry had caught on right away that he wasn't a regular mechanic. Sure, he could change brakes and oil and tires, but the Frenchman went further. His expertise was in making vehicles faster and finding ingenious methods of smuggling liquor in them. The cars he had shown Jerry this afternoon had been rigged with hiding spots, just like the city's hotels, manufacturers, and docks, many of which boasted tunnels and secret rooms beneath them.

"The gas tank in this Whisky Six," the Frenchman was explaining, his rosy cheeks bright. "She is split, *oui*? You only need a small amount of gas, really. You're not going so far, uh? But over on this side of the tank is so much room. Think how many bottles you can fit in here! Or you can do like some I have heard, who siphon the liquor into false gas tanks and spare tires. Once they get over there, they pour it all into bottles."

"Show him the Packard. Underneath," John nudged.

"Of course!" He grabbed Jerry's elbow and brought him to a shiny blue Packard. Flinging the back door open, he knocked on the floor. "You hear that? It's hollow, *oui*? Fake floor. Underneath, you can fit almost five hundred quarts at a time along the whole length of the drive shaft. You think you can keep up with that, eh?"

Jerry was more than impressed. The Frenchman, he was learning, was full of clever ideas.

"Look at the back seat," John said.

The interior of the car looked perfectly normal, but when Jerry peeled back the black leather seat cover, he discovered that's all there was. No cushions or springs beneath, just a wide box for storing cases of bottles, covered by the cloth.

"What did I tell you?" John said to Jerry. "He knows all the tricks."

"*C'est incroyable*," Jerry said, making the mechanic grin.

"Well, I have one more, *mon ami*. Come and see this Studebaker."

"He's got them all outfitted. He's just giving us a choice of cars," John explained.

The Frenchman opened the car door and touched the fabric ceiling. Working his fingers into a seam, he pulled the panel open and demonstrated that the ceiling was separated from the car's hard roof by covert, four-inch pockets sewn inside. "You can fit 180 pints in here."

"How does she drive over rough roads with all that weight?" Jerry asked.

The Frenchman pointed to the steel bars under the chassis. "We reinforce the suspension, you see? So they drive smooth. For the winter, I make big, big skis to attach to the front axle so you can cross the river. But I got no guarantee on how thick the ice is, *n'est-ce pas*? That is up to you."

John already had the river covered for when it wasn't frozen. In addition to the cars, he'd bought them an old fishing boat and hired a former navy man who knew almost as many tricks as the Frenchman. Jerry's favourite was the one where he'd hide bottles in nets that could be cut free if their boat was stopped by the authorities—but they wouldn't forfeit a drop. The nets also contained buoys weighed down by chunks of salt. Once those melted, the booze bobbed back to the surface.

The Frenchman was still talking, obviously enjoying his work. "Some fellows drag chains behind their cars, making a huge cloud of dust. Can you imagine? The police would be waving their hands, trying to see . . ." He clapped a hand on Jerry's shoulder, laughing. "The things we do for money, eh?"

But Jerry's mind was already elsewhere, calculating how many bottles he and John could hide in one car. One hundred and eighty pints was about twenty-two and a half gallons, and that was just in the ceiling panel. Five hundred quarts underneath would be about a hundred and twenty-five gallons. All together, that meant one car could hold almost a hundred and fifty gallons of their booze, not including whatever fit in the empty gas tank.

That left him stunned. From his figuring, if they fully loaded up the car and sold each case for about a hundred fifty dollars, they could make over five thousand every time they sent a shipment over the river.

"You look like you just thought of something," John said.

He had, but Jerry didn't know the Frenchman well enough to say it out loud.

"I'll tell you later." He studied the car again, still calculating. With almost a thousand bottles, he'd need two men: one to drive, another to protect the hidden crates with the might of his shotgun. Or pistol. Or tommy gun. Whatever Jerry could get his hands on. It was all going to add up, but he could see now that it was also going to pay off in a big way. *Thanks, Pa.*

"I'll take this Packard for now," Jerry told the Frenchman. "And the Ford over there by the back, without the modifications."

John raised his eyebrows. "Are you giving me Pa's Ford?"

Jerry laughed. "It's not mine to give. But this one will be used as a decoy. Walter suggested it as a precaution in case the police get wind of a big shipment. We send two cars—the police will stop the first one, but even if they strip it down to its bare bones, they'll find nothing." He gestured to the Packard. "Meanwhile, our Trojan horse chugs by unnoticed."

"Thank you, Wally," John said, grinning.

Jerry turned to the Frenchman. "All right. *Combien?*"

He told them the price, and Jerry counted out the money. They arranged to pick the cars up the next day, then Jerry and John hopped in their Ford and drove out to the river and the *boozorium* they'd rented. With its padlocked doors and barred windows, the little building reminded Jerry more of a fort than a warehouse, but that was good. Nobody was going to get in there without his say-so.

One by one, the many threads of their operation were coming together. They'd worked hard to get to this point, and every new braid gave Jerry satisfaction.

They'd come a long way since that first night at the Edgewater. Jerry had woken up the next morning with a blistering hangover, but after observing everything around him and listening to his cousins' stories, he also had a better sense of what he and John might be able to do with their father's still. Specifics about liquor sales and buyers across the river were rather murky because of the evening's libations, but between what he did remember and the notes from their father, he had been increasingly confident about their direction forward.

Muttering something about the hair of the dog, John had poured whisky into his coffee then held the bottle toward his brother's cup, but Jerry waved him away. He needed a clear head to sort through all this. Too many thoughts and emotions had been stirred up at the Edgewater, and if he was going to move forward with this business, he'd have to cut back on drinking. It made it too easy for the unwelcome memories to creep in, and for him to possibly miss a step along the way.

"So?" John said, settling onto his chair with a cigarette. His skin looked slightly grey, the black shadows under his eyes deep with the aftereffects of too much celebrating. Jerry didn't have to look in a mirror to know he looked the same way. "You thinking yes?"

Jerry nodded.

"It'll be rough work from the sounds of it."

"We've handled rough work before, and we've survived. This one, though, it's a big moneymaker. If we do this right, well then, Pa set us and our children and our grandchildren up for life."

A little colour seeped into John's cheeks. "We'll make him proud."

"Let's start with something easy," Jerry said, clearing the lump in his throat. "We need a name for the business. Something that lets people know our whisky's the best around."

"We could call it The Best Whisky."

Jerry rolled his eyes. "A little more imagination than that, brother."

After a moment, John's face broke into a wide smile. "I got it. How about Bailey Brothers' Best?"

It was perfect. Jerry could almost picture the label already. "I like it. Pour another coffee. Let's get to work."

Together, they sat down with their father's journal, which had become Jerry's textbook. In it, their father had written his secret recipe, lists of connections he had made among suppliers and buyers, and invaluable notes on his opinion of who was or wasn't trustworthy. But just as importantly, beyond the journal, he'd left the boys with a lifetime of learned experience working alongside him on his still.

A still that would need to be expanded if it was to live up to Jerry and John's plans.

"I want to talk with Uncle Henry about possibly moving it to his pig farm and expanding," Jerry said. "Nobody'd suspect him. That's just the beginning, though. I'm not quite sure . . ."

There were the physical logistics of the still, contacting the suppliers, building a web of networks. There were the threats they didn't yet know. There were the—

"Jerry. You gonna let me in on your thoughts, or do I have to guess?"

He understood his brother's frustration, but John had always been an impulsive man. Jerry, on the other hand, was a planner, and he wouldn't do this thing halfway. If he and John were going to run a business, it'd be big, and it'd run smoothly. That's the only way he saw it.

"I get that we need to plan," John was saying, but all Jerry could hear was his father's voice. *Pay attention to the little things.* And in that moment, Jerry saw all the questions and solutions laid out in front of him, clear as could be. He looked up slowly, savouring his brother's exasperated expression.

"Don't tell me you haven't already worked it out, Jerry, because I know you have."

"Of course I have."

John stubbed out his cigarette. "Knew it. Tell me everything. What do I need to do?"

On a fresh page of the journal, Jerry began outlining the details as he saw them. "This is the setup. I'll be in charge of manufacture, suppliers, finances, and general planning. You'll look after the buyers, runners, vehicles, and protection. Pa wrote a lot of names in here, but we'll need more."

"All right."

"We'll rent a bigger warehouse not too far from here and hire men to guard it. A place with an office. That'll be our headquarters. I'd like to hire some of the men coming back. The ones who can't get regular work."

John's eyes narrowed. "You're talking about a lot of hiring. Warehouse would be what, shifts of two?"

"Yeah, to start. As soon as production is going, there will be four of us at the still, cooking, bottling, and loading trucks. Two drivers taking different routes, each one with a guy riding shotgun. As we get rolling, we'll switch up runners to keep it interesting for anyone watching. So with shift changes, we'll need somewhere around a dozen men for now."

"This is going to be expensive."

"That's just the start of it, John. In the beginning, it's all about spending. The first job is to pay everyone off: the suppliers, the runners, the buyers. Payoffs will put us high on everyone's list."

"How are we supposed to do that? I mean, we got some savings, but we'll have to pay the muscle—"

"Pa's safe." Jerry tapped the page. "Only we know where it is, and he put the combination in here. He also hid fifteen casks in the barn under a hill of straw, and five more in the cellar. That's over five hundred beautifully aging gallons of whisky. The law says whisky has to be aged two years, and we have loads of that. If I'm calculating right, we hold on to Pa's stock for now then gradually release it once our own production is underway."

"I get it," John replied. "Give the people a taste of Bailey Brothers' Best and whet their appetite for more. When do we start?"

Jerry set the pencil down and leaned toward his brother, needing to make his next point clear. "We have to plan everything down to the last drop of whisky. We have to get it right the first time. While we were gone, people around here have been honing their businesses. Like Willoughby. We might hate it, but we gotta take him seriously. He's a kingpin these days. Guys like him will take us out at the knees if we're not prepared."

John's mouth twisted to the side. "Don't worry about Witless. You and me will watch out for each other like we always do. We'll be fine. We always are."

So began months of dedicated work. First, they visited Uncle Henry, who agreed to move the original still to his unassuming pig farm and help them build three more.

"But I won't be part of the business beyond that," he told them. "I won't bring that kind of risk into my home."

"That suits us fine, but we'll pay you rent for the space," Jerry said, looking around. "Where's Walter today? I got a question or two for him."

The minute they mentioned their plan to Walter, their cousin took the risky step of walking out on Willoughby's burgeoning enterprise. "I'd rather work for family," he said. Charlie had wanted in too, though he admitted his role would be limited due to his disabilities. There was never any question in Jerry's mind, though. Besides being family, the boys had a wealth of information between the two of them that only someone who'd been living the rumrunner's life for a while could know. Right away, Walter and Charlie helped the brothers hire the right men for the job, ensuring the business would flow as smoothly as the whisky itself.

Over the next two years or so, the business had come neatly together. Jerry and John had produced hundreds of casks of whisky that were just now coming of age. With the cars from the Frenchman, the final detail was in place.

Jerry shifted gears, accelerating the Ford. Both brothers were eager to get to the warehouse; Jerry could feel John's excitement sparking in the air.

Today was inauguration day.

"Nice work on the cars," Jerry said.

"Thanks," John replied. "And I have something else for you. Just finalized it yesterday. You remember our old friend Tuck?"

"Of course." They'd grown up going to school with Tuck, but Jerry hadn't seen him since the war.

"Well, he's a policeman now."

"Okay," Jerry said slowly.

"Nope. It's the opposite. Tuck knows us. He knows what kind of men we are. He says he has bigger fish to fry than us, and he'll help us out. Give us the heads-up when he can."

"Well done," Jerry said, giving his brother a smile. "You don't get all the news though. I've got some of my own."

"Oh yeah?"

"I've set up our first American buyer: The Two Way Inn in Detroit. The owner's ready to buy anytime we're set."

"It's really coming together, isn't it?" John said thoughtfully. He lit two cigarettes, handed one to Jerry. "You ever think about how lucky we are? I mean, did you think we'd make it back here?"

Jerry took a deep drag. "I didn't," he admitted.

"What was the best day of the war for you?" John asked. "Besides the day it ended. Can you think of one?"

"Sure," Jerry said without hesitation. "The day the Krauts tried to slice my face off."

John barked out a laugh. "That's your best day? Shit, Jerry. The others must have been worse than I thought!"

"Yeah, that was the one good day."

A smile crept over his brother's face. "Oh, I know why. That dame. That nurse. Naughty boy. She was a nun."

"Nah. She told me she wasn't."

"You ever see her outta that stiff blue dress?" John teased.

Jerry felt an unexpected flare in his chest, offended for her, but he knew deep down John meant nothing by it. "When would I have had a chance to do that?"

His mind went to the night of the hospital bombing, when she'd run into the inferno in her nightgown, her blond hair falling loose down her back. Then later in the rain, after she'd lost her friend. Not without her gown, but yes, he'd seen her without her veil. And without her guard up. He hoped she had survived the war. He knew a number of nurses hadn't.

"She's probably forgotten all about me anyway," he said. He'd asked around Windsor for the first few months, seeing if anyone knew her, but no one did. Grudgingly, he'd given up the search, but he'd never forgotten her. "Still, that was the best day. I never thought I'd meet someone so nice out there. She was all class. Even with blood all over her, she was graceful. Girls are amazing that way."

John was watching him closely. After a moment he said, "I bet that was her best day too."

Jerry let the comment go. It didn't do any good to think about something that was over with. It was time to move forward. Everything for the business was in place, and that's what mattered now.

When they arrived at the warehouse, Jerry headed to a shelf lined with recently bottled whisky. The liquid gold inside was still a little raw, because it was their own, not their father's, but that didn't matter to Jerry. This first glass was just for them. He pulled a bottle out then turned toward his brother.

"It's time, John."

John grabbed two glasses from a shelf over Jerry's desk. "Yes, indeed. I'll drink to that."

Jerry handed him the bottle, and John held it up to the light, admiring the amber liquid rocking within. Then he turned it slightly so he could see the label Jerry had had printed up.

"My, doesn't that look good." He cleared his throat then read out loud. "Bailey Brothers' Best. Windsor, Ontario. 1920."

"Like it?"

"I like it a lot." John cocked his head, curious. "What's this little bird in the corner?"

Jerry's cheeks warmed a little. "It's a bluebird."

John didn't skip a beat. "Only right," he said, passing the bottle back. "Without her, you wouldn't be here."

With great ceremony, Jerry opened the bottle and poured a glass for each of them.

John lifted his in a toast. "Here's to Bailey Brothers' Best. May we get richer than we ever imagined and make a lot of people happy while we're at it."

"I'll drink to that." They watched each other's face as they clinked the glasses together, then Jerry grinned. "Here's to the future of the Baileys."

twelve

ADELE

⌘

— May 1921 —

Clipboard in hand, Adele paused in the doorframe between the treatment rooms and the waiting room, scanning the half dozen people sitting quietly within the medical clinic. A headache was starting up behind her eyes, but she had only herself to blame. She never should have allowed herself to go without lunch, but it had been a busy morning, and she'd lost track of time.

"Mrs. Chalmers?" she called.

A woman Adele estimated to be in her late twenties limped toward her. "Sorry. I'm a little slow."

"That's quite all right." Cursing her growling stomach, Adele opened the door wider, ushering Mrs. Chalmers inside the treatment room. "Please have a seat on the examination table. Now, what's the trouble?"

"I've cut my leg," she said, carefully removing her boot. "I tried to bandage it myself, but . . ."

"Let's take a look." Adele peeled back the soiled bandage on her patient's calf to reveal a deep gash about three inches long. Fortunately, it had stopped bleeding. "That is quite a cut," she noted, setting aside the bloody dressing. "You were smart to bandage it, but you'll need stitches. How did you get this?"

The woman gave her a smirk. "I slipped."

Adele raised an eyebrow. Mrs. Chalmers had no bruises on her, and her hands were free of scratches. She suspected she knew the real cause. "And what made the cut? Should I look for anything sharp in the wound, like glass, perhaps?"

The woman sighed. "Okay, I didn't slip. I was carrying pints in my rubber boots. I bumped one too hard, I guess."

Adele reached for her needle and sterile catgut thread, unsurprised. "Well, I'll make sure the wound is clear of any glass then stitch you up. Shouldn't take too long."

Since she'd started working for Dr. Knowles, she'd seen the full gamut of bootlegging injuries, from minor cuts like this to serious bullet wounds. She'd treated one slender but clumsy man who had wrapped rubber tubes filled with booze around himself then hidden the evidence beneath his spacious coat. Unfortunately for him, he'd tripped on his own invention and broken an arm on the curb. Looking sick with regret, he'd admitted to Adele that the impact had split one of the tubes, and liquor had sprayed like a fountain into the street.

People would do just about anything for a drink these days, it seemed. Adele had been impressed with all the creative methods they'd come up with to smuggle booze: women tucked bottles into brassieres, bloomers, and corsets, even into their baby's blankets and carriages. Adele had even heard—though she wasn't convinced it was true—that one man had emptied two dozen eggs of their natural liquid and used a syringe to refill them with whisky. Then he'd carried the carton across the frozen river to Detroit. Mrs. Chalmers's cut wasn't the first of its kind, and it wouldn't be the last.

Adele finished her careful sewing then applied a fresh dressing.

"There you are. That should heal nicely, but you may have a small scar."
She smiled. "Try to be more careful?"

Mrs. Chalmers laughed as she rolled her stocking back up. "With all
the money I'm making, I can afford a few stitches."

Adele bid her patient farewell then returned to the treatment room to
clean up the bits and pieces left behind. As she tossed the dirty linen into
the garbage, a memory returned of the days when she had plucked shrapnel from men's bodies and brains before throwing their bloody sheets
and bandages into a laundry bin to be washed and sterilized and used
again for someone else. Back then she was so exhausted she could barely
stumble back to her tent before falling asleep. Now that she was here,
working on cuts, scrapes, and the day-to-day demands of Dr. Knowles's
office, when she wasn't treating more serious wounds, like the occasional
stabbing or shooting, life was easier. It kept her busy, which she needed.
For the most part, that allowed her to put the war behind her.

But there were things about her time overseas that she sorely missed: the
dangers of surviving in the worst of places, the rewards of seeing a terribly
wounded man healed, and the companionship of her friends. Dr. Knowles
was a sweet man, but he could never replace the wonderful chatterboxes
she had lived and worked with for four years. She missed Hazel and Lillian terribly, and the distance between the three girls seemed even more
now that both of the others were married and pregnant. And though Adele
was happy for them, they had left her behind when they joined that special
club of motherhood of which Adele was not yet a part. Her sister, Marie,
was already on her second, a little boy named Arthur, and understandably,
her letters had become more sporadic as she juggled both a toddler and a
newborn. On her mother's advice, Adele had tried to make friends at
church, but it hadn't amounted to much. Most of the girls there had no
idea what she'd experienced, and their priorities were mostly fashion and
landing the perfect husband. Many of the men she met seemed to view
her wartime experience as either distasteful or scandalous, which reminded
her of Fred's judgemental views, and she cut those conversations short.

Adele was happier now. She was safe, and work gave her purpose. She loved being around her family again. But deep down, she longed for a friend.

Once she'd tidied up, Adele returned to the waiting room for her next patient, Monsieur Lamar, a middle-aged gentleman with rosy cheeks and leathery skin who sat hunched on a chair. He rarely said much, but he came into the clinic almost every week for the same reason.

She leaned against the doorframe with a wry grin. "Monsieur Lamar, nice to see you again. Has your prescription run out already?"

He looked up and clutched his hat between his hands. "It don't seem to be getting better yet," he said, giving a little cough.

"I see. I'll get the doctor for you."

These days, the affliction that brought most people to the clinic was their apparently unquenchable thirst for alcohol. Ontario's temperance law allowed doctors to prescribe alcohol to anyone who needed it for medicinal reasons, but what those reasons were wasn't specified. Just the other day, Adele had walked past a drugstore where a line of people stood, waiting to hand in their prescriptions. Since buying their own liquor locally wasn't allowed, they basically shopped at the pharmacy. The irony wasn't lost on any of them, and Adele didn't judge.

As she had told Marie, Adele believed people had a right to drink. Especially those who had been to war. She'd seen some severely inebriated patients, usually veterans who had tried to drown out the memories by drinking to excess, but they had Adele's sympathy and understanding. Since returning home, she, Guillaume, and Maman had enjoyed a few drinks from his private stock, and it had done no one any harm. On the contrary: it helped to temporarily quiet her demons. Of course, there were always those who went too far or consumed bad, homemade hooch that was too raw for their bodies to handle, but she figured outlawing booze wasn't going to stop those men anyway.

Adele knocked on the door to Dr. Knowles's office then waited to hear his voice. As a nurse, she could treat most of the ailments they saw at his small practice, but the pharmacy still required the doctor's signature on prescriptions.

"Come in," Dr. Knowles called.

He sat behind a heavy oak desk, frowning at a stack of paperwork, but he lifted his bushy white eyebrows to her in question.

"Pardon me," she said. "Monsieur Lamar is here for a refill."

He nodded then pulled a prescription pad and pen from one of his drawers. He wrote the required language, signed his name in something akin to a scribble, then gave it to Adele.

"Remind him of the poker game tonight, would you? The good Monsieur Lamar somehow forgot the money he owed me last week."

She chuckled. "I will, sir."

Out in the waiting room, Adele handed the paper to Monsieur Lamar. "Here you are."

"*Merci, merci,*" he said, without a trace of a cough.

"And Dr. Knowles asked me to remind you—"

"The poker game, yes. Tell him I will be there *with* his money."

No sooner was he out the door than two men hobbled in off the street. One was bleeding from his forehead and leaning heavily on the other, who appeared unharmed. Adele rushed to the other side of the injured man, immediately assessing the source of the blood to be a wide laceration on his upper brow.

"Are you injured anywhere else?" she asked.

"Just his head," the other man replied for him.

Adele's eyes flitted over the speaker. He was close to six feet tall with a strong physique and a full head of coiffed brown waves. Next to him, his friend seemed small and out of place.

"Let's get you into an exam room," she said, refocusing on her patient. "What's your name?"

Again, the other man spoke. "His name's Richard. He crashed the car. Dickie's always driving too fast."

Richard groaned as Adele and the tall man helped him onto the exam table. He was young, barely older than a teenager, Adele realized, as she took a closer look at his face.

"Are you sure you're not injured anywhere else? A car crash can be quite traumatic."

Richard's eyes darted toward his companion who declared, "He's fine. Just cut his head."

It seemed strange that the patient wasn't saying anything at all, but when she held his gaze, he gave nothing away. She raised his chin and dabbed at the blood. The flow was slowing, but the cut was deeper than she'd expected.

"You're very fortunate," she told him. "I don't often see such localized damage from a car accident. I can stitch this right up." She retrieved her suture kit from the cabinet and prepared an injection of cocaine. "This might sting a little," she warned. "But it'll numb the pain."

Richard sucked hard through his teeth at the small prick. While she waited for the anaesthetic to take effect, she threaded her needle.

The other man watched her closely as she began to sew. "You seem to know what you're doing. I expected the doctor would tend to this type of surgery."

She kept her eyes on her work. The boy's brow had a messy tear, and the tissue was very thin, but it was nothing she couldn't handle. "I've done more than my share of sutures."

"I haven't seen you around here before," he said, leaning back so one elbow rested on the counter beside her. "I thought I knew all the pretty dames hereabouts. Are you from the area?"

"I am," she said, biting her lip as she finished off the last stitch. "I'm from Petite Côte. But I was . . . away for a few years." She clipped the thread, set the needle aside, then reached for a bandage. "There you go. Put some ice on it tonight if you can."

"Thank you, Nurse," Richard said weakly, uttering his first words.

He started to get off the table, but his friend put a hand on his shoulder, forcing him to sit back down.

"Hang on a minute, Dickie. The lady and I are having a conversation."

That's when Adele noticed the man was missing a few fingers. A war wound, she surmised sadly. So many had been disfigured in some way over there. It was a travesty.

"I'm a sucker for solving little mysteries," he was saying, his deep brown eyes on Adele. "You say you were away a few years and that you've done your share of sutures. Pardon me for prying, but were you overseas?"

"Yes, I was," she said.

"They were lucky to have you. I expect men would have run toward the enemy, just so they could have a nurse as beautiful as you."

"Of course not," she said, her cheeks warm.

He checked his watch. "Listen, I hope this don't sound too forward, but I'd like to thank you for looking after Dickie here, as well as all those poor boys over there. I'm real impressed. I don't know one other woman brave enough to do that. So I'm wondering, it's after five o'clock. Closing time, right? Would you consider letting me buy you dinner at Watson's Tavern just down the street? Nothing fancy, but it'll be delicious, I promise."

Her stomach growled at exactly the wrong time, and she pressed a hand quickly against it. "Oh, I don't think that's such a good idea. I don't even know your name."

"The name's Ernie Willoughby," he said, giving her a broad smile. "At your service."

"Adele Savard," she replied, still unsure. He might be polite, but he was still a stranger.

Ernie placed both hands over his heart. "You're safe with me, Miss Savard. You can ask anyone in this town. They all know me, right, Dickie?"

Dickie gave a tiny, almost imperceptible nod.

He patted the boy's shoulder again. "And Dickie here is looking so much better already. Please allow me to thank you properly."

How long had it been since she had gone out for supper with anyone? And wasn't Maman always encouraging her to meet someone new?

Adele was twenty-seven, after all. And since Mr. Willoughby had fought overseas, it might be therapeutic to talk with him about the war. To have a normal conversation. Besides, it was early evening and he was inviting her to a nearby, public restaurant. She voted now, for Pete's sake. She should feel liberated enough to go out to dinner with a man. She took in the wide cut of his navy suit, recognizing good quality, then blinked into his brown eyes and made her decision.

"I'll be finished here in about a half hour," she said with a smile.

"Sounds great. I'll drop Dickie off at home and come back for you then."

True to his word, Ernie returned for her, and as they walked down the street to Watson's Tavern, she noted the way so many people greeted him with deference, even stepping off the sidewalk to make room. She'd assumed Ernie was merely a wealthy gentleman looking for conversation, but from the looks of it, he had earned a lot of respect in the community as well.

She'd never been inside Watson's Tavern before, but she'd walked past it plenty of times since she'd been home. Its original grim, dark exterior had been freshened with a coat of white paint. Ernie opened the door for her, and as she stepped into the dim light of the tavern, she inhaled the most delicious aroma of frying onions.

"What a nice place," she said. "It smells wonderful."

"Have you never been in here before? They have a marvellous cook. The owner's a friend of mine."

She shook her head. "I'll be honest. I've never even been inside a tavern before."

"You're in for a treat, then."

"So sorry to keep you waiting," said a young man in a black waistcoat, appearing before them. "If you'd follow me, Mr. Willoughby, sir?"

As they were led to a small table in the corner, Adele took in the white-panelled walls cut in half by dark wainscotting, the muted lamps over every table, offering both repose and privacy, then the mirrored bar, lined by dozens of colourful liquor bottles. The tavern was fairly crowded already with the supper crowd, and she saw most had a glass of something in their hands. The sight gave her a lift of anticipation: this was a side of Prohibition she hadn't considered.

A waiter appeared with menus and remained beside the table. "Good evening, Mr. Willoughby. As always, it's a pleasure to see you."

Ernie gave him a noncommittal nod then looked to Adele. "What would you like to drink?"

"A cup of tea, I believe," she said, suddenly shy.

He cocked an eyebrow. "Whisky. My regular," he told the waiter. "And I'll have the boiled lamb. Miss Savard?"

She quickly scanned the menu. "The chicken fricassee looks delicious."

"Excellent choice."

The drinks came quickly, and Ernie—he insisted she call him by his first name—held up his glass.

"A toast to you, Miss Savard, and to your nursing skills, used so courageously in the most perilous of places. It's a rare woman who has that much pluck."

Adele blushed, blowing over her steaming cup of tea. "You're very kind. Please call me Adele."

"Adele," he repeated. "Such a lovely name." He reclined in his chair, but his eyes never left hers. "Tell me. Why did a pretty girl from Petite Côte choose to become a nurse when she could have stayed home like many others?"

"I suppose I got restless. If you asked my mother, she would say I was always meant to be a nurse. My dolls were usually wrapped in some sort of bandages, and I was always bringing home injured birds, though I'll admit I don't remember if they left my care flying or not. She encouraged me to go to nursing school in Toronto, and I was eager to see more of the world, so I hopped on the train."

"Then onto the ship bound for Europe."

"My mother was less enthusiastic about that, but it seemed the right thing to do," she replied. "I wanted to be of use, and I was trained for exactly what they required. I was glad to go."

"I admire that. A woman who seizes an opportunity without fear."

"Oh, I can't say there wasn't any fear," she replied wryly. "We shipped out fairly early in the war, so we didn't really know what would be expected of us until we were in the thick of it. I probably should have been far more afraid than I was."

His brow creased. "I cannot imagine what you went through."

She thought it a strange comment since he'd seen conflict as well. Then again, everyone had their own experience. What mattered was that they'd survived.

She took a sip of her tea, feeling herself open up a little. "It's difficult to describe, isn't it? The war itself was so vast, so we'd all have come away from it with different memories and thoughts. I'm glad I went. I took strength and pride from helping those poor men. We saved a lot of lives. And I made a lot of friends while I was there."

"Where were you stationed?"

"I worked in a clearing station, so we moved a couple of times. We started in France, but most of the time I was in Belgium. We were close to the Front, but not actually *in* it. The men came to us straight from the battles, though."

"You must have seen some terrible things."

Her mind returned to the chaos of the hospital, the commanding shouts of doctors and the cries of suffering men. The quiet sobs that leaked into rare moments of silence when men and nurses broke. When she let herself remember, she could see butchered wounds pulsing blood from weakened hearts as clearly as if she was still there. She could see again the exposed bones; the streaming, blinded eyes; the severed, abandoned limbs set to the side of the operating table while she and the doctor focused on sewing what was left of a man back together.

Yes, she'd seen a lot of things.

"I did," she said, drawing a ragged breath.

Concern shone in his brown eyes. "I'm sorry if I've upset you."

She pushed the memories back and squeezed out a smile. "Oh no, you haven't at all. This happens sometimes, often when I least expect it. It's like I get flashes of things that happened over there. Memories I'd rather forget." She took another breath, grounding herself once again. "Perhaps I will have that glass of whisky after all."

"Certainly." Ernie signalled to the waiter and pointed at his drink. A glass of amber liquid appeared almost instantly in front of Adele.

"Thank you," she said, enjoying the warmth of the first sip. "Enough about me, though. I imagine you would have seen things, too."

"How's that?"

"Where did you serve?" Her gaze went to his missing fingers.

He grimaced and slid his hand under the table. "That happened when I was a boy. The military wouldn't take me without a full hand. I would have been there otherwise. I would have been proud to fight."

His shame pulsed hotly across the table, and she rushed to cool it. "Of course you would have. I'm sorry I assumed. How did it happen?"

"An accident."

Hundreds of hushed conversations with wounded men had taught her to follow their cues. "I understand if you don't want to talk about it."

"It's all right," he said, softening slightly. "I barely notice it anymore, though it was hard when I was young. I had to learn to do a lot of things all over again, and the other kids, well, you know how they can be."

"That must have been very difficult," she replied, meaning it. How awful for a boy to have to experience such a thing, then to suffer at the hands of his friends because of it. "Children can be cruel. What about your family? I imagine they helped you along the way."

His face clouded. "To be honest, I didn't come from what you might call a loving home. My older brother drowned in the river when we were young, and my parents . . . they were never the same after that. So I learned to stand up for myself. The only way you can get hurt is if you let people get away with it, right?" He sipped his whisky. "My parents died years ago, and I've been on my own ever since."

Instinctively, she reached for the hand he'd left on the table. "I'm so sorry, Ernie."

He turned his hand over so her fingers rested on his palm, then he folded his on top. "That's nice of you to say, Adele. I don't talk about my childhood much. Thinking about it reminds me of the family I never had." A moment of silence passed between them, then Willoughby straightened and recovered his charm. "Here I am rambling on about my little life when I'm dining with a war hero. I feel truly humbled in your presence."

She started to look away, embarrassed, but something in his expression released butterflies in her chest. "Now you're just being silly."

"Not at all."

The waiter appeared just then with their meals. "This looks delicious," Adele said, smiling up at the server, but his attention was entirely on Ernie.

"May I get you anything else, Mr. Willoughby?"

"Another whisky."

He was off like a shot, returning within seconds with Ernie's order.

"They're really efficient around here," she noted, cutting into the chicken. She closed her eyes briefly, savouring the flavour. The chicken was moist and tender, the creamy sauce exquisite. "This is divine."

He nodded, a bit of lamb on his fork. "I'm pleased it's to your taste."

"It's delicious," she replied. "Did you say you knew the owner?"

He swallowed, dabbed his mouth. "Manny Watson. We do some business together."

"What line of work are you in?" she asked.

"The export business. I work with taverns and such, here and in Detroit." He tapped his knife against her glass. "How's your whisky?"

"It's lovely," she replied, then realized what he was inferring. "Oh, you're in the liquor business?"

He smiled. "I am indeed."

She sat back, intrigued. She'd never have imagined this man with his smart suit and affable manners would be a rumrunner. She'd had a much different impression of those men. Evidently, she had much to learn.

"You're surprised?"

"A little, yes," she admitted. "I mean, I don't have a problem with alcohol, obviously"—she touched her glass—"but I am curious. I've heard so many rumours. Is rum-running as dangerous as some say?"

"Dangerous? No, no." He tilted his head slightly, considering. "Well, I suppose it can be, depending on what you're doing. There are rivalries in every business, and thanks to Prohibition, there's a lot of money at stake, so things can get heated. But I'm in a position of authority, so I look out for my employees."

"Like Dickie," Adele said. "That's good of you. To be honest, I've come to think of Prohibition as a failure. Just because booze is banned, that doesn't stop people from drinking. As a nurse, I see evidence of the ways people get around the rules every day."

Ernie nodded. "Make something illegal, and everyone will want it. It's unfortunate that regular folks just trying to make a living are treated like criminals."

Adele looked at him, thoughtful. Fred and Marie had preached that alcohol was at the root of all evil, but since crime had only increased in the past couple of years, it really did seem that the prohibition of liquor was causing more trouble than the drink itself.

"Penny for your thoughts?" Ernie asked.

"I was just wondering what my sister would say if she knew I was having a meal with a rumrunner. She's quite an avid member of the temperance movement."

"But you're different," he said, watching her closely. "A war nurse such as yourself isn't afraid of a little booze."

"No, I suppose not," she said, emboldened.

At Ernie's request, the waiter brought each of them a slice of pineapple upside-down cake—Adele's first taste of the decadent delight—then Ernie smoothly turned the conversation in a different direction.

At the end of the evening, he escorted her to her car and opened her door. "Thank you for agreeing to have dinner with me tonight. I apologize for the spur of the moment invitation, but I've really enjoyed your company. Truly. It's been a pleasure."

"It has been. Thank you, Ernie."

He helped her into the car and closed the door gently behind her. "Would you consider joining me for dinner again, perhaps on Friday night?"

She looked up at his face, admiring how his chocolate eyes glinted with gold under the streetlamp. "I would like that very much."

"Until then," he said, smiling.

As she drove away, she glanced back over her shoulder at the tall, sturdy man still standing in the middle of the street. It had been a long time since she had connected so quickly with anyone. Especially a man. Not since Jerry Bailey, she realized. Ernie might not have shared her wartime experience, but he had suffered his own losses and come out the other side, just as she had, and she was looking forward to seeing him again. She didn't know what lay ahead, but her heart warmed at the thought that she might not have to travel that road alone.

thirteen

JERRY

❧

Jerry stepped back from the stack of whisky cases he'd piled against the wall, rotating his shoulders to ease his muscles. He'd arrived early that morning, sleeves rolled up, hoping to finish his inventory count before anyone else arrived. A new shipment would arrive from the still tomorrow, and he needed everything in the warehouse counted ahead of time. Too many people in the same place, all of them talking at once, made it more difficult to concentrate. Fortunately, everyone else seemed to have slept in, so Jerry was able to work in peace.

Life sure had changed for John and him since their toast over a year ago. From their first shipment across the water to their full list of buyers on both sides of the river, Bailey Brothers' Best was doing a fine business indeed. Expenses were down, profits were up, and everybody knew their name. The stills were working overtime, and he'd hired more men, almost all of whom were fresh back from the war and needing a practical way out of the past. Their whisky was washing past a great many lips, smooth and bold and exactly what people wanted. Sure, he and John were breaking a law or two, as far as Prohibition went, but they were filling pockets and helping men, and so far, they had steered clear of any kind of violence.

The brothers made a good team. Jerry oversaw production, arranged contracts, and balanced finances while John managed the rumrunners and smuggling logistics. Their roles played to their strengths, and their natural partnership made it all run smoothly. But Jerry thought John seemed a little distracted of late, and he'd noticed empty bottles had begun to pile up around the house. He didn't like the look of John's cracked knuckles or the dark circles under his eyes. He'd seen it before. While Jerry turned to the irrefutable, dependable accuracy of the numbers in his ledgers for escape from the past, John sought it in alcohol. Jerry understood that. It was easy to drink away the memories, even if it was just for a little while. But John wasn't good at putting the cork back in the bottle, and all the booze did was stoke his temper. Jerry stepped in when he could, diffusing situations, but he had started to worry that the day might come when he wouldn't be there to hold John back from a fight he couldn't win.

A few nights ago, he'd talked John into staying home for supper for a change. He fried up some fish and tried to be subtle about placing a cup of coffee in front of them both. John had eyed his cup, but when Jerry made no comment, he didn't either. Over their dinner of fried fish, they talked about business, rumours, friends, and memories of anything that did not involve the war, and eventually, Jerry asked about John's scraped hands.

"It's nothing," John told him, dismissing the questions. "We had a bit of a tussle at poker the other night."

"You're sure? You're doing all right, then?"

"Never been better. In fact, I'm thinking about getting a new car," John said, tipping back his whisky.

"You wanna show off for that new gal," Jerry acknowledged, letting his concerns go. There was no point in having an argument over this. Not unless it got worse. "What's it been? Two whole weeks this time?"

"Yeah," John replied, oblivious to Jerry's teasing. "Betty. She's the one, I'm telling you."

"She's a peach," Jerry agreed.

The only things as prevalent as roadhouses in Windsor were cathouses. On some streets the two businesses practically alternated, so a man in that frame of mind could go for a whisky, put money on the horses, visit a girl, then move directly onto the next drink. John was drawn to all the vices. His was the laugh heard over the crowd, the hand that poured drinks, and the heart that fell in love—over and over again.

"Hélène's from Quebec," he'd told Jerry one day as they were bottling. "Eighteen. Prettiest little thing, with those big brown eyes . . ." The following week it was, "How haven't I noticed Suzette before?"

"Who?" Jerry asked.

"Suzette. With the long red hair and the . . . well, you know."

Now it was Betty.

"When are you going to get back in the game, Jerry?" John asked.

Jerry gestured at his face. "I don't think this is what the ladies want."

"You're wrong about that, brother. There's a whole lot of pretty gals eyeing you up, but you ain't taking any of them out for supper."

Jerry had kept his eyes on his meal. When they'd first come back, he'd let himself dream for a little while about running into Adele, but it had been three years. He'd grudgingly given up on that hope. Still, none of those pretty gals John was talking about interested him much.

He was thinking of that as he finished his inventory, straightening the last bottle so the little bluebird on the label faced out. Satisfied, he settled onto his desk chair and pulled out his ledger to check the previous numbers against his latest count. He slid his finger slowly across the columns, then paused, noting a discrepancy in the stock. Four cases missing. A hundred bottles. He rubbed his hands against his face in frustration; it wasn't the first time bottles had gone missing.

He knew the stock hadn't been stolen from here: the warehouse was locked and closely guarded, and they were always careful about anyone following them to and from the location. Tuck had been helping out whenever he could, giving them notice of any planned police raids on their shipments, but some were to be expected, and there were other thieves out there—rival gangs—eager to waylay a shipment for their own gain. If the Baileys' rumrunners were stopped, the customer still came first. The rule was that they had to return to the warehouse, replenish the stock, and get the liquor out to the buyer as quickly and covertly as possible.

He'd noticed a definite uptick in seized shipments lately. His gut told him it was Willoughby, but he had no proof. Jerry tapped his pencil on the ledger, puzzling out this latest problem in the columns. Usually John told him when a delivery had gone awry. Had he forgotten to do that, or had something else happened to the bottles?

"Jer," Walter said, walking in.

Jerry looked up. "What is it?"

He shifted the toothpick in his mouth. "You got a visitor."

"Who?"

"Slim Baines."

Concern flitted through Jerry's chest. Slim was Willoughby's man. This was out of the ordinary; everyone knew any sort of business meeting had to be conducted far from the warehouse. Away from Bailey territory.

"Have you seen John?" he asked.

"Not yet today."

Jerry sighed, resigned. "Might as well let Slim in."

As Walter left, Jerry pulled on his suit coat. His father had always said he should dress well if he wanted people to respect him, so while Jerry worked in a plain shirt and trousers, he always kept a coat handy. After a moment's deliberation, he secured his pistol on his hip and stood to wait. A suit wouldn't make Slim respect him, but the gun would.

Walter opened the door, and sunlight lit the dark space, bringing Slim Baines with it. He was a short, wiry man who had worked for Willoughby for a couple of years, doing his behind-the-scenes dirty work. Slippery as an eel. Never set foot on a battlefield in his life.

"Baines," Jerry said, knowing Slim preferred everyone to use his nickname. "To what do I owe the pleasure?"

Slim's small eyes roved the space, taking in Jerry's stock. "Big Will's tired of playing nice," he said.

Jerry pulled out his silver cigarette case, letting Slim see his weapon, and lit a smoke. "I wasn't aware he and I were playing," he said calmly. "I have my business; he has his."

"Who you kidding, Jigsaw? Everybody's business is Big Will's business."

"Big Will," Walter snorted. "That's such a stupid name. He's not much taller than I am."

"I hear you got stood up again," Slim said, ignoring Walter.

"What would you know about that?" Jerry asked.

He shrugged, but the mocking look in his eye confirmed what Jerry already thought: Willoughby was behind the recent raids. Had Willoughby's hired police force confiscated the booze themselves, or had they passed it over to Willoughby to relabel and resell? Jerry returned to the chair behind his desk and wrote *Tuck* in tiny letters on the paper in front of him, out of Slim's view.

"You want Big Will's protection, you're gonna have to pay the tax."

Jerry's eyes rolled up at Slim. "I need protection from Willoughby like I need another hole in my head."

"Listen up, Jigsaw. I'm here with a message. He's had enough of your mouth. It's your business he wants now. He'll take sixty per cent."

Behind Slim, Walter's eyebrows shot up.

"Not from me," Jerry replied. "He can ask someone else for that. He's already stealing my liquor. I'm not gonna pay him to do it."

"Fifty-five."

"Get this through your head. I'm not paying Ernie anything. And he'd better back off my shipments."

"Or else what?"

"Don't be stupid."

"He can't help it," Walter said wryly.

Jerry took a drag from his cigarette, then turned back to his ledgers. "If there isn't anything else, it's time for you to leave."

Walter caught his cue. He took out his own revolver, made a show of checking the safety.

Slim's thin lip pulled up in a snarl. "We ain't done, Jigsaw."

"That's where you're wrong," Jerry said, not bothering to look at him. "Walter, would you please see our guest out?"

"With pleasure," Walter replied, giving Slim a shove toward the door.

"You're gonna regret this," Slim called back.

The door slammed shut behind him, and Jerry let his mask of calm drop, his mind racing. Willoughby might be a bully, but he wasn't stupid. His enterprise was taking in a cut of the hard work of all the other rumrunners—he didn't make whisky himself—and he had paid off the cops for good reason. He was protecting his own interests while putting everyone else who didn't fall into line out of business. Jerry knew the authorities didn't really care about the Baileys' relatively small operation, but with Willoughby, it was personal. If he offered them enough money, they might put the screws to John and him. He could just as easily put his own gang of thugs on him. Willoughby had his choice of methods, most of which would leave the Baileys vulnerable.

As soon as Jerry heard Slim's tires spin out on the gravel road, he grabbed his hat and headed out the door. "Walter," he said. "We need to double up security for a while."

"All right. Where you going?"

"To the house. I gotta find John. Don't let anyone in the warehouse until I'm back. Nobody, got it?"

"Got it."

By the time Jerry parked in front of the house, he'd worked through a sliver of a plan. It was the last thing he wanted to do, but from what he could see, it was the only way to ensure that Willoughby didn't get his hands on their inventory and destroy everything they had worked so hard for.

Inside, Jerry found John hunched over a cup of coffee, his skin grey and clammy from another hangover.

"Good time last night?" he asked, keeping his voice even.

"I think so," John replied. "Some parts are a little cloudy."

Jerry took a seat. "Listen. Slim Baines showed up at the warehouse."

John sat up, alert. "What?"

"Yep. There's also more stock missing. A hundred bottles. Did you know about that?"

John's face fell. "Yes. Our run to Woodbridge Tavern was held up." He counted back the days. "Two days ago. Sarg fulfilled the order, but I should have told you. Sorry about that."

"Well, we know for sure now that Willoughby was behind it, so I'm assuming he's behind the rest of the hijacks. Slim basically said that Willoughby's offer of protection would ensure the cops on his payroll backed off. And that we'd regret saying no."

"That scum—"

Jerry cut him off. "Have you talked to Tuck lately, John?"

His brother studied a knot in the table. "No, I was supposed to meet him last week, but Betty wanted to go dancing." He dropped his head into his hands. "I'm sorry. I've let you down."

Jerry softened. "It's all right. But I've been working on a plan, and I need you back in the game." He angled his head toward the liquor shelf on the wall. "And you gotta cut back."

John nodded, looking contrite. "Whatever you need."

"We're gonna have to lean more on Tuck for a while. We haven't asked him for much so far, but we can compensate him if he keeps his eyes and ears open for any information about Willoughby sending the cops after our warehouse."

John's eyes widened. "If they raid the—"

"Yeah. I'm worried about that. It was a direct threat, sending Slim there instead of meeting me somewhere else. I have Walter doubling security."

"What's the plan, Jerry?"

He took a breath. "We dig a tunnel under the barn then build a storage room for the booze underground. No one but you and I can know about it."

John was incredulous. "Just the two of us? It would take forever to dig a room big enough to house everything."

"It's not for everything. We're going to split up the stock. We'll keep some at the warehouse, store the rest here at the house."

"But you just said they might raid the warehouse. You still want to leave some there?"

Jerry nodded slowly. "Yeah. I want it visible. If we are raided and half our stock is here, they won't get everything. Willoughby will think he's put us out of business if he takes what he can see, but he never will."

"That'll make him crazy," John said with a smile.

But Jerry wasn't smiling. "In order to do this, we will have to go underground."

That was something neither of them ever wanted to do again.

John paused, then lifted his chin, resignation in his eyes. "Guess we'd better start digging. You mark the entrance off. I'll go get the shovels."

At first, it wasn't so bad, but as soon as they'd hollowed out enough of a hole that they were able to stand underground, Jerry's chest constricted. It was silly, he knew, and it lasted only a blink, but he didn't think he'd ever be able to go under the earth again without this kind of fear. When John lit a match for the lanterns, they both stared at it out of habit. In the tunnels, where breathing clean air meant life or death, they'd learned that if the match only burned red, there wasn't enough oxygen for a man to survive. Now, the flame bloomed yellow, and they both exhaled.

"All right," Jerry said, shrugging off the claustrophobia. "Let's keep going."

It was a different colour dirt from so many other tunnels he'd dug,

but it was dirt just the same. Heavy and thick and endless. In the beginning, all Jerry heard was the crack of the pickaxe, then the scrape and
push of their shovels. After three days, they'd moved so far underground
that Jerry had to remind himself to unclench his jaw. And while he told
himself that men were not dying above him, he couldn't help listening for
explosions, and for German shovels coming from the other side.

John was watching him. "Do you hear them too?"

Jerry nodded, aware his hands were shaking. They hadn't done that
for a while.

"We should sing," John suggested, then he launched into an old
song they'd sung when they were done with their shifts and clear of the
tunnels, safe to use their voices again. The men had squeezed the words
through their strained throats to ease the fear they all felt.

> *Oh what a life! Oh what a life!*
> *Living in a trench.*
> *Oh what a life! Oh what a life!*
> *Fighting for the French.*
> *We haven't got a wife or a nice little wench,*
> *We're all quite happy in an old French trench.*

And for a little while, Jerry let himself forget.

fourteen
ADELE

❧

— June 1921 —

Adele fidgeted, hugging her shawl tight around her for reassurance as she stared up at Ernie's house. Really, it was a mansion, with its four storeys, at least a dozen bright and welcoming windows, and an illuminated walkway filled with a stream of guests. A rainbow of merry women in short, shiny skirts and floor-length satin gowns swept along the path accompanied by gentlemen in white shirts and long, dark coats, black fedoras sitting jauntily on top. Everyone smiled and laughed as they walked, and she watched them disappear through the open front door, welcomed by the music playing inside.

When Ernie Willoughby had invited her to the annual party at his house, her first reaction had been to decline. She wasn't good in crowds. Especially one filled with strangers. She wouldn't know anyone, she said, trying to wriggle out.

"When's the last time you went to a party?" he'd coaxed. "I promise it will be like nothing you've ever seen before, all black tie and caviar."

He was right about her nearly empty social calendar. When she was younger, she'd enjoyed a few parties and met a lot of people, but the war had changed her; she rarely went out for fun anymore.

"I have nothing suitable to wear," she protested, but she was weakening and Ernie sensed it.

"I'm sure you do. Don't worry, I'll be with you the whole time. I'll keep you safe." His smile was warm. "I'll send a car for you."

"No, no. Just tell me the address, and I will drive myself," she said, planning to have an escape car at hand if needed.

He wouldn't hear of it. "The prize jewel of the party driving herself? No, no, the car will pick you up at seven o'clock precisely. I can hardly wait."

In the end, she had gone out to buy a dress, justifying the use of her savings by reminding herself that she really wasn't spending anything otherwise. When she told the saleslady where she was going, the woman's eyes nearly popped out of her head. She tugged Adele to the back of the store, where she draped her in all the latest fashions, from long Greek evening gowns made with layers of chiffon, to dresses with a defined, dropped waist over a fuller skirt.

"Is everything sleeveless?" Adele had asked, turning sideways in the mirror to inspect a beautiful pink number, the bust shiny with metal sequins. "The evening might be chilly."

"Oh, yes. It's all the rage. But we have shawls and stoles."

"This neckline feels . . ." Adele frowned, trying to find the words. "A little heavy. Like it might slip too low, if that makes any sense."

"Of course, dear. Let's find a dress with fewer sequins. They're metal, so naturally they're heavy. It doesn't matter, though. You don't need too much sparkle with your beautiful complexion." Her eyes lit up. "I have just the thing. And it's blue. With your eyes, blue is definitely your colour."

She brought out the gown, and Adele slipped it on, marvelling at how it clung to her figure as if it had been sewn especially for her. The smooth satin fell halfway down her calves, and at first glance she shied away, thinking it too brazen. Then the saleslady handed her an overdress as light as air, and its light blue, netted mesh layered loosely over top of the sheath, making both dresses dance as one. The lacy, dropped waist was delicately defined by an embroidered belt, its thread a deep sapphire blue, and the bottom of the skirt flared slightly, swinging as she turned.

"You look stunning," the woman declared, hands clasped in front of her chest.

And she did. Adele turned full on to the mirror and stared, starting at the little white beaded shoes, moving up through the gown, and finishing with her long blond hair, which the saleslady had quickly pinned up in a style Adele hadn't tried before. For a moment, she couldn't speak, struck dumb by her reflection. The woman before her was soft and feminine, elegant in the best possible way. How long had it been since she'd seen herself not as a working nurse but as a woman? Had she ever really done that? And this, this was what Ernie would see, and knowing that made her glow even more.

Maman was speechless when she came out of her room the night of the party. "*Ma belle petite fille*," she gushed. "How it sets off your eyes. Look here: Monsieur Willoughby has already sent over flowers." She pointed to a bouquet of dark red roses. "It seems you have indeed charmed him."

Guillaume was just walking in the house, and he stopped in his tracks. "Look at you. Most beautiful girl in the world, other than your maman."

"She's going to a big, big party tonight. At a rich man's mansion. He's a rumrunner, she says, but he is a gentleman. He is sending a car! *C'est bien.*"

"He sounds nice." Guillaume reached for a newspaper and headed toward his favourite chair in the living room. "What is his name?"

Her mother picked up the card from the flowers and waved it in the air. "Ernie Willoughby," she said. "Oh, I'm very excited for you, *ma belle*. So lucky!"

"Thank you, Maman!" She pulled her into a hug, looking over her shoulder at Guillaume. "What do you say?"

He hesitated. Was it her imagination, or did his smile look strained? "I'd say he's the lucky one, *ma petite*. Be careful. A big party with rum-runners could mean trouble."

"Or it could just be a lot of fun," Maman said, then she'd hugged her again when the driver knocked on the door.

Now she was here, staring up at the mansion. She felt an urge to spring back home, high heels and all, but the chauffeur held out a hand, waiting.

Adele took a deep, reassuring breath. "I've gotten through German bombardments," she reminded herself. "I can do this."

She joined the queue and was relieved to see Ernie standing at the entrance, looking dapper in a pinstripe suit. His face broke into a wide, appreciative smile at the sight of her.

"I've been waiting for you," he said. "Adele, darling, you are a vision. Blue is most definitely your colour."

She felt the warmth of his lips as he kissed the back of her hand. "Thank you," she said. "I'm glad you approve."

"Truly. You've exceeded my wildest dreams tonight. Like Cinderella arriving at the ball." He took her arm and led her to the side, out of the way. "Before we go in, I have something for you."

"Oh?"

He circled behind her, and she felt his fingers on the back of her neck as he fastened a necklace in place. Dropping her chin, she stared in disbelief at the diamond and pearl pendant hanging just above her breasts.

"It's beautiful, Ernie, but it's too much. We've only been seeing each other a short while." Her fingers went to the back of her neck to unclasp the little hook. "I can't possibly accept this."

His hand pressed against hers. "Of course you can. A beautiful woman deserves beautiful things. Please, Adele. You know what you mean to me, I think. I want you to have it."

At first, she was self-conscious, aware of the gem's weight on her chest, but then Ernie tucked her hand through his arm and led her proudly into a crowd that sparkled with its own jewellery.

His voice dropped to a whisper. "Don't let them intimidate you. You've got more class and beauty than all the women in Windsor, but I'll be right here in case you need me."

A waiter paused beside Ernie, a drink tray in hand, and Ernie claimed two glasses of champagne. Adele regarded hers with a hint of trepidation—she'd never tasted champagne before—but after one ticklish sip she was enamoured of the drink.

"Shall we?" Ernie asked.

"Lead on," she said.

"That's my girl."

They walked arm in arm through the crowd, and at Ernie's summons, people came to greet Adele, their smiles and enthusiastic compliments almost fawning. She wasn't sure if it was her glamorous gown, the bubbly drink, or Ernie's dedicated attentions, but she felt aglow with excitement. She couldn't stop smiling. It was as if she was an entirely different person, and the power of that feeling made everything even more exhilarating.

"Adele Savard," Ernie said regally, "I present Felix and Ruby Arrington."

"So this is the great beauty we keep hearing about," Felix boomed.

His wife smiled brightly, revealing a smudge of red lipstick on her tooth. "The nurse, right? Oh, is it true you were in the war? What an amazing young woman you are! You'll have to tell us all about it."

"Well, I . . ." Adele reached for her practiced response, and a bit of her elegant self slipped out of place. "I did my duty, that's all. It was an honour to serve."

Behind Ruby, Adele noticed a few others around them, listening in, making honeyed comments about what she'd said. Was this how the evening was going to go? Would she be peppered all night with questions about the war? She felt a stab of disappointment, realizing that. She could wear the most dazzling dress in the world, she realized, but she would always be regarded as "that woman from the war."

Ernie must have sensed her discomfort because he deftly turned the conversation to other matters. "Felix and Ruby recently moved from Detroit."

Ruby didn't skip a beat. "Felix kept saying that this was the place to be! And with parties like this, who could argue?"

She continued on, talking of the new friends she'd made here, and after a while, Adele felt the tension in her shoulders release.

As promised, Ernie stayed by her side, one hand on her waist, helping her with names and leading the chitchat to safer ground. She started to think she'd been silly before, worrying so much, when a man as thin as a scarecrow slid toward them. She looked at Ernie expectantly, but for the first time all night, he didn't introduce them.

"Excuse me, Adele," he said, and took a step away.

Whatever the man whispered in Ernie's ear caused him to scowl, and he turned back to Adele. "I'm so sorry, my dear, but there is some business I have to attend to."

"You're leaving?" she asked, anxiety creeping up her arms, reaching for her neck.

"Just for an hour. I'll be back as soon as I can."

He kissed her lightly on the cheek then swept away, leaving her alone in a sea of strangers and cigarette smoke. Over the next hour, she did her best to join the conversations around her, but she had no idea what to say. Now that Ernie had left, people no longer seemed interested in her.

"Wall Street is the place to be," she overheard as she sipped. "If you're not buying stocks right now, you're missing out. The thing to do is buy on margin."

"Darling, those earrings are simply gorgeous. Wherever did you get them?"

"That fella always begging outside the Sandwich post office. What a sight. Wonder what he looked like before."

"I'll get my broker to telephone you next week, shall I?"

She'd been right after all, she realized. She shouldn't have come. She didn't fit in. She was here for the host, and he had left almost an hour ago—though she seemed to be the only one put out by that fact. The heat, the noise, the smoke, and the champagne were clogging her thoughts, and she felt a wave of nausea roll through her. She needed fresh air. Squeezing between guests, she headed toward the door, but before she could reach it, Ernie returned, striding like a benevolent king back into his castle.

"Where were you?" she asked, then she despised herself for the desperation even she had heard in her voice. Where was the courageous war nurse now?

"Just taking care of some business that I had hoped was already handled," he said, passing his coat to a servant. "I feel terrible, leaving you alone, but I promise I am yours for the rest of the night. Oh, you need a drink."

He raised a hand to signal a waiter, and Adele noticed a spatter of fresh blood on his cuff. She was about to mention it to him when she realized the knuckles of his right hand were split and bleeding.

"You're hurt," she said, reaching for his arm. "What happened?"

The waiter appeared, and Ernie pulled his arm out of her grip. He handed her their drinks then dabbed the accompanying napkin over the blood. "Nothing to worry about. Banged my hand is all. Sweet of you to worry about me, though."

The nurse in Adele pressed forward, and she set her glass back on the waiter's tray. "May I take a look at it?"

"I said it was nothing. Please don't henpeck." Then he flashed her his charming smile. "Shall we dance?"

Adele blinked up at him, confused. Had he been fighting?

She said nothing as he whisked her onto the gleaming hardwood floor, proud as a peacock, sometimes watching her, sometimes yelling to a guest at the other end of the room, always entertaining someone.

The effort seemed redundant, considering everything he'd put into this party. She recalled something he'd told her the first time they had gone out, about never having had a family, and the wounded expression he'd worn as he said it. Maybe that's what he had created here, she thought, feeling a little sad for him. Certainly his guests had come when he'd invited them, but had they really come for him? Or was it for the free liquor, the glamour, the prestige of being invited to such an event?

Around and around they danced, and despite the guests moving out of the way for Ernie, the space was crowded, and the air was getting stuffy. Deep in her chest, Adele felt a flurry of panic, a need to escape the shrinking room. The necklace he'd fastened around her throat suddenly felt too tight. When at last the song ended, he released her hand, but the arm around her waist remained as he led her off the floor.

"That was nice. You're a good dancer." When she didn't respond, he peered at her face. "Adele? Are you all right? You're looking pale."

"Honestly, Ernie, I have a terrible headache," she managed. "It must be all the excitement. I need to call it a night, I'm afraid."

He scowled slightly. "But I don't want you to leave yet. I have one more surprise for you."

She pressed two fingers to her temple, which really had begun to throb. "Ernie, I—"

"That's all right," he said brightly, checking the gold watch hanging on a chain from his waistcoat. "We can do it now."

He flagged a passing waiter and whispered something in his ear. The man nodded and vanished back the way he'd come.

Ernie chuckled. "You're going to love this. It's just for you. Grab your wrap and come outside with me." He looked around the room then raised his voice. "Everyone come outside, please!" Somehow, not everyone seemed to have heard him, so he yelled more sharply this time, making her flinch. "I said, 'Come outside'! Now!"

Hearing this grand announcement, the level of conversation rose from silence to animated, and after she'd retrieved her shawl, Adele had no choice but to swim with the tide of people heading toward the front door of the house. When everyone was out, Ernie faced them all.

"It's been quite a year, hasn't it? A wonderful year. Well, there's no better way to celebrate than with friends like all of you, and I'm pleased you could all be here. Are we all having fun?" A scattered chorus of approval rose up, and Ernie's face darkened slightly with frustration. He tried again, and Adele frowned. She'd never seen this aggressive side of him. "I said, 'Are we all having fun?'" This time the whole crowd roared in agreement, so Ernie rewarded his audience by holding up a fresh glass of champagne and beaming around at them. "That's what I thought! Let's celebrate with a bang."

In the next instant, Adele threw herself to the ground, covering her head against the bullets that cracked overhead, the shell fire—

"Adele!" Ernie said, laughing as he hauled her to her feet. "What are you doing down there? Up! Up you get, my dear."

High overhead, fireworks exploded in cascades of colour, but Adele could barely breathe through her panic. She looked around at the other guests, most of whom were gawking up at the display, cheering with appreciation. But there were others, like her, who flinched every time another firework went off.

Adele turned to Ernie, fighting the urge to run. "I have to go now."

"Now?" His brow drew in. "These things are expensive, and I got them for you."

"I'm sorry, Ernie. I'm just very tired, and my head . . . I need to get home. Thank you so much for inviting me, and for"—she glanced up, catching her breath as another burst of fireworks went off—"for such a memorable party."

"Well, if you must. I'll call the driver." He whistled through his teeth and signalled to someone inside the house, then he turned back to her and held out his arm. "I'll walk you out."

Once they were away from the crowd, he softened. He gestured toward the sky, where a veil of grey smoke dwindled in the darkness in the aftermath of the fireworks. "I'm sorry if this was too much. I just wanted to do something special for you, my little war hero. I didn't think about the noise. I'm terribly sorry."

The car pulled up, and he opened her door. Before she could step inside, he took her hand.

"I hope you enjoyed yourself tonight."

She almost regretted letting him down. Almost. But his apparent need to bend people to his will was disturbing. Trying to hide her discomfort, she forced a smile.

"I did. And thank you again, for the gift." She touched her necklace.

"It looks cheap on such an elegant neck." He fingered the chain around her throat. "Adele, you were the most beautiful woman here tonight, just as I knew you would be."

He leaned in to kiss her, but she turned her face to the side.

"I'm sorry, Ernie. It's too soon."

His forehead creased, but he released her hand. "Of course. You're tired."

"Thank you again," she said, retreating into the car.

"Goodnight, Adele."

She smiled and waved at Ernie until he disappeared from sight, then she wrapped her arms around herself and sank into the leather seat, wishing she could stop trembling. The fireworks had really knocked her for a loop. A gift, he'd called them, like the necklace. The thought, however extravagant, had been sweet, hadn't it? Just wasted on her.

As the car rolled onto the highway, the dwindling smoke from the fireworks gave way to a velvet sky, twinkling with stars. The peace helped her breathe normally once more. The music and colours and razzle-dazzle were like nothing she'd ever seen before. Exciting, like the fireworks should have been. He'd done all he could to ensure she enjoyed herself, and yet the sense of claustrophobia still squeezed her. She touched the diamond hanging from her neck, thinking about the way he had looked at her, then how he'd shown her off to the others. What was she to him? Was he genuine in his interest, or was she just another pretty thing to add to his collection?

She reached behind her neck and unclasped the necklace, wondering why the weight of it around her neck made her so uncomfortable. She dropped the beautiful piece of jewellery into her bag and immediately felt better. More like herself. It just didn't suit her. He wouldn't be happy to hear it, but she didn't want to keep his gift. Then she thought again about everything she had seen in him tonight, and it dawned on her that she wasn't sure she wanted to keep him, either.

fifteen

JERRY

❧

Thirty feet beneath the ground, Jerry sank his shovel into the dirt floor and swept his forearm across his sweaty brow. It hadn't taken Jerry and John long to fall into the rhythm of digging, nor for their hands to develop the familiar calluses that turned the skin of their palms and fingers to sandpaper. They'd made good progress over the past couple weeks, as evidenced by the twenty-foot tunnel they'd dug. From there, they had begun to dig a room.

As much as the brothers hated being back underground, at least it was less terrifying this time. No one was actively trying to kill them here, though they never went into the tunnel without a gun. The entrance through the barn was camouflaged beneath a cabinet when no one was in the underground space, but if anyone were to somehow discover it, the brothers had to be prepared to defend themselves. They were also slightly reassured by the general construction of the tunnel. Unlike the dicey, splintering wood they had been forced to use back in Europe to keep those tunnels solid, here they had strong posts of oak. Still, their safety wasn't guaranteed, and Jerry couldn't help but regard those overhead beams with trepidation. Regardless of the condition of the wood, they supported hundreds of tons of dirt, all of which loomed over the brothers' heads.

But overall, it was easier work. They even had a wheelbarrow, so they shovelled the discarded dirt into it rather than filling hundreds of sacks, then dumping them in the field behind the barn.

John returned with the empty wheelbarrow now. "I heard Sammy McDonald was beaten pretty bad in that fight," he said, picking up their conversation. "Walter says Sammy owed Willoughby money. He must have been in big trouble, turning to Willoughby."

"I wouldn't call it a fight," Jerry muttered. He knew of Sammy only from a distance. Just a regular man with a wife and three kids and a tiny bootleg operation, but he'd been beaten to within an inch of his life on his way home last night. "Willoughby's men held him down while he taught him a lesson. I'd put money on that."

"Pretty rough lesson."

"It's more than rough, John. It's a reminder to you and me. The violence is getting worse. Right now, it's like we're stuck in a tunnel with men who care even less about the law than we do. We gotta listen to the walls, or they're all coming down." He scratched his head. "I gotta tell you, the way things are building these days, I have a bad feeling we might not get out this time."

Yesterday, they'd invited Tuck over to their place for supper. He'd looked tired but determined, and Jerry could see his frustration as he listed off all the cops, lawyers, and judges he knew were on the take. He kept shaking his head, naming men he'd worked with for a long time before this. *Good* men, he kept saying.

"Speaking of which." John slid an envelope of cash across the table to Tuck. "We want you to have this."

Tuck pushed it back, looking disappointed in John. "Don't want it. That's Willoughby's way, not yours."

"If Willoughby's cops hear about you helping us . . ." John said.

He shook his head. "They won't. Besides. Money won't stop them if it comes to that."

"You'll have us at your back if anything happens," Jerry assured him. "And this envelope will be ready for you if you change your mind."

Tuck had left without the cash, and though Jerry admired him for his tough moral code, he was sure Tuck could use the money. A constable who might usually take home $600 a month could now earn ten times that, just for looking the other way.

"I'm hungry," John said now. "Let's go for lunch."

"I don't know. We have a lot to do here. We're running low on time."

"All this will still be here when we get back."

Jerry set his shovel aside. "All right. But we're coming back to do more later."

The Chappell House was a brick hotel and tavern standing three storeys tall on Sandwich Street West. Mr. Howard, the manager, spotted the brothers coming in and gave them a wave.

"Here for lunch?"

"Please," John said. "A couple of plates of ham, please."

"Whisky?" Mr. Howard offered.

"Not today," John answered, making Jerry smile. John had been taking it easy on the liquor lately, and Jerry could see he was looking healthier already.

A few minutes later, Mr. Howard brought their lunch, and Jerry asked him to join them. "We haven't had much time to tell you we think you're doing a great job here, taking over from Trumble."

"Thanks," Mr. Howard said. "I appreciate that."

The previous owner, "Babe" Trumble, had been fatally shot last November by a local minister obsessed with cracking down on bootleggers. Leslie Spracklin, or the "Fighting Pastor" as he became known, had been appointed as a special temperance enforcement officer, and he sicced his gang of righteous thugs on anyone who carried the slightest whiff of alcohol on them. Trumble and Spracklin had a beef that stemmed back to boyhood, and it all culminated when Spracklin decided to put a stop to the Chappell House's successful liquor business once and for all.

He broke into the tavern at 3:00 a.m., shattering the window and waking Trumble's family. Trumble had gone downstairs to investigate, gun in hand, but Spracklin's Colt 45 went off first. His bullet had severed Trumble's femoral artery, and he died in his wife's arms.

Jerry had been somewhat surprised by the attack, because Police Chief Masters was on the payroll for Chappell House. But Spracklin's thirst for temperance was unquenchable. He demanded a complete cleanup of the police. That, everyone knew, was laughable. There were so many cops on the take they'd never be able to get them all.

Still, Trumble's death had shocked a lot of people, including Jerry and John. It felt too close to home. They'd paid closer attention after that.

"We're throwing a couple extra crates into your next delivery as a thank-you for your business," Jerry told Howard now.

"I'm much obliged," he replied. "You boys always give me a good deal, and your hooch is first-rate. A lot of folks will buy your whisky over others priced the same."

"We're just following our father's recipe," Jerry said modestly.

"Your pa was a good man," Mr. Howard replied, rising from his seat. "Don't worry about the food. It's on the house."

After lunch, they lit a couple of cigarettes and sat back, delaying the moment when they would have to return home and go underground. As John blew circles of smoke over his head, Jerry squinted across the sun-dappled road at a group of well-dressed men disembarking from three parked cars. They were likely from Detroit, Jerry surmised, here for liquor. Sure enough, a moment later he spotted Dutchie, one of the Bailey brothers' competitors, approaching the group, his shock of white hair gleaming in the sunlight. Jim Dutch was a poker-faced former POW who didn't put up with nonsense. He shared some of the same buyers with Jerry and John, but neither of them had encroached on each other's business out of respect for their wartime experience.

"Is that who I think it is?" John asked.

Jerry followed John's gaze. Another car had pulled up behind the entourage, and the broad-shouldered figure of Ernie Willoughby emerged, adjusting his fedora. Slim and a few other goons trickled out of the vehicle after him.

"What's Dutchie doing with that idiot?" John said, getting to his feet.

Jerry was wondering the same thing, but he hung back, cautious. "Leave him, John," he warned.

John wasn't listening. He grabbed his cap and stepped toward the door. Jerry sighed, then did the same. He couldn't leave John to his own devices.

Outside, the group had moved down the road and around a corner, and Jerry and John trailed at a distance, stopping behind a thin stand of trees. Hidden from the street, Willoughby and the Americans had circled around Dutchie. From their stances, Jerry could sense the friction between them, though he couldn't make out what they were saying.

"We can't go out there," Jerry whispered. He had no doubt that each man had a weapon nestled on their hip under their fancy suit jackets.

John nodded. "Too many guns."

The discussion before them was deteriorating fast. Dutchie now stood chest to chest with Willoughby, his face bright red against his white hair. He jabbed his finger over and over into Willoughby's chest until Willoughby tilted his head in a signal toward one of his men, who dragged Dutchie away then punched him in the face. Dutchie stumbled to the ground, blood streaming from his nose, but he got up like a jack-in-the-box, his eyes trained on Willoughby. The man had survived a German prison camp; he could withstand more than a broken nose. Willoughby said something to Dutchie that ended the conversation, then he turned to leave.

"If Dutchie's involved with Willoughby, it's against his will. Let's go," Jerry said, and they quickly returned to the main street then slowed their pace, disappearing into the crowds on the sidewalks.

"Witless is such a bastard. Somebody's gonna put a stop to it eventually. I hope it's me."

"Stay away from him, John," Jerry said. "I mean it. We can't aggravate him any more than we already are. No matter what, he's always gonna have a bigger army." He took out the key to the Ford. "C'mon, we have work to do. We can't avoid it forever, as tempting as that is. Willoughby is getting pushier. He'll be coming for our booze again soon."

John sighed, then started to cross the street toward the general store. "Fine. Just let me get some more cigarettes. I'm out. If a man can't drink, at least let him smoke."

While they waited for the shopkeeper to ring up their cigarettes, Jerry's gaze went to the people walking past. June had brought out the light, colourful clothing, and now that coats and scarves were gone, he could see people's smiles. His own faded at the sight of Willoughby, who, having finished shaking Dutchie down, was heading up the sidewalk, chatting amiably with a woman at his side. Jerry's gaze dropped to Willoughby's companion, and he froze.

So many faces he'd forgotten since the war, but never hers. *Why, I grew up in Petite Côte!* Suddenly, he lay on a cot in Belgium's grey, damp cold, his face wrapped like a mummy's, his mind counting the minutes before she returned to tend him. The best part of the war. The only good thing about it.

Now Nurse Adele Savard, the woman he'd reached for when his nightmares were unbearable, was looking up at Willoughby, her hand raised to shield her eyes from the sun. She wore a simple yellow dress, and her long blond hair was pulled loosely back. He'd never seen anything more beautiful.

Jerry seized his cap and bolted toward the door, holding out a hand so John wouldn't follow. He didn't pause to explain, to laugh with him about what a small world this was, to marvel at how happy it made him just seeing her. He couldn't, not when she was walking next to the man responsible for so much of the violence and chaos in their town. How had a beauty like her ended up next to that beast of man? Did she know who he really was?

The two were walking about twenty feet ahead of Jerry, not quite touching, and Willoughby's bulk took up most of the sidewalk. He was droning on about something, and she glanced over, listening and offering a quiet smile. With everything she'd had to deal with over there, he knew she could take care of herself. Still, Jerry was unable to walk away.

From a few paces back, he watched them turn the corner and stop in front of a building. A doctor's office, Jerry noted. Then Adele pulled out a key and opened the door, and Jerry's thoughts began to spiral as Ernie Willoughby followed her inside.

sixteen

ADELE

D r. Knowles must still be out at lunch," Adele told Ernie, setting her purse on the front counter with as much nonchalance as she could muster. "He's having lunch with his wife. It's their anniversary, but he'll probably be back soon," she added.

"Don't worry. I'll leave before he returns. Can't be seen distracting his beautiful nurse." Ernie winked. "I'm actually glad we ran into one another just now. I heard Sammy McDonald was here, and I wanted to make sure he was doing all right."

Alarm skittered up Adele's neck at the mention of Sammy's name. The poor man had been brought to Dr. Knowles' office from the rail yard that morning; his body was covered in bruises and blood, and his face was barely recognizable. Adele had witnessed the carnage men inflicted on one another on the battlefields, even tended a few gunshot and stab wounds here in this office, but she had never expected to see this kind of brutality. Hadn't they fought enough overseas?

Sammy's jaw needed to be reset, so Adele had assisted Dr. Knowles with the intricate surgery. When they were done wiring Sammy's jaw closed so the bones could begin to heal back together, they stood back and hoped for the best. Dr. Knowles had ruled out any serious internal bleeding, but only time would tell if Sammy would make a full recovery.

"Should we call the police?" Adele had asked.

Dr. Knowles shook his head. "Not one of them is gonna step in for this poor fellow. I have a hunch that this is gang-related. The man who did this, well, he probably has the cops on his side."

He wouldn't tell her anything more, saying he might be mistaken— and he didn't want to end up in a similar condition to Sammy.

Adele's next patient, a woman with a two-inch gash above the back of her elbow, was more forthcoming. "Did you hear they found a man almost beaten to death by the rail yard?" she asked as Adele fetched her suture kit.

"I did." She said nothing about Sammy, heavily sedated in the next room.

Her patient lowered her voice. "Some say he owed money to that rumrunner, Big Will, though why anyone would be so stupid as to borrow from that man is beyond me."

Adele's mouth went dry. Maybe it was a coincidence. "Big Will?"

"He's a big man in the racket. Booze, gambling, whores . . ."

The image of Ernie's bloodied knuckles filled Adele's vision.

"Nurse?"

Adele blinked.

The woman's eyes were round with fear. "I shouldn't have said anything. You won't tell anyone, will you?"

"Of course not," Adele managed, but she had to work to still her shaking hands as she finished up her stitches.

Now Ernie stood before her, asking politely after the man whose jaw she had laboured to repair a few hours earlier. After what she'd heard from her patient, she couldn't help but wonder if Ernie was responsible for Sammy. Was it possible that the same man who listened to her so attentively and sweetly kissed the back of her hand had beaten a man to within an inch of his life only to return to a party after, cool as ice? She didn't want to believe it, but now, she saw once again the still fresh cuts and the bruises on his knuckles.

"How do you know Sammy?" she asked casually.

Ernie tilted his head. "We do business together from time to time. I wouldn't want to bore you with the details."

"It's such a shock what happened to him," she said. "You're very kind to take such an interest in his well-being."

"Can I see him?"

"I'm afraid not. He's unconscious. Even if he was awake, he couldn't speak with anyone, because his jaw is wired shut."

"Is that right? For how long?"

"I don't know. Weeks, I suppose. It takes a long time to recover from something so . . . traumatic."

"Will he survive?" Ernie pressed. "And eventually be able to speak?"

Was he asking out of concern? She couldn't help thinking that the most likely reason for this line of questioning was that he was afraid Sammy might blow the whistle on him.

"He'll survive," she said. "But I doubt he'll ever talk again. Not so anyone could understand what he is trying to say, anyway." It was a half-truth. She couldn't possibly know how Sammy's speech would do, but she felt compelled to protect him in that moment.

"Poor fellow," he said coolly. "You'll let me know when he's able to talk, will you?"

Her blood stilled, hearing his voice harden. "Of course. Since you're friends."

He smiled genially at her, as if nothing had changed between them. As if he was still Ernie, not *Big Will*. But Adele saw a different man before her now. A man who could lead her around the dance floor with another man's blood on his hands. Ernie Willoughby was not the courteous protector he had claimed to be, she realized. He was a man from whom people needed protection. Suddenly, his charm felt wrong and manipulative, and she felt sick that she'd fallen for it. When had she become so naive? She had let him wrap that necklace around her throat and promenade her in front of all his flashy friends as if she belonged to him, and she'd never said a word about it. Now she had to put a stop to it, but she would have to choose her words carefully.

"Ernie, about last night," she said.

His expression collapsed with sympathy. "I know you were nervous around all those people, but really, you fit right in. They were all quite taken with you, as I knew they would be."

"That's nice of them to say," she replied, but since no one had paid any attention to her after he'd left for that fateful hour, she knew any remarks about her had likely been made for Ernie's benefit, not hers. "I wanted to thank you again for a lovely time. I've enjoyed spending time with you these past weeks."

"As have I," he said, taking a step toward her.

"You've made me feel like a princess, truly, but I must tell you that I'm not prepared for anything more. I'm sorry if I've made you think otherwise."

He hesitated. "Is something wrong? Have I upset you somehow?"

"No. It's not that at all. Please understand, Ernie."

"Adele, I'm crazy about you," he said. She could hear the frustration in his voice, but also a great deal of hurt. He was like a little boy, desperate not to get left behind. "Let me show you. I could give you the world."

"I know you could, Ernie, but I've seen enough of the world. I'm quite content with what I have." She retrieved the necklace from her bag, its diamond briefly catching the light from the open window. "I'd like to return this to you."

He ran his fingers through his slicked-back hair, his desperation hardening to bafflement. "I don't understand. What can I do to convince you?" When she didn't answer, his brow drew in. "Am I not good enough for you? Because you're not gonna find anybody better around here."

"It's nothing like that. It's not about you, Ernie. It's me." She dangled the necklace closer to him, but her hand shook, making the pendant wobble. "Please, Ernie. Take the necklace and go. Before Dr. Knowles returns."

"I don't think you understand," he said slowly, his voice low. His hands flexed at his sides, and her concern became fear. "I want you, Adele, and I always get what I want."

In an instant, he closed the distance between them. She wanted to shove him away, to make a run for it, but she felt frozen in place under his towering gaze. Then his lips pressed hard against hers, his teeth colliding with hers. She tried to squirm out of his grasp, but his hands were clamped on her hips, holding her in place.

"Let me go!" she cried, turning wildly in his grip, then she remembered the open window behind him. "Stop!" she screamed, hoping someone would hear. "Stop! Get off me!"

She heard the door fly open but she could see nothing. In the next instant, Ernie's hands were ripped from her body, and a man stepped between them, his back to Adele.

"Get away from her," he growled.

Anger bloomed on Ernie's face. "This has nothing to do with you, Jigsaw. Get lost."

"It has to do with a lady saying no. Now back off."

Adele caught her breath. She knew that voice.

"Who's gonna make me?" Ernie taunted. "Your big brother ain't here."

Her rescuer glanced back, and she saw a flash of sharp grey eyes and a familiar scar.

"Jerry?" she whispered, suddenly dizzy.

"Stay back, Adele," he said, quiet and calm, just as she remembered him.

Ernie's nostrils flared like a bull's. "You two—"

Jerry wrapped his fingers around the edges of Ernie's shirtfront and shoved him against the wall, pinning him there, but Ernie spun out of his grip and swung his elbow around so it crashed into Jerry's face. Jerry staggered sideways, momentarily stunned by the blow, then he pulled back his fist. In the next instant, a scarlet fountain erupted from Ernie's nose, spraying the wall and the floor.

Bile shot up Adele's throat at the sight of the blood. "Stop!" she shouted. "Please! Stop!"

But neither appeared to hear her. Their attention was entirely on each other, and as they circled, she saw the deep contempt on both their faces. Ernie was hunched like a boxer, hands out front, panting slightly. Jerry was just out of his reach, waiting, calculating.

Suddenly, Ernie's fist shot out, but Jerry ducked. He came up from under, slamming the base of Ernie's jaw. The impact sent Ernie arching backward, and when he looked about to lose his balance, Jerry swept his foot behind Ernie's legs, bringing him to the ground with a crash. Before Ernie could move, Jerry had dropped on top of him and was punching his face again and again and again, his expression tight with purpose.

"Stop, Jerry! You'll kill him!" Adele shouted, rushing in and grabbing his arm before he could strike again. He resisted, as if he didn't feel her there at first. She had to use all her strength to hold back his next punch. "It's done! It's finished!"

Jerry stilled, and for a moment, the only sound in the room was the laboured breathing of all three of them. Then Jerry got to his feet and wiped the back of his hand across his mouth, clearing some of the blood, glaring down at Ernie.

"You might think you're king of Windsor these days, looking down on us peasants from your castle, but you're forgetting gravity. Once you're up that high, you got a lot farther to fall." He jabbed his boot into Ernie's side, making him grunt. "Listen to me, Willoughby. Listen good. I have two things to say to you. Number one: you have your business, and John and I have ours. You stay on your side of the road, and we'll stick to ours."

Ernie grumbled something Adele couldn't make out, and Jerry leaned down, his voice a hoarse whisper she barely heard. "Number two: if you ever come near Adele again, I will have no problem taking you down."

Willoughby dragged himself out of reach, his face a wreck. From an inside pocket, he pulled a white handkerchief and pressed it to his nose.

"We're not done," he snarled through bloodied teeth.

Jerry closed his eyes, calm again. "You still don't get it. We *are* done."

Willoughby rose slowly, then he bent to grab his hat. "We're not," he repeated.

"Ernie," Adele said, and he turned.

She held out the necklace. He looked from it to her, his eyes sharp with anger and humiliation, then he thrust out his hand and grabbed the jewellery, shoving it into his pocket as he left.

"You all right?" Jerry asked after he was gone.

She wasn't sure whether to laugh or cry. She took a deep breath, fortified by Jerry's steady gaze. "I am now."

seventeen

JERRY

❦

Shame pulsed through Jerry, beginning in his fist where the skin had torn. One eye was swelling shut fast, and the inside of his mouth was metallic with blood.

He couldn't even look at her.

He'd let it out. All this time and he'd never let the fury out like that before. There would be consequences to what he'd just done. There was no going back with Willoughby now. This whole time he'd been worried about John, but he should have been worried about himself. The worst was knowing she'd been there, witnessing the whole thing. She'd seen what Jerry had become.

Hugging his ribs against the pain, he turned toward Adele, taking in her pale beauty with anguish. He knew what she saw: his face smeared with blood, his eyes bloodshot from exertion, his shirtfront drenched. He'd dreamed so many times of seeing her again, but never like this.

"Jerry," she whispered, disbelief sparkling in her blue eyes. "I can't believe it."

"I'm sorry," he said. "You shouldn't have had to see that. I'm usually more . . . controlled."

"You rescued me," she said simply, and Jerry thought in that moment that Willoughby could be the king of the castle all he wanted, just so long as Jerry could be her knight.

"Willoughby and I, we have a long history."

"I gathered that," she said. "I just . . . I can't believe . . . Come here, would you? You're bleeding, soldier."

He sniffed. "Guess I am."

She took his elbow, guiding him to a chair, and he smiled, watching her get her kit, take out the needle and thread, the antiseptic, the gauze.

"Here we are again. Just like old times," he said wryly. His gut twisted when he saw a tear slide down her cheek. "Please don't worry. I'm all right, Bluebird."

She wiped it away and smiled, and his heart soared. "It's a happy tear," she said. "Now, let me see your face. Oh, he tore your scar. I can fix that quickly, but what a shame. It had healed so well."

He couldn't take his eyes off her. He didn't flinch when she wiped the area clean then injected anaesthetic into his cheek, didn't say a word. Neither did she, as she carefully sewed him back up again. But he was achingly aware of her fingertips, light on his face, so gentle, as they had been years before, cleaning his throat and ruined face with that cool, damp cloth.

"There," she said eventually, and he watched her put her tools away. "He hit more than your face, though. Your ribs—"

He jumped slightly when she touched his ribs, and her eyes creased with laughter. "Why, Jerry Bailey. You're ticklish."

"Don't tell anyone. I have a reputation to protect."

For a heartbeat, then another, they held each other's gaze.

"It's so good to see you," he said.

She paused, still taking him in. "The last time I saw you, you were on that truck, heading back to fight. I didn't know if I would ever see you again."

"I thought maybe we'd have run into one another by now, and when we didn't . . ." He blinked, startled to feel the emotion tightening his throat. He hadn't cried in years. "I'm so glad you made it back."

She took a shaky breath. "Me too. And your brother? Uh—"

"John," he said. "He's great. And your family?"

"Good. Everyone is fine."

"Lucky folks in this place, having you as a nurse."

She gave a little shrug. "I discovered I wasn't much good at not working. It's a different pace, but I like it. What about you? Did you become an accountant, like you'd said?"

An accountant, he thought wryly, then one side of his mouth lifted. "Sort of."

They fell silent, and while he normally didn't mind that, this time he scrambled for something to say. He never knew the right words. Should he talk about how good she looked? How memories of her had helped him through his darkest times? That he'd been determined to live through it all on the tiniest chance that he might see her again?

Then something shifted in the air between them. All those years ago, those blue eyes had promised comfort. Help. Friendship. Now they offered something different. *Hope*, he realized.

"I can't believe you're here," she said softly.

"Well, I had to come," he said gently. "I owed you a dance."

He glanced down, suddenly remembering the condition he was in, then he looked back at her. God, she was pretty. "Would you go out with me sometime? When I'm cleaned up, I mean. I'd like to take you someplace nice."

"I thought you'd never ask." Her smile lit up places in him that had long gone dark. "But I think we ought to put off the dancing until you heal a bit. Maybe we could start with dinner."

"Friday? I can pick you up, if you'd like. Where do you live?" She told him the address, and his pulse picked up again. This was really happening. "I'll be there," he promised.

"Good. I don't want to wait another three years."

PART
— three —

eighteen
CASSIE

✤

—Present Day—

By the time Cassie dropped the tubs of bottles off at the Maison François Baby House museum, her tears had dried. She had been hoping to sneak in and out without being seen, but she should have known. Mrs. Allen, the head curator, saw everything, and she lifted an eyebrow, seeing Cassie at work on her day off. Cassie just smiled and waved, then disappeared outside again, heading to her car. She would tell Mrs. Allen eventually, but for now, she was still feeling a bit raw after visiting the old house.

With her mind a little clearer now, she drove to her apartment building and let herself think about what had happened. As rattled as she'd felt back at the house, all her memories stirred up along with the drywall dust, she couldn't deny that a lot about the old place still brought her comfort. From what she could see, Matthew was doing a good job, and she was glad that he seemed to care about properly restoring the place.

As for the bottles he'd found, well, those had stirred up a whole lot of questions. What were they doing there? As a child, she'd heard so many stories about the Bailey brothers from her grandmother Alice, but she had never even hinted at a secret cache of whisky. Especially one in their very own living room.

Cassie pulled open the front door of her apartment building then climbed the three stories to her bachelor apartment, her mind ticking through a mental list of the archives she wanted to access at the museum. Before she did any of that, she planned to go through her personal collection of the Bailey family history.

She dug in her bag for her key, unlocked her door, and stepped inside. Having just been in her spacious childhood home a half hour before, her little dwelling suddenly felt smaller than ever. She'd gotten the apartment a few years ago, after she turned eighteen and left foster care. The very first home of her own. She had filled it with objects that mattered to her, often perusing the local antique store for preowned items that, at one point, had meant something to someone and now called out to Cassie: a stained glass lamp and a black typewriter from the 1920s, a dark maple bookshelf from the '40s that had required three people to carry it, and a dented brass cigarette lighter. Some might see a mishmash collection of secondhand things, but to Cassie, they were a connection to the past that brought her comfort.

Setting down her bag, she went to the bookshelf and withdrew the shallow wooden chest that her grandmother Alice had given her so long ago. At the time, she'd told Cassie the box had once belonged to *her* grandmother, whose name had been Elizabeth. And since Cassie always seemed so interested in her family's stories, Alice said she thought it should remain with her. Together, they had brought the wood back to life by oiling and buffing it, then they attached a new hinge so the matching lid would close tightly. The inside had been lined by a sheet of dark green felt. But it was what the box contained that drew Cassie to it now: the family scrapbook.

After her mother died, Cassie had been put into foster care. What little she was allowed to take with her consisted of her clothing and one item of her choice. She had chosen the family scrapbook. Even as a little girl, the photos and stories in that book had been important, and to her young, grieving heart, it represented everything she had lost: her father, her grandmother, her mother, and her home. Years later, Cassie had been informed by a lawyer that her grandmother's small estate, as well as the minimal proceeds from the sale of the house and furniture, had been put into a trust for her, but until that time she'd had practically nothing of her own. That made the book matter even more.

The tattered old book had travelled with Cassie from foster home to foster home, and when she felt truly alone, which was quite often in the beginning, she would study the photos of her family in the happier years before the cancer. Then she'd turn to the intriguing black-and-white photos from generations past. The album hadn't been in pristine shape to begin with, but Cassie had always treated it as she had the box her grandmother had given her, with the utmost respect.

Her third—and final—set of foster parents had been a kind, older couple who understood her, at least a bit. They encouraged her to restore the precious book and even gave her a little money for the project. With it, Cassie bought the best acid-free album she could find, a pair of white cotton gloves, and a fine point, permanent marker. Using a regular pen on the backs of the photos might damage them, she'd learned, plus the ink would fade over time, so the marker was important. Her foster parents cleared a space for her at the desk they used for their bills and taxes, and she set to work removing all the photographs from the old album. Over time, some had lost their black adhesive corners, but others clung stubbornly to the old paper. For each of those, she turned a blow dryer on very low, giving the photo just enough heat to melt the remaining glue, then slid dental floss underneath to free it. She neatly transcribed the dates and names on the backs of the photos then reordered them in the new album, using fresh notes in corresponding margins.

When it came to the few bits and pieces of newsprint in the album, she had more of a challenge. The poor-quality paper, originally manufactured inexpensively out of unpurified wood pulp, was barely holding together by that point. Among the articles was the announcement about Jeremiah and John Bailey's departure for Europe in 1914, then their return. She also had one that spoke of her grandmother Alice's brothers—John Jr. and Edward—heading to the next war. Cassie couldn't do anything about the damage that had already been done to the paper, but she was determined to prevent it from getting any worse. After fixing what she could, she had transferred the photos to the album as carefully as if they were broken glass.

Now, Cassie brought the box to the cracked leather armchair in the corner of the room. Tom, her cat, hopped silently onto the armrest and pressed his soft, grey head against her. A year ago, she'd come across him at the side of the road, the newborn blue still bright in his eyes. His mother had been hit by a car, and little Tom mewed helplessly at her side. Scooping him up in her arms, Cassie had brought him to the closest vet then carried him home.

"Let's be orphans together," she'd whispered into his little ear.

As she settled in with the box, he lay down next to her, his purr vibrating against her hand. With her other one, she raised the lid, and she felt a rush of nostalgia at the sight of the heirloom inside.

Usually, she perused the book for her own entertainment. Today she had a mission. She removed the scrapbook and set the box aside, intent on rereading the small number of newspaper articles, in search of any clues that might hint at the secret bottles in Matthew's wall. But she lingered over the photos of Jeremiah and John, hearing again the thrilling stories her grandmother had told her—about how the brothers had had the courage of lions, digging tunnels beneath the battlefields of the Great War, then how they had come home and dove into the rum-running business, which came with its own perils.

Whenever Grandmother Alice spoke of her own father, Jeremiah, she described him as a quiet, bookish man, and while he wasn't very talkative, he was a loving father. She didn't know much about her uncle John. He had died before Alice was born, and her father rarely mentioned him, just like he rarely mentioned the Great War. Alice's impression of John came mostly from the way people in town talked about him. Like he had been a wild man. A dangerous man. But sometimes, when her father was out, Alice's mother would tell her a different story. She said her uncle John was a good, courageous man. She said he had saved Alice's father's life time and time again. That was why they had named Alice's older brother, Johnny. But the shadow her uncle John cast had never completely faded. When Cassie or her mother did anything remotely crazy, Grandmother Alice would claim that it was because of the "wild Bailey streak," coming straight from John.

Cassie's gaze lingered on Alice's older brothers, Johnny and Teddy. They had gone off to fight in the next war, but they had died months apart during the campaign to liberate Italy from the Germans. Every time her grandmother got to the memorial announcements in the newspaper, she would pause, tears in her eyes. She was the youngest, born eight years after Teddy, and as of 1943, she became an only child. She told Cassie that the house was so much quieter after that. Alice did what she could to care for her devastated parents for the rest of their lives, but nothing was the same.

Finally, Cassie turned the page and touched the photograph of her grandmother, missing her with a pang. Beside it was one of her mother in her wedding gown, looking happy next to her dad. All these people, once young and vital and living their lives, were gone.

It had taken Cassie a long time to convince herself that she was not to blame for her mother's death. She could never forget how it had ended, though, with her standing helplessly to the side as her mother crashed down those stairs. Not that a ten-year-old girl could have prevented that fall, but still, it weighed on her. As she got older, she understood the role grief and alcohol had played that day, but even that knowledge couldn't entirely erase her guilt. As soon as her mother had taken that fateful last step, Cassie had been left alone. She was still alone, all these years later. Maybe she always would be. And maybe she deserved it.

Matthew thought her interest in the bottles and house was simply because of her job, but it was so much more than that. The faces staring back at her now were the reason she cared so much. There was one little detail she hadn't mentioned to him. One thing she'd kept to herself: Cassie was the last of the Baileys. She was the only one left.

———

Monday morning, Cassie threw herself into her work, planning to concentrate on the archives. It was good timing; Mondays were slow, with few visitors. She set Matthew's original bottle on the back desk as inspiration, then started flipping through files of local newspaper clippings, photographs, and interviews, all from the 1920s. There were mentions of raids and robberies involving local gangs, and sure enough the Bailey name came up a few times, usually in reference to John, but another name kept popping up as well, often in connection to the brothers. And it was one Cassie didn't recognize: Ernie Willoughby. She bookmarked each mention, then began a new search for information on him. Almost right away, she came across all different sorts of articles, including social announcements.

YEAR-END BASH A HUGE SUCCESS

Well-known businessman Ernie Willoughby hosted his annual event of the season last Saturday, with a stunning array of guests dancing in their finest and a wondrous exhibit of fireworks to cap it all off.

An hour or so later, Mrs. Allen swept silently into the room, her spectacles hanging from a delicate gold chain around her neck. Cassie sensed her coming up behind her, and in a moment was aware of the older woman peering curiously over her shoulder.

"Working on a new project?"

Mrs. Allen was a quiet, serious woman, the epitome of what people might expect of a museum curator. Her enthusiasm for history carried over in the way she always encouraged Cassie to look into projects that might bring more value to the museum. Mrs. Allen was closing in on eighty years old, which meant she knew some of the legends from the area. That could be very useful to Cassie in this particular situation. As much as Cassie had planned to keep this project to herself, she'd run into a bit of a brick wall. She was forced to admit she could use some expert help.

"Well, it's kind of a long story," she said.

"History is full of long stories," Mrs. Allen replied. "And I am here for history. If you'd like assistance, tell me how I can help."

So Cassie told her the story of Matthew's discovery, keeping her own personal history out of the telling, at least for now.

"How wonderful. I know that house. It's been neglected for years. So you're helping him find out more information?"

"I've been trying to learn more about the Bailey brothers and figure out why fifty bottles of their whisky would have been permanently left in their living room wall," Cassie said.

Mrs. Allen looked impressed. "Fifty bottles! It sounds like that Matthew fellow might have come into a small fortune. Are you investigating their value for him?"

"Not yet, but I will. I want to understand the story behind the bottles first."

The curator frowned slightly. "Well, abandoning them there wouldn't have been done on purpose, Cassie. Something must have gone wrong. Perhaps you should be looking into events that were going on around that time. Something that could have endangered the Baileys."

"That's what I've been doing," she said. "The only suspicious thing I could see was this article."

MISSING PERSON: ERNEST "ERNIE" SAMUEL WILLOUGHBY OF WINDSOR

Police are requesting the public's help in determining the whereabouts of Windsor businessman Ernest Willoughby, who has been missing for three days. Sources close to Mr. Willoughby report that he was not planning to leave the city. In fact, he was expected at a few meetings that he ended up missing...

"From everything I can read, he was never found. He's mentioned alongside the Baileys a few times, but they didn't seem all that friendly with each other. They may have had a rivalry. Can you think of anything else that might have been going on around that time?"

"Ernie Willoughby," Mrs. Allen said, tapping her fingers on the desk. "He was a bit of rumrunner royalty around here. He had a little army of thugs, from what I recall hearing. Like a smaller, local version of Capone, one might say. You're right, I don't think he was ever found. There were rumours he had owed money to someone and escaped to Florida, but there was also speculation that he could have been murdered. I'll take a look in my records, see if I can come up with something."

"There's one other thing that makes me wonder," Cassie said, shifting her papers and uncovering two of the articles she'd printed out. "The Bailey brothers were raided on this day in 1921, see?"

BAILEY BROTHERS' BEST CLEANED OUT!

In broad daylight, police raided the warehouse of Misters John and Jeremiah Bailey of Windsor, where they seized every last drop of their illegal whisky cache.

"That happened two months before the article about Mr. Willoughby came out. And strangely, it is the last article I have found on Jeremiah and John Bailey. It's like they disappeared from sight too, almost."

Mrs. Allen was leaning over her, reading the article. "That is interesting. It could be purely coincidental, but then again, it might not. What a lovely puzzle you've come up with. I'll see what I can find out."

The mystery had existed for a century, so Cassie supposed it might be unrealistic for her to crack it in one day, but she was determined to get to the bottom of it. After all, it was her own family's story. She'd always assumed the Bailey business had stopped along with the end of Prohibition, but with all this new information, she wondered if the raid could have had something to do with it. If only she had thought to ask her grandmother for more details. Alice had been born ten years after the raid, but she would have heard something about it from her parents, wouldn't she? And shouldn't she have known about the bottles in the wall?

Frustrated, Cassie turned off the microfiche and turned on her computer to research the value of the bottles, hoping to solve one thing today. She looked up an evaluator with whom they often dealt and gave him all the neccessary information about the bottles. He took everything down and said he would get back to her with an estimate as soon as he could.

When her phone rang, she saw the incoming number and her pulse quickened. "Hello, Matthew," she said.

"Hi, Cassie. Listen, I hope you don't mind my calling you like this, but something came up."

"No trouble at all. How can I help you?"

"Uh," he said, hesitating. "I think it's the other way around. Did you tell me that Jeremiah Bailey, the guy that made the whisky, dug tunnels in the war?"

"I did."

"Huh. Well, then I think I have found something you might want to see."

nineteen

ADELE

୧ৡ৸

— July 1921 —

At the sound of tires rolling on their drive, Adele's heart skipped a beat. Jerry was here. She smoothed out the skirt of her favourite dress, a simple pink one that fell almost to the floor and was dotted by small bouquets of flowers. She was glad Jerry had mentioned he wanted to take her somewhere "nice" so she'd known how to dress.

"Do I look all right, Maman?" she asked.

Her mother tucked a strand of Adele's hair inside her matching ribbon. "You look perfect. And if all he remembers is you in that uniform, he's not going to believe this."

"I'm so nervous," she whispered.

Maman touched her cheek. "My, he must have made quite an impression on you."

When Adele had mentioned to her mother that she had run into one of her wartime patients, and that he was taking her out for dinner, she raised an eyebrow with interest. Right away she'd asked if it was the tunneller with the facial wounds.

Adele's jaw had dropped with surprise. "How did you know?"

"Just a lucky guess. You were so adamant about keeping your distance from your patients, but you wrote about him more than the others. I always wondered if you were fond of him," Maman replied, then she asked, "but what about the dashing Monsieur Willoughby?"

Adele looked away. "I'm not seeing him anymore. He wasn't who I thought he was."

Her mother tried to press her for details, but Guillaume stepped in.

"She served in a war, *mon amour*." He winked at Adele. "She knows trouble when she sees it."

He had no idea how right he was, she thought. In any case, it was better that they not know the full truth about Ernie, for their own safety. She'd had to be a little more up-front with Dr. Knowles, who had returned from lunch just as she was cleaning up the waiting room. She'd fibbed about the blood, claiming it was from a patient's cut and looked worse than it was, but she did tell him that a man had been in, asking after Sammy. She suggested that if Dr. Knowles was right about the attack being gang-related, they might want to transfer Sammy to another doctor's office. Dr. Knowles agreed, and they'd sent Sammy to Grace Hospital, just to be safe. To Adele's great relief, Ernie hadn't come back so far.

A few moments later, they heard a knock, and Adele flew to the door, trying to quell the butterflies in her stomach. When she opened it, the man who'd rescued her from Willoughby, the man she'd dreamed about for years, stood before her, looking far different from the last time she'd seen him. Instead of a bloodied face and sweaty shirt, he wore a gentleman's short black coat and waistcoat over a white shirt. A silver watch chain hooked on his waistcoat glinted in the sun, and his face was shadowed by a black fedora.

His bruises were still evident, faded to a shallower colour, but the swelling was down. He wore a small white bandage on his cheek where she'd stitched him up, but that was all. To Adele, none of it mattered. To her, he would always be the thoughtful soldier who'd won her affections in a hospital tent in war-torn Belgium. And the most handsome man in the world.

He slipped off his fedora, his grey eyes soft on hers. "There she is," he said. "The most beautiful woman in the world. I hope I'm presentable, Lieutenant Savard?"

"You look very handsome, Corporal Bailey."

"I see you still haven't gotten your eyes checked," he said, then he held out a bouquet of violets. "These are for you."

She clutched the flowers to her heart. "Thank you. They're lovely. Please come in while I put them in a vase," she said, stepping back.

Her mother was all smiles as she greeted Jerry. "It's nice to finally meet you, Corporal." Her gaze flickered to the fresh bandage on his cheek, and Adele realized that she should have given her a warning, not of Jerry's scars, which her mother already knew about, but of his new injury.

"Just a scratch," Jerry said good-naturedly, noting her gaze. "I've endured much worse, as you can see. This is your daughter's handiwork, by the way."

Adele's cheeks warmed with the compliment, though he exaggerated. They both knew it was the doctor's work. Still, she kept quiet, not wanting to interrupt their conversation.

"She wrote to me about you. Lots of things."

"Maman!" Adele said.

Her mother paid no mind to her embarrassment, and really, Adele didn't mind that she'd said it. It was true, after all. "Adele said you were a tunneller. I cannot imagine. You were very brave to serve as you did."

Jerry was saved from responding by the entrance of Guillaume. He hung his hat on the hook and asked, "Who has the nice Ford in the driveway?"

"Guillaume," Adele said as he turned to face them. "I'd like you to meet—"

"Well, well!" Guillaume said, holding out his hand. Adele stared at the two, taking in their twin expressions of surprise. "*Ça va bien*, Monsieur Bailey? What's this? Looks like you went a round or two. Glad to see you made it out of the ring."

Jerry's smile was warm. "It is nice to formally meet you, Guillaume."

"You know each other?" Adele asked.

Guillaume chuckled, his gaze holding Jerry's for a beat longer than it had to. "Ah, *oui*! I helped him out with a few cars. Nothing special."

"I'd beg to differ," Jerry said, a funny little smile on his face. "You're the best at what you do."

Confused by their furtive glances, Adele turned to her mother for an explanation, but she just shrugged.

"Guillaume, Monsieur Bailey is the courageous soldier Adele met overseas."

"Is he? Then I feel I know you better already. It's a small world, is it not?"

"As far as I'm concerned, your daughter is the courageous one," Jerry told her mother.

Maman beamed, but Adele could tell by her pinking cheeks that tears were coming. Any talk about Adele's part in the war made her emotional.

"We're very proud."

"The doctors and nurses put their lives on the line just like we did," he said, "but at least we were armed and trained. All they had were bandages and scalpels. When I was laid up in the hospital, we saw some pretty heavy action. Adele and the other doctors and nurses never flinched, never panicked. Everybody was running for safety, but they ran *into* the shelling, making sure we all got out. Your daughter's a very brave woman."

"We did our duty. Like you," Adele said quietly.

"I didn't want her to go," her mother said, her eyes shining. Her hands clasped tightly together. "I couldn't imagine losing her. But her heart was set on it."

Adele had never gone into detail about the dangers she'd faced, wishing to spare her mother, and she could see it had affected her. Hearing it from Jerry somehow made it sound better than if she'd had to describe it.

"I promised I would come back. You know I always keep my promises."

"She has always been that way," Guillaume told Jerry. "Brave. *Compatissant.* Like her father."

Her heart squeezed.

"I can see that," Jerry said, watching her.

After a moment of silence, Guillaume wrapped an arm around his wife's waist. "*Mon amour*, I think maybe these two have a lot to catch up on, *non*? They don't want to stand around with us old folks all night."

Her mother blinked then opened the door for them. "*Oui*, of course. Have a lovely evening, you two. It was wonderful to meet you, Corporal Bailey."

Outside, they paused, and Adele saw her own shyness reflected briefly on Jerry's face. Then he tilted his head toward his car. "I have a reservation at Abars. Have you been?"

"I've only heard of it, but it sounds very nice."

"I hope you like it." He opened the passenger door for her and offered his hand as she stepped onto the running board.

Once she was settled, she watched him walk around the car then get into the driver's seat, and she found herself unable to look away. He glanced over as he started up the car, and he smiled self-consciously.

"What?"

Her cheeks flared, and she turned away. "Oh, nothing. I'm so sorry. I don't mean to stare. It's just . . . I still can't believe this is happening."

"I know exactly what you mean."

For a couple of minutes, they chugged along in silence, and Adele's anxiety began to get the best of her. They had so much to talk about, didn't they? How terrible this might be if they couldn't find a topic of interest.

"It was a lovely day today," she tried. The weather was always a good starting point.

"It was," he agreed.

She watched the fully leafed-out trees swishing past. "I just love summer, don't you? Everything's so . . . green."

"Yeah," he said politely. "It'll be a warm night, I imagine."

"I hope so."

"Me too."

And that was that. With a sinking heart, she started spiralling into thoughts she'd never wanted to have. Maybe she'd been wrong all along. Maybe it had just been the right circumstances in Belgium, but at home, they didn't have anything in common. Maybe he was sorry he'd invited her along. Wondering if he might be thinking the same awful thoughts, she glanced covertly at him, and she was struck by the relaxed slope of his shoulder, the easy stillness of him as he drove. His face was calm, the corner of his mouth curled into a gentle smile. He wasn't anxious. He was at peace. It all came back to her then, the fact that, unlike Ernie, Jerry simply didn't feel the need to constantly fill the silence. Not unless there was something to say. She'd valued their conversations for their simple honesty. The quality of their words, not the quantity.

Relief washed over her, and she relaxed in her seat. If there was something to talk about, they'd talk about it. There were so many things she wanted to learn about him, but she didn't need to rush in with all her questions. They had time.

About a half hour later, they were headed down Riverside Drive in Windsor, and she spotted Abars. The big, redbrick building wasn't particularly pretty, but it was in a beautiful spot: right on the Detroit River, across from Belle Isle. At the door, the maître d' personally welcomed Jerry, then he showed them to a table with a beautiful view of the waterfront and the island beyond.

A waiter appeared a few moments later with menus and asked what he could get them to drink.

Jerry turned to Adele. "Would you like to share a bottle of wine?"

"I'd love to."

He passed her the wine list. "You choose."

That made her laugh. "Oh no. I don't know any of these. I know I like white wine, but that's all. You pick, please. Otherwise, who knows what we'll be drinking?"

The waiter took his order then returned to pour the wine, and Jerry raised his crystal glass. "A toast. To you."

"To us both," she said, touching her glass to his.

She brought the glass to her lips and took a sip, and he did the same. A beat of silence stretched between them, and she could see him thinking the same thing. They'd spent nearly every day of his convalescence talking late into the evening, and now it was as if neither knew quite where to begin.

"You changed your bandage," Adele said, defaulting to her nursing out of habit.

He touched the dressing lightly. "John helped me out. His hands are rougher than yours, but he got the job done."

Adele smiled fondly. "I remember him being very protective of you."

"He still is," Jerry said, then he lifted his eyebrows, looking contrite. "He's typically the one getting into fights these days, though, not me. Usually I'm pretty good at controlling my temper. I just lost it when I saw Ernie coming after you."

"But what a welcome surprise that you arrived when you did." Now it was she who wanted to apologize. "I suppose you're wondering why Ernie was there in the first place . . ." She trailed off, unsure of how much she should say.

Jerry shook his head. "You don't owe me an explanation. I told you a long time ago that I'd always fight for you, Bluebird. I just wish I had found you sooner."

"Me too," she said. "But you're here with me now. You and I have all the time in the world."

She held her breath, worried she'd been too forward, but all her fears were put to rest by the look in Jerry's eyes. He held up his glass again. "Here's to that."

After the waiter arrived to take their orders, they both sat back and stared at each other again.

"I want to hear everything," she said at last. "Your parents must have been overjoyed to have both you and John home again."

An unexpected shadow crossed his features. "They never actually saw us. They died of the flu a month before we got there."

"Oh, Jerry!" Her hand went to her heart. "I am so, so sorry. How horrible for you."

He frowned at the tabletop. "It was rough. I won't lie."

"I hardly know what to say. I can't even imagine your pain."

"Not the best news to come home to." He summoned a smile. "John and I are doing all right, though. We're running a business together, and it's doing very well."

She opened her mouth to ask about that, but the waiter arrived with two small plates of oysters on the half shell and another of lemon slices, which he set in front of them.

"What's this?" she said, inhaling the buttery sauce.

"Oysters Rockefeller," said the waiter, then he gave a little bow. "On the house for Mister Bailey and his guest."

"They know you here," she said as the waiter left. "I'm impressed. Are you here a lot?"

"They're a client of mine," he said, then he looked over at her plate. "Do you like these?"

"I have no idea."

He smiled. "May I help you with it?"

"Oh yes, please."

First he squeezed lemon juice over both plates, then he showed her how to loosen the oyster with a fork.

"Some people just kind of swallow them, like this," he said, tilting his head back and letting the oyster slide into his mouth. Once he chewed and swallowed, he said, "But you might be more comfortable putting the whole thing on your fork."

She grinned. "I'll try it your way."

The oysters were delicious, and she sat back with anticipation when the waiter brought out the main dishes. She'd ordered sugar-glazed ham, and he went with braised short ribs. Both were beautifully served, with a swirl of duchess potatoes on the side.

"This smells wonderful," she sighed, picking up her cutlery. "How lucky for you that they needed an accountant."

Jerry set down his fork, looking a little uncomfortable. "There's something I need to tell you."

"Should I be worried?"

"No, no. It's just . . . You should probably know that I'm not exactly an accountant, though I do some accounting as part of the business."

She waited, and he took a fortifying drink of his wine.

"When I got home, I found my father's journal. In it he had a lot of things, but the most noteworthy was what he'd written about the whisky business. He'd been making his own booze for years on the side, but with Prohibition happening, he was suddenly making a lot of money. So when I found the book and read everything he'd written, I felt like he'd left it for me on purpose. Like his legacy, in a way. So the truth is, John and I run a successful whisky business. That's what Ernie and I were arguing about the other day. He and I have a long, unpleasant history. You know he's in the business, right?"

She nodded, not knowing how to respond. She'd been so overcome at seeing Jerry again, she hadn't picked up on what he'd said to Ernie the other day. Now it made sense.

"I'm not a runner," he rushed to say. "I'm a manufacturer. But I work with all different kinds of men to make it work. That's why I know Guillaume—I had no idea he was your stepfather. He insisted we call him the Frenchman. When we were first starting out, he sold us vehicles we use for our runs."

For a moment, she was speechless. She was less surprised about Jerry's confession than the news about Guillaume, but if the last three years had shown her anything, it was that everyone in this town was somehow involved in the booze business—even her stepfather.

"What a coincidence," she finally said.

"Everyone's making money these days, including him. All the fellas I hire were fighting overseas, and most of them came back broken. Our business has given them purpose and cash. I'm proud of that. It's not quite the accounting job I was planning," he admitted, "but it pays a lot better." His smile faded, seeing her expression. "I'm sorry to spring this on you. I should have mentioned it earlier. I can see that it bothers you."

"No, it's not that. I don't believe in Prohibition."

It was the other side of the business that worried her. All she had to do was picture poor Sammy, with his jaw wired shut. She hadn't thought about Ernie putting himself in harm's way, she realized, but this was different. When it came to Jerry, she minded very much. She had worried about him at the Front, she'd worried about him in the years between, and she worried about him now. That was just the way it was between them. Didn't he know that?

She looked up at him through her lashes, needing him to understand. "After all this time, I've only just found you. I'd like you to stay in one piece. I don't always want to have to sew you up."

He dropped his chin to his chest, taking that in, then he lifted his eyes to hers. "I'll be careful, Adele. Especially now that I've found you. I'll be fine. Besides, John would never let anyone come anywhere near me."

She knew that to be true.

"I'm sorry if this put a damper on supper, but I had to tell you before..." It was his turn to flush. "Before anything happened between us."

But something already had happened, long before they'd returned from the war. As much as Adele hated the thought of Jerry ever being in danger, it didn't change her feelings toward him.

She reached out her hand and placed it over his. "Thank you for telling me. I should have known. Accountants don't usually have so much dirt under their nails."

Jerry chuckled, a warm, genuine sound that instantly evaporated any of the tension still between them.

"Now that we got that out of the way," she said, digging into her ham, "tell me more."

Bit by bit, they caught up on all that had happened since they'd last seen one another. Jerry told her how John was doing, with his ups and downs, then he spoke of his cousins, Walter and Charlie, who she thought sounded like good, loyal friends. She was glad to know he was surrounded by that kind of protection. Then he asked about her nursing friends, saying he remembered Hazel and Lillian, so she told him they were both happily married with children on the way.

"And your sister?" he asked. "She'd just had a baby when we met."

"You have a very good memory," she said. "Little Madeleine is almost three, and Marie just had a baby boy named Arthur. We don't see them much, unfortunately. They're nervous about coming to Windsor because of the amount of rum-running activity out here. Fred, her husband, has strong opinions about alcohol ... and other things," she said, thinking of his reaction to her nursing experience. "Marie wasn't always so strict, but she's joined the temperance movement now."

"It must be hard not to see your family."

"It is," she admitted, leaning back as the waiter came to collect their empty dishes. "But I respect her decisions. We've taken the train up once or twice to see her, of course. I'm just disappointed that she doesn't come out our way. It's hard on my mother as well. I write to her, and I've promised she could leave the little ones with me so she could relax for a change. From her letters, she seems a bit worn out lately."

"Dessert, mademoiselle?" the waiter asked.

"Oh, I couldn't. I don't think I could manage another bite."

"Are you certain?" Jerry asked, and when she hesitated, he asked the waiter to bring the house special, with two forks. A moment later he returned with a large slice of bright white cake.

"Lemon-filled coconut cake," the waiter announced.

"We can't leave until you try this," Jerry said, so she had a little taste.

It wasn't long before they were down to the last bite. He insisted that she take it. As she did, she noticed the sun setting across the water, which meant it was about nine o'clock, she realized with disappointment. She had wished the night would never end.

She finished her last sip of wine and smiled at Jerry. "Thank you for tonight. It was wonderful."

He tilted his head. "We're just getting that warm summer night I was talking about earlier. Care to join me for a walk along the river?"

As they stepped outside, dusk was easing its royal blue mantel over the earth, bringing out the winking lights of warehouse lanterns on both sides of the river.

"It's very pretty down here," she said. "And it's quiet. I think I expected more than a few boat engines and bullfrogs."

"It's a slow night. It'll get louder soon. What do you mean—you expected something different? You've walked here before, haven't you?"

"It's a bit of a rough area for a woman to walk alone, Jerry."

"Good thing you're no longer alone," he said, tucking her hand through his arm and filling her chest with butterflies. "You warm enough?"

"It's a little chilly," she admitted, so he paused to layer his coat over her shoulders, and in its fibres she smelled a spicy hint of cologne along with a whisper of oil from the car. When his hand bumped hers, she reached out and took it, and her thumb gently stroked a callus on his thumb. The way he smiled after that warmed her even more than his coat did.

"It's amazing to me that we both grew up along this river, but never met," she mused. "Didn't you say you used to play hockey out in Petite Côte?" She was surprised to see him stiffen, but he didn't stop walking. "What's wrong?"

"It's not important. An old wound," he said, his voice thick.

"I know a thing or two about wounds," she said gently. "Bandages help, but they need air to heal."

He stopped walking and let out a long breath. "I suppose you're right. And if you're going to put up with me, I guess you'll need to know stories like this one. I'm warning you, though, it's not a happy story."

He dropped her hand and turned toward the river, his face partially lit by the yellow of a lantern hanging nearby. She waited while he took a package of cigarettes from his trouser pocket, and when he offered her one, she took it. She hadn't smoked in a while, but this seemed as good a time as any. He lit them both then shook out the match.

"I told you Ernie and I had a long history. It all started on this river. You see, I've known him all my life. John and I used to play hockey with him and his older brother." He paused, breathing in his cigarette. He sank his other hand into his front trouser pocket. "Frank."

Adele stilled, the smoke curling from her cigarette as she remembered what Ernie had said about his brother. He'd said he'd drowned.

"Frank and John were the same age. They were the loud ones. The leaders. Everyone wanted to be around them, including Ernie and me. We were the younger brothers, and we were like ducklings, following them wherever they went. The winter of '05, the four of us were out on the ice nearly every day, passing the puck around. Come March, we were still playing, but we shouldn't have been, and we all knew it. The ice was making noise. It was going to bust through any day. But it was spring, you know? After a long, cold winter, it's irresistible. We wore sweaters instead of coats. We didn't need hats. We were young. We were stupid."

Jerry stamped his heel absently on the ground as if to warm his foot, but it wasn't that cold. A sense of foreboding came over Adele.

"I didn't hear the ice break, actually, or the splash. John had just scored, and he and I were yelling about it, but Frank had dropped his stick and was racing toward this gaping hole in the ice."

"Ernie had fallen in?" He hadn't mentioned that to Adele.

Jerry nodded. "We both kept yelling at Frank to lie down." He waved his hand, and the little orange circle at the end of his cigarette cut through the night. "My father always told us that if the ice broke, we needed to distribute our weight, and the best way to do that was on our stomachs. But Frank wasn't listening." He sighed. "Just as he got close to Ernie, the ice gave way beneath him, and he went under, too. John and I dropped down right away and crawled toward the two of them. They were splashing and screaming so loud, it's surprising no one heard us. Anyway, we knew having both of us on the thinner ice at the same time was too much of a risk, so we made a chain of sorts. I was smaller than John, so I crawled in front of him, holding out my stick. John hung on to my ankles so he could pull me back." He took a long drag of his cigarette, and a faraway look came into his eyes. "The ice was so thin."

Instead of a man, Adele pictured a scared little boy. Instead of the gentle lapping of the river beside them now, a crackling, broken river of ice.

Jerry cleared his throat. "When we got close, we saw that Frank had a grip on the edge of the ice, but Ernie was flailing around in a panic. He wasn't a strong swimmer, and Frank shouted at us to help him first. So we did. I held out my hockey stick, but Ernie was splashing too much to grab on. John and I kept telling him to calm down and grab the stick. He finally did, and we hauled him out of the hole, over to the safety of the shore. We left him there so we could go get Frank.

"By then, the ice was in real rough shape. It took us a long time to inch back to Frank. Too long." He paused, shaking his head. "I can still see him. He kept on fighting, but he was getting weaker and weaker every second. When we finally reached the edge of the hole, Frank was gone. We screamed his name, peered through the ice for a glimpse of him, but we couldn't find him. I swear I almost dove into that hole after him, but John held me back. We heard the ice start to crack again, and he pulled me out of there right away."

Jerry took a ragged breath. When he lifted his cigarette to his lips, it was shaking. "I'll never forget Ernie's face when we returned to the shore without Frank. His lips were blue, and he was shaking with cold, but I could tell. None of that mattered. It was his heart that hurt most of all."

Adele felt a fresh wave of sympathy for Ernie, hearing Jerry describe the forlorn boy waiting by the shore. Waiting for a brother who would never return.

"Is that how Ernie lost his fingers?" she asked. "From frostbite?"

"No, that happened a little while later. Ernie's mother took Frank's death hard; not long after the accident, she had a heart attack and died. His father had always been a drunk with a short temper, but Frank had protected Ernie from the brunt of it. Without Frank around to step in front, Ernie suffered the full weight of his father's rage. He blamed everything on Ernie. One day, when he was well beyond drunk, he saw Ernie cutting firewood and he snapped. He went after Ernie, forced his hand onto the block, and severed three of his fingers."

"Oh, God." Adele's hand flew to her mouth.

Jerry grimaced. "He told Ernie that since he had failed to use those fingers to save his brother, he had no use for them anyway."

Tears blurred Adele's vision. "The poor boy," she said quietly. "It wasn't his fault."

"No, it wasn't. It wasn't anyone's fault," Jerry agreed. "But Ernie was never the same after that. He became hard, merciless. He took it out on everyone around him, and he's still doing it. Ever since then, he's blamed John and me for what happened to Frank, and to his hand. He never misses an opportunity to pick at that wound. So what you saw that day, with me and him . . . it's more than business between us. I wish it wasn't."

"I see," she replied.

It explained so much, she thought sadly. Going all the way back to their first date, when Ernie had told her in passing about his brother, and the family he never had. She thought about the party, how everything had been glittering and extravagant—his way of ensuring his guests loved him, she supposed. Then how he'd turned, bullying them when they didn't listen, beating Sammy nearly to death for some sort of slight Adele didn't know. Oh, it all explained so much.

Beside her, Jerry had stopped speaking. He was staring at the river, the moonlight making it a pale blue highway. She remembered the night of the hospital attack, when he had gone back into the tent over and over again to bring out men, how he had stayed with Trent until his death, then refused to leave his body behind. It all came back to Frank, she realized: the boy he couldn't save.

"You don't blame yourself for Frank's death."

He stomped out his cigarette in the grass, still looking over the river. "I'll always think there was something more I could have done," he said, and she saw anger flex in his jaw. "But mostly, I will always feel guilty that John and I walked away unscathed, and Frank and Ernie didn't. It's like the war. How did I make it out when so many others didn't? Why did I survive the flu when my parents didn't? What makes me so goddamn—pardon me—special?"

"Do you remember what you told me when Minnie died?"

"I do."

"I was not to blame just because I gave her my ticket. But a part of me will always regret that. I'll always wish I'd never given it to her," she said, then she reached for his hand again. "I want you to know that I understand. We don't know why we're still here, but I am so glad we are."

A boat started up a few boathouses down, spitting to life with a roar, and Jerry stepped closer to her.

"You ever wonder if you'd go back to the war if you knew then what you know now?"

She smiled. "I've asked myself that question a hundred times. I'd go back. What about you?"

He shook his head slowly, and she imagined everything spinning through his mind. The insanity of war. The cold, tomb-like tunnels they had dug so they could blow up the enemy from below. How many men had he killed? How could a sane man go on, knowing he'd done that? And yet so many had.

"I'm a different person than the one I was back in '14," he said. "The war changed everything. But yeah, I'd go back." He lifted one hand, and she didn't move when the backs of his fingers slid smoothly down her cheek. "I'd go back so I could meet you again."

She couldn't speak. She could hardly breathe.

"I have to say something to you, Adele, and I don't want to," he said, his voice almost a whisper. He was so close she could feel his breath on her face. "I'm not the right man for you. I don't deserve you."

"Let me decide that."

"You don't understand. My world, the one I'm in now, isn't a nice place. It's full of risks. It's complicated and competitive, and it can be violent. The truth is, Adele, I want to offer you the world, but it's not the right world for you."

This time it was she who lifted a hand and touched his face. She loved touching his skin, even if it was torn. She skimmed her fingers over the lines and indentations, remembering when the damage was so deep she had no idea what his face looked like. When he'd asked for a mirror, taken a look, then nodded with simple, uncomplicated acceptance. When she had watched over him late at night, the golden warmth of the hospital's lanterns playing over his features. She'd loved him all along. She wouldn't let him leave her behind this time.

"I'm not afraid, Jerry. Not for me. Since the moment I met you, I have thought of little else but you. You understand me like no one else does, and I think I understand you as well. After you left, I was afraid every single day, but it wasn't for myself." She swallowed, forcing back tears. She didn't want to cry. Didn't want to show any kind of weakness at that moment. "I know what it is to be afraid, but I'm stronger than you think. I just found you again. I can't lose you. Please don't push me away."

His blink was slow. Deliberate. Then he bent down and kissed her, changing both of their lives forever.

twenty

JERRY

❧

Jerry was still thinking about that kiss when he got home. When he opened the door, John was waiting for him, along with two crates of whisky.

"Is this the last of it?" Jerry asked.

They'd finished the tunnel and the new room just yesterday, and now they were under a tight deadline. Ever since Jerry had humiliated Willoughby in front of Adele, he'd known they were in his sights. Willoughby wasn't going to let Jerry get away unscathed. That meant everything to do with moving the liquor had to be done as quickly as possible. John had said he was going to finish stacking everything in the new room. Jerry was a little disappointed he hadn't.

"It is."

"Why'd you leave these out?"

"No room," John said. Then he lifted an eyebrow. "How was dinner?"

Jerry hung his coat and hat on the hook on the wall, then he sat across from his brother, cigarette already in his mouth. "Abars makes an excellent short rib," he said, striking a match.

"Oh, I see. That's how we're playing it," John chuckled. "Well, all I know is that Witless ain't impressed with you stealing his girl."

Jerry shook his head, gazing into the smoke, thinking of her. "Not his girl."

"He doesn't seem to know that. Tuck told me Witless is in a rare mood, thanks to you."

Jerry closed his eyes. He would have liked to hold on to tonight a little longer, but as he'd told Adele, his business was a demanding one.

"He's planning a big raid on the water tomorrow night. Cops have been told to stay away. Bastard's making a fortune off everyone else's back," John said. "That business with Dutchie? He's trying to squeeze him out too."

"First, Sammy, now Dutchie," Jerry said. "Willoughby's getting rougher."

John put his elbows on the table, looking his brother in the eye. "I have a plan, but we need reinforcements. I need you to talk with Dutchie."

Jerry raised an eyebrow. "He won't be interested in a partnership."

"I bet he would. This would be a temporary thing. We get the High Tides and the Green Boys too. Band together. And we'll keep it up until Willoughby gets the message."

Jerry drummed his fingers on the table. "Let's hear it."

The following evening, Jerry and John headed to the docks to join Al, the retired-navy-captain-cum-fisherman-cum-rumrunner John had originally hired to pilot their boat. Al was an older, weathered man with a scruffy, grey-speckled beard. It was difficult to tell exactly how old he was, since the man looked as rough as gravel, but Jerry thought he was closing in on fifty. He could tell he was embarrassed to have the Baileys riding along with him tonight, though he tried not to show it.

"You didn't have to come. I brought my son Bill, and we got guns," Al told the brothers, gesturing to his son. "We wouldn't let Big Will touch your booze. Not again."

"You're not the only one he's stealing from," Jerry reminded him.

The river was stirred up by the wind tonight, rising and falling beneath the boat. Jerry was trying to ignore the motion so he could concentrate on the job at hand. Both he and John had brought rifles, and they had known Al and his boy would have theirs. But considering the size of Willoughby's well-financed little navy, those wouldn't be enough.

He couldn't get Adele's face out of his mind. *I'll be careful*, he'd told her. *I'll be fine.* He wasn't sure how this should go. Would a man in his position tell her about this later, or was this something he could safely keep to himself? He let his gaze travel over the cases of whisky and decided it was probably better if she didn't know.

John's big hand patted Al's shoulder. "It's a big night, Captain. There's a plan in place. All I need you to do is get us across the water. Regular speed. We'll take care of the rest."

"What's happening?" Al asked, unconvinced.

John gave him a wink. "It's all under control. Trust me."

Al gave him a glare, then he leaned toward his son. "Something's up. Stay low."

As the captain started up the engine, Jerry hunkered down beside John, out of sight of the Windsor shore. The boat began to motor across the Detroit River, and Jerry kept his eyes peeled for Willoughby's men. When they were about a third of the way across the river, Jerry turned to John.

"See anything?"

John shook his head, disappointed.

"Maybe we need to cast a little bait," Jerry said.

"Slow 'er down a little, Al," John called over the wind.

"Eh?"

"Slow down!"

Shaking his head, Al cut the engine back, and Jerry felt the boat slow.

"There," Bill said to his father, pointing toward the shore.

Sure enough, Jerry spotted the lights from three boats. They were headed straight for them.

"Those are Big Will's boats," Al said, one hand on the throttle. He was a tough veteran with years of experience behind him, but rum-running warfare was something completely different. He had good reason to be nervous.

"Hold steady," John told him.

Jerry could see the disbelief in the man's eyes.

"You sure you know what you're doing?" he exclaimed.

"Yes," Jerry said, trusting his brother's plan.

John brandished his rifle, his smile gleaming in the dark. "Let them come."

The three boats roared across the river, water frothing against their bows, and Jerry's hand tightened around his rifle. The trick to an ambush, they both knew, was to play dead. Be a rock. So Jerry hardened himself as he had so often before. He hunkered down as he'd been trained, but even then he couldn't stop the nerves from zinging through him. He wasn't the only one. John was leaning forward, scouting the water, concern tightening his expression. They were sitting ducks out here, and a big piece—in fact, the most important piece—of the plan was missing.

"Dutchie gonna double cross us?" Jerry asked, keeping his voice down.

John shook his head. "He wouldn't. He hates Witless as much as I do."

Willoughby's men had almost reached them; Jerry could just make out the determined set of their faces when Bill pointed beyond the incoming trio. "Look! I count . . . eight boats."

"What?" Al cried, but before he could race out of there, John grabbed his arm.

"Those are the good guys, Al! This is going to be legendary."

Victory swelled in Jerry's chest at the sight of a whole battalion of vessels coming in fast behind Willoughby's men. There were Dutchie's boats, but also representatives from the other rumrunners—and each one was loaded with men and rifles.

"Today is our lucky day," John said, grinning as Willoughby's boats split up to escape the oncoming naval bombardment. "All right, Captain, turn this boat around and show me what you did in the war."

"With pleasure," Al said, then he gunned the engine, giving chase.

Willoughby's trio was no match for the charge, and within minutes, John's battalion of boats had corralled them back together. Dutchie aimed his rifle at one of Willoughby's captains, then he yelled at them to cut their motors. A hush fell over the water, and Willoughby's goons glared sullenly at the enforcers surrounding them.

John was absolutely loving this, and Jerry had to fight hard to keep his smile hidden. His brother stood on a crate, rifle at his side. "There'll be no more pirating of our liquor," he announced, loud and clear. "The Bailey Brothers, Dutchie's gang, the High Tides, the Green Boys, we're out of bounds for all of you. You let Willoughby know what I said."

"You don't own the river," one of the trapped men yelled.

"No, but we own this liquor, chump," he replied.

"You can't stop us!"

Jerry knew the next step in the plan, and he had to admire John for coming up with it. He didn't think he could have done something so brash, but it was exactly what they needed.

He sat back and watched John nod at Dutchie, who raised his twelve-gauge shotgun, aimed it at the side of one of Willoughby's boats, and fired. Two of his men followed suit, and the marble-sized, lead slugs they'd used instead of the usual pellets hit exactly the same spot, blowing a beautiful, four-inch hole in the starboard side. The men on board scrambled back, but nothing could keep them dry. The boat sank quickly, and the men toppled helplessly into the river. Sputtering and splashing in the cold, they swam as fast as they could to the other two, and yelled until their compadres hauled them in.

Once they were all out of the water, Dutchie looked them over, aiming the mouth of his rifle at every face in turn. "You heard what John Bailey said, right? Out of bounds."

The man who had first taunted them shook visibly with cold, but his face was a furious shade of red. "You won't always be here."

Jerry cleared his throat. "Sure we will. We'll be here every day and night until you get the message. And when others learn what we've done here today, I think they'll join us."

John waved a hand, dismissing the remaining two boats. "Run along home and tell Little Will the new rules, kids."

"You'll be sorry," the man yelled.

They watched the two boats limp back to shore.

"He's probably right," Jerry said. "Willoughby's gonna lose his mind."

Dutchie pulled his boat up alongside Al's. "I don't know about you," he said to John, "but I feel like a drink is in order."

Al still had his route to finish, so the brothers climbed into Dutchie's boat. The rest of the fleet would stay out all night, guarding each other as they made their deliveries.

They headed to Dutchie's watering hole, the Dominion House, and Jerry had to laugh at the tavern owner's expression as four of the more prevalent, competing gangs in Windsor, over two dozen hardened men, walked into his place, laughing like old friends. He doubted the man had ever seen anything like it. As Jerry watched, he turned to his wide-eyed barmaid and told her to start pouring and just keep going.

Dutchie, glowing with victory, slung an arm over Jerry's shoulder. "Now *that* was a good time."

"You just did something good for other people, Dutchie," John said. "Miracles do happen."

"You know, if I learned anything in Europe, it's that the men in charge are constantly underestimating everyone else. Didn't matter what country we were from, if we banded together and used our heads *and* our numbers, we were able to change the rules. The more the merrier. But it doesn't always happen as spectacularly as tonight." He threw back his head in a big booming laugh. The unexpected sound was contagious, and Jerry found himself laughing along with him. "Oh, boy. Willoughby's not gonna like that."

John was still chuckling, saying something to Dutchie as Jerry headed over to the bar and ordered a whisky for his brother.

John looked surprised but appreciative as he accepted the drink. "To-night was all you, John. Not sure I could have arranged anything near as good as this."

"Not bad, huh?" John grinned. "I never thought I'd say I enjoyed a plan more than an all out fight, but this came pretty close."

He headed over to a couple of the High Tide boys, enjoying this brief truce, and Jerry turned back to the bar, smiling to himself. It had been a good night for the good guys, he thought smugly. The victorious men filled the tavern's coffers for another hour, then they all drifted apart, heading back to their own turf.

"I have a couple of boats going in the morning," Dutchie reminded Jerry on his way out.

"We'll be there," he promised. "It'll be a long week, but it'll work."

Dutchie hooted out another laugh. "I hope we haven't made things even worse. Willoughby hangs on to his grudges. But it sure was fun."

"It sure was," Jerry agreed, turning back to the bar for one more celebratory drink. But as he lifted the glass to his lips, he heard again the man on the boat, shouting at them they'd be sorry. Normally, those words meant nothing to him. Typical male bravado. Flexing muscles for show. But they felt a little different now, and Jerry felt strangely uneasy at the threat. Because for the first time in his life, he realized, seeing Adele's smile in his mind, he had something to lose.

twenty-one
ADELE

❧

— August 1921 —

Adele spotted Marie before the train had even come to a stop, and she waved madly, trying to catch her attention. A smile broke out on her sister's face, and the next thing Adele saw was little Madeleine popping into view, her fat little hands pressed up against the window. Adele could hardly wait to hold her niece again.

She had been cajoling Marie into coming to Windsor for a visit for the past three years without any luck. So it had come as a complete surprise when her sister had written that she was coming to see them in two weeks. She said it would just be her and the children. Adele had been too excited to ask any questions.

"You're finally here," she cried, sweeping Marie, Madeleine, and little Arthur into her arms. Her sister's cheek felt warm against hers. "I thought you'd never come."

"I'm sorry it's been so long," Marie said, squeezing her back. "But I'm here now." She turned and signalled a porter, who came to carry all their bags to the waiting car.

"And you!" Adele said, scooping up her niece. "You and I are going to have such fun. Your *grandmère* cannot wait to see you. She has been baking sweet bread all morning. Tell me, who is that your mother is holding?"

"That's my little brother. Arthur doesn't do much. He just cries."

As if on cue, Arthur began to fuss. "Sorry," Marie said, rocking him. "He's probably hungry. It was a long trip."

"Of course," Adele said, noticing the dark lines under Marie's eyes. "You must be exhausted. Shall we go?"

"I can walk," Madeleine declared, leaning toward the ground. Adele put her down then felt a rush of affection when the little girl took her hand.

"She's a little bossy," Marie said as they headed toward the car.

"Nonsense. She just knows what she wants. Just like her mother." She opened the trunk of the car, and the porter packed everything inside. Marie put a coin in his hand, then they all climbed into the car, with everyone piling on top of each other in the front seat.

"I'm so happy you're all here," Adele said again. "You have to tell me what happened. What did I finally say to convince you to come? You sure made me work for it."

Marie shrugged. "You haven't met Arthur. I thought it was about time you did." She gazed out the window, and Adele saw a hint of a smile on her face, though it seemed a little sad. "Oh, it's more beautiful than I even remembered."

"So's that sweet baby of yours," Adele said. "He looks so much like Fred. How is Fred, anyway?"

"Oh, he's fine. Fred's always fine. Working hard as ever."

"My daddy's very important," Madeleine said, and Adele caught her sister's eye, trying not to laugh.

"Now tell me about this new beau of yours," Marie said, sitting a little taller. "Fred wanted me to ask what line of work he's in, but I just want to know if he's handsome."

Adele had planned her response in advance. She didn't want to start the visit off with the shocking news that she was in love with a gangster of sorts. "I happen to think he's the most handsome man in the world. As for his work, he's a businessman. And here's the best news: Maman has invited both him and his brother, John, over for dinner tonight, so you can meet them both."

"Tonight?"

Adele's spirit fell a little. "Oh, but we'd all understand if you were too tired after this journey. I'm sure we could postpone."

"No, no," Marie said. "In fact, I think some fresh company might wake me up."

From the minute her mother had suggested the dinner, Adele had been a little nervous about Marie meeting Jerry. Her mother hadn't batted an eyelash when Adele told her about Jerry's business, she'd just gushed on about how adoringly he looked at her daughter.

"I can tell, *ma chérie*," she'd said. "That man would never do anything to put you in danger. Don't worry about what Marie says."

Of course, Guillaume already knew all about Jerry's work, and he'd fessed up cheekily to the connection when Adele had come home after that first dinner.

But now Marie was coming, and the truth was, Adele wanted to share this news with her sister because she had never been happier. Whenever she was in Jerry's presence, a sense of calm came over her, whether they were talking or not. It was often in those quiet moments that they remembered the war, but the memories weren't so bad when Jerry was holding her hand. She still worried about him—she always would—but he assured her that he had taken care of things with Ernie, at least for now, and she had no reason to doubt him. Over the last couple of months, she hadn't seen hide nor hair of Ernie, and Jerry promised that all was going well—even better than usual—for Bailey Brothers' Best.

"We're here," Adele said, turning into the driveway. "Look, Madeleine! There's Grandmère!"

No sooner had she turned off the engine than her mother came rushing out to greet them, pulling Marie into a fierce hug. When they broke apart, Adele wasn't surprised to see tears in their eyes. It had been far too long this time. Their mother took little Arthur into her arms, cooing over him, then reached down to Madeleine, marvelling at how tall she'd grown since she last saw her, her words blending joyfully between French and English as they walked.

Madeleine thrilled at her grandmother's pronunciation of her name. "Mad-*leen*," she echoed, studying her grandmother's lips. "Mad-*leen*."

"*Oui, oui!* Madeleine, the Queen!"

The little girl beamed at her mother and aunt. "I'm the Queen."

"Now you've done it," Marie said. "We'll never hear the end of it."

"That is all right. While she is here, she is the Queen," Maman declared. "And this little man is a prince."

The little prince, who had fallen asleep on the drive, woke up at that moment, and began to wail, his face turning an angry red.

"He has a healthy set of lungs," their mother said, smiling.

Marie rushed to take him. "He needs to be fed. Then he'll probably fall back asleep."

"Come along," Adele said, leading the way to Marie's bedroom. "And when you're done, maybe you'd like to hand the reins over to Maman and me. We can entertain Madeleine and make dinner. You look like you could do with putting your feet up for a while."

Marie drooped slightly. "That would be very nice. But you'll wake me in plenty of time to be ready for supper?"

"Of course."

Her mother was already bending down, addressing Madeleine in an adult voice that the little girl seemed to appreciate.

"Would you like to help me prepare tonight's feast, Your Majesty? We have some handsome princes coming as well."

"*Oui, oui,*" Madeleine chirped.

As they prepared the meal, Madeleine counted cutlery and set the table as she saw fit, singing bits of songs most of the time. When Marie emerged from her room an hour later, the previous strain was gone from her face, and Adele was relieved to see she seemed rested. She rustled up a cup of tea for her sister, and they all bustled about the warm kitchen.

Just when Adele didn't think she could get happier, in walked Guillaume, laughing with Jerry and John. It was so good to see the brothers together after all this time. She'd given John a proper hug when they'd reunited the week before.

Guillaume went to Maman and gave her a peck on the cheek. "Smells delicious in here, *mon amour*. Let me just wash up."

From across the room, Jerry caught Adele's eye.

"I'm so glad you came," she said, heading toward him. She leaned in for a chaste kiss on her cheek. "You too, John. You look very handsome, both of you."

John gave a mock bow. "I aim to please, Nurse Savard." He sniffed. "That smells delicious. What are we having?"

"Roast beef," she replied. "It's a celebration, after all."

"Are you sure it's all right for us to be here?" Jerry asked quietly. "After what you said about your sister and her thoughts on liquor, I thought we'd make things awkward."

She took his hand and cocked her head toward Marie. "Come and see. She'll be very civil, I promise." She winked. "Or she'll answer to me."

They had just started toward Marie when John stopped short. "And who is this?" he asked, peering down at Madeleine. The little girl was standing at his feet, staring way, way up, and wearing her most regal expression.

"Oh, this is Queen Madeleine," Adele replied.

"Your Majesty," he said, squatting in front of Madeleine. He took the little girl's hand, kissed its back, then gave her a smile that could win over a wicked witch from any fairy tale.

"And this is the Queen Mother," Adele said, smiling as Marie came out of the kitchen. "Jerry, John, I'd like you to meet my sister, Mrs. Marie Everett."

The smile Marie gave them both lit Adele's heart. Gone were the weary lines beneath her eyes and the weak attempt at conversation from earlier. The nap had certainly helped.

"What a pleasure, meeting you both." She winked at Jerry. "I've heard *so much* about you."

The table was a noisy celebration, the loudest of all the voices being a tie between John and Guillaume. Both seemed determined to outdo the other on making everyone laugh. Fortunately for Marie, Arthur had chosen to sleep through the entire supper rather than join them. John was in fine form, encouraging conversation from Marie, then leaning down and teasing Madeleine, who sat beside him, staring in awe. If Adele hadn't known better, she'd say Madeleine had developed her first crush.

Across from John, Jerry was quiet and introspective as always, but she could see he was happy to leave the spotlight to his brother. Adele looked between the two, feeling like the luckiest woman in the world. Charming John might look every bit like a man from the pictures, but it was Jerry, with his quiet calm, who had captured Adele's heart before he'd even been able to speak a word out loud.

She couldn't help but observe Marie throughout the meal. She'd missed her terribly, and she wanted her to have so much fun that she'd come back again and again. It was more than a selfish thought, though. It was hard to tell, but Adele had a strong feeling that something more than travel fatigue was going on with her sister. Marie appeared to be in fairly good spirits, occasionally jousting with John, even eating with enthusiasm. And yet there was a sadness behind her eyes that only Adele—and possibly their mother—could see.

"You're a nurse as well?" John asked, though he knew the answer perfectly well. Adele had told them both all about her so they'd be prepared.

At the same time, Jerry had given John a warning that Marie was a supporter of temperance, and they'd agreed to keep their line of work out of the conversation.

Marie patted her lips with a napkin. "I was a nurse, yes. But I only got to work for a few months before I got married."

"Ah. You sacrificed work for love. Sounds like a good choice," John joked.

At that moment, Madeleine dumped an entire spoonful of mashed potatoes with gravy onto her dress, then screamed with alarm. "Mommy!"

Cooing at her daughter, Marie picked up what she could of the potato and dabbed at the dress. "Don't worry, darling. We'll fix it later. Please don't cry. We're having a nice, adult supper." She looked at John. "Sometimes I'm not sure I did make the right choice." But she was smiling as she said it.

"We take care of lots of messes in nursing," Adele said lightly. "You can't escape them."

Madeleine's lip was stuck out, making it clear she was still primed for a little pouting, so Marie leaned down to her ear. "You know that adults don't pout. I want to see your happy face now. If you cannot manage that, you will go to bed immediately."

Madeleine's eyes widened at the threat, and she pasted on a huge, desperate grin, making everyone laugh.

Maman stood up and held out a hand. "Come with me, Madeleine. We'll get you a clean dress to wear."

"Anyhow, I never could have done what Adele did," Marie continued, as her mother and her daughter toddled down the hallway. "I was not made for war."

"None of us were," Adele assured her.

"Ain't that the truth," John agreed. "I'm sure you would have been just as courageous as she was. Though I gotta tell you, she sure was impressive when I met her, rushing from sickbed to sickbed, her pretty blue gown covered in blood—"

"John," Jerry said, seeing Marie's eyes widen. "Pardon my brother."

John apologized with a sheepish grin. "I forget myself sometimes. I apologize."

"And what about you?" Marie asked as if nothing had interrupted them. "Tunnellers? Why does one become a tunneller?"

The brothers exchanged a glance. "We were assigned to it," Jerry said with a shrug.

"Trust me," John put in, "if I had to choose between going down there and getting married, I most certainly would have chosen to become a wife."

Everyone laughed again, but Marie still seemed interested. "I know you were underground, so does that mean you actually saw fighting? Were you in the battles? Or just digging?"

The table fell quiet for a moment, and Marie's cheeks flushed. "Was that rude?"

"No, no," Adele said, jumping in to save her sister. "It's fine."

"I apologize. I'm completely lost when it comes to etiquette about this sort of thing, but I can't help being curious, can I?"

John was the first to rebound, and he swept the conversation neatly away. "Well, let's not worry about etiquette, Marie. Let's not worry about war at all. There's nothing fun in that. Instead, I think we should go out after supper," John said, turning to Jerry. "Why don't we stop in at the Riverside Inn tonight?"

Jerry raised his eyebrows, but he seemed to like the idea.

"Here we are!" Adele's mother announced, presenting Madeleine in a different dress.

"Thank you, Maman," Marie said, her gratitude genuine.

Since Marie had asked about the men's jobs overseas, Adele wondered, not for the first time, what her life was like. She was securely tied to Arthur, obviously, but the day-to-day labour of keeping a curious, intelligent toddler entertained as well, then tending to Fred and the baby and the apartment . . . it all must get exhausting. Marie had always been very sociable. Was she finding any time at all to meet with friends? John's idea suddenly appealed even more.

"I think we should go," she said. Other than at Ernie's party, she hadn't actually been out dancing, but it had looked like so much fun. And this was a perfect excuse. "You'll love it, Marie."

"Sometimes there's an orchestra," John added smoothly. "And there's always dancing."

Under his gaze, Adele saw her sister consider the offer for a moment before demurring. "Oh no. Not me. I can't. The children—"

Maman swooped in, right on time. "Tell me, *ma petite* Madeleine, would you like to have a fun evening with your *grandmère*? Just you and me and Arthur? Maybe we shall make cookies!" She glanced at Guillaume, who was already nodding. "If your *grandpère* is not working, perhaps he can stay and watch."

Madeleine hopped up and down. "*Oui!*" she cried, using her one and only French word. "*Oui! Oui!*" Her face suddenly shifted, becoming serious. "But don't let Arthur have cookies, Grandmère. He's too little."

"All right. Those will be for you and me. And maybe Grandpère."

"All right. Maybe him, too," Madeleine allowed. "But only a few."

"Maman," Marie said, observing their back and forth. "I can't ask you to do that."

Their mother feigned confusion. "You didn't. I want these little angels all to myself, and I want you and Adele to have a good time together."

Adele reached for her sister's hand. "Oh, you'll love it, Marie. Dancing is so different these days. No one worries about anything, and no need to wear fancy clothes. We just go for fun."

Marie wavered. "I don't have anything to wear."

"I have just the thing," Adele said. "It'll be so pretty on you." She glanced at Jerry, and somehow he picked up her silent plea. John suddenly looked at him, startled, and she had to assume his brother had kicked him under the table.

"John and I would like to look after these dishes," Jerry said. "To show our appreciation for such a fine meal."

John blinked, then joined in. "Of course. Madame Savard, if you would, show me to your soap and towel."

Glowing at the sight of the two brothers at the sink, Adele led Marie to her room and pulled out the blue gown she had worn to Ernie's party.

"Oh, Adele," Marie breathed, draping it over the bed. "It's gorgeous."

"Try it on. It'll make you feel like a princess."

"I don't know . . ."

"About the dress? Or the dancing?" Adele asked. "The Riverside is a classy place, so this dress will be perfect. I should warn you, however, that there will be booze there. I know how you feel about that, but please don't make that your deciding factor. You don't have to drink."

Marie frowned slightly. "I'm not quite as . . . militant about alcohol these days," she admitted, lowering herself onto the bed. "In fact, I'm no longer a member of the Woman's Christian Temperance Union. I've gotten myself into something else entirely."

Adele took a seat next to her, intrigued. Apparently, Marie had changed in more ways than one since her last visit. "What happened?"

"I've seen things recently that have moved me to learn more. When I saw a veteran on the street, missing limbs and having no one to talk to, it broke my heart. They gave so much over there, and we seem to have mostly forgotten them. Then I started seeing more and more of them huddled in doorways, sleeping in parks . . . I saw them everywhere."

Adele had as well. She was proud that a few had built better lives since they'd started working for Jerry and John. "What did you do?"

"I did two things. The first was that I started approaching the men, seeing if they wanted to talk. I thought it would be more difficult since the children were around me all the time, but then I discovered Madeleine's dear little face encouraged conversation more than I could. A lot of the men didn't want to say much, and just like you three, no one wanted to discuss the war. But they seemed glad I was there. They needed to know someone was listening, I think, and I was happy to do it. Sometimes their words were a little garbled, or they said things that didn't make much sense to me, but they seemed grateful for a cup of coffee when I brought one. Sometimes, they asked me for a drink of something stronger. I looked at their faces, and I thought about what you said." She swallowed. "Then I bought three or four pints of whisky and gave them out. It seemed to ease their misery, and I started to understand."

Adele was listening closely, a sense of wonder rising in her chest. "You said there were two things. What was the other?"

Marie twisted her mouth to the side, a sure sign that she wasn't sure how much to say. "A few months ago, I read something in a magazine about a new organization in the city that was focused on amputee veterans. You had written to me about Jerry's wounds as well as those of his cousin, and so naturally I was interested in learning more. The very next day, I told Fred I was meeting friends for lunch, but in fact I went to knock on the organization's door. It's called the Amputations Association of the Great War, though they have shortened that long title in conversation to the War Amps of Canada."

"I've heard of it," Adele said quietly. "A very good organization."

She nodded. "It isn't just for show like some other organizations. It does what it says it will do. It was actually started last year by a lieutenant colonel who had lost most of one leg, and it's really caught on. They connect with amputee veterans across the country. I have come to admire their work greatly." She straightened a bit. "Of course I couldn't attend their convention, because that was for the men only, but I do contribute to their national newsletter, *The Amputations' Quarterly*." She stood and went to her suitcase, producing a thin magazine that she handed to Adele. "I wondered if it would be too forward of me to leave this here for Jerry."

Emotion caught in Adele's throat. "That is so thoughtful. What does Fred say?"

She scoffed. "I never told him, but one of the men at his office must have seen me going into the building, because I came home that night to an angry, pacing husband."

"Oh no."

"He said he wouldn't allow me to do it, and since I was very pregnant with Arthur at the time, I went along with him, let him have his way. But Arthur is a good baby who has no trouble napping when I am at the office, and Madeleine has a new friend across the hall and is invited to play there whenever I am going out. It's all come together splendidly. Fred is the only trouble."

"What will you do about that?"

"You might recall that I am somewhat stubborn."

That made her laugh. "Somewhat," she agreed.

"I know what's important, and this organization is. I am needed there, and oh, it is so nice to know that I am doing some good. For the longest time, I was just going with the crowd, nodding when I should have been thinking for myself. But after you visited me the first time, and we argued, I couldn't help wondering why we were spending so much time and energy fighting over something like alcohol prohibition when we could be using that to help these poor men." She shook her head. "I felt very foolish. I have told all that to Fred." A smile curled her mouth slightly. "I think I might have frightened him a little, because he has not brought up the subject in a while. But I know it is on his mind. He is not happy, and I will admit it is causing some strain between us. Coming here is medicinal for me, I think."

Adele was speechless. "I had no idea. I'm in awe of you, being a mother and a wife, and still giving up your time."

"It's nothing compared to what you've done, Adele," Marie said, taking her hand. "I know you don't talk about what you went through, but Maman did mention your friend Minnie to me. I'm very sorry for what happened to her. But then you came back here and got right back to nursing. I'm so proud of you. I missed that feeling of being useful, and while it's only volunteer work, the War Amps have made me feel like I am making a difference. Motherhood is one thing, and of course I love my children, but sometimes I envy you your freedom."

"And this whole time I've been dreaming of what you have," Adele said with a small laugh. "Well, tonight, you can have a taste of that freedom, if you like."

Marie touched the blue gown, lying on the bed beside her. "This place we're going must be safe if Jerry would take you there. Don't think I didn't notice how you two look at each other. Good thing his brother is a good conversationalist, because it's fairly obvious you and Jerry only have eyes for each other."

"Trust me, we will be perfectly all right tonight. Those boys out there doing dishes wouldn't let anything happen to us, no matter what. And if you're the slightest bit uncomfortable, just give me a signal, and Jerry will take us home. Oh, let's go, Marie. I promise you'll have fun."

"I don't want to ruin the evening for you three."

"Don't be silly. We're going because you're here," she said with a wink. "Now let's get ready. I'm dying to see this dress on you."

Once changed, Marie was a new woman. Adele put on an older, brown dress that she'd altered by raising the hem by about a foot then sewn in a bit of flair with sequins and feathers. She added a little headband, complete with matching decorations.

"Ready!" she said, leading Marie out to the front room again. The men were sitting with Guillaume, each with a cigar, but all three rose and smiled with appreciation, seeing the girls transformed.

"We'll be the envy of the whole club," John said.

Marie gave the children quick kisses after making her mother promise it was all right. Maman assured her over and over that yes, she knew how to take care of children.

"I raised two perfect ones already," she said, kissing them both goodnight.

From the back seat of the Ford, Marie stared out the window, impressed by the well-lit, busy streets of Windsor and the lines of traffic slowing them down.

"Fred might be right," she said to her sister. "I can't imagine this is all legal."

"Oh, it's not," Adele assured her. "But the laws need to be rewritten."

When they pulled up the long driveway to the Riverside Inn, a magnificent white building that could have held four of her family's homes inside of it, the music flowed outside toward them, and a trumpet soared over a chorus of saxophones. Marie beamed at Adele, and she knew everything was going to be just fine.

Adele had only heard stories about the place, and she was not disappointed. The inside was even more glamorous than the outside. The main restaurant was a very large room with a bright, cheery feel to it and more than twenty tables were set around the perimeter. White tablecloths adorned every one of them, as did a vase of fresh flowers, and the clientele were all elegantly dressed. In the middle was a wide, wood-panelled floor with an orchestra at one end, and couples were taking full advantage of the snappy music filling the air. Swaying a little as she walked, Adele followed the host to a table with a picturesque view of the river; the sun had set, but lanterns blinked along the shore. It was all very romantic.

"This is nice," Marie said as they sat down. Adele had made sure her sister had a window seat to best enjoy the sight.

Jerry held up a hand, signalling a waiter, and Adele turned to her sister. "Will you have a drink with me?"

"Just one," she replied cautiously. "I think I'll need something to even attempt those dances," she added, nodding toward the couples who moved effortlessly across the floor to the latest popular tune. "What's good here?"

"They make great cocktails," John said. "You could try a Negroni. It's gin, sweet vermouth, and Campari."

"Maybe cut it? Add water so it's not as strong," Jerry suggested thoughtfully.

Marie nodded. "That's what I'll do."

Then he looked at Adele, a twinkle in his eye. "I hear they have excellent whisky here. Might I recommend one with a Sidecar of lime?"

It took her a second to figure out where that twinkle was coming from, then she understood. Apparently, the Riverside Inn was another one of the Bailey Brothers' customers. She gave him a conspiratorial smile. "How could I refuse?"

The waiter arrived, and Jerry placed their orders, adding two straight whiskies for him and John. "And chicken for everyone," he said.

"Yes, sir," the waiter replied, then he walked away.

"Why did you order chicken?" Marie asked. "We already had a big supper."

"It's the law," Jerry explained as the song came to an end. "You have to order food if you want a drink. You don't have to eat it, though I recommend it. They make great meals here."

"Oh, that's right. I had heard of that. Too bad I'm not hungry."

John rose at that moment and offered his hand, smooth and confident as a Hollywood star. "Maybe I can help you regain your appetite. Care to dance, Mrs. Everett?"

"Don't tell me you can do all that fancy footwork."

"A bit. C'mon, I'll teach you."

"Okay," Marie said gamely, and took his hand.

Adele watched them walk onto the dance floor, smiling in sympathy as her sister gestured apologetically at her feet, declaring she had two left ones. John laughed with her, then he showed her how to start.

"Your sister isn't quite who I imagined," Jerry said as they watched their siblings.

"Well, I'm happy to say she isn't who I expected, either. She's changed since the last time I saw her. She's more of her old self, thank goodness. I don't suppose she'd mind me telling you about her volunteer work."

Jerry hadn't heard of the War Amps, and he was intrigued.

"You'll get to read all about it. She brought you a magazine from there, thinking you could share it with others."

"I look forward to it."

Back on the dance floor, John must have suggested that Marie look up at him instead of at her feet, because she smiled and did so. After that she seemed to catch on.

"It's kind of John to be so attentive to her."

"He's a natural flirt," Jerry said. "I know it's kind of a front, but it's a good one at least. I think he needed tonight. I haven't spent much time around him lately."

"Oh?"

Jerry smiled. "You see, there's this girl in Petite Côte."

Butterflies swooped in, filling her chest. "Is that right?"

"She's all I can think about these days."

She couldn't look away, but she leaned back when the waiter returned with the drinks. The song ended, bringing a flushed John and Marie back to the table. Marie's face was lit up like it had so many years before. What a wonderful night this was turning out to be.

"Here's to the four of us," Marie said, holding up her glass.

"I'll drink to that," John said, and they all clinked their glasses together.

When the whisky touched Adele's tongue, she closed her eyes and held it there a moment, swishing it lightly around her mouth and letting all the different tastes register before she swallowed. She liked the taste of whisky, the spicy smoothness of it, the balance of the oak and the vanilla. Anything they'd drunk overseas had been cheap, but she'd tasted good blends as well. Guillaume often brought home bottles to sample. The one she was tasting now was excellent. When at last she swallowed, she savoured the burn as it washed down her throat. Just enough peat, but not too much. What was that last teasing flavour? She opened her eyes and discovered Jerry watching her, studying her reaction.

"Citrus?" she asked quietly, making him grin with appreciation. "It's delicious, Jerry."

A few moments later, Jerry gently tapped his foot on Adele's under the table. "You may not remember this," he said, "but I promised you a dance once upon a time."

"I never forgot that."

When she took his hand, her skin buzzed at the touch. He'd waited for a nice, slow waltz, and when they reached the dance floor, she felt the gentle pressure of his hand at the base of her spine, then the subtle tightening as he brought her closer, and she understood. Just as she'd longed for this moment, so had he.

"You know, I've tasted your whisky before," she said, gazing up at him.

"Oh?"

"Guillaume brought some home the other day. Bailey Brothers' Best. It wasn't too much of a leap to figure out it was yours. It's very good, Jerry."

"It's our father's recipe. We just play with it a bit."

"I have a question about it."

He tilted his head, curious. "About the whisky?"

"Sort of. It's more about the label."

She didn't miss the way colour flooded his cheeks in that moment, and she loved it, because she thought she knew what it meant.

"There's a little bird in the corner," she said. "Why?"

"I think you know."

"Tell me."

He paused, gazing into her eyes in the most mesmerizing way. She didn't think he even knew he was doing it. She thought he was trying to read her, to make sure he could say out loud what he was thinking.

"Did you know that bluebirds are a symbol of happiness and good health?" he asked in a low voice. "I read that somewhere, and it rang true to me. You started with the health part, but ever since I met you, I've never felt happier. That's what you've given me." He took a breath. "So yes. It's a bluebird on the label, Adele. It's for you. It's all for you."

Goose bumps rose all over her body. She'd never heard anything so beautiful. "You changed my life, Jerry. You brought the best part of me alive. I feel like . . . I feel like I'm whole when I'm near you."

She could feel the pull between them, the physical need to get even closer. Her gaze flicked to his lips then back to those hypnotic eyes, partly shaded by his long dark lashes, and she knew beyond any question that she needed him in her life for all time. This was the man she had always needed. The one she would always love.

It didn't matter what the orchestra played. She had no idea if anyone else was still in the building. It was just the two of them, holding each other, and that was all that mattered.

Then someone bumped into Jerry, his hand raised in a quick apology, and they realized they were standing still in the middle of the dance floor. The music had switched tempo, and the people around them were bluffing their way through a new dance craze she'd heard of, called the Charleston.

"Let's get out of here," he murmured into her ear.

Their plates of chicken were waiting for them when they returned to the table, and despite the roast beef dinner of a couple of hours ago, both men dug in. Adele watched them a moment, not yet hungry. Her whole being still sparkling from the dance floor.

"You ladies have to at least try the mashed potatoes," John insisted. "This place is famous for them."

Marie obliged, and her eyes widened. "These are delicious." She migrated to the chicken, and to the beans at the side. "Adele, you have to taste this."

Adele had a bite of chicken, then she glanced at her sister with a new thought. "I have something you need to try too," she said, placing her glass of whisky in front of Marie.

Marie studied it dubiously. "Whisky? Will I like it?"

Adele could see Jerry watching her from the corner of her eye. "I hope so."

"All right." She sniffed, wincing slightly at the fumes, then she took a sip. They all watched her taste then swallow it, silent with anticipation. "Not bad."

"I'm impressed," John said. "I didn't think you'd do it."

"Do what? Drink whisky?"

"Because your sister told us that you—" He stopped suddenly. "Uh, she said you only liked sherry."

Marie sighed and looked at Adele. "You told them about the temperance thing, didn't you?" She shrugged. "Well, that's all over with now."

"That's a really good thing," Adele said, looking at Jerry. "Really good."

Marie put down the glass. "Why? What's going on?"

Adele let out a long breath. "Because John and Jerry made the whisky you just tasted. They made it, bottled it, and sold it to this place."

At first, Marie said nothing, merely dropped her eyes to her glass and ingested what she'd been told, and Adele worried that she'd misread Marie's change of heart earlier. Then she looked up, her expression more interested than shocked. "You're dating a rumrunner?"

Adele beamed. "He's much more than a rumrunner, Marie."

Jerry pressed his foot against Adele's, and from his smile she could tell he was impressed that she'd told her sister. Relieved too, she imagined.

"All right," Marie said, nodding slowly, then her face creased into a wry grin. "I have no idea how I'm going to break this to Fred." With that, she took another sip of whisky, and John let out a hoot of a laugh.

When their plates were empty, Jerry winked at Adele then turned to Marie. "I think it's time you tried dancing with someone who knows what he's doing." He got to his feet. "May this rumrunner have a dance?"

Marie accepted, and they moved to the dance floor.

"Quite a night, isn't it?" John said to Adele.

She tilted her head, feeling on top of the world. "Thank you for showing my sister such a good time."

"I can behave like a gentleman, despite the rumours."

"I know that," she said. "I've always known that about you, John. From the first minute I met you."

He tasted his whisky, watching her through eyes that were so like his brother's. "You know, I never did thank you. For saving him, I mean. Not properly, anyway. I trusted you with my brother's life, and you kept him safe." He lifted an eyebrow. "And now, from the things he's been saying about you, it looks like I'm going to have to do it again. This time I'm gonna have to trust you with his heart."

"His heart is safe with me."

He nodded, already knowing that.

"But John, I owe you a thank-you as well. And it's long overdue. You saved him that day. You dug him out, then you brought him to me. I'll always owe you for that."

"No need."

Her throat ached with every emotion. "I have a favour to ask. I need a promise from you."

"Whatever it is, you know I'll say yes."

She blinked, and a tear escaped one eye. "I need you to promise you'll never stop looking out for him. I know what it is you do out there, and I need to know you'll keep him safe."

John shook his head. "You don't need to ask, Adele. You never will. You just need to understand, that's the way it is between us." Then he flashed the smile no woman could resist, she was sure. No woman but her. "Lucky for you, Adele, if you're with him, you're stuck with me as well."

"I wouldn't want it any other way," she assured him, then she reached up and kissed his cheek. His reaction, soft and grateful and a little bit embarrassed, was adorable.

On the way home, Adele sat with Jerry in the back seat, their thighs pressed against one another in an atmosphere that shivered with desire. John and Marie sat in front, chatting companionably, pretending not to notice the wall of heat behind them.

At the door, John took Marie's hands and bid her goodnight. "You're a helluva dancer, Mrs. Everett. Your husband's a lucky fellow."

"I'm sure my feet will be feeling it tomorrow," she said, then she turned to all three. "Thank you all for showing me such a good time. It really was wonderful." She winked at Adele. "Now I'd better get in there, make sure Maman survived my children."

They watched her go inside, then John pulled Adele into a hug. "Thanks," he said. "That was a great night." He shoved Jerry back a step. "Don't stay out all night, Jerry. I'll be waiting in the car."

"He's a good man," she said, watching John's back.

"Subtle as a brick," Jerry agreed.

She stepped closer to him. "And then there's you."

"Then there's me." He tucked his hands in his front pockets, but she could tell he was pleased with himself. "I'm not too bad either."

She kept moving toward him. "No, you're not."

The corners of his eyes crinkled with his smile. "Well, maybe a little bit bad. I am a rumrunner, after all."

"My rumrunner," she said, then she rose up on her tiptoes and wrapped her arms around his neck.

"My bluebird," he replied softly, bending to kiss her in the most beautiful way.

twenty-two
JERRY

Jerry took the ring out of John's palm and raised it to the light over his desk, admiring the way the diamonds seemed to catch fire.

"You're sure?" he asked. "It's rightfully yours."

John shook his head. "None of the ladies I know are ready to take that big step. Or maybe it's just me. Anyway, Ma would've like seeing it on Adele's finger. I think the two of them would have been good friends."

"I like to think so."

"Aunt Judy and Uncle Henry send their best. They're already cracking open champagne in your honour."

Jerry gave him a look. "She has to say yes first."

"You know, Jerry, the only other thing she might say beside yes is 'it's about time.' By the way, I saw Charlie when I was picking that up from Aunt Judy," he went on. "He said to let you know that Willoughby lost another customer today."

Jerry smiled, still looking at the ring. "So we have a new customer, do we?"

"The last time I saw Witless, he was not looking pleased with me."

"That's always good news. Just be careful."

John gave him a bear hug just before Jerry left the warehouse on his way to pick up Adele. "I'm looking forward to gaining a couple of sisters," he said into Jerry's ear. "Congratulations, brother."

When he drove up and parked at Adele's house, she was already waiting outside for him. That was by design, though she had no idea. When Jerry had asked Guillaume's permission for Adele's hand, Guillaume had suggested he meet her outside. He said he didn't think he and his wife could keep from grinning.

Before he could get out of the car, Adele slipped into the passenger seat of the Ford and leaned toward him so he could give her a kiss.

"Where are you taking me, soldier?"

"It's a surprise," he said, driving back toward the road.

He'd wanted to show her the house for a long time. Ever since the moment he knew he wanted to spend the rest of his life with her, which, if he was honest with himself, was back in Belgium. Then again on the day he walked in on her with Willoughby. Then every day since. Now, his heart hammered with nerves. She peered around as he turned down the long drive, passed the six elms, then sped toward the big white house with its tall, sharp roofline, its friendly bay window, and the wide, welcoming porch wrapping around the front door area. As they got closer, Adele leaned forward, taking it all in. He glanced at her face, noting her interest with pleasure. The three-sided window at the front was dark for now, since John had left them alone for the night. It was on the east wall, and Jerry couldn't wait for her to see how much light would flood in every morning.

"This is my house. My father built it."

"It's beautiful, Jerry," she said.

"Let me show you the inside."

His whole body hummed with nerves as they walked to the front door. He'd gone underground hundreds of times, somehow surviving beneath the worst of the war, and yet he'd never felt jitters like this before.

He opened the door and stepped aside, welcoming her into the living room.

"Such a big space," she said. "So friendly, the way the sitting room and the dining room are all one. Then the kitchen is right there. I bet you can hear everything that's being said on the whole first floor."

"Pretty much," he replied, coming up behind her. "When my father built it, he wanted it wide open."

She glanced his way. "I remember you telling me how they used to dance in here. So I have him to thank for your superior dancing skills." She turned to the framed portraits on the wall, looking closely at their faces. "Are these your parents?"

"Yeah," he said quietly, aching that they weren't there to meet in person. John was right, he thought, fiddling with the ring in his trouser pocket. They'd have loved her.

"You have your mother's eyes. And John, too. I wish I could have met them."

"They would have loved you."

At that, she turned to him and waited for his arms to wrap around her waist. She leaned in and kissed him, and his pulse picked up again.

"There's something else I wanted to show you," he said, then he went to the bookshelf and retrieved the brown paper package he'd put there this afternoon.

"What is it?" she asked.

"I guess you'll have to open it."

She eyed him curiously, then tore the paper. The moment she saw the cover of the book, a wide smile broke out on her face. "*The Thirty-Nine Steps*," she marvelled, skimming her fingers over the cover. "Oh, Jerry. What a wonderful gift. We never did finish it, did we?"

He took a deep breath for courage. "I'm hoping maybe now we can," he said, then he knelt before her, his entire body buzzing.

She took a step back, the sweet softness of her lips parting slightly with surprise.

"I never stopped thinking of you after I went back to the Front," he said, the words bubbling to the surface at last. "The world kept blowing up around me, and all I wanted was to get home alive so I could see you again."

Her eyes had widened while he spoke, their magic blue almost swallowed up by the depths of her pupils.

"Then I got back, and nobody I asked knew you. I gave up. And when I gave up on finding you, I gave up on myself, I guess. Nothing mattered much. And then one day, there you were." He could still see her in that yellow dress, her long blond hair tied into a tail and tickling down her back. "I've known all along that you were the one for me. No one understands me like you do. Nobody sees me like you do either. They see a monster, but you see *me*. You've always seen me, despite everything."

She looked as if she was going to say something, and he knew what it was going to be. She was going to reassure him, tell him he was no monster, that he was a good man who'd had an unfortunate accident. She was going to smile at him and hold his hand, and he'd come undone before he could even ask her the question.

"I love you, Adele." He reached into his pocket, hooking his mother's ring between his thumb and forefinger, then he offered it up to her. "Marry me?"

She was in his arms before she said a word, her lips on his, her scent all around him. He took her face in his hands and felt the warmth of her tears trickle onto them, under them. He held her there, needing to understand, gazing into those eyes with all he had.

"Is that a yes?" he whispered.

"Yes," she said against his mouth. "Yes, Jerry. I'll marry you. I want to live here with you. I want to dance with you in your father's big room." She threw her hands into the air. "And I want to fill this house with your children." Her arms lowered so they were around his neck again, and she pressed her cheek to his chest, breathing there. "Oh Jerry. I've always loved you. You must know that."

For the first time in a very long while, he felt tears burn in his eyes, and this time he did nothing to stop them. The cool, emotionless man he knew everyone else saw when they looked at him was nowhere near. He was far away with the woman he loved, the woman who had sewn him up and made him whole. *She loves me*, he thought, incredulous.

Their hands trembled as he slipped the ring onto her finger, then they both stared down at the beautiful gold band with the flower on top, made of bits of diamonds.

"I hope you like it," he said, loving the look of it against her skin. Like it was made for her.

"It's stunning. It's like nothing I've seen before."

"It was my mother's," he said quietly.

At that, she looked as if she might cry again. "Jerry, you do me an incredible honour, giving me this ring."

He pulled her close again, drawing strength from her kisses. This is what it would be like. The two of them, doing this whenever they wanted, holding each other, walking life's paths hand in hand. "Your future brother-in-law asked us for a favour. I told him it was bad timing, but—"

"Of course, Jerry. What is it?"

"He said that if you said yes to me, he had something to give you. He's waiting for us at Chappell House."

"Now?"

"You know John. He doesn't exactly think ahead. He gets an idea in his mind and goes with it. So yes. Now. If you're not in the mood, I can—"

She got to her feet, grabbing his hand to pull him up. "Let's go."

The whole way into town, she was smiling. He couldn't stop watching her, the way she was admiring her new ring, turning her hand this way and that, and the way she kept looking at him, happiness shining in her eyes. That's all he wanted, from this day forward.

It was still relatively early, the sun barely touching the western horizon. To Jerry, the voices in the street were light and merry, not an unpleasant thought in the whole town. How could there be? The most wonderful thing had just happened, and his life was only going to get better from here. He stepped out of the car and went around for her door, then he helped her get down. He held her hand as they walked to the door, and he kissed her again just before they stepped into the building.

"Surprise!"

They both jumped at the unexpected shouts. Right away, Charlie hobbled over, shaking Jerry's hand and wishing Adele all the best. He was followed by the rest of the crowd. John stood in the middle of it all, arms folded, smiling with satisfaction as he watched everything going on.

"Aunt Judy!" Jerry cried as she came over. "Adele, this is my mother's sister. They were twins, so you can almost see what Ma would have looked like. Aunt Judy, this is Adele," he said, still shocked at how happy he felt, "the love of my life."

"Wonderful to meet you," Adele said, accepting his aunt's embrace with a laugh.

"And Uncle Henry," he warned her, watching her brace for the incoming hug.

"Maman!" she said, then Guillaume was there, shaking Jerry's hand with a grip of iron.

While Adele's mother gawked over her engagement ring, Jerry looked across the room for his brother.

"Did I surprise you?" John shouted over the crowd. "Nobody spilled the beans?"

"You amaze me," Jerry replied.

"Let's get some whisky pouring!" John yelled, and Bob Howard started pulling out bottles of Bailey Brothers' Best, then sending them around to tables with glasses for all. Someone had brought a fiddle, and though it was difficult to hear it sometimes over the celebration, it brought a sweet, homey feel to the room. Over the next hour or so, the door kept opening, letting in more guests, surprising Jerry every time.

"Dutchie?" he exclaimed. "Why, I never expected to see you!"

"You should know that I never miss a party where the whisky's flowing," his rival said. He glanced appreciatively at Adele, who was busy speaking with Aunt Judy. "Congratulations, Bailey. I hope she knows what she's signed up for. She's much too good for you."

"Don't I know it," Jerry agreed. "Did you get your drink yet? We're serving BBB tonight, not your lousy hooch."

Dutchie snorted. "On my way."

Just then John's expression changed, his smile hardening to a scowl. He was looking past Jerry, so Jerry turned and came face-to-face with Ernie Willoughby.

"Well," Willoughby said. "This is quite a gathering."

"I'm certain you weren't invited," Jerry said, heat surging into his face. "Brave of you to walk into this crowd of folks who won't work with you, let alone speak to you. Probably the bravest thing you've ever done."

But Willoughby wasn't finding humour in anything. The look he gave Jerry was flat and expressionless.

Adele appeared at Jerry's side almost immediately, her hands on his arm. "Hello, Ernie," she said civilly. "I'm surprised to see you here."

His gaze dropped to her ring finger, where the diamonds glittered despite Willoughby's shadow, and he sucked in his cheeks. "I understand congratulations are in order, but this is such a waste of a beautiful woman."

From behind them, Jerry felt the crowd giving way, then John barged through. Jerry put out a hand to stop him. He didn't want any fighting tonight.

"Get the hell out," John hissed. "Closed party."

Then Dutchie was there, and to Jerry's surprise, Guillaume stepped up beside him, the big Frenchman's arms crossed over his barrel chest.

"You should leave now," Jerry said.

Very slowly, Willoughby took a step back, then another. He didn't say a word, and his dark eyes, so full of threat, never left Jerry's. Just before he reached the exit he paused, and his expression changed the tiniest bit, the hint of a smile coming to his lips. Jerry waited for Willoughby to say what was on his mind, but he only nodded. In that moment, Jerry saw something in Willoughby's eyes that froze him in place. It felt like a message. No, more than that. A warning. Deep inside himself, Jerry shuddered, fighting a memory that threatened to bury him in the cold blackness. Jerry could hear the voices on the other side of the tunnel wall again. The enemy had a plan.

twenty-three
ADELE

❧

The morning of the wedding, Adele was a ball of nerves. The day she'd dreamed of was here, and she could hardly wait to see what it would bring. She stared at her gown, hanging in the window. Sunlight streamed through the window, setting the silver threads alight, dappling the floor through the delicate lace sleeves. Adele had thought the cost was frivolous, but she had been unable to stop Maman and Guillaume from buying it for her.

"Imagine Jerry's face when he sees you in it," Maman had said, and that was the end of the matter.

"I can help you put it on," Marie said now, from the door of the room. "Maman is dressing Queen Madeleine."

Adele smiled. "She'll be a beautiful flower girl."

"And you a beautiful bride. Come here. You'll never get those buttons on your own."

Marie had arrived two days before to help prepare for the wedding. No one was surprised to hear Fred wasn't coming, though Adele was disappointed on her sister's behalf, but she was proud with how Marie had handled the situation. When Fred refused, she had informed him that he would be taking care of Arthur, which he hadn't liked. Nervous at the idea of being alone with the baby, he had called in reinforcements in the form of his aunt.

At supper the night she'd arrived, Marie had accepted a glass of champagne and chuckled. "She's a well-meaning woman, and she won't let Fred hide away. We'll see how he feels after a couple of days of burping and diaper changes."

Now, Adele felt her sister's fingers working at the back of her neck, finishing the row of tiny pearl buttons.

"There you are. Oh, Adele. You are a vision." She held her hand toward the mirror. "Take a look."

Adele hardly recognized the woman before her. Whoever she was, she looked very sophisticated, she thought, turning a bit to see the profile. So confident. Her wedding gown was threaded throughout with exquisite patterns of beaded flowers, not unlike the diamonds on her ring. What a difference from the first time Jerry had seen her. *He loves me*, she thought for the hundredth time, awed by the very idea. Soon she would be his, and he would be hers.

She had already received her first wedding gift, and it was more meaningful than the giver could have imagined. She'd told Dr. Knowles of her impending nuptials, then she'd watched conflicting emotions play over his rosy face. After congratulating her with the utmost courtesy, he had chewed a moment on his lower lip, and she knew he had more to say. Eventually, he worked up the courage he needed then peered at her through myopic eyes.

"I understand my breach in etiquette, Mademoiselle Savard. I am aware the idea of married women retaining a career in nursing is generally frowned upon." His lips tightened slightly. "But I am wondering if you might consider staying on here. You are the most qualified nurse I have ever worked with. The patients and I would consider it the greatest of personal sacrifices on your part if you would remain."

In truth, she had been planning to ask him about that, whether it was considered socially acceptable or not. She knew without asking that Jerry would have supported her choice to continue her work. He understood it wasn't just a job to her; it was a calling. Still, she had clarified with Jerry before agreeing, because she knew it was the right thing to do. From now on, she would be sharing her life with someone, not just forging ahead on her own. She assured Dr. Knowles that she had no intention of leaving his employ, and the relief that spilled over the doctor's face in that moment was worth any hesitation she might have had.

Today, Adele would become Mrs. Bailey, but that would never change the fact that she would always be Nurse Savard. Or perhaps Nurse Bailey, going forward.

At John's insistence, the couple had happily agreed to hold the wedding, then the reception at the Bailey house. At first, he had grumbled a bit, since he'd wanted to throw a rip-roaring party for the newlyweds at one of the speakeasies, but Jerry had drawn him aside and explained why he didn't want to do that. After the feeling he'd gotten from Willoughby the other night, he'd decided the wedding would include only family and close friends, which meant there would be no excuse for their rival to wander in again, unwelcomed. John had reluctantly agreed that Jerry was right. Any possible issues with Willoughby would be dealt with after the big day.

As the best man, John had ensured Jerry was nowhere near the house that morning. He'd taken him to the warehouse, then out to the Dominion for a bracing drink, but they were back now. From the room upstairs where Adele had gotten dressed, she could feel the love crowding into the big room downstairs. It had probably been a good thing that Hazel and Lillian weren't able to come, because there simply would not have been enough room. They'd both sent their best wishes and regrets from the east coast, explaining it would be too far to travel with their new babies, but promising to come see Jerry and her when they could. They remembered him fondly—just as they remembered the glances that had been shared between the two when Adele had thought no one would notice.

Now that Adele was dressed, a crown of pearls pinned to her hair along with its attached veil, it felt to Adele as if the house held its breath, waiting. Then Guillaume appeared at her bedroom door, a bittersweet expression of pride on his face, his arm held out in invitation, and the waiting came to an end.

"Your groom awaits," he said.

"Your turn," Marie whispered to Madeleine. The serious little girl was all dressed up in a pretty pink dress Marie had made for her, complete with a stylish dropped waist. "You get to go first. Remember what I told you. You take this little basket, and you be very careful on the stairs. When you get to the bottom, you sprinkle these pretty petals all the way across the room to Grandmère. She will be waiting for you."

Madeleine frowned. "That will be messy."

Adele held in a laugh. It would have been a relief to let it out and shake up all the nerves that had congregated in her stomach, but she kept it inside.

"Yes, dear," Marie explained to her daughter. "It's just for today. Aunt Adele will be walking over the flowers like a princess. I will be right behind you, but it's your job to go first. All right." She hugged her little girl then ushered her toward the door. "Go!"

Then she turned back to Adele, her eyes glistening. Adele held her breath, and for a moment it was just her and Marie, sisters as children, and now sisters on a whole new level. Her best friend her whole life.

"I'm very glad for you, little sister. You and Jerry will be so happy together." A sound of appreciation carried from the living room as the little flower girl arrived, and Marie started to follow. At the last moment, she looked back. "Don't chicken out now. I'll be waiting for you."

The living room was packed with loved ones, including Jerry's cousins, aunt, and uncle, but as Adele and Guillaume reached the bottom of the stairs then entered the petal-littered space, all she could see was Jerry's striking figure, tall and proud and waiting for her by the fireplace mantel. Behind him, the portraits of his parents looked down, and she smiled, feeling their approval. Guillaume led Adele to Jerry, then he took a breath and laid her hands in his. He sniffed lightly as he backed toward Maman, and nostalgia welled up inside her. She was no longer Guillaume's little girl, no longer her mother's baby. She was a grown woman, marrying a man who loved her over all others. A man she knew deep in her soul that she could always depend upon. For a heartbeat, she felt afraid, stepping from one lifetime into another, but his beautiful grey gaze held hers, and the love radiating from him filled her heart to overflowing.

She faced him, both her hands in his, so caught up in him that she barely heard the minister begin the service. Then it came time for their vows, and the corners of Jerry's lips curled slightly, reassuring her.

"Do you, Jeremiah Alexander Bailey, take this woman, Adele Yvonne Savard, to be your lawfully wedded wife, to have and to hold from this day forward, for better, for worse, for richer, for poorer, in sickness and in health, until death you do part?"

Adele had thought about those words so many times, she had them memorized. She knew the commitment might seem frightening to some, but not to her. Not to Jerry. She thought of the day they'd met, and her memories replayed his convalescence, with her always at his side. The scars weren't just his, they were theirs. They'd already been through so much. She wasn't afraid of anything except being without him.

"I do," he said without hesitation, strong and sure.

She tried to say her own "I do" without tears of happiness trickling down her cheeks, but couldn't. Jerry's fingers squeezed hers to give her comfort.

On cue, John stepped forward and placed a ring in his brother's palm. Adele held out her trembling hand as Jerry spoke.

"With this ring, I thee wed. With my body I thee worship, and with all my worldly goods I thee endow. In the name of the Father, and of the Son, and of the Holy Ghost."

The whole room joined in with a hushed, "Amen."

Then Adele turned to Marie, who was right there waiting, holding

Jerry's gold ring. She took it, her attention on the precious gold promise, and she gave a silent thanks.

When Adele had first come home and announced her engagement, her mother had burst into tears then run into her room. She returned moments later, holding a man's gold ring.

"This was your father's," she said. "Now it will be Jerry's."

Adele had never thought about that before. "Why me? Why not Marie?"

"Fred did not want a ring. It passes to you, if you want it."

"Oh, Maman. Of course I want it." The gold had been engraved with a tiny, antique scroll, a subtle design on a perfect ring. "Jerry will love it."

Now she slipped it onto his finger, speaking her vows, promising him everything she had and everything she would ever have. There was no hesitation in her heart or in her words.

Then the minister addressed everyone in the room. "Jeremiah Alexander Bailey and Adele Yvonne Savard, through their words today, have joined together in holy matrimony, exchanging their vows before God and witnesses. They have pledged their commitment each to the other, and have declared the same by joining hands and exchanging rings. I now pronounce that they are husband and wife. Those whom God hath joined together, let no man put asunder." His gaze dropped to Jerry. "You may now kiss the bride."

The moment Adele kissed her husband's lips, John let out a whoop, and the celebrations began. Jerry's uncle Henry brought out champagne for a toast, and Guillaume followed with a tray of glasses. Adele looked into her sparkling glass and couldn't help briefly remembering her last taste of champagne, in another lifetime at Ernie's party. There, everyone had been talking and laughing, but she'd sensed no true affection in anyone's smiles. Here, love was all she saw.

"This is just to start, folks," John assured everyone. "Whisky's on its way. For now I ask you to raise your glasses for my brother and his beautiful wife. Jerry's my best friend. Always has been." John's eyes found hers, and her throat tightened at the sincerity she saw in them. "In all the world, I never could have imagined a more perfect match for him than Adele, and I love her as I love him." He looked back at the others, smiling. "I know you all stand with me as I wish them a lifetime of happiness, love, and prosperity. May you always be as happy as you are today. To Adele and Jerry!"

Jerry's aunt Judy had put out a table full of food that the women had prepared in advance, then she added punch, which she put beside John's bottles of whisky. Standing beside Adele, Jerry pointed out little Madeleine practically crawling up the table leg for a cookie, but they only laughed, and Adele assured him she was ready to step in if the tablecloth started to slip. By then Marie had taken over the gramophone, playing from discs she'd brought, and was insisting that everyone dance. As John spun a giggly Madeleine around the room, Guillaume took Maman in his arms, and Jerry stretched out his hand to Adele.

"Care for a dance, Mrs. Bailey?" he asked. She took his hand and snuggled in close with her eyes closed, knowing he'd lead her expertly around the other dancers. "Are you happy, Adele?"

She looked up at his gentle smile, at the lines on his face she knew so well. "I have never been happier in my whole life," she said, and he leaned down to kiss her.

"That makes two of us," he replied, holding her close.

A half hour or so later, Adele was dancing with Guillaume when she noticed Walter and John going to the door. They spoke briefly with someone standing outside, then turned back. Unease rippled through her as they walked directly to Jerry.

"Warehouse was raided," John said quietly, but Adele overheard. She dropped Guillaume's hand and joined the brothers.

"Is everyone all right?" she asked, concerned.

John shrugged. "A few cuts and bruises. No need to trouble a nurse over it."

"How much did they get?" Jerry asked calmly.

"Sounds like everything," John said tightly. "Walter and I'll head over now and see what's what."

Jerry nodded, and she was surprised that he was smiling slightly. Maybe she was wrong, but shouldn't he be more concerned if his livelihood had just been stolen?

"We saw this coming," Jerry was saying. He put an arm around his brother's shoulder as they walked toward the door. "That's what we've been doing all this work for. He has no idea about the tunnel."

Marie appeared, looking nervously at the departing men. "Is everything all right?"

"I think so," Adele said, reassured when she saw Jerry returning to her. "Jerry doesn't seem concerned, at least."

Marie nodded toward the couch, where Madeleine had fallen asleep despite the noise. "Your flower girl needs to go to bed, and it looks like Maman is close behind. Will you be awfully upset if we take our leave now?"

Adele thanked her sister for everything, and soon the rest of the guests dwindled, and the newlyweds stood on their porch, waving goodbye under a waning moon. When the last had gone, Adele turned to Jerry, remembering what he had said to John earlier.

"What's the tunnel?" she asked.

He let out a sigh. "I'm sorry I didn't tell you before. I should have, but I thought if I kept you out of all this business stuff, you'd be safer."

"I'm not afraid, Jerry. I'm tougher than that. And I'm your partner now."

"The tunnel leads to our secret vault." He indicated an empty space on the lawn between the house and the barn. "John and I dug it out. Most of our whisky is hidden away in there, just in case something like this happened."

She stared at the yard, amazed. "You have a plan for everything."

"I try. My pa said if I paid attention to the important things, the rest would fall in line," he said, then he pulled her around to face him. There was a new look in his gaze that stirred her inside. His eyes were hooded, his mouth soft. "You're the most important thing in my life, Mrs. Bailey. It's time I paid some special attention to you." Suddenly, he scooped her up in his arms, making her laugh out loud. "I'm gonna start by carrying my bride over the threshold."

His face, so dear to her, with that scar she knew so intimately, was an inch from hers. His breath was a little sweet from the evening's whisky, his jaw lightly bristled.

"I can walk, you know," she said softly. "I'm capable."

"I know what you're capable of, Nurse Savard."

"That's Nurse Bailey now."

Holding her against his chest, the silvery white of her gown pressed against his beautiful black suit, he angled them both through the front door. It was the same room they'd just spent hours in, but the atmosphere was something else entirely. The quiet proof that they were alone.

He set her on her feet, then bent his head and kissed her deeply. This place, this moment, this man. This was everything.

Moving slowly, Adele took his hand. "You didn't show me the rest of the house before."

He led her up the stairs. "This first one's John's room," he said, "and this is the spare room. I've been using it as an office, keeping records and things. I hope it will be a nursery eventually."

She shared his hope. One day . . . At the next door, she paused. "And this?"

He grinned. "I think you'll like this." He swung the door open to reveal an indoor bathroom.

"What an extravagance," she gasped as she stepped inside the narrow room. She ran a finger along the bathtub's smooth white porcelain, then she paused at the sink, with its exposed pipe sticking out from the wall behind.

"My father had started it, so John and I finished it. It took some work, but we figured it out. We wanted to have it ready for you."

His quiet pride was irresistible, and it was obvious this construction would have been more than just a little bit of work. "Thank you for my toilet," she teased.

"It's no more than you deserve," he said sincerely. Then his hands curled around the sides of her waist and his voice dropped. "If you're interested, there's one more room to show you."

With a rush of desire, she followed Jerry into their bedroom, taking in the pale swirls of green on the wallpaper and the delicate pink roses edging the crown moulding overhead. As she moved with him toward the elegant four-poster bed, she had the impression of crossing into the unknown, like when she'd been afraid to board the ship home so long before, and she shivered with nerves.

Jerry took her fingers in his and kissed the backs of her hands, calming her as he always did. "You have nothing to be afraid of, Adele."

"I'm not afraid. Never afraid when I'm with you."

He hesitated, one eyebrow cocked. "Well, I might be a little. It's important to me that you're happy."

"I don't think there's anything you could do that wouldn't make me happy," she said, and a delicious new fire burst into flame inside her.

She reached up and tucked her finger into the knot of his tie, wiggling it loose, and he bowed his head so she could slip it over his head. He didn't move as her fingers undid the buttons of his shirt, but she saw his nostrils flare slightly when she pushed it back off his shoulders. Her gaze travelled over the muscular slope of them, strong from all that digging, paused on the active pulse at the side of his throat, then she skimmed her fingertips down his chest. His belly rippled.

"I forgot you were ticklish," she said, then she kissed the centre of his chest. When she looked up, his eyes were closed, and he wore the calmest, most blissful smile. She stared at him a moment, in awe, and something bloomed within her.

Jerry Bailey was hers. To have and to hold. And she wanted very much to do both.

"I'll need help with my dress," she said, turning her back to him.

His calloused fingers were gentle, wrestling the little buttons, and his breath hitched at the same moment she felt cool air hit her bare back. She let the spiderweb-thin lace of the cap sleeves slide off her shoulders, then all the way off her arms, and when she faced him again, maybe just a little bit afraid this time, she saw his grey eyes darken with desire. Then, for the second time that night, he lifted her off her feet, cradling her against him. This time there were no sequins or bits of lace between them. No cotton or wool or hesitation. The warmth of his skin pressed against hers, chest to chest, his bare arms on her body, and she shivered with anticipation. He carried her to the bed and laid her down, his lips on her neck, her arms, her mouth. He moved above her, holding himself up with his arms, and his eyes searched hers.

She reached up with one hand to trace the lines of his scar, to remind him there was nothing between them.

"Don't be afraid, Jerry," she whispered.

PART
— four —

twenty-four
CASSIE

❧

— Present Day —

Matthew was leaning against an unpainted pillar on the front porch when Cassie drove up to the house, his arms folded, eyes on the tail lights of a receding Lexus. He smiled at her as she parked, and a part of her melted at the sight of it. Every time she saw him, she liked him a little more.

She handed him a coffee. "If you want cream or sugar, I have it in the car."

He took one of each, and she added that to her growing list of things she knew about him.

"The porch looks brand new!" she said, admiring the new boards and walking toward the bay window. "And you fixed up the window. Looks great." She lifted a hand, shielding her eyes from the sun, and glanced back down the road. "Who was that?"

"A developer. He just offered me half a million bucks to build a condo here."

She stopped in her tracks. "Oh," she said. "Are you considering it?"

"I'd be lying if I said that the money didn't matter. The renovations are costing a small fortune."

She cupped her hands around her eyes and peered through the bay window, not wanting Matthew to see how much that hurt. It was good for him, though. Half a million dollars was a great deal, she tried to convince herself. Through the glass, she could see he had finished the wide-open living room, and the walls glowed with a fresh coat of paint. Now he'd let them bulldoze it? Unless . . .

"You know, the bottles might be worth something."

He eyed her. "Really? Any idea how much?"

"I called my guy today, and he'll get back to me with an estimate soon. There are a few factors to consider for the valuation. They're not from a major distillery, but they're old, and there's probably a tale to go with the bottles, so that would add to the value to a certain extent. I don't want to guess."

"I'd love to hear that tale. Why would they have hidden them in the wall?"

"I have no idea, but I'm working on it. When I was digging in the archives, I discovered the Baileys' business was ruined after a police raid. They lost it all—except what you found, of course. Riches to rags overnight. After that, there was basically nothing about them in the papers. The mystery is so intriguing." She sipped her coffee. "I did read about a few other things going on at the time, and it would be very cool if they somehow connected, but I really have no idea so far. It seems there was a big gangster around here who disappeared mysteriously in 1921 some time after the Bailey brothers had their warehouse seized. My boss, Mrs. Allen, seems to recall reading somewhere that they had a rivalry. If the bottles have anything to do with that kind of legendary gang stuff, it might increase their value. I don't know. I'm still working on it. Luckily, Mrs. Allen is a whiz at local history. If anything can be found, she'll probably be the one to find it."

Matthew gave her a slow, drawn-out smile that fluttered in her chest. "Well, whether or not they are connected, I've found something else that makes this mystery way more interesting. It's over here."

He led her from the porch and past the barn, stopping at the sinkhole where she could see that he had been digging. A ladder leaned against one side, and a shovel was sticking out of the earth. The hole was quite deep. It would have taken him a few days. At the bottom he had spread out a towel.

"This area didn't feel natural to me. In construction, we don't usually see something like this unless there's been a collapse of some kind. Then I remembered you saying that Jeremiah and John were tunnellers, and my mind went to all the tunnels and secret hiding spots people had back then, and I got curious."

She peered into the deep hole again, feeling that same sense of curiosity. Like when her cat, Tom, felt something unseen in the air. "And you found something?"

"I did." He hesitated. "Do you have a strong stomach?"

"That's a scary question. I'm not sure."

He led her to the ladder, then at the bottom, he lifted off the towel. Cassie stumbled backward, stunned.

"That's a skull," she said breathlessly.

"You're a museum person," he said. "You've seen bones before."

"Yeah, but . . ." She squatted by the find. It wasn't just a skull. She could see most of a skeleton here as well. She shuddered, wondering if the bones might belong to one of her ancestors, then her thoughts shifted to the stories she'd been reading earlier that day. She looked up at him. "What if this is that missing gangster? Dead on Bailey land?" She stared back at the bones, trying to figure it all out. "But wouldn't my grandmother have known?"

Matthew cocked his head. "What does your grandmother have to do with anything?"

Her stomach rolled, realizing what she'd just said. She hadn't been thinking. She backed away from the skeleton.

"Cassie? Your grandmother?"

She stopped at the base of the ladder, realizing it was finally time to tell her story. "Listen, I need to tell you something, Matthew."

He looked intently at her, arms folded. "That doesn't sound good."

"It's not that it's bad, it's just . . ." She bit her lip, trying to keep her eyes averted from the bones. "My last name, Simmons—that's my dad's name. My mother's maiden name was Finnegan."

His eyebrows flicked up. "Are you trying to tell me that you're Irish?"

"It's a little more complex than that." She rubbed her hands together, her palms suddenly sweaty. "My grandmother Alice, her maiden name was Bailey." Feeling slightly ridiculous, she held out her hand to shake his. He took it, a funny smile playing on his mouth. "My full name is Cassandra Bailey Simmons. Jeremiah Bailey was my great-grandfather."

twenty-five
JERRY

❧

— November 1921 —

Jerry rubbed his forehead, hoping to ease the headache that had settled behind his eyes. He was in the spare room, his ledger before him, lit by the brass desk lamp Adele had insisted he buy for himself. It was late, well past midnight. Adele was asleep in the next room, her breathing slow and calm and at peace. For so many years, sleep had been Jerry's enemy. Lying next to Adele, he found he could finally share in that escape. He longed for that peace right now, but he wouldn't find it tonight. Jerry had spent the last three hours in the tunnel, counting the remaining stock with Walter, hoping, somehow, that he'd been wrong. But he had always kept good records, and the numbers didn't lie.

After Willoughby raided their warehouse on their wedding night, Jerry hadn't been overly concerned. This was, after all, what the plan for the storage room had been for. And for a while it worked. Jerry had just enough aged booze hidden underground to quietly fulfill the remaining orders of the year before the next batch was ready. It would be tight, but they could make it work.

But Jerry hadn't counted on Willoughby continuing to pilfer their shipments, and he was angry that he hadn't. He should have known Willoughby would be mad as a hornet's nest. At first, things had been quiet, with Willoughby pleased to have struck what he thought was a lethal blow against the Baileys, but that hadn't lasted. Slim had spotted some Bailey Brothers' Best in one of the taverns across the river, and the owner hadn't known enough to claim it was old stock. So Slim promptly reported back to Willoughby that the brothers were still in business. Ever since then, their runs had been trailed and raided. More and more, Willoughby was chipping away at the hidden stock.

It ate both brothers up inside that Willoughby was making a profit off their hard work. And that he was using them as an example as he bullied other gangs. That really stung.

"I wish you'd let me kill him," John had said one night after one of their rumrunners had been stabbed on a run. Walter had found the hijacked vehicle with the driver gasping in pain, then he'd driven him to Jerry's home. They'd laid him out on the kitchen table, and Adele had sewn him up without asking questions. But the look in her eyes told Jerry she was not happy about this at all.

"We're not killers anymore, John," Jerry had replied.

"Speak for yourself. Given the opportunity, I'd do it."

"You'd go to jail, and I'd have to do all this work by myself. I'll come up with a plan."

"You better think of one soon. Willoughby won't stop until he's taken every last drop from us."

But Jerry hadn't come up with anything this time. And day by day, he could feel the increasing pressure of Willoughby closing in on them. Walter felt it, too. Before he left for the night, he told Jerry that he was pretty sure he was being followed.

They'd run into another wrinkle, too. With so much threat hanging over their heads, they had taken as much liquor as possible from Uncle Henry's farm to keep him out of danger. That new stock, combined with the well-aged whisky, meant there was no more room underground. Crates were stacked inside the house, shoved into his office, the cellar, and wherever else they could find space. That had caused the first friction between him and Adele. So Walter had joined the brothers underground, and they'd dug a larger space, nearly doubling the size of the room. Then, under the cover of darkness, the three of them carried everything from the house to the barn, down the shaft, and through the tunnel. The raw, unaged whisky was stacked in the storage room. While it aged, the booze that was already over two years old was moved into the tunnel for their rumrunner to pick up.

That night, Jerry had come back inside, sweaty and tired, and discovered four more crates in the living room. John was sitting on the couch beside them.

"What's this?" Jerry asked.

"I have an idea."

Jerry was tired, and it bothered him that John had purposefully held up the process. He'd wanted it all finished tonight.

"I want to keep these in here," John said. "Our emergency cache of a hundred bottles."

"Right here," he said. "You want to leave them right here in the middle of the house. With my wife. I see a problem with that, John."

John rolled his eyes. "I'm not stupid, Jerry. Bear with me." He held his arms straight out in front of his chest. "I see us building a wall. Right here in the main room. And the bottles will be in that wall. We'll put the bookshelf in front of it for access and use it only if we need it. No one would ever imagine we might hide them here in plain sight."

He understood what John was saying, and he had to admit it was brilliant. Sometimes it wasn't possible to get out to the tunnel for whatever reason. Having a hidden stash like this made sense. But his thoughts had gone immediately to their father and mother, then to him with Adele on their wedding night, dancing in the big open space.

"I hate to give this up."

"Pa would say it was a smart move," John said.

Adele had pursed her lips but said nothing. Sewing up that man on her kitchen table had changed her perspective a little.

Now Jerry was trying to reconcile the crates and casks he'd counted tonight with the numbers in his ledger, and they weren't lining up. Far too many rumrunners were getting waylaid—and more and more, they were getting hurt. Something had to change.

"You're still up?" Adele appeared at his office door in her nightgown, her long blond hair tussled from sleep. He saw the dark circles under her eyes. He saw those an awful lot these days, and he hated himself for causing them.

Marrying Adele had been more than he'd ever dreamed. Sometimes he still couldn't believe she was his, and that she loved him just as much as he loved her. Secretly he doubted that was possible, because to him, she was the sun. The last two months had been wonderful, full of loving and laughter, but the stress of the business just kept creeping in. He'd promised her a good, safe life, but he'd done just the opposite, and his guilt was weighing on both of them.

Their first argument had happened after the stabbing. The second, when he'd started sleeping with a rifle by the bed. She said she'd seen far too many times what those things could do, and she didn't want to see it anymore. He couldn't blame her, but he couldn't give in on that point.

"I'll come to bed soon."

"I can't sleep without you beside me," she replied. Her gaze dropped to the dirt on his fingers. "You've been doing inventory again." She sighed and left the room. "I'm going to pour you a bath."

His mind might have been occupied by the ledger, but his body craved the bath. A few minutes later, he got out of his chair and switched off the desk lamp, though his eyes lingered on the numbers even in the dark. Pulling his shirt off over his head, he followed her into the bathroom. She sat beside the tub, her hair falling down her back, her fingers trailing in the water as she waited for him. He climbed in and melted into the heat. Almost immediately, he felt his muscles begin to relax after yet another day of hard physical labour.

"Lean forward," she said softly, and when he did, she smoothed a wet cloth slowly over his back. He sighed, loving her touch as he always had. She was constantly healing him in one way or another.

"It isn't going to stop," she said gently. "Ernie will never stop coming after you. His anger for you has become an obsession. It's like he *can't* stop. And it frightens me, Jerry."

He didn't say anything. It frightened him, too.

"Everything has gotten worse," she continued, squeezing the cloth over one of his shoulders. "Dr. Knowles treats more stabbings and shootings each day, and I've seen a few of your own rumrunners in there. You may think you're hiding me from the truth, but you can't. And you know I don't like guns in the house. Every time I see that rifle beside your pillow I want to cry."

"I'm sorry, Adele. I'll figure something out."

The cloth pressed across to the other shoulder. A little more pressure. "I need to ask you to do something for me, Jerry."

"Anything."

"I want this to stop."

"I'm trying. I'm working as hard as I can."

"No," she said, her hand paused behind his neck. "I mean I want this business to stop altogether. We have plenty of money. You could sell the rest to Dutchie or something."

He frowned at her, incredulous. "I can't do that."

"Give me one good reason. Explain to me why this isn't enough. You're out there where anyone could kill you, and you'd never even know who it was. Haven't we had enough of war?" She sat back, and he saw the tears in her eyes. God, he hated making her cry. "We have everything we could ever want here. But if someone kills you, none of it is worth a cent. I can't live without you, Jerry. Not again."

He'd never really considered that his life mattered until she'd come along.

"Especially now," she whispered.

He straightened. "What's that mean?"

She took a deep, shaky breath. "I hate to add one more complication to our lives, but I'm afraid I have. I quit my job today."

"What? Why? I thought you loved your job."

She wiped away a tear, but she was smiling. "You're gonna be a daddy, Jerry."

His jaw dropped. "You're pregnant?"

She nodded.

The bathwater sloshed against the sides of the tub as he reached for her. "Adele, why, that's wonderful news. That's, oh, I don't even know what to say!"

She laughed at his confusion. "Are you happy about this?"

"More than you can imagine, my love." He read so many questions in those blue eyes of hers, and he wondered if he'd ever be able to answer them all. A father? Could he do that? Could he teach his boy what his father had taught him? Or . . . what if it was a little girl? A daughter, looking at him like Adele was now. And suddenly, he saw his life in a whole new way. He had everything he'd ever need now. But one stray bullet, one sharp blade, and he'd lose it all. He'd lose her. With that, it was settled.

"I'm sorry I've been so slow to understand," he said. "I'll talk to John tomorrow. I love you, Adele. I won't jeopardize our family."

―――――――――

The next day, Jerry took John to the Dominion House for lunch. He ordered them both a whisky and lit a cigarette.

"What's up?" John asked.

"I have a plan."

"At last! What's happening?"

Jerry blew a stream of smoke to the side, avoiding the moment he'd have to look his brother in the eye. "You're not gonna like it."

"Try me," John replied, frowning slightly as he lit his own cigarette.

"It's gotten too dangerous lately," Jerry began. "We need to put an end to the violence."

"It's always been dangerous."

"Yeah, but there are no rules now. It's been a while since that day on the water, and since then our alliance with Dutchie and the High Tide boys has gotten more than a little shaky. Think about it, John. Everyone around here suspects someone of something, and they'd be just as likely to stab you in the back as not. It's happening everywhere. Fellows like Rocco Perri in Hamilton. There's a new one in Chicago I heard of the other day, name's Capone. Tuck says he's suspected of a bunch of murders, and he's been seen in these parts as well. We're fighting off the Purple Gang every day and barely surviving. They're the worst sons of bitches I've ever seen. Fearless." He put his cigarette to his lips. "And then there's Willoughby. He's lost his mind, and I'm tired of fighting him. I'm tired of all the fighting. And I don't want to be responsible for someone getting killed running a shipment of my booze." The smoke curled out of his mouth. "It's time to shut down the still."

John sat up, alert. "That's your plan? The runners will still go, just with someone else's booze."

"Maybe, but it wouldn't be on my conscience. You're welcome to take over the entire operation, if you want, of course."

John leaned back, staring at his brother. "I can't believe you'd even suggest that. The label says Bailey Brothers' Best, not John's Best. I can't do this without you."

"I get it, John. I'm sorry." He tapped his cigarette on the ashtray. "I did say you wouldn't like it."

He watched John ingest what he was saying, knowing he would need a little time to think about it. To come to terms with the same thing Jerry had the night before. It wasn't like the war. No one was forcing them to get out there and risk their lives. They already had more money than they could ever spend, but what was the point of all that if they weren't around to spend it?

"I'm tired of dodging bullets, and there's more to life than making whisky." John still didn't look convinced, but that's why Jerry had left the best for last. "I'd like my kid to meet his wild uncle John."

John's mouth dropped open. "Is Adele . . . ?"

"Maybe play ball with him someday."

John threw his head back. "I knew you had it in you, Jerry! That's terrific. When did you find out?"

"Last night. And I made her a promise, John. I'm done."

"Damn," John said, almost to himself, then he slowly nodded. "I understand now. I guess you just realized you're not immortal."

"I guess I figured out the same about you, brother. Let's just retire, you and me. Enjoy life. We've earned it."

John breathed in his cigarette again, observing Jerry through the smoke. "All right," he said simply. "I promised your wife that I'd keep you safe, and quitting this life would definitely help me keep that promise."

Hearing those words was a relief. He was grateful for the acceptance in John's expression. Jerry had hoped John would do the smart thing and leave the business behind, but a part of him had been unsure that his brother was ready. That thought had kept him up last night. How hard it would have been, knowing John was out there on his own. Like when he'd been in the hospital, and John had been fighting the enemy without him.

"But what about all those bottles underground? What are we gonna do with those?"

Jerry smiled. With a question like that, John was definitely with him. "I have a plan for that, too," he said. "I just need to know if my brother is willing to help me on one last run."

twenty-six
ADELE

❧

Adele reached for a bottle of whisky in the wall of their living room and placed it in the crate lined with straw, then groaned as she straightened. At least she felt better at night. Mornings were not fun these days, and the sympathy she had received from Maman was not helping. When she'd written to Marie about how sick she was getting, Marie wrote back suggesting eating crackers and going for walks. Neither of those had helped either. So Adele had resigned herself to riding the waves of nausea every morning. It was all worth it, she kept telling herself, for she'd joined a new sisterhood. She wouldn't have to envy her sister or married friends for much longer. Then again, Adele thought, her experience was turning out to be a little more trying than theirs had been. None of them had been tasked with helping to move a stockpile of illegal whisky.

The half crate of bottles she was carrying to the tunnel wouldn't be ready to drink for another six months, but at least it was out of her house. Originally John had wanted to hide a hundred bottles in the new living room wall, but only fifty had fit, so she'd taken on the job of packing the extras up and bringing them to the men. Jerry had only agreed as long as she promised to carry a half crate at a time. This was her fourth half crate. Then she'd be done.

Jerry had already sold off the last of the aged whisky to his customers, delivering the news that they were going out of business at the same time. Now he, John, Walter, and Charlie were delivering the raw whisky to Dutchie a truckload at a time, having struck a deal with him. After that, Dutchie would hand the Baileys a fortune.

And that would be the official end of the business.

She knew both brothers would have regrets, but they hadn't argued about it at all. At least not in front of her. She'd actually been surprised by how easily John had adjusted. She'd been fairly sure that he was going to put up a fight, maybe even try to run the business on his own. Seeing John acquiesce to Jerry's request without a fuss, Adele understood why Jerry loved his brother so much. John was the most loyal man she'd ever met. She would have to thank him again for keeping his promise.

Then again, he seemed almost as excited about his future niece or nephew as Jerry was. And he was dating a nice girl now. Maybe, incredibly, the most eligible bachelor in Windsor was getting ready to settle down.

Once the decision had been made to shut down the still, everything had gotten better. After Jerry made the deal with Dutchie, it seemed his shoulders were suddenly lighter, and he spent more of his energy doing what he said he loved the most, which was making her happy. When all was done, it might take him a little time to learn how to relax, but she was looking forward to more nights with him in their bed, not underground. Thinking of those precious moments, she smiled to herself, thinking of how he touched her, of how his solid muscles were so soft on hers. She had married a beautiful man. And soon they'd have a little one to keep them busy. Jerry would be a wonderful father.

The brothers had been busy over the past two days, carrying the heavy crates of raw whisky back through the tunnel, back up the shaft, and toward the truck parked in the barn. Charlie had figured out how to drive without his right side, so with Walter riding shotgun, he had been looking after Dutchie's deliveries. Unfortunately, the cousins' car had broken down early that morning. So while Walter took the vehicle up to Guillaume's for repairs, Jerry divided his time between working underground with John and delivering shipments himself.

Nights came in faster and darker now that they were nearing December, and Adele picked up her step to get to the barn before she got too cold. She carried the half crate to the others, hidden back in the corner, then started to pack them together. Once that was done, she climbed down the shaft to check on the brothers, see how the room was looking.

At the bottom, she peered down the well-lit tunnel. She couldn't see them, which meant they were either in the storage room or off on a delivery. John's coat had been left on the floor, so she knew they must be hot from working hard. Maybe she should just wait here, she thought. They'd be out soon, and she'd only be in the way if she went in.

It was much colder down here than it was up in the barn and outside, so she shrugged on John's coat as she gazed at her surroundings. The first time she'd toured the tunnel and the storage room, she'd been so impressed by how secure it was. Everything had been done exactly right, which was what she had come to expect from Jerry. Her husband didn't do things halfway. So the posts were straight and true, the walls as smooth as they could make them. Even the low ceiling was flat, braced by long overhead beams.

"Don't touch those," John had teased, though he'd known she wouldn't touch anything. "Pull that beam down and the whole thing goes," which reminded her how awful it must have been for them during the war. As she stood there, feeling the walls closing in on her, it struck her again how horrible those years underground must have been for them. They must have hated making this place. It was a shame, she thought now, that this amazing structure would soon be empty after so much work.

She stamped her feet against the cold and hugged John's coat closer around herself, then she felt the lump of his wool cap in one of the pockets. She fished it out and was just starting to pull it over her ears when she heard a voice behind her.

"Long time no see, Adele."

All the breath in her body left her in that moment, and she spun around. "Ernie."

He stood tall and smug, his handsome face shadowed, but there was no mistaking Ernie Willoughby. "You're looking well. I miss seeing you around. How is married life treating you?"

"What are you doing here?" she asked, whispering over the hammering in her heart.

"Is that any way to speak to an old friend? I've come to find out what's been going on over here at Bailey Brothers' Best headquarters, that's all." He held out his arms as far as he could in the small space. "And what an interesting thing I've discovered!"

"You need to leave here. Right now."

"I'm not leaving, Adele. You should know that."

He reached behind him and pulled a gun from the back of his trousers. Instinctively, she placed her hand on her belly. Ernie didn't notice; he was looking at the chamber of his gun, checking each cylinder for a bullet. Satisfied, he smiled back at her.

"Now, what were you saying?"

She had to keep him away from the storage room, from Jerry, and John—especially John. There was no way that would end well. All she could imagine was bullets flying around in this tiny space. Somehow, she had to get Ernie out of here.

"Ernie, please," she said in the calmest voice she could muster. "You don't have to do this. Please, please put that away. There's no reason to do anything drastic. They're shutting down the business—did you know that? They won't be competing with you anymore. There's no reason to hurt anyone."

That caught his attention. "They're shutting down the business?

How interesting. Why would they do that?" He winked saucily at her. "Is the old ball and chain making him do it? Oh, I'm just teasing. So they're in there right now, clearing it out?"

"No. They're not," she stammered. "It's just me. They're out making a delivery."

"Oh good. You're back," John's voice came from the other end of the tunnel, and Adele realized with a sick feeling that he'd heard them speaking. "Come help me with this, Jerry."

Adele's stomach plummeted.

Willoughby clicked his tongue in admonishment. "I didn't think a girl like you was capable of lying. But then again, you didn't quite end up being the woman I thought you were, did you?" In a flash, he whipped her around so her back was to his chest. "Let's go for a walk, shall we?"

She dug her feet in. "No, Ernie. You can't do this."

"You're wrong," he said quietly. "I can do anything I want. I always do. And people love me for it."

"They love your money," she said. "Or they're afraid of you. That's not love, Ernie."

"That's enough." He shoved her forward, into the tunnel. "Let's go see what your husband and his brother are up to."

"Ernie, stop," she pleaded, pressing backward to no avail. "You used to be friends. You were just boys. You played together. Please stop," she begged. "There's no need for this, because there's no business anymore."

"Silly girl. This isn't about business." She felt the cold, hard mouth of his gun at her temple. "Now, move!"

Ernie Willoughby was a madman. He wouldn't hesitate to pull the trigger, and she had to warn John before he found him and killed him. She grabbed on to the arm that had locked around her neck and screamed at the top of her lungs.

"Ernie is here! He has a gun!"

twenty-seven
JERRY

Jerry shut the door to his car and headed into the barn, wondering how much John had accomplished while he was gone. They were doing well with moving stock, but this last shipment to Dutchie was going to keep them busy for a couple more days, he thought. Still, it was encouraging, seeing the boxes and bottles leave his hands for the final time, knowing he would no longer have to worry about deadlines and quality control as well as everything else. Soon he would be done, taking his wife out for the night, watching her belly grow with his child.

As he reached the top of the tunnel, he saw the two crates hidden back in the corner. That meant Adele had finished her job of pulling together the last fifty bottles from inside the house for delivery. It was a chilly night, and he hoped she was all bundled up inside now, keeping warm in front of the fire. Maybe working on that tiny white sweater she'd been knitting last night.

He had just placed his boot onto the top rung of the ladder when he heard a sound that cut through him like a blade. A woman's gasp, caught on a sob. Adele was here. She was afraid. Everything in Jerry's body flashed with anger.

"Let her go," he heard John growl. Jerry held his breath, listening for the response, though he already knew who it would be.

"That would be a stupid move on my part," Willoughby replied calmly. "I have all the advantage here, don't I?"

"*You should have let me kill him,*" John had said. Jerry wished with all his strength that he had.

"What are you doing here?" John demanded now.

"I wanted to see for myself how the famous Bailey brothers were still in business. Pretty easy, since I've got eyes and ears everywhere. They led me straight to your house. Then I saw this pretty little thing carrying a crate to the barn and I thought, No, they wouldn't be stupid enough to keep their stock on their property. But it appears you are indeed that stupid."

Jerry was hot with fury. For the past week or so, he had ignored the vague warning pulsing in his chest that told him he was being watched. Never should have done that. *Listen, Jerry! Never stop listening!*

He had to get down there undetected. Travelling back in time to another tunnel, where silence was everything and listening was even more, he moved down the ladder like a cat, checking for loose gravel before he put his foot on the ground at the bottom. No rocks or dust in sight. Nothing to give him away.

From his belt, he grabbed his gun, then he turned toward the tunnel, his arms held straight in front, but what he saw froze him in place. Willoughby stood about eight or nine feet ahead of him, taking up most of the space in the tunnel, but he could see a little bit of blue at the bottom: the hem of Adele's dress. Every part of her was shielded by Willoughby. There was no way to get a shot off unless he wanted to shoot through them both. His only option was surprise.

Adele made a little sound, like a hiccough, tearing Jerry's heart. "Stop, Ernie," Adele pleaded. "You don't have to do this."

"Let her go." It was John's voice. He was trapped at the far end of the tunnel. They'd never dug another entrance. There was no escape.

Willoughby was moving slowly forward, closing in on John, so Jerry edged forward a little faster, knowing the terrain so well. That's when he saw Willoughby had Adele around the neck, his Colt 45 pressed against the side of her head. She was gasping back tears, trying to be brave, and in that moment, he wondered if it was possible to love someone so much he could actually die. Because seeing her there, witnessing her terror, was ripping him apart. He clenched his teeth together, knowing he had to focus. Solve this problem.

He was closer now, could see John, his gun raised, but neither of them could take the shot with Adele in front of Willoughby like a shield. No matter how John felt about Willoughby, Jerry knew John would never endanger her. John would give his life for hers. His brother's eyes flitted to him for the briefest second. He didn't want Jerry to interfere.

"What do you want, Willoughby? Our booze? It's yours. I won't even fight you for it." John sounded a little more confident now, knowing Jerry was there, but Willoughby didn't hear it. Willoughby never heard anybody but himself.

"If I wanted your booze, I would already have taken it. I think I've proven that. It's you I want now, Bailey. You and your brother. You've humiliated me at every turn. You are gonna pay for what you did. I want you gone."

"What do we owe you?" John asked. "How are we supposed to pay for saving your life?"

A slight pause. "Don't try to turn this around. Frank would be here if it weren't for you. I'd have a full hand and I could have gone out there to fight for our country. Come to think of it, if I'd gone, I could have shot you over there instead."

"Many tried," John said, rolling his eyes upward, pausing at the ceiling in an exaggerated way.

That was for Jerry's benefit, and his heart constricted, realizing his brother's intention. There had to be a better way. There had to be. He mouthed a no, but John never saw it.

In that moment, Willoughby shoved Adele to the side and fired off a shot, but John was already ducking, rushing at Willoughby. Adele dashed out of the way just as Willoughby raised the butt of his pistol and brought it down on the back of John's neck. John dropped like a stone.

Without a second thought, Jerry leapt forward, one hand on his gun and the other reaching for the back of Willoughby's coat, yanking hard to throw him off balance. He was heavy, and he fell with a thud.

Adele stood trembling against the wall, frozen, and Jerry reached for her hand. "Get out of here, Adele. Right now. For our child's sake."

She took off running, and from the sound of her breathing he could tell she had made it to the bottom of the shaft. He turned to check on her, and in that split second, Willoughby rose and went for Jerry like a steam engine, bowling him onto his back, closer to the shaft. His hands closed around Jerry's throat, and his knees slammed down onto Jerry's wrists, freeing his gun. It all happened so fast. Jerry was aware of the pressure, of the thumbs cutting into his neck, and he gasped for breath, struggling against Willoughby's hands as spots began to appear in his vision. Then all at once the weight was gone, and Jerry gasped in air.

Wheezing, he staggered to his feet. John had drawn Willoughby deeper into the tunnel, toward the storage room, where he'd be trapped. The two big men were tussling over a gun, the meaty sound of fists on flesh traveling through the earthen walls. Jerry blinked to clear the lingering spots in his vision and found his gun, lying a few feet from where he'd fallen. He scooped it up, but before he could aim, a gunshot cracked through the air.

For a moment, neither Willoughby nor John moved. Then John looked down, an expression of disbelief on his face, and Jerry saw the bloom of blood that was opening fast on his brother's chest.

A second later, John locked eyes with Jerry. And he smiled.

And Jerry suddenly knew exactly what his brother was going to do.

"No!" he screamed.

Willoughby spun back toward Jerry, his gun pointed directly at his chest. He wouldn't have missed this time, but John changed all that. With a triumphant shout, he grabbed the beam that connected most of the ceiling—the one he had warned Adele never to touch—and using all his might, he hauled it down. There was a hideous *crack!* like frozen river ice breaking apart. Before Willoughby could even think of pulling the trigger, the world collapsed in a roar, dousing the lights, and throwing Jerry back into the tunnels of Belgium. Except this time the earth didn't fall on him. It thundered down in a solid wall, knocking him back under the shaft and choking him with dust, but letting him walk free.

John had made sure Jerry was clear before he'd done the unthinkable. Darkness.

Silence, broken only by a loose rock trickling down the devastation and Jerry's thundering pulse.

"John," he whispered into the blackness. No one answered.

Struggling to breathe, Jerry stood and reached out both arms to brace himself between the walls, knowing the paths he and John had dug, side by side, brother by brother. He took only three steps before his boot hit a solid wall of dirt. He could go no farther. Thirty feet of earth had crushed the tunnel, the storage room, and the two men within.

"John!" he cried desperately, but there was never a chance he'd hear his brother's voice again. "John!"

On his hands and knees, he began to dig, sobbing as he clawed through the dirt. His hands were useless against the infinite earth. A thousand shovels could not have reached John in time. But how could Jerry stop? How could he let his brother go?

The earth had finally come down. It hadn't taken a hundred thousand boots after all. Just one brave man and a promise to keep his brother safe.

epilogue
CASSIE

❧

— Present Day —

From the corner of her eye, Cassie watched Matthew peer out the window of her car, looking intrigued but slightly uncomfortable, squeezed into her tiny Prelude. The sight made her smile.

"Where are you taking me?" he asked, not looking the least bit put off.

"It's a surprise," Cassie replied coyly.

"Haven't we had enough surprises lately?" he teased, his brown eyes warm. "At least tell me that wherever we're going there's food."

She nodded. "You won't be disappointed, Mr. Flaherty."

She'd decided to take him to the Dominion House Tavern for supper, to thank him for everything. Especially considering everything that had happened over the past few weeks. So really, to thank him and to celebrate. And as a Flaherty, she thought he'd appreciate the Irish pub, as well as the history behind it.

After discovering the skeleton buried in the sinkhole behind the barn, Cassie had reached out to a professional team of archaeologists so they could excavate the site and confirm Cassie and Matthew's suspicions that it could have been a tunnel or even a hidden storage room for the Bailey brothers. Mrs. Allen had been overwhelmed with excitement with everything that was happening, and Cassie had actually feared for her heart when Matthew suggested he would take time off his renovations so she could take what she wanted from the house and use it to expand on the museum's Prohibition exhibit.

"You've been amazing about all this hassle," Cassie said. "You haven't had a day alone there since you found that skeleton. I bet you're sorry."

"Not at all. I told you that day you came to the house that I think history's important to learn. Too many people thinking about the 'now' and not the 'then.' Plus it's exciting. I never thought I'd be in the middle of an archaeological dig."

"Well, thank you for not getting angry at me for hiding my connection to your house. I don't know why I didn't just say it up front."

"You didn't know me. I wouldn't have expected you to tell me anything, so there's no apology needed. Actually, it makes the house even more special, knowing that one of the owner's descendants is literally walking in it." His mouth twisted to the side a bit. "I should probably tell you something too, since we're sharing family secrets. I told you that my dad and I used to work in construction. He's the one who showed me the satisfaction that comes from rebuilding old houses. He'd love what I'm doing now. Anyway, a few months before he died, we had a fight over something stupid. I don't even remember what it was anymore, but I reacted by leaving home without a word and heading to the oil rigs. After a while, I thought about coming back, tail tucked between my legs, but my pride got in the way." His gaze travelled to the window. "I wasn't there when he died. He never knew how sorry I was in the end." He cleared his throat. "So there's my guilty secret."

Cassie kept her eyes straight ahead, trying to keep her expression neutral. "I'm so sorry, Matthew." How alone he must have felt. She knew that kind of loneliness. "I bet he knew you were sorry."

"Maybe. My mom always said I got my stubbornness from him."

"You know you can't blame yourself, right? His death wasn't your fault."

He hung his head. "That's what people say."

"So then you came all the way to Windsor? Why here?"

"I remembered him saying something when I was a kid about a second cousin twice removed living here once upon a time. He always said he'd like to come here someday."

"You came here for him." She looked over at him. "You're working on that house as a tribute to him, aren't you?"

He shrugged lightly. "I guess I am."

"And now you're rebuilding your life and a house at the same time."

His smile returned. "Yeah, and I was doing fine with that until I found that bottle, then you showed up talking about legends and smugglers."

She laughed. "I messed up your plan, didn't I?"

"You did," he said, but he was smiling, showing those deep laugh lines around his mouth.

"Should I be sorry?" she asked.

"I'm not," he replied, and a warm tickle of nerves fluttered in her chest.

For so long, Cassie had blamed herself for her mother's death, and with that guilt had come the belief that she'd caused her own loneliness. That she deserved it. But then Matthew had walked through the museum doors, and being around him was changing her. She could feel herself coming more alive every day, just like the old house. Maybe she'd been wrong. Maybe it wasn't really her destiny to be alone.

"I'm thinking of stripping some of the wallpaper and painting a couple of highlight walls in the house," he said, changing the subject. "Kind of updating on a small scale."

"You think people would prefer updates to the original when you're selling?"

He looked shocked that she would even ask that. "Who's selling?"

Relief rushed through her. "I'm glad to hear that."

"So as I was saying, for wall colours, what do you think of a light green in the living room, to complement your great-grandmother's awful sage cupboards?"

She laughed. "They're not that awful." She pulled into a parking spot near the Dominion House Tavern and turned to him. "Ready to go back in time?"

The pub was one of her favourite places in the city, even when it was crowded with university students. She could hardly blame them. The furniture might be worn down, but the old white house oozed history and smelled like comfort food. Cassie and Matthew grabbed one of the booths, then they both ordered a beer and a burger. He added extra fried onions to his.

Looking around appreciatively, he said, "So this is where Jeremiah and John swigged whisky, eh?"

"Here and a lot of other places. Before the food gets here, I wanted to show you something," she said, then she reached into her bag and pulled out her precious family scrapbook, along with a clean white cloth. She set the cloth over the table, placed the leather-bound book on it, and slid it across the table to him. "This is the story of the Baileys."

He looked at her, eyes bright, then carefully opened the book. "This is incredible," he breathed after a moment, taking in her work. "You did this?"

She beamed, pointing at the first photograph. "Those are my great-great-grandparents, Robert and Elizabeth."

He leaned in. "That's my house when it was being built," he said. His finger traced the familiar door, the windows. "This is amazing."

She flipped the page. "And this is the infamous Jeremiah with his brother, John, just before they went to World War I."

"They don't look so tough."

"This is Jeremiah afterward. Looking a little tougher now? He got his scars in an accident in the tunnel."

Matthew studied the cool, serious face of Jeremiah, then he turned back to the earlier photo, before the war. He looked directly at Cassie, fascinated. "Did you know that you look like a female version of Jeremiah? I mean, give or take a hundred years, you could be twins." He jabbed a finger at Jeremiah's brow. "That's the same look you get when you're focused on something."

"That's what my grandmother Alice always used to say." She drew his attention to a photo of a woman in uniform. "This is Jeremiah's wife, Adele Savard."

"I stand corrected," he said. "You might look like Jeremiah when you're serious, but that smile is pure Adele. Wow. DNA is amazing."

She glowed, hearing the affection in his voice. "Adele was an incredibly brave woman. She served as a Canadian nurse in World War I. They were called Bluebirds because of the colour of their uniforms. Apparently, she and Jeremiah met in a field hospital. He was so taken with her that he put a bird on his whisky label to honour her."

Matthew raised an eyebrow. "She's a brave woman to get involved with rumrunners, but I suppose she'd seen it all during the war."

She showed him a small newspaper announcement featuring a photo of a smiling young woman with an older gentleman in a white coat. "This is one of my favourite articles."

MEDICAL CLINIC ANNOUNCES IT IS READY FOR BATTLE!

Dr. Wesley Knowles is pleased to announce that Nurse Adele Savard has been hired to work with him at his medical clinic on Sandwich Street. Nurse Savard, with her captivating blond hair and piercing blue eyes, comes to the clinic with a surplus of medical experience, having recently returned from her position as a Canadian Nursing Sister at a Clearance

Station Hospital in Belgium. This reporter is looking forward to his next visit!

The next page included the newspaper articles Cassie had found about the Bailey brothers and their rival, Ernie Willoughby. At the bottom of the page was John's death certificate, which Mrs. Allen had uncovered after a bit of searching through the city archives. For a few moments, she and Matthew were silent, reading between the lines of the newsprint, filling the gaps with the new information they'd found in the tunnel.

When Matthew had first dug up the skeleton, Cassie had assumed it belonged to Ernie Willoughby, since she'd just been researching the missing gangster at the museum. She suspected the worst, thinking that her wild ancestor John Bailey had stooped to murder over the raiding of his warehouse and ruination of his business. Then the archaeologists dug deeper and found evidence of a second body—as well as bullet fragments. After a few days, they uncovered what they believed to be a storage room, filled with broken green bottles. To Cassie, it felt as if the last puzzle piece was sliding into place.

Given the violence of the day, the documented rivalry between Willoughby and the latter's disappearance, and her grandmother's stories, a shootout seemed the likely explanation for what they'd found. During her research, Cassie had been so focused on Jeremiah that she'd never really paid attention to the fact that John had died the same year the business went bust. If John and Willoughby had both died in that tunnel, it explained why the business had ended so abruptly. She became convinced that the second body belonged to John, and she'd submitted her own DNA to test against his remains, just in case.

But that was all she could find out about the mysterious Bailey boys. The rest was lost to time.

"It must have torn Jeremiah apart to lose John," Cassie said. "If only they'd quit even one day earlier."

Matthew looked thoughtful. "I wonder if that's why he boarded up the wall with those bottles. Grief, regret, probably guilt."

"My grandmother Alice said that her father rarely spoke of his brother. But his firstborn son was named Johnny. That tells me they were very close. Too close for Jeremiah to talk about." She flipped to the next page in the album. The photo was a casual family scene outdoors, taken on a warm summer day. It was interesting to see the past mixed in with the present in this photo, because Adele was sitting on the very porch Matthew had recently rebuilt. On her lap she balanced a tiny girl with black ringlets. Jeremiah stood nearby in a white shirt with the sleeves rolled up, wearing casual trousers and suspenders, with two young boys on either side.

Cassie pointed at the taller of the boys. "That's Johnny." Her finger slid to the other son. "This is Edward, but everyone called him Teddy. And this little girl on Adele's lap is my grandmother, Alice. She was a surprise, I think, coming along eight years after Teddy."

The next page featured the formal photographs of Johnny and Teddy Bailey, both with matching silver-grey eyes, both in military uniform. "They never came home," Cassie said softly.

He whistled quietly. "Jeremiah and Adele lived through the First World War and everything else, then lost their sons in the next one. And his brother in between. I can't even imagine how that must have hurt."

"Alice was Jeremiah and Adele's only surviving child. She told me she sometimes heard stories from relatives and family friends, talking about Bailey Brothers' Best and the rowdy age of Prohibition. She loved hearing about her heroic mother, stitching up rumrunners on the kitchen table. She said that she remembered seeing her parents dance in their living room, and that even as a little girl she could feel the love between them." Cassie moved through a few more pages, the photographs jumping decades. "Here she is with my mother, and that's me in her arms."

"Cute baby," Matthew said.

"My dad took the photo—it was a couple of years before he got sick. That's probably the last photo of us all together and happy."

"What happened?"

"My mother never recovered after Dad died. And about a year after that, my grandmother passed suddenly from a stroke. Mom loved me, and she meant well, but her heart was broken. Sometimes she spent days in bed, depressed. And sometimes she drank more than she should have.

"Then one day, when I was ten, she got really drunk. She started following me around, wanting to hug me, I guess, but I ran ahead and she fell down the stairs trying to catch me. She died." Cassie hesitated, the brakes in her heart slamming hard as they always did when she thought about what had happened. Then she looked at Matthew, seeing understanding and encouragement in his dark eyes, and realized it was all right to share the pain. "You remember that first day I came to see you at the house and I ran out like it was on fire? That was the first time I'd been there since she died. All the memories flooded back."

He listened quietly, giving her room to speak. "I'm sorry that happened to you, Cassie. You never deserved any of it." Then he reached for her hand and held it between his own. "Someone very wise recently told me that I shouldn't blame myself for my dad's death. I'm not all that wise, but I hope you know you never deserved any of that sadness. And none of it was your fault."

She took a shaky breath, waiting for the grief, but there was something about the strength of his hands that took all that away. She felt warm inside. And safe.

"So that's my story. I'm the last Bailey."

"It's your ancestors' story," Matthew clarified. "Yours is your own."

Their burgers arrived then, so she set the book aside and they dug in. As soon as she was done, Cassie took a swig of her beer, preparing to give Matthew the good news.

"I'm glad you're not going to sell the house," she said.

"Yeah, it's going to be tight, paying for everything when I finally get back to the renovations, but I really like the old place. Especially now that I know the stories behind it."

"Well, I thought you might be interested to hear that I have an auction house interested in your forty-two wonderful, full bottles of Bailey Brothers' Best whisky." She paused for effect. "Matthew, they believe each bottle could sell for up to five hundred dollars. In a few weeks, you could be twenty thousand dollars richer."

He shook his head in astonishment. "That's amazing! That will more than cover it." He looked toward the bar. "Do you think they have champagne?"

Cassie grinned. "Don't you think we ought to celebrate with whisky instead?"

When their glasses arrived, they looked at each other for a couple of moments, neither of them saying anything, then Matthew raised his and clinked it softly against hers.

"Cheers," he said, and this time, she knew she wasn't imagining the tenderness in his eyes.

She took a sip then swirled her glass. "I've been thinking about how you and I got to this point. A buried treasure, a century-old murder, and now here we are, sipping whisky."

"Sounds like a happy ending," he said.

"To me, it sounds like the story's just getting good," she replied with a wink.

He beamed. "I would definitely drink to that."

Smiling, she took another drink of her whisky. Once upon a time, the shelves behind the bar would have carried bottles of her great-grandfather's whisky, and flappers and bootleggers would have lined up to enjoy them. The labels, she knew, had said **Bailey Brothers' Best**, the simple words bold and just a little bit cocky, as a tunneller would have had to be in order to survive. And above those words flew a dear little bluebird, healing their wounds, guiding them out of the darkness, and helping them live again.

Bailey-Savard Family Tree

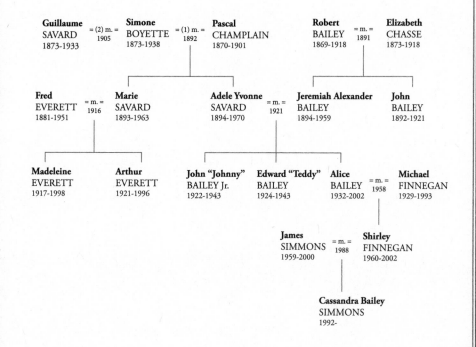

Guillaume = (2) m. = **Simone** = (1) m. = **Pascal**   **Robert** = m. = **Elizabeth**
SAVARD   1905   BOYETTE   1892   CHAMPLAIN   BAILEY   1891   CHASSE
1873-1933   1873-1938   1870-1901   1869-1918   1873-1918

Fred = m. = **Marie**   **Adele Yvonne** = m. = **Jeremiah Alexander**   **John**
EVERETT   1916   SAVARD   SAVARD   1921   BAILEY   BAILEY
1881-1951   1893-1963   1894-1970   1894-1959   1892-1921

Madeleine   **Arthur**   **John "Johnny"**   **Edward "Teddy"**   **Alice** = m. = **Michael**
EVERETT   EVERETT   BAILEY Jr.   BAILEY   BAILEY   1958   FINNEGAN
1917-1998   1921-1996   1922-1943   1924-1943   1932-2002   1929-1993

James = m. = **Shirley**
SIMMONS   1988   FINNEGAN
1959-2000   1960-2002

Cassandra Bailey
SIMMONS
1992-

A Note to Readers

Ever since I began writing Canadian historical fiction, readers have suggested I write about the Roaring Twenties and Prohibition. In the Maritimes where I live, there was a lot of rum-running, and everybody seems to know somebody who did it. I thought about the subject again when I was in the Crowsnest Pass, Alberta, researching my book *At the Mountain's Edge* and came across the story of Emilio Picariello and Filumena Lassandro, a pair of bootleggers charged with the murder of Alberta Provincial Police Constable Stephen Lawson on September 21, 1922. With so much research laid out in front of me, I did plan to write about the subject at one point. Then two things happened that made me realize there was no time like the present to dive into that story.

The first was an article in the *New York Post* about a couple in Ames, New York, who had just purchased a 105-year-old house that had been built by a bootlegger. During their renovations, they were removing some rotten outdoor trim when an old package wrapped in straw, paper, and string toppled out of the broken wall. I cannot imagine how their pulses must have raced, unwrapping the mysterious package and finding six bottles of Old Smuggler whisky from 1923. Turns out the entire outside wall was packed with bottles, as was a spot under the floorboards in the mudroom.

The second was the Netflix series *Peaky Blinders*, of which I've become a huge fan over the last few years. The violent, but visually stunning series focuses on a post–World War I crime family in England who navigates underground schemes and battles, vicious turf wars over gambling and the alcohol trade, crooked cops and politicians, and the general social movement of the often chaotic, extravagant Roaring Twenties. The family's leader, Tommy Shelby (played by actor Cillian Murphy), is who I envisioned in my head whenever I wrote about Jerry. He is brilliant and unafraid of death, but he is also suffering from shell shock (PTSD) following his years as a tunneller. He is only able to find solace in the arms of his wife, Grace, who provided my vision of Adele. While the scenes in the television show are extreme, they inspired me to finally put pen to paper about Canada's own rich drama from this era. What an exciting catalyst!

As with every one of my books, I began my research by learning the five W's of the historical period, trying to capture a black-and-white snapshot of Prohibition. I was fascinated by the "Who." The men and women of the Roaring Twenties had already lived through so much. The Great War—the greatest conflict the world had ever known, with over forty million casualties, half of those being deaths—was still in their rearview mirror when a new enemy reared its head: the Spanish Flu. Estimated to have killed between twenty and fifty million people, the disease decimated a world already reeling from the aftermath of war. Imagine trying to pick up the pieces after all that! But humanity, however diminished, was determined to survive, no matter the conflict. The dead must be buried and mourned, but then life must be lived. I knew I couldn't write about Prohibition without exploring the men and women of the Great War. And since I was writing in the middle of a pandemic, it only seemed appropriate to touch on the Spanish Flu.

I mentioned above that the character of Grace in *Peaky Blinders* inspired the face of Adele in this book, but Adele's actual character was very different. The only parallel is that both represent the progress of women in that time period. Grace might have been an undercover detective, but to me, Adele was the one with the courage. Canadian women have always served in times of war. During the First World War, daughters, sisters, mothers, aunts, grandmothers, and friends mostly supported the war effort from the homefront: rationing, buying war bonds, and join-ing the workforce, filling the civilian roles in industry and manufactur-ing that the men had left behind. That's in addition to raising children and running their own homes. But the only *overseas* position available to Canadian women during the Great War was as a nurse. The original Nursing Sisters were nuns; however, as the conflict dragged on, it became obvious that superior nursing skills were more necessary than a religious affiliation, and so that requirement was eliminated, and in January 1915, the call went out for nurses interested in serving in the war. Over 2,000 Canadian women eagerly applied for seventy-five positions. Those suc-cessful at securing an interview brought with them their graduate nurse's certificate, which was an endorsement of their character and skills, and hearts full of compassion. For the hundreds of thousands of men suffer-ing in battle, one was almost as essential as the other.

To be eligible for the Canadian Army Medical Corps (C.A.M.C.), the nurses were required to have British citizenship, high moral charac-ter, physical fitness, and be between the ages of twenty-one and thirty-eight. With few exceptions, most were unmarried and once given the official rank of lieutenant, they were readily accepted into the British In-ternational Nursing Corps, Queen Alexandra's Imperial Military Nurs-ing Services, or the various branches of the Red Cross, where they found themselves at bedsides across England, in the coastal resort towns and villages of Belgium, and on Mediterranean islands. Four even ended up in Russia in the middle of a revolution. Many paid for their own travel arrangements, and they remained at their destinations for the duration of the war. The only acceptable excuses to leave were personal illness, "daughterly duties," such as death or illness in the family, and matrimony.

The C.A.M.C. nurses were nicknamed "Bluebirds" early on for their distinctive, robin's-egg blue dresses and white veils. To the wounded in cots, the bright colour gave the nurses the look of "ministering angels." To the Imperial and Red Cross nurses who were assigned a dull grey uniform, the blue was a source of envy—as was the fact that the Canadian nurses were permitted to attend military social events and dances with fellow officers while the British nurses were not. At such events, the Bluebirds wore a dress uniform, which was a darker blue, with two rows of brass buttons, the two stars of a lieutenant, a scarlet-lined cape, and a brimmed hat.

I found it interesting that nurses of the C.A.M.C. worked for $4.10 per day, and their positions came with paid room and board amounting to about $2.60 per day. In comparison, the men fighting and dying on the front lines made about $1.10 a day. My only thought was that perhaps the government expected the women to survive the war and therefore be able to use the money. But not all of them did. At least fifty-eight Bluebirds died over the duration of the war from enemy fire, disease, or drowning, including the fourteen aboard the *Llandovery Castle*. Two C.A.M.C. hospitals in Europe were bombed in 1918, killing three people and burying two nurses under rubble. When you read about Adele and her friends racing into the hospital tent under shellfire, you were seeing my version of the true story of Eleanor Thompson and Meta Hodge, two Canadian nurses who, despite having been struck by a falling beam, dug themselves out then raced through the hospital, putting out fires, turning over coal heaters to prevent patients' beds from catching fire, and evacuating patients. They only stopped because they lost consciousness due to their injuries. They were later honoured by becoming two of the nine Canadian nurses awarded the Military Medal for Gallantry.

When the Bluebirds returned from the war, they were celebrated at soirées and receptions where they told their stories and enthralled listeners, but that was all. During my research, I found very few quotes from them, though there were a few secondary sources. In 1920, Margaret Macdonald, the wartime Matron-in-Chief of the C.A.M.C. Nursing Service, reached out to all the Bluebirds and asked them to recount their experiences or share a "characteristic incident, a telling photograph, or authentic circumstance of historical value that came under [her] personal observation." Out of thousands of nurses, she received eight responses. Over the years, a few of them did write their own memoirs, including

Humour in Tragedy: Hospital Life behind 3 Front's [sic] by a Canadian Nursing Sister Illustrated with 64 Very Original Pen & Ink Sketches by the Author by Constance Bruce, but even then, those obscure published works were considered a lighter "peep behind the scenes," as Lord Beaverbrook wrote in his introduction for Constance's book.

With all the books, museum exhibits, memorials, movies, essays, websites, and more dedicated to sharing the stories of the First World War, I wondered why we know so little about these courageous women. Was it due to their small numbers? Perhaps their gender? Or was it something else entirely? Could it be that these women, having been raised and trained to be modest, unassuming "angels of mercy," felt their stories were private, personal experiences to be kept between them and their charges? Or maybe they, like the broken men in their care, still craved the silence that had been so absent during the chaos.

Writing about the attention given to Florence Nightingale of the Voluntary Aid Detachment and to the larks referenced in Lieutenant-Colonel John McCrae's poem "In Flanders Field," Canadian historian Susan Mann notes that when it comes to the war, larks and nightingales fly high in people's consciousness. She asks, why then, are the Bluebirds left behind? Every Remembrance Day, we remember the terrible sacrifice made by the men who fought in the Great War on behalf of future generations. On a rare occasion, a wreath might be placed in honour of Canada's Nursing Sisters. At the Canadian National Museum of Civilization in Ottawa, they appear in a few paintings, and they are quietly memorialized on occasional war memorials in bronze, marble, brass, stone, or in photographs. It's only in the past twenty years that their records have been publicized. I hope *Bluebird* will help shed a little light on these courageous women.

As with all my novels, I needed a partner for my leading lady who was as equally important to history but perhaps in a role that was not as well-known as some. I knew he would be a soldier, one of the 630,000 Canadian men who served, and he would meet Adele because of a grave injury. Quite by accident, I discovered the Canadian Tunnelling Companies, of which there were three, and while there is lots of information about the tunnelling companies from Britain, Australia, and New Zealand, there was significantly less about the Canadian tunnellers. The majority of tunnellers were chosen because of their experience as miners, mining engineers, and geologists, but I took a little creative license making Jerry Bailey an aspiring accountant instead to suit my larger story about Prohibition.

When we think of World War I warfare, our minds often go to the trenches, which, by late 1914, ran all the way from the Belgian coast to the Swiss frontier. The opposing forces dug into place, creating a violent standoff, and to break it, both sides employed tunnellers. Referred to as clay-kickers, moles, and other derogatory terms, these men were tasked with digging long, narrow tunnels in the clay soil underneath the trenches where they would plant mines, destroying the trenches completely and hopefully giving an advantage to their allies battling above them.

Of course, the key to successful tunnelling was silence. To avoid detection, the men used a specific technique. Deep beneath the surface, in a cold, dark, narrow space often filled knee-deep with water, the digger lay on his back, braced against a wooden cross, and pushed the clay—he couldn't kick it because that could make noise—with his shovel. The thick earth he loosened was placed in a bag by a second man, who handed it on to another man responsible for taking it to the surface to be wheeled away. It was all done by the light of a candle. With them, the men usually had a canary or mouse in a cage, the only indicators of whether they'd run out of oxygen. Hopefully, they would notice in time.

The soldiers in the trenches were uncomfortably aware of the subterranean threat and had their own ways of detecting the tunnellers, though I imagine they might not have been very effective considering all the noise of battle going on. The first was to drive a rod into the dirt, then put the other end between their teeth to feel for underground vibrations. For the second method, the men in the trench sank a water-filled oil drum into the floor then took turns placing one ear in the water to listen for any sounds made by the tunnellers.

Digging a tunnel could take months, but the strategy was effective at turning the tides of war. The most famous example of tunneller warfare was the Battle of Messines on June 7, 1917. By that point in the war, there were thirty Tunnelling Companies in the British Expeditionary Force alone—more than 25,000 men—and after a year of digging under the German trenches at Messines Ridge in Belgium, they were ready to complete their mission. The evening before the attack, the British commander said to his men, "Gentlemen, we may not make history tomorrow, but we shall certainly change the geography." In the morning, more than one hundred feet beneath the surface, the British forces detonated six hundred tons of explosives, destroying the German trench entirely and creating one of the largest non-nuclear explosions the world has ever seen. The reverberations were felt all the way to London. About ten thousand Germans died that day, and thousands more were captured in a state of shell shock.

Now on to Prohibition, where Jerry and John and so many others took risks and banked on making big money. The Temperance movement, a social campaign that had risen to prominence, claimed drinking alcohol was both unhealthy and immoral, and it blamed booze for all of society's problems, including poverty, abandoned and abused women, broken families, and increased criminality, not to mention mental illness. The group had been working toward the goal of Prohibition for decades, calling for moderation or total abstinence from liquor. The push against alcohol even shows up in 1842 in a children's verse:

> *Touch not the foaming, tempting glass*
> *Nor look upon the wine!*
> *A serpent vile is hid within*
> *The liquid of the vine.*

In 1878, the Canada Temperance Act moved their efforts ahead a little by giving local governments the option to ban the sale of alcohol, but it wasn't until 1900 that Prince Edward Island became the first province to go fully "dry." The rest of Canada, including the Yukon and Newfoundland, eventually followed suit, though they all had different rules regarding sale and consumption. In 1918, the federal government introduced national Prohibition, banning the importation of alcohol of more than 2.5 per cent, any inter-provincial trade of alcohol, and all production. Most provinces repealed Prohibition, "the noble experiment," throughout the 1920s.

But in the U.S., Prohibition laws were much stricter and lasted much longer. In 1918, the state of Michigan went dry, followed by the rest of the United States in 1920, and wouldn't be lifted until 1933. And for all those Canadian distillers, the party had just begun.

The overall result of Prohibition was that drinkers and manufacturers went underground, and individual illegal stills ("distillers") popped up all over the country. As the infamous Chicago gangster Al Capone said, "Prohibition has made nothing but trouble."

Needless to say, when Adele and Jerry arrived home in Windsor from war, they found that the quiet city they remembered had changed. Not just the buildings and the commerce, but the people themselves. And where once there had been a focus on industry and etiquette, now there was stubborn resolve, and for many, a sense of adventure and opportunity—particularly when it came to the smuggling of liquor across the Detroit River.

Rum-running was a busy enterprise Canada-wide, but the most active point was at the Windsor-Detroit border, or "Funnel" as it became known, and this was because of Michigan's early ban. The Canadian government charged export taxes on every bottle that crossed the Detroit River, so they generally kept quiet about how they were creating trouble (albeit legally) for their neighbours to the south. It was estimated that proceeds from liquor export taxes during the Roaring Twenties amounted to 20 per cent of all government revenue in Canada. In 1929 alone, the export tax on alcohol brought in twice as much revenue as the income tax.

The Prohibition era is famous for a lot of things, but to me, the story of the Roaring Twenties is about the colourful characters and the ways they changed the rules. In those days, warehouses and docks stockpiled with liquor lined the Detroit River on both sides all the way from Lake St. Clair to Amherstburg, and hundreds of boats designed for smuggling booze bobbed on the water. A rail line serviced the warehouses, carrying the liquor directly to the wharves for loading. One smart business owner, Vital Benoit, extended Windsor's streetcar tracks directly to his establishment, Chateau LaSalle, specifically for pickup and delivery of alcohol. Since booze wasn't yet allowed to be sold in restaurants or taverns, owners became creative, relabelling their establishments as speakeasies or blind pigs where customers were charged for food or entertainment, then provided with complimentary alcohol. Sometimes, these establishments were also hotbeds of gambling and prostitution. Anyone with skin in the game, like Ernie Willoughby, knew a large segment of the police could be bribed with cash and free drinks just for looking the other way.

Roy Greenaway, crime reporter for the *Toronto Daily Star* at the time, claimed more than a thousand cases of liquor crossed the Detroit River into the U.S. every day during Prohibition. When he interviewed Al Capone—also known as Scarface because of the three carved lines in his cheek—he asked about his Canadian connections. In response, the smooth-talking bootlegger claimed, "I don't even know what street Canada is on!" Greenaway soon partnered up with "The Fighting Pastor," Leslie Spracklin, certain that the fire and brimstone preaching pastor of Sandwich's Methodist church would be a gold mine for stories. He was right. With his Colt 45 on his hip, Pastor Spracklin raged against the open debauch of alcohol from his pulpit while his goons searched his congregation's cars for booze. He was twice charged with the 1920 murder of Beverley "Babe" Trumble, his childhood rival and the owner of the infamous Chappell House Tavern. Despite all the evidence, Spracklin was found not guilty both times.

Within a few years, the violence became unstoppable on both sides of the border. From across the river, the Purple Gang, an ever-expanding group of vicious mobsters with roots in the city's Jewish community, ruthlessly hijacked shipments, not the least bit concerned about killing to get what they wanted. They had such a terrifying reputation that Al Capone used them as a supplier rather than compete with them. In Windsor, Harry Low, an auto industry machinist turned pool hall owner, supplied the Purple Gang, as did Blaise Diesbourg, a self-named character called King Canada. Unfortunately for King Canada, the only thing he did better than make money was spend it, and he died penniless.

The newspaper headlines were filled with stories of gangsters all fighting for a piece of the Prohibition pie. Bloody turf wars between the Sugarhouse Gang, the Westside Mob, and the Vitale gang filled the pages of the Detroit press with murder and mayhem. The Little Jewish Navy openly attacked the police's cleanup operations on the lakes and rivers. Some runners even fixed a cannon to the bows of their vessels and turned the game around, giving chase to the police. And while the police force did what they could to patrol the illegal goings-on—only approximately 5 per cent of the total amount manufactured was ever confiscated—the local cops knew who was selling alcohol, and they were divided in their loyalties. They were constantly being offered bribes to either protect hidden stills or cast a blind eye to any sort of liquor-related activities, and it would have had to be a stubbornly moral man who refused: as Jerry said, a constable who might usually take home $600 a month could earn ten times that just for looking the other way. Jacques Paul Couturier, author of *Prohibition or Regulation? The Enforcement of the Canada Temperance Act in Moncton, 1881–1896*, summed it up as: "relations between members of the police force and the liquor community were fluid," and the bribes covered all branches of the law, including prosecutors and judges.

By the late 1920s, the obsession with gambling taking place in the speakeasies and dens of ill repute spilled over to Wall Street. Everyone who could, whether they were rich or poor, invested their savings into stocks. When the market crashed on October 29, 1929, it threw the country into the Great Depression. By then, Prohibition had lifted in most of Canada, but as much as people really would have needed a drink to take the edge off, very few people could afford a drop.

The abundance of historical treasures during this unique moment in time provided a rich backdrop for my novel, and I included as many historical places as I could. Abars, Dominion Tavern, Chappell House, and Edgewater were all real establishments, as was the infamous Edgewater Thomas owner, Bertha Thomas. Riverside Inn is based on Shore Acres, which I wanted to include because it was so popular among the "right people," but it was actually being used as a hospital in 1921. Sadly, most of these old landmarks are gone now, erasing any evidence of the secret passages and trapdoors these daring, reckless bootleggers built. One of the last of the big speakeasies in Windsor, Chappell House, suffered a devastating fire in 2006 and was demolished soon after. The Dominion House, Dutchie's favourite watering hole, is alive and well.

Also true and fascinating were the tales Adele, Jerry, and Cassie recalled about the inventive methods the rumrunners used. Yes, even the one about the man crossing the frozen river with two dozen eggs, all filled with whisky! Fabulous little details like these, as well as the incredible stories of our war veterans—including the Bluebirds—captured my imagination and inspired me to write this book. As the world found its way back into the light after the dark ages of the Great War, so did its people, and they did it in the most courageous and ingenious ways.

Unlike Cassie, I am not a real historian, but I am so grateful to those who are, and who have devoted their lives to researching moments in the past. It is only through their dedication and passion that I can do what I do, which is to bring those moments home to you.

Sources

The following publications are just a few of the many that provided factual information about the story's time and place and the people involved.

BOOKS

Francis, Daniel. *Closing Time: Prohibition, Rum-Runners, and Border Wars*. Vancouver, BC: Douglas & McIntyre, 2014.

Gervais, Marty. *The Rumrunners: A Prohibition Scrapbook*. Windsor, ON: Biblioasis, 2011.

Hunt, C. W. *Whisky and Ice: The Saga of Ben Kerr, Canada's Most Daring Rumrunner*. Toronto, ON: Dundurn Press, 1996.

Quinn, Shawna M. *Agnes Warner and the Nursing Sisters of the Great War*. Fredericton, NB: Goose Lane Editions, 2010.

Schneider, Stephen. *Iced: The Story of Organized Crime in Canada*. New York, NY: Wiley, 2009.

ARTICLES

Mann, Susan. "Where Have All the Bluebirds Gone? On the Trail of Canada's Military Nurses, 1914–1918." *Atlantis: Critical Studies in Gender, Culture, and Social Justice* 26, no. 1 (2001).

Rosenberg, Zoe. "Couple Discovers Walls of Whiskey Hidden in 'Bootlegger Bungalow' Upstate." *New York Post*. October 29, 2020. https://nypost.com/2020/10/29/upstate-ny-couple-discovers-whiskey-hidden-in-bootlegger-bungalow/.

FILM

Watts, J. P., dir. *The War Below*. 2021; Norcross, GA: Vital Pictures.

BLUEBIRD

GENEVIEVE GRAHAM

A Reading Group Guide

Topics & Questions for Discussion

1. The novel follows Adele Savard, a World War I Nursing Sister working at a Clearing Station in war-torn Belgium. Had you known about the history of the Bluebirds before this book?

2. The Bluebirds were in the war in a dual capacity as medical workers and caring citizens. What are some examples of how Adele fulfills these duties? And what does the need for compassion as much as medical training reveal about the nature of war? Consider the fact that Adele—and many nurses—had no idea of what they would see overseas.

3. The horrors of trench warfare are often discussed in relation to World War I. In *Bluebird*, the author shines a light on tunnel warfare by having Jerry and John Bailey serve as tunnellers, digging beneath the trenches and setting mines. Were you aware of tunnellers and their function in the war? What are some of the dangers they faced as they waged war below the battlefields that perhaps the soldiers in the trenches did not?

4. Both Adele and Jerry's fathers served in the Boer War, but the Great War was the first war to be fought on the global stage. In its wake, nearly everyone suffers from shell shock, or PTSD. Discuss how the scale of the death and devastation haunts the characters after peace is reached.

5. Similarly, how is personal trauma a theme in the novel? Consider what each generation of the Bailey family endures, including Cassie in the present day. How do love and family help heal these wounds? And what does this tell us about the strength of the human spirit?

6. Matthew tells Cassie that "these days we live in the 'now' so much that we kind of forget the world was full of stories long before we came along." How do the past and present storylines intersect over the course of the novel? What does this technique highlight about the legacy of history for both the personal and the public record?

7. When Adele and Jerry return home to Windsor, they find a city changed by the dawn of Prohibition. How do the losses they faced in the war and the subsequent Spanish Flu affect the choices they make in this dazzling—and sometimes dangerous—new era? How have their values changed? What are they willing to risk in order to feel alive again? And what aren't they?

8. The Roaring Twenties boasted increased freedoms for women and men, a burgeoning of wealth and finance, and a general questioning of traditions. What are some examples of how the characters embrace these changes? Is there a difference between those who went to war and those who did not?

9. Comparing Adele and Marie, discuss the opportunities and expectations for women of the 1920s. How do marriage, children, and work shape their lives? And what do they desire for themselves deep down?

10. Marie is an avid supporter of the Temperance movement at the beginning of the novel. What is her reasoning? Do you think there is any merit in her position? Why does she later change her mind?

11. Al Capone said, "Prohibition has made nothing but trouble," and Adele says that Prohibition is a failure. What evidence do they have? Do you agree?

12. When Jerry and John find their father's distilling recipe, they decide to go into the whisky business, even though it's illegal. How do they rationalize their actions? Do you think Jerry and John are in business for the same reasons?

13. Discuss the theme of survivor's guilt. Which characters experience this and why? How do the characters try to redeem themselves?

14. Sibling relationships are at the very heart of this novel. Discuss the dynamics between Adele and Marie, and those between Jerry and John. How do the events of the book test those bonds?

15. Compare the brotherhood between Jerry and John with that of Ernie and Frank. How does loss affect who the men become?

16. The rivalry between Ernie and Jerry goes deeper than business, but knowing the formative event that shaped them, did you have greater sympathy for Ernie? Which actions can be chalked up to the heated turf wars of the day and which are rooted in personal hurt?

17. How does the ending in the past storyline bring the characters full circle? How are the themes of sacrifice, redemption, and compassion at play in that closing scene?
18. Discuss the symbolism of tunnels—and what they hide. How does the act of digging and uncovering take on different meanings in both the past and the present?
19. Consider the title, *Bluebird*. What do you think the bluebird represents?

Enhance Your Book Club

1. If you're curious about the history of the Nursing Sisters in Canada, check out the Veterans Affairs Canada website here: https://www.veterans.gc.ca/eng/remembrance/those-who-served/women-veterans/nursing-sisters
2. To find out more about Prohibition across Canada, visit *The Canadian Encyclopedia*: https://www.thecanadianencyclopedia.ca/en/article/prohibition
3. For a detailed look at rum-running in Windsor—including the famous names and places—read this article in the *Windsor Star*: https://windsorstar.com/life/from-the-vault-prohibition
4. The Amputations Association of the Great War, which came to be known as War Amps, started in 1918 in British Columbia. Find out more here: https://waramps.ca/about-us/history/
5. The little-known story of the Black sleeping car porters, all of whom were called "George," is just one detail in the struggle for Black labour rights on Canada's railways. Read more about this important chapter in history here: https://humanrights.ca/story/sleeping-car-porters

Acknowledgments

When I write, I disappear. I research so much that I become a part of the history, and I dig so deeply into how the people of the day existed, I become one of them. When I begin writing a book, I start with the history I want to understand. I read and I watch and I listen, and from those facts emerge my characters. I love my characters—even the wicked ones—and if all I had to do was follow them around and write their lives, I would be fine. I would write all day long. But the trouble is, a regular individual's life doesn't usually create much of a story. A story comes from pulling all the strings together, the most important of those being the research, the characters, the over- and underlying messages, and, of course, the plot. My plots come to me in stages, like curtains lifting one behind another, and they only make sense after I have begun to create the characters. After all, without characters, there can be no story. And if I have "become" one of the characters, I cannot possibly see the plotline before it occurs. Sadly, because of that, my approach isn't organized, and sometimes when I finish writing my first draft of a story, that becomes painfully obvious. And so, how does a story like that become something like what you just read? I'm glad you asked. Because it's so much more than just me behind the scenes, dear Reader.

When I first begin to collect information about a subject, I start at the library. A librarian will fill my arms with more books than I could possibly read in a lifetime, then they'll often volunteer to look up whatever strange author questions I might have after that. Since I write about things that happened across this country, I can't possibly visit all their physical locations, but I do want to acknowledge them here. I also want to thank those libraries who have been inviting me to speak with readers at their virtual presentations. I enjoy those events so much. They are wonderful opportunities for me to meet fascinating people and help others learn about these parts of our country's history.

Museums are obviously a research destination as well, and I have been contacting quite a few online these days. Shoutout to my friend Kaley Stewart, who helped me with my initial introduction to Cassie and the Maison François Baby House, a National Historic Site of Canada in Windsor, Ontario.

After my initial visits to the library, I am constantly online, trying to find the answers to random questions that most people would never even consider. Have you seen the joke online about how authors hope the authorities never look up their browsing history? That most definitely applies to me.

Sometimes, unexpected diamonds magically appear in my email inbox, and whether I can use them in my finished book or not, I am so honoured that the sender actually thought to send something to me. There is one in particular that I was able to use in *Bluebird*, and that came from Patricia Sinclair. She wrote to me about a Canadian soldier of the First World War, Lt. Leslie H. Miller, who returned home with oak acorns that he planted on his farm, which he subsequently named "Vimy Oaks." Nine of the original trees remain. If properly maintained, she told me, this type of oak (*Quercus robur*) will last a thousand years. I loved the idea that Jerry and John might have met Leslie along the way, and I was so glad to include the story. Thank you, Patricia.

All my readers are so important to me. The thought that you are out there holding this book and waiting for the next, possibly even preordering before it hits the stands, is astounding. I have always written my stories for me, so I can learn, but now I find I am only one of many seeking the facts of our history. Since *Tides of Honour* came out in 2015, I have written one novel every year, and to thank you all for your incredible support, I promise I will keep up that staggering rate for as long as I'm able. I am already well into work on my next book. It's going to be a good one!

Many of you accidentally happened upon one of my books in libraries (hurray again for libraries!), some might have received one as a gift, and many more discovered them in bookstores, which is still—even after ten novels—such an incredible thing for me to understand. For the books to make it onto those shelves then home with you, an experienced team of experts is required. Simon & Schuster Canada has treated me with the utmost respect and care for the past eight years and are always there when I need support. Huge thanks to my friends up here in Canada: Nita Pronovost (Vice President, Editorial Director), Shara Alexa (Director of Sales, National Accounts), Adria Iwasutiak (Vice President, Director of Publicity and Canadian Sales), Felicia Quon (Vice President, Marketing and Communications), Lorraine Kelly (Manager, Library and Special Sales), Jessica Boudreau (Designer), and the big boss, Kevin Hanson (President and Publisher). Very, *very* special thanks to the wizard of a woman who keeps me organized, Mackenzie Croft (Marketing Associate and former Publicist), and to my editor, Sarah St. Pierre...but you'll read more about her in a second. I would also like to send my sincere gratitude to two very special Simon & Schuster ladies in the U.S.: Paula Amendolara (VP Director Retail Sales) and Lexi Dumas (National Accounts Manager). I am so thrilled that Americans are looking for my books these days as well as Canadians!

As always, thank you to my literary agent, Jacques de Spoelberch, for all the things he does for me behind the scenes.

There are two more people I need to thank, and without them I never could have written this book, which I hope you love. *Bluebird* was a very special book to me. I knew it would be different from the others in mood, and over its creation it became one of my favourite stories of all. I love Adele and Jerry and John and the rest of the cast, and I love that their story became, in the end, so much more than I dreamed it could be. Its strength came from conversations I had with my editor on the phone and on Zoom, then back and forth in dozens of emails. Having Senior Editor Sarah St. Pierre as my editor is the greatest gift I could have been given, and I cannot imagine writing without her. Her depth of insight, imagination, and intelligence has not only shown me where my writing could go, it has given me the courage to go there. Thank you, Sarah. Oh, and thanks for that brilliant solution at the end, Harrison!

As with every book, my final thank you goes to my husband of almost thirty years, Dwayne. Whether it's brainstorming ideas with me in our "plot tub," calming me down at midnight when my characters are demanding attention, patiently carrying boxes of my books to events, running the house when my fingers are glued to my keyboard, or simply bringing me that cool glass of Pinot Grigio at the end of the day that makes me go *Ahhh*, he is the wind beneath my wings. He's the one you have to thank for my ability to produce a book a year. Here's to number ten, Dwayne, now on to lucky number eleven!

ALSO BY
GENEVIEVE GRAHAM
#1 NATIONAL BESTSELLERS

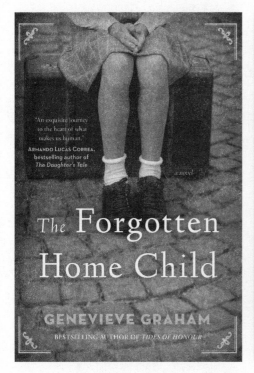

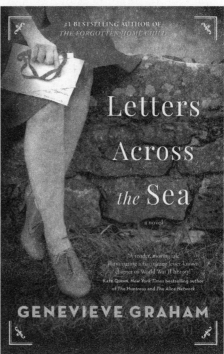

"Time and time again, Genevieve Graham
shows us just how fascinating our past is."

JENNIFER ROBSON, bestselling author of *The Gown*

ALSO BY
GENEVIEVE GRAHAM
NATIONAL BESTSELLERS

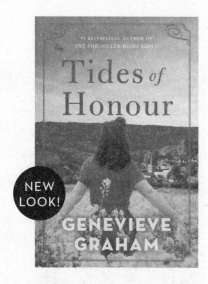

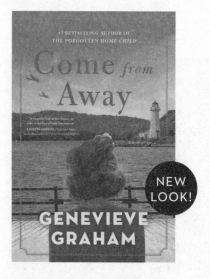

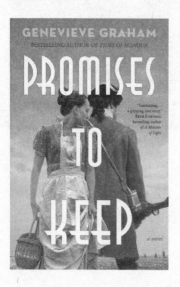

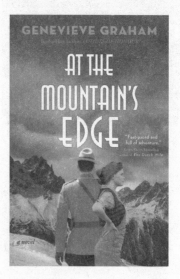

SIMON &
SCHUSTER